SAVAGE
TEMPTATION

LEGAL NOTE

Savage Temptation, by Stephanie Amaral

First paperback edition 2024
Book design by Stephanie Amaral
Editing by: Michele Mencer, Angeliese Maggio
ISBN 9798873232130 (paperback)
ASIN: B0CLDHG7ZD (ebook)
www.stephanie-amaral.com

LORDS OF THE COMMISSION

BOOK 1

Dedication:

To all of you who think you can't.
YES, you fucking CAN!
Whether it's taking it all like a good girl or becoming a
neuroscientist. Yes, you fucking can.

Blurb

Jamie

New York was supposed to be a fresh start.

An uncomplicated, clean slate where I could draw a new me and forget the Jamie who'd ran from her past. But my clean slate got covered in coffee when I accidentally bumped into a devil in a tailored suit just before my life-changing interview. He was rude and entitled. Dangerous and dark. Little did I know that he would be making a mess out of my life, too.

I wanted to run. To avoid the train wreck I knew he would make of me, but he forced me to stay and work for him.

Soon I would find out that this devil had darker shades than I could handle, but still, he'd be the one to shine a light on the person I was supposed to be.

Liam

I was sure angels walked in Hell now that I had seen one with my own eyes. She bumped right into me in the middle of the street, tempting me with her light at a time where everything around me was dark and grim.

One hard look at her was all it took to know that she would be trouble.

All I ever did was consume. Everything in my life was about taking without permission, and even after trying to fight it for her sake, that's what I did to her, too.

She was desperate for a job and like the predator I was, I took all her choices away, forcing her to stay. Because after tasting her lips for the first time, I was addicted. No amount of self-reasoning was enough to take her off my mind, even if I was dragging her into a life of sin and depravity.

Jamie was my weakness, and in my world, having weaknesses was a deadly affair.

Savage Temptation is a full-length, interconnected stand-alone romance novel with open-door steamy scenes and a guaranteed HEA, written in dual POV.

This is the first book in the **Lords Of The Commission – New York** series and it's a lighter shade of Mafia romance, featuring forced proximity and office romance tropes amongst others. There are dark subjects throughout, but it can't be considered an overly dark story. Content warnings do still apply.

CHAPTER ONE

Jamie

At ten a.m. today, my life was going to change.

I'd either be able to stay in New York and pay my rent or be forced to leave and face my past. The outcome of the second round of interviews I was getting ready for would dictate that fate.

I needed that job like air to breathe.

I studied my effort to look professional in the reflection of a shop I would never afford to set foot in, waiting to cross the street. The mannequin in the window seemed to mock me. I sighed, hoping no one could read through the façade of the wannabe fancy clothes and colored lipstick I had put on to hide my fear.

Straightening the perfectly pressed fabric of my suit jacket, I took another deep breath I hoped infused me with the amount of courage and determination I needed to survive this day. I needed it all and then some.

AD Architects was a high-end, world-renowned architectural firm founded and run by the one and only Adrian Dornier.

The man was a legend.

He had forged his way to the top with nothing but hard work and disruptive designs, setting himself amongst the biggest names in the industry. Nothing an inexperienced nobody like me would *ever* find intimidating.

I couldn't help but shrink a little at that daunting thought.

Who am I trying to fool? I will never make it through.

There was more than the status of the man I was about to meet shaking my confidence, though. That kind of self-sabotage ran deeper than just the nerves that preceded a life-changing interview.

There was this constant, familiar voice I'd hear. Diminishing and degrading, as always. It was far away now, but it still kept tearing me and my dreams to pieces, whispering my determination into oblivion. Bad memories and a traumatic past weren't space or time bound. No matter how many miles I had put between us, those thoughts were part of my essence.

I squeezed my eyes shut, forcing myself to remember that I had passed the first round. I must have done something right!

Besides, I had run out of options. There was no way out besides back, and *that* would be my last resort even though fate seemed to be forcing my hand.

Living, or should I say surviving, in New York City on the miserable paycheck from the 7-Eleven I was working at was damn near impossible. Never mind now that it had suddenly closed down last week without any notice.

I had been here for three months already, and my bank account wouldn't be able to support another if I didn't find a decently paid job.

So saying today was a big deal was a huge understatement.

This was my new start. Being who and what I wanted to be, far away from ghosts that were still pretty much alive and well.

Focus, Jamie! Leave the past where it belongs and focus on the future.

I held my head high, balancing the best I could on these heels, aiming for graceful but settling for not falling while making my way through the busy streets of New York.

"Shit. Nine-thirty already," I hissed to myself as I tapped on my phone for the hundredth time in the last ten minutes. I could swear all the damn lights were turning red against me.

Finally the freaking light turned, and I resumed my bee-line between the swamp of people crowding the streets. A ping of an incoming email caught my attention. All those soul-crushing thoughts of self-doubt and unworthiness came rushing back, no permission needed.

My heart sank to my feet as I saw it. It was from AD Architects. Surely no good news could come from an email right before an interview.

I warily opened it, my eyes glued to the slow device as I rapidly swerved between the oceans of people. I expected to see a dismissal or information that the position had been filled while forcing my hopes to tell me otherwise.

'Dear Jamie, we're looking forward–'

I could hardly get past the greeting before I slammed into what seemed to be a stone wall. The impact was so violent that I was thrown back, immediately stumbling to the ground.

This will definitely hurt tomorrow!

Just before my ass hit the ground, I felt a strong pull around my waist lifting me up.

My feet were off the ground, and my body was safe and guarded by the most incredible feeling of warmth that smelled like oak and fresh trouble.

What the hell?

My hand flew to the arm around me, holding onto this perfect stranger for dear life. Strong arms and the fine threads of a perfect suit pulsed under my touch as I hovered in the air.

I was suddenly staring into a pair of hypnotizing, long-lash, emerald green eyes. His stern glare seemed to pierce through my flesh and see straight into my soul, melting away all and any coherent thoughts.

No blink or words to stain the moment.

Truth be said, I couldn't speak if I tried. He seemed to be studying me, a deep frown on his face hiding concern or maybe confusion. It was damn intimidating but so alluring. I was totally lost in the intensity of this stranger's unwavering stare.

Those eyes, the strong grip around my waist, the feeling of those strong muscles under my fingertips.

All of it was sending a strange feeling down my spine before it settled in my stomach.

He was so close I could feel the warmth of his breath on my face. Under this spell, the busy streets of New York had gone void and quiet.

My daze ended just as quickly as it started.

The tight grip loosened, and I stumbled back onto my feet. Strangely, I found myself wanting to be there again.

"Watch where the fuck you're walking!" His low, menacing voice blurted with palpable irritation, catching me off guard.

After the stare-off we just shared, I was counting on something... a little more charming? I sensed the tension, and I was almost positive that I saw him shake his head before speaking as if he was trying to snap out of his thoughts.

"Oh! Forgive me, Your Highness, king and ruler of New York City!" My sarcasm was not masked, heightened by my mock bow in fake submission. "Maybe next time you should try watching where the fuck *you're* going!" I tried to match his words, but somehow mine fell short in comparison. Seemed he was much better versed in cruelty than I was.

"Watch it!" He gruffly warned, but his attention was quickly dispersed beyond me. His neck craned as he scanned our surroundings as if he were searching for something or someone. I didn't follow his motion. Not even those crude words were enough to break the stars still shining in my eyes. I should be wise to recognize those red flags by now, but I couldn't help but crave those eyes back on me.

"Or what?" I defied, catching his attention. I dealt with a bully my whole life, and I knew I was pushing it, but there was something about him that didn't inspire any kind of fear in me. The pristine three-piece suit he wore did nothing to tame the dark and dangerous vibe he had going on.

"Brats don't do too well in this part of town. You might want to adjust your attitude," he said, taking a step forward, the most basic of the basic intimidation tactics.

"Sorry it doesn't cater to your ego, Sir. Now, if you and your high horse don't mind stepping aside, I have places to be." I was poking the bull. Sometimes my stupidity knew no boundaries. What the hell was wrong with me?

"Just fucking great! Now I'll have to go back to that never-ending line," he grunted, pointing at the iced coffee stain on my white blouse, his paper cup soiling the sidewalk.

My eyes widened in disbelief.

This can't be happening!

I would never have time to go back home to change. I couldn't go like this to a possible life-changing interview, either.

Anger welled tears in my eyes as my gaze swerved from the brown stain to him and back.

"Don't worry, Sweetcheeks. At least now we all smell the coffee before the country girl on your clothes."

Whatever sass I had in me left my body as I registered the disaster this could be.

"You ruined it!" I yelled while more tears started prickling behind my eyes.

Pushing him out of my way, I darted towards a café across the street.

"Asshole!" I shouted almost from the middle of the road with rigid arms and clenched fists. I was trying as hard as I could not to let these tears fall at the possibility of losing this opportunity because of some entitled fucker. "Bathroom, please?" I asked the barista, who simply pointed to his left to a pair of black doors.

I ran into the bathroom, praying I could clean up the mess that dickhead had made all over my clothes and still make it to AD on time.

People shouldn't judge on appearance alone. I just learned that two minutes ago when a Greek God who saved me from a bruised ass turned out to be nothing but an insufferable idiot. Yet that same principle doesn't apply when you're being reviewed like I was going to be in a few minutes.

First impressions last long, and arriving with a big fat coffee stain to a place that lives and breathes class, beauty, and exuberance, didn't exactly play to my advantage.

I took my blazer off, followed by my white silky blouse, and started washing out the stain with water and soap, standing only in my lacy bra. I mumbled every dirty word in my dictionary, cursing that perfect stranger for possibly ruining my life. As the stain spread wider, I couldn't hold a couple of stray tears from falling.

I was done for.

"I believe this is yours?" I jumped from the unexpected deep, manly voice that rang from behind me. I could hear his grin in those words without even having to look at him.

A new rush of heat and embarrassment flustered my cheeks in all shades of red as I stood half naked in front of this stranger.

He held my phone in his hand, stretched out to me, his eyes dropping to my waist before slowly climbing back to set on mine.

He studied every inch of exposed skin while my reaction came slow and late. I covered my chest with my arms as my eyes searched the small space for my jacket. It was lying on the vanity right beside him. Too far from my reach, too close to him.

"Could you…" I finally asked, pointing to it, rushing to wipe my face as his eyes diverted to my jacket.

"Come get it." He dared me. But I couldn't move.

I'd self-combust if I stood that close to him again. Instead, I stared back at him, my breathing making me even more aware of my naked chest. For a moment there, I thought he was going to move forward and close the space between us. For a moment there, I wished he did.

"I hum…"

"Don't flatter yourself!" He grunted after clearing his throat, tossing my jacket to me. "You've got nothing I haven't seen before. Not the best sample either."

I might be innocent, but I'm observant, too. His words didn't match his actions at all. His tongue had swept across his lips. The still-wet trail of saliva shining on them was proof of his unrestrained reaction. That was all it took for the heat on my cheeks to travel south and settle between my legs. He wore rudeness and bluntness just as well as that damn alluring suit he had on.

But that little lie? I caught it.

My chest filled with a strange sense of pride at that realization. I needed to revert to the problem I was facing to bring my mind back to earth.

"This is the ladies' room! Can't I get some privacy?" My supposed anger came out weakened by his unrelenting stare. The heat of his gaze was setting me ablaze, disconcerting me together with my focus.

"You dropped your phone." He wiggled the damn thing in front of me again. "But I get how throwing a tantrum can get you blindsided." He turned the phone in his hand, inspecting it with a scowl. "Do they only sell last century's devices where you come from? I understand if you don't want it back. I can just throw it away and do you a favor." This man was all arrogance and good looks. Damn fucking enticing in all the wrong ways.

"Give me that. Now get the hell out!" I yanked the phone away with my free hand and turned my back to him, shielding myself from the effect those magnetic emeralds had on me.

"You're welcome. And by the way, it's a common bathroom and not a 'ladies' room.'" He mocked me with a poor imitation of my voice while pointing to a sign that said 'His and Hers.' "Have a nice life, *Smallville*."

Through the mirror, I saw him staring at me for another second, nodding in disapproval before finally leaving, allowing me to breathe and blush in peace.

That masked 'good deed' was nothing but an excuse to taunt me.

His arrogant tone hit a nerve deeply braided in my body, but truth be told, I was mostly unsettled by the heavy pounding of my heart against my chest, paired with that flutter in my stomach and weak knees.

Why was my body reacting this way to such a prick? I couldn't deny that he was irrevocably good-looking. He had a bad-boy-worse-man vibe going on, despite the classy and expensive-looking black suit that hugged every inch of his perfect body.

That man might have just ruined my once-in-a-lifetime opportunity, and here I was, swooning and daydreaming about him. He was infuriating and a complete jerk, yet somehow, there was something about him that pulled me in like a magnet.

He ruined everything with his arrogant and condescending talk, paired with the way he belittled me with his gaze just as fast as it had feasted its way up my skin.

I shook my head to get him and his bad manners out of my mind. I had to clean myself up and run if I still wanted a chance at this interview.

Scrubbing to no avail, I decided to go without a shirt, pulling my suit jacket on and fastening all the buttons. It gave me more cleavage than I wished for, but if I was careful enough, it wouldn't reveal more than what was appropriate for these situations.

There was no time for another glance in the mirror. I rushed out of the café, heading as fast as my heels would take me towards AD's headquarters, hoping to God I could still make it there on time.

CHAPTER TWO

Liam

"**D**on't even think about missing our appointments. Otherwise don't bother coming back." My father barked at me as I was entering the elevator.

"I'm going for coffee, Dad. I'll be back before your parade starts," I bit back.

"Don't make things difficult, Liam."

"I wouldn't dream of it. It's your company, after all. I'm just here thanks to parental obligation, right?" I let the doors close on that, not waiting for his response. There was no need to hear it, I already knew his speech by heart.

I gripped the metal bar behind me, trying to steady my breathing. My jaw pulsing rhythmically while my father's distrust in his own son soared through my veins. It burned its way through me all over again, as if it was the first time I was experiencing his skepticism. It wasn't, though, yet I couldn't deny its sting even if I tried.

Half an hour.

Half a fucking hour was all I could set aside for a breather this morning, and even that was pushing it. These past couple of weeks had been a walk through Hell, and I needed fresh air before I did something I'd regret today.

I had my assistant, Michelle, push back all my appointments for the day except *that* one.

My father had blocked out half my morning and the entire fucking afternoon just to have the pleasure of my company while he picked and chose his version of a babysitter for his incapable son.

He didn't trust me. He was too afraid I'd stain his perfect little enterprise with my "lifestyle," as he called it.

To be fair, I could ruin it in under a minute, and that wouldn't even be my best record. But I was not the stupid, selfish boy he thought I was.

All I ever wanted was to be a welcomed part of the company, not burn it to the ground! Show him that despite everything else, I was here to stay. More now than ever before.

So excuse me if I was more than fucking fuming by yet another display of his lack of faith in me.

I needed a drink. Yet, the convention says that I shouldn't have a tumbler filled with malted gold at this time of the morning, nevermind the three or four it would take to start to ease me up. So I had to settle for a sloppy second – coffee.

The long line and indecisive patrons took the last ounce of my patience, making me run later than I had anticipated, adding more fuel to my burning temper.

I'd never hear the end of it if I decided to skip the meetings as I was tempted to do.

My mind got lost in that thought, playing out the war it would start with my father as I made my way back to AD.

We were holding on by a thread, our relationship had never been in the gutters as much as it was now.

I'd been going through some hard shit these past few weeks, and instead of cutting me some slack, he just tightened the noose on our already strangled connection.

I was deeply lost in thought, sinking deeper in the shadows that darkened my mood, when suddenly an angel ran straight into me, erasing those corrosive thoughts from my brain, even if for just a second. She stumbled back after impact, losing her fight against gravity.

I grabbed her, hooking my arm around her waist, raising her off the ground and off her feet. A vision of light and life was now held tightly against my chest as I prevented her from falling straight to the ground.

Her deep brown eyes stared intensely into mine, reaching my troubled soul and drenching me in a foreign peace I had never known.

I was paralyzed.

Trapped in a moment that I wanted to eternalize, captive by a beauty I had imprisoned within my arms. She clung to me as if her dear life depended on it, her eyes never leaving mine. She looked like a goddess, and for the first time, I mourned my hellbound soul.

Her nails were carved in my arms. The light sting surged as a pleasurable pain, submerging my brain in an image of lust. A vivid image of those same nails leaving red trails down my back as I made her mine. As I claimed her light and buried her in my darkness.

She was thinking the same depravities I was. I could see it in the way her eyes dipped from mine to my lips and back up again. If I squeezed her tighter she could feel each one of my thoughts hardening under my pants.

Her sweet scent hit my nose like a ton of bricks, pulling me deeper under her spell. Damn, she was so close I could almost taste her.

Her slightly ajar mouth was inviting me in with a silent plea for intrusion, and right then I felt the strangest urge to crush my lips to hers, taste her until her pouty mouth was bruised and swollen and molded to mine.

I almost did.

These thoughts are dangerous. Too dangerous. Stop it, Liam!

I couldn't afford any distractions, not today and not ever. I could see this girl would be a fucking big one if I let her in. And from her reaction, she would unknowingly and unquestionably fall hard.

I shook my head, waving off those incredibly juicy thoughts, letting go of her as brutally and coldly as possible, making her stumble back onto her feet.

I had to push her away, make her erase that look from her face. The one that painted me as Prince fucking Charming. I had seen it before on so many other girls, it was hard not to recognize.

She stood there in front of me, her perfect shape alluring me like a moth to a flame. Her long brown hair framed the most beautiful face I've seen, while a look of disappointment furrowed her brow.

She looked too good to be true, which normally meant it was.

All my alert signs were triggered as I saw just how idyllic she was for me. As if she was handpicked to meet all my preferences. I couldn't have done it better if I had built her myself.

And then there was the other thing. The similarities to a ghost I wished I'd never met.

Red fucking flag. Someone sent her. It's too much of a coincidence to be just that.

"Watch where the fuck you're walking!" I roared, staring intensely at her with a deadly glare and a menacing tone. I saw her flinch as she took the unexpected hit of my words. It didn't match whatever had just flowed between us as I held her against my body, but she had to know I would figure her deception out.

"Forgive me, Your Highness, king and ruler of New York City!" She scoffed back with a theatrical and sarcastic bow. "Maybe next time you should try watching where the fuck you're going!" She was either stupid or just oblivious as to who I was.

The edge and sass in her voice added another ingredient to an already perfect mix. Whoever put her up to this had been studying me closer than I would like to admit.

"Just fucking great! Now I'll have to go back to that never-ending line," I blurted, pointing to my spilled coffee. Just my fucking luck!

She was visibly disturbed by the sight once she noticed. I was sure I saw her eyes sparkle from newly formed unshed tears. She looked like a spoiled brat, a superficial daddy's little girl crying over her ruined outfit.

She quickly spun on her heels, crossing the road in the tight jog those cock teasing high heels allowed. I watched as she cursed and gestured the whole way. Her round and sexy ass swaying, making me want to go get her back and finish what I almost started.

No, no, no. Walk away.

She would have been an interesting fuck, that was for sure. I couldn't recall ever tasting the sunny colors of the countryside before. It's been city girls mostly, if my memory doesn't fail me.

My spilled coffee leaked a long trail down the sidewalk, almost reaching a lost device I could only assume was hers. A broken, lit screen flashed from it. It was hardly salvageable at all. Still, I picked it up and followed the perfect stranger into the café she had disappeared into.

There was no trace of her inside. I scanned the cramped space with my eyes before settling on the tall, skimpy man covered in a brown apron behind the counter.

"Bathroom," he mouthed immediately.

I pushed the door open, craving another bite of her sharp tongue, yet I wasn't prepared for what my eyes landed on. I never thought I would catch her half-naked, but fuck did I enjoy the view. I took my time, lingering a little longer than necessary before speaking, just admiring her without her even noticing.

I'd had my fair share of pussy. Tasted so many that by now they had all blended together. Almost faceless women, eager enough to blow me and walk away with no promise for a tomorrow. One night stands after the other.

I hadn't touched this girl and somehow I had already staked a claim I couldn't fulfill.

Damn she was perfect.

Mine.

That word rang in my head in a loop as I looked at her. I hadn't even asked her name and yet thoughts of possession had swamped my brain without permission. There was no rhyme or reason to what I was feeling, and still, I was feeling it all.

She had broken my numbness with a severe case of pins and needles — relief and pleasure with a thick baseline of pain.

For damn sure she was different from all the others. Perfect. So perfect it could only be wrong.

When I finally spoke, she jumped in surprise, covering up. But it was too late. I had seen it all. And fuck, did I approve!

Again, I was rock hard without her even trying. Her body, her hair, her smell, even that sweet, innocent look that sparkled in her eyes. Everything about her spoke to me in a deafening volume.

The same red flag was now flashing before my eyes. She had everything I could ever dare dream of in one sexy-as-fuck package. It could only be orchestrated.

My cock quickly deflated as reason finally came back to my senses. Whoever sent her knew me fucking well, but not well enough to think I would fall for it.

I'm on to you, whoever you are.

I left her in that bathroom, along with half of my brain. I needed to get back to the office ASAP, but not without a fresh cup of coffee. I needed the punch of a straight-up black and sour cup before I had to deal with what was coming. Yet those thoughts that had been burning me inside the whole morning were nothing but a distant whisper. She had taken over, overriding everything else. Maybe I should have fucked her in that bathroom and got it over with, get her out of my system.

I focused on the only trait of hers I despised. That temper tantrum she threw after seeing her ruined clothes told me she was nothing but an airheaded bimbo. Superficial and materialistic. After a couple of minutes, I had convinced my brain that was all she was.

Distractions came at a high cost and I had more pressing matters to attend to. One of them was walking straight towards me as I exited the elevator back at AD.

"Mr. Mercier, what brings you to this side of the country? I thought we would call you once we had the first drafts ready," I saluted the old man my father was so eager to get into business with.

"Liam, it's always good to see you," he replied, patting my shoulder as we shook hands, "I came to support the Mayor in the bid to bring the Formula One race to New York. Seems like he can use all the support he can get."

"Mixing business with pleasure, I see." There was something about this man that didn't inspire any confidence. I had eyes on the back of my skull every time we met for no specific reason other than a strong gut feeling.

"No harm, no foul, right? With my support, I secured his. The City's Department of Buildings has just signed off on the paperwork to start the Verten construction. The project will pass inspection, whatever it is." If I had any doubts Mr. Mercier dabbled in less than lawful circles, he had just cleared them all. "I hear you'll be in charge."

"That's correct," I replied with a fake smile, sensing his reticence.

"It's a big and important project meant for more seasoned professionals. I thought your father would be supervising it himself."

"There's nothing he can do that I can't. Verten is in good hands, Mr. Mercier. Don't worry." He nodded in acceptance, even if reluctantly, while stepping into the elevator.

"Don't disappoint me then, and everything will be just fine." Was that a threat? I narrowed my eyes, my face failing to hide the annoyance his little nuance had filled me with. "Oh, and Liam? Have fun with that one for me, will ya?" He finally said, pointing to the conference room just before the doors closed.

CHAPTER THREE

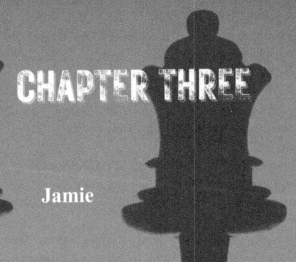

Jamie

Walking like a child in her mother's heels, I rushed over to AD's building, mumbling incoherent cusses along the way, half lost between hope and defeat. There was no way I would ever get there on time.

I held one hand over my overly pronounced cleavage as I walked as fast as I could, trying to cover up what shouldn't be on display in the first place. My judgment had been a little off when I thought this wouldn't be too revealing.

It didn't matter now, because finally, here I was, ready to shoot my shot, if I still had one in the first place.

I stared at my reflection on the glassy building, home to one of the most prestigious architectural firms in the world, my own image harshly judging me for my state. I did my best to tame the wild nest my hair had become from the morning breeze and obstacle course I'd run to get here, but I could only do so much.

If it weren't for that smug, handsome asshole, I would have been here as planned — on time, without looking as if I'd plugged my fingers in an outlet.

My confidence was now vanishing like melting ice in the summer. To be honest, I wasn't sure what I was still even doing here.

I wouldn't hire myself!

Being late for the interview, looking like a mad woman gasping for her next breath, didn't exactly scream, '*Hire me, I'm trustworthy.*'

But what did I have to lose? I'd be going back to Jacksonville with my tail unwillingly snuggled between my legs if I couldn't somehow pull my weight.

Game. Over.

It was only when my lungs burned that I noticed that those thoughts had my breath caught in my throat and my heart sinking to my feet.

Get it together, Jamie. You are not going back to that.

I took a sharp breath, drawing strength and hope from deep within my gut, as I walked into the pristine space with my head held high. *Fake it 'till you make it.*

I let the massive foyer swallow me whole as I took in the grandness of the triple-height-ceiling space. White marble coated the floor while light wood accentuated a feature wall right across the entrance where a slim, stainless-steel sign hung proudly behind the reception counter — AD Architects.

No expenses have been spared here, that much is clear.

I was the opposite of all this opulence. A small-town girl with less than ten dollars to her name. All I had to go on was my love for the art and my will to work my freaking ass off if need be.

That definition seemed to have a new name as of today — *Smallville.* Was I that obvious?

Spinning on my heels, I lost myself in the grandiosity and purity of the light-filled place for just a couple of seconds, my head tilted back, framing every detail in my mind.

I had consumed so many pictures of this place and of Adrian Dornier's work, it was as if I'd been coming here my entire life. Yet nothing prepared me for the overwhelming feeling I had once I was truly standing here.

This was it, this was the dream. I was just one teeny tiny step away from having it come true. Nothing major. Just being hired amongst a sea of other applicants, probably more experienced and more suitable than I was for the role. Not to mention *on time* and properly dressed for the part.

"Ma'am." The mid-fifties lady sitting by the edge of the counter snapped me out of my reverie. "Do you have a purpose for being here, or should I call security?"

"What? No, no." I jogged towards the desk, realizing I had wasted even more time, as if I had any to spare. She met my gaze with a raised eyebrow, still waiting for my full reply. "Hum... I have an interview at AD today?" It came out more as a question, unconsciously. I wasn't sure the appointment was still up.

"Under what name?"

"Jamie Harden."

"Fifty-fifth floor. Check in with the front desk, they will tell you where to wait."

"Thank you." I got nothing above a curt nod and a finger pointing towards the pair of stainless-steel doors to my right.

A damn elevator! Of course. How had that escaped every dream I've had of this day?

My heart skipped a couple of beats as I tried to get a grip on the crippling panic that tingled its way up my fingers, through my arms, and straight to my chest.

I hated closed spaces, and elevators were just the worst kind. It was like dangling over a death sentence. At least if it came to that, I'd be long passed out before the end arrived.

I had managed to overcome my fear just enough to start using these things again, but stairs would always be my first option, given the chance.

But going up fifty-five flights of stairs was a solid no. Hopefully, I won't be suffering in vain.

Just keep your thoughts elsewhere, and you'll be fine.

I watched the numbers on the display above count down until they reached one. My oxygen intake decreased at the same rate those numbers did until the doors opened smoothly without a single sound.

I took a sharp inhale of courage and stepped inside, the fear now slowly spreading from my chest to my legs, too.

I looked around, trying to focus on the details so that my mind kept away from its ride to *Panicville.*

Focus, Jamie.

I willed my eyes to see beyond the cloudy fog of fear, focusing on the details.

Even the simple elevator matched the rest of what I've seen of the building so far. Luxurious and high-tech, all covered in white glass, light wood, and stainless steel.

The numbers were displayed on a touchscreen on the right, where I typed the floor number to start my dreaded ride.

I took a step back, leaning against one of the walls, both my hands gripping the metal bar so hard we were almost fused together.

This isn't working. Think about something else. You're in another place, somewhere nice and safe.

I focused on breathing slower, my eyes shutting tight not to face the closed space as I pulled my mind off the ledge, forcing better images into it.

Anything would do right now.

Almost without a struggle, my mind roamed off to that hot, rude dickhead I ran into earlier. I couldn't believe my knees even gave in when I was pressed against his hard, warm chest.

I could still feel the pressure of his arm around my waist, wrapped in a tight grip that stirred my insides. His alluring green eyes hypnotizing me into a land of lust and longing. I had never been that struck by a man before, never mind a total stranger.

Whoever he was, he would be haunting my dreams for a long time. His touch lingered on my body and my skin felt those delicious tingles all over again, as if I was still pressed against him.

His handsome face was eternally engraved in my mind. His deep voice still replaying in my ears with promising words of both safety and depravity.

I was spiraling into a not-so-innocent vision of the both of us, together inside that bathroom. If I had walked towards him to get my jacket, would he have somehow caved? Would I?

He was just too sinful to be true. I couldn't be blamed for imagining lustful things about him. His taste, his touch, his…

Oh my God! STOP! What the hell is wrong with you?

The doors finally opened on the fifty-fifth floor, pulling a sigh of relief from my chest. That ride was far less problematic than the intruding thoughts of that mystery man. Those had worked me up in a way I absolutely didn't need to be right now.

I quickly strode over to the reception area where a blonde, blue-eyed woman was standing behind a desk exactly the same as the one down in the lobby. She had a professional look going on with her dark blue pencil skirt suit, high heels, and a chiffon blouse under her open suit jacket. She was extremely beautiful and fit right in with the surroundings.

The whole place was impeccably decorated, a clean but luxurious look to it. Again, light wood and white was the style that covered the entire place, from the walls to the furniture. It had a Nordic decor feeling to it all, much classier and definitely more expensive, but still simple.

Exuberant! That's the word.

And so was she. The personification of corporate elegance.

"Good morning," I said as I approached the desk. "My name is Jamie Harden. I had an interview scheduled for today?" I was wrong when I thought I had the jitters before. I was full-on shaking right now.

"Good morning, Miss Harden. As I've mentioned in my email, we are a little delayed today, so I will have to ask you to please wait for your turn in the waiting room. I am so sorry for the inconvenience. It's right down the hall to your right," she said, flashing me a bright white smile that contrasted with her burgundy lipstick.

My heart flipped in my chest at the sound of her words. I hadn't seen the email. The word *delayed* had never sounded so good to me in my whole life.

"Thank you so much." I smiled back before turning towards the hallway, my walk gaining a new springy effect as I contained the victory dance I wanted to do.

My opportunity still wasn't lost!

That email she mentioned must have been the one I started reading before bumping into tall, dark, and troublesome. That man just swept every rational thought from my mind. I hadn't given my phone a second thought after our encounter.

The waiting room was a men's only club. Testosterone ranked as high as the sky as they all looked me over like the odd one out.

I was.

There were five of them waiting, most of which were around my age, maybe a little older, except one that was surely in his late fifties, if I was being kind.

Funny enough, he was the only one who made me uncomfortable. His gaze was deep and unsettling, sending a frozen shiver down my spine. His ice-blue eyes clung to me like leeches, sucking my blood from my face and draining me of all color. The crooked smile that crept onto his lips was too suggestive of the thoughts he had running through his mind.

Red fucking flag.

He sat straight in a poise of regal posture, as if he had something over all of us, allowing just his eyes to dip onto my pronounced cleavage.

I clung to my suit jacket, shielding my body from his unwanted stare.

I didn't hesitate to take the most isolated seat I could find, still next to another one of the men waiting, but if push came to shove, I'd sit on a pile of needles if that meant being away from that man.

Creep.

I wasn't sure why my palms had started to sweat while my knees danced to the pace of my uneasy heart. Reality was hitting me like a ton of bricks. If I didn't get this job, I wouldn't be able to stay in New York for much longer.

Crawling back to Jacksonville and giving my father the satisfaction of witnessing my failure was something I'd try to avoid at all cost.

I'd had enough of his degrading words. I'd had enough of him telling me how big of a disappointment I was. I'd had enough of the guilt he tried to throw on me for…

"Jamie Harden?" A tall brunette interrupted my thoughts. "Mr. Dornier is ready to see you." I nodded once, getting up from my seat and walking towards her as I fixed my jacket again, trying to look as conservative as it would allow me while purposely ignoring the pair of eyes I felt following me.

The woman looked at me with a warm smile and an amused expression on her face, waiting to guide me through the double doors behind her.

"Nice to meet you, Miss Harden. My name is Tracy Parker," she greeted, holding her hand out for me to shake. "Your name is quite ambiguous, you know? They're expecting another man. I'm glad we have a lady applying today. We could use more in this men-driven business." I smiled at her remark, treading behind her into the place where my fate would be sealed.

There was no mistaking who Mr. Dornier was. As soon as I was in the conference room, my eyes landed on an extremely handsome man with a steel-bending presence. His hair was as dark as night, sprinkled with a couple of silver streaks on the sides, matching the ones in his dark beard, granting him the elegant and refined look of a silver fox.

From this distance, it was hard to perceive the correct color of his irises. They weren't brown or green, but they held me pinned in respect, and to be honest, a little fear. His stare was stern under a furrowed brow of confusion. Together with his pristine gray suit and impeccably white button-down, he had me almost ready to salute.

There was another man sitting next to him, his presence much less overwhelming. Both of them rose once I was in front of them, respectfully greeting me.

"Miss Harden," Mr. Dornier said, with a curt nod in a deep voice laced with an under-toned French accent, before sitting back down and pointing to a vacant chair right in front of them. "Please, take a seat."

The brunette who had met me by the door took the seat at the end of the table, leaving an empty one between her and Mr. Dornier. That could only mean someone else was missing.

Four people interviewing me? This just got a lot more nerve-wracking.

"My name is Adrian Dornier, CEO and founder of AD Architects." *As if I didn't know that already.*

I was practically fan girling internally to finally be meeting a living legend in flesh and bone.

Before he could say anything else, the double doors behind me burst open with a loud noise, banging shut right after, rattling the frame with its force.

I kept my focus on Mr. Dornier since his eyes were still strained on me, unaffected by the intruder. It would only be disrespectful to break my attention, but God did I want to. I was dead curious to see who would have the nerve to burst in here like that.

Mr. Dornier's expression grew darker. He was beyond pissed, annoyance clear in every faint wrinkle on his forehead.

"You weren't going to start without me, right?" A deep male voice said from behind me, his tone connecting instantly with my gut. I'd heard this man before; both his voice and that presumptuous tone were now branded on my mind forever.

His tauntingly slow footsteps resounded in the room as he walked over to us, finally coming into my line of vision.

Holy shit on a stick! It's him!

My heart sank to my feet as soon as I saw his face, fluttering in my stomach on its way down.

Adonis held nothing on him, but then again, Lucifer probably didn't either.

"Just my fucking luck!" He cursed as soon as his eyes met mine, all my hopes deflating together with my heavy exhale as soon as I saw him.

"Liam!" Mr. Dornier's harsh voice resounded through the room. "Language!"

"You?" His voice was low and heavy, his eyebrow raised in suspicion or maybe annoyance. I couldn't help but shut my eyes trying to find the motivation to face this interview. I could sense it was about to be nothing short of a total disaster.

His eyes dipped towards my chest making my cheeks flush all shades of red, the intensity in his stare burning me to my core. Having him look at me that way shouldn't harvest this kind of reaction. I should feel offended, yet somehow, all that invaded me was a strange pride and a need for more.

"Good morning," I muttered in a flat tone with a fake smile, hoping my voice would break his reverie. With a small shake of his head, he finally broke contact with my steep cleavage, averting his gaze to the rest of the people sitting at the table.

"Is my schedule right or have you moved things around?" He asked Mrs Parker, flipping the pages of the thin stack he held in his hands. "I thought we were starting with a Mr. Harden."

"This is *Miss* Jamie Harden, Liam," Mr. Dornier clarified. "I understand you know each other?" Somehow the implication in his question didn't seem innocent or platonic.

I opened my mouth to refute, but Liam was quicker on that trigger.

"No! *Miss* Harden over here bumped into me this morning and spilled my coffee. I'm starting to wonder if it was as much of a coincidence as it was made out to be." His eyes practically pierced through me, waiting for an answer or reaction to his accusation. "Seeing that you're here and all…"

A sarcastic, disdainful grin spread on his face as he took the fourth and final vacant chair on the opposite side of the table, right next to Mr. Dornier and in front of me. The derogatory tone under his insinuation was clear to everyone in this damn place, making me shift in my seat as exasperation crept up my spine.

What could I say to that? And why on earth would I ever feel the need to purposely bump into such a self-centered prick? He thought a little too highly of himself, that was clear.

All I could do was sarcastically chuckle as if I was silently asking everyone here if this guy was for real. Other than that, what was brewing to come out of my mouth wasn't at all suited for Mr. Dornier's ears.

It was best to say nothing.

"Miss Harden, please excuse my son. Sometimes he is under the impression that the whole world is out to get him. Let's just forget your… *incident* this morning and proceed." Son? Did he just say son?

Liam was right, *just my fucking luck!*

"First of all, thank you for coming. As I was saying, I'm Adrian Dornier, this is my assistant, Alex Durst, and this is AD's Human Resources manager, Tracy Parker. This here is my son Liam Dornier." He continued calmly as if he hadn't just detonated my whole future. There was absolutely no way I would ever get this job now!

"I'm sure you are aware the available position is for our creative department, under Liam's supervision. We are in the running to win an important project for a green energy company, so we will be looking to blend aesthetics with high-tech sustainability," Mr. Dornier explained, and although I was doing my best to focus, I couldn't help but keep Liam in my peripheral vision. "That's where your portfolio stands out. You seem to incorporate quite a few self-sufficient and green ideas in your projects in a pragmatic yet aesthetically pleasant way."

There was something magnetizing about Liam. I was drawn to his every move like a moth to a flame. Only I knew for certain I was getting burnt.

He had unfastened his suit jacket when he sat down, displaying a fitted black waistcoat that snuggled around what I could clearly see was a toned torso. Tight and stretched, just like a tailored second skin.

Status, wealth, and a fine ass had him sitting on a damn high horse, looking down on the rest of us mere peasants. Since the first moment we met, he had treated me like annoying gum stuck on his shiny designer shoe. He could be my boss, or he could be God for all I cared; I was done being treated like shit.

I was lost in thoughts on how I could ever have a professional relationship with a narcissistic asshole while my eyes had wandered to the wonder that was him. Fuck, how could the package advertise such a lie?

He was too easy on the eyes. Too. Damn. Easy.

I swallowed dryly, watching his biceps strain under the white shirt as he shifted in his seat. I was drifting between him and his father, trying not to be too obvious, yet *he* hadn't strayed for a second. I could feel the heat of his eyes set on me. My face, my fidgeting fingers, my chest.

"So, Miss Harden," Mr. Dornier snapped me out of my thoughts, "You have an extremely interesting portfolio. Quite innovative and disruptive design ideas. Yet you seem to be lacking field experience." A victorious, crooked smirk spread on Liam's lips, sure this was the end of my chance.

I needed this too damn much to leave it at that. Again, he was quicker and spoke first.

"Well, I guess we're done here then. Field experience is a must and I have no time to be schooling inexperienced little girls," Liam chimed, still holding that smug smile.

"Yes, that is a fact. I'm sure that's not a decisive trait or I wouldn't be here today. What I lack in field experience, I make up with a photographic memory. I learn fast, and I'm not afraid of a new challenge. I can adapt to new situations without a struggle," I managed to say without so much as a stutter. Yet I wasn't finished, and the last part of my reply was directed to the entitled asshole in the room. "Besides, the job description said internship. I'm sure I'd be learning a lot more than that if my direct supervisor was willing to share knowledge."

"I'm sure you're extremely flexible," Liam quickly said in a mocking, derogatory tone. "Yet we are looking for someone who can pull their own weight. This isn't charity, *Smallville*. It's long hours and hard work that I'm not sure your manicure can handle. Besides, that little stunt you pulled this morning won't help your case. Stalking me to seduce your way into the company isn't the way we do business here. We don't gratify that kind of conduct. So, if we could stop wasting time, that would be perfect."

Did he just call me a slut?

My blood had passed boiling point by now, heating an unsettling fire under my ass and a fresh blow of wit and conviction into my veins.

That was the last straw for me. There surely was no way we could have a civil, professional relationship after that. I came here to stay away from that kind of toxicity.

I didn't know Liam. I could never guess how far he would go. Even though this was my last opportunity, it was a hard pass as of now. I was thinking as straight as I could, trying not to focus on the consequences of what I was about to do.

Slowly, I stood up, collecting my notepad from the table and shoving it into my handbag. I could see him trying to act calm and collected, relaxed into the back of his chair, an ankle resting on his knee. But I could also see the tight grip he held on the edge of his armrest. He wasn't as calm as he made out to be.

"Mr. Dornier, I'm sorry to have wasted your time. I'm a die-hard fan of your work, and it was a dream come true to work and learn with you, but I don't want this job. I didn't realize I would be supervised by a self-centered, egotistical, rude prick, no offense to you, of course. I truly am underqualified for that." I turned to Liam before continuing,

"And by the way, I can't think of a single person who would like to bump into you by mistake, never mind going out of their way by orchestrating such a far-fetched plan of doing so intentionally. There is no earthly good enough reason to ever want to be in that position. I'm just a naturally unfortunate person."

Liam moved forward, ready to unleash hell, but I wasn't finished yet, and I'd be damned if I let him rattle my sudden burst of confidence. I held a finger up in his direction, showing him I wasn't done.

"If you didn't bribe your way through college, you must have heard the expression 'less is more.' You should probably take that life lesson to heart. Your ego desperately needs to slide into minimalism. I don't see it deserving more than a pale palette since it has close to nothing to go on." It was an obvious lie, and he knew it based on the way his brow arched, but still maintained the rest of his face unreadable. "Going by your blank expression, I might need to make my point a little easier to follow for the sake of your simple mind. Don't flatter yourself, Mr. Dornier. I've seen better." I threw his words right back at him, straining to hold back a little victory smirk. "Mr. Dornier, Mr. Durst, Mrs. Parker, thank you so much for considering my application. I am truly sorry to have wasted your time." I grabbed my stuff, ready to leave the room with my dignity intact. I might not have gotten the job, but it felt damn good standing up for myself for the first time since maybe... ever.

CHAPTER FOUR

Liam

I hated superficial women. Bimbos who preyed on daddy's money and depended on a precious trust fund for the rest of their meaningless lives, measuring their value with the amount of Louis Vuittons they owned.

Hard pass.

That was how Jamie had come across when I bumped into her this morning, despite her look not matching the description. Throwing a fit over a stain on her precious clothes came across that way. That image was far from the confident woman I was now watching, completely stunned as she handed my ass over to me in front of an audience. *Simple mind, ah!*

Women never spoke to me that way. *No one* ever spoke to me that way!

But fuck me, do I find her sexy as hell doing it.

I couldn't find the words in me to reply. I was stuck looking at her, glowing in the victory she thought she had achieved. She was mesmerizing. And that was reason enough for me not to want her here. She was perfect. So perfect that she seemed almost tailored to my taste.

I had a gut feeling she was trouble. I just couldn't pinpoint why I felt that way and so strongly about a stranger. But something about her set off the red flags in my brain, leaving me a little more than just uneasy.

Little did we both expect the bomb my dearest father was about to throw into this pit just as Jamie was about to leave the room.

"You're hired!" He said in a firm tone, drenched in finality, stopping her straight in her high horse march before reaching the door.

"WHAT?" Both Jamie and I practically shouted in utter disbelief. How the fuck was he even considering hiring someone so inexperienced? I already had a stack of work I could hardly finish, never mind having to babysit a fresh out of college, provincial loudmouth, architectural toddler.

"You can't be serious," I immediately protested. We had agreed that it would be a mutual decision, and yet, once again, Mr. Adrian Dornier couldn't help but shove me into the corner and take the wheel alone.

The eye roll my father directed my way was the only reply I got.

"On your way out, please provide your information to Michelle at the front desk. She'll see that your contract and payment terms are sent to your email for acceptance. You start Monday."

"Mr. Dornier–"

"Liam will be personally supervising your integration, Miss Harden." My father cut Jamie off, "He'll see that you don't have any trouble settling in and getting acquainted with the *Verten* project. *I'll* see that you don't have any problem with *him*. If you do, please come straight to me." There was no hesitation in his voice and it was my turn to reply with an eye roll.

There it was again. His lack of trust in me was crystal clear in just a simple one-liner.

"Mr. Dornier, I truly appreciate this opportunity, but I don't think this will be a good fit for either of us." Thank God she was displaying some brains.

"Miss Harden, I was under the impression you actually wanted this job. Am I wrong?"

"No, Sir, not at all. It's just that–" Jamie averted her eyes to me, pleading for help or maybe considering her options. Her whole demeanor had shifted, losing the confidence I saw just a minute ago. She grasped her jacket above her chest, hiding her cleavage and shrinking into herself, showing me her whole hand – her earlier assertiveness was nothing but a poorly held-up mask. *Smallville* apparently couldn't handle the pressure after all.

"I do believe I'm perfectly capable of judging the people I hire myself. I'll see you on Monday, Miss Harden. You may leave."

Jamie stood there stunned, her words lost in her perplexion.

"Miss Harden," Mrs. Parker said, holding the door open for her.

"Oh, hum... Thank you," Jamie mumbled while she struggled to keep her composure, grasping her stuff tighter against her chest as she left the conference room. It was more than clear to me now that this was all a setup. My dearest father was setting me up to fail. What he probably didn't count on was me seeing through his bullshit.

Did he really think I would drop the ball because of a hook up? As alluring as she was, my mind was set, and AD was what I wanted as my future.

The challenge had now tripled in complexity. I had to deal with Mr. Mercier and his sketchy shit, an intricate project with colossal proportions, and now an inexperienced, spoiled brat to call my right hand. On top of all that, I couldn't deny how distracting Miss Jamie Harden was.

I can't wait to start!

I took a deep breath and waited for everyone to vacate the conference room, stealing a moment alone with my father.

"Why?" I simply asked as soon as the door closed.

"Why what?"

"Are you so invested in seeing me fail that you don't care if you jeopardize the company and lose the Verten project?" I tried my best to reel in my anger using proper vocabulary in place of all the foul language running free in my mind.

"Quite the contrary. Miss Harden is perfect for the position. Her portfolio is impressive and more than experience, she'll excel at keeping you grounded. Obviously she doesn't refrain from saying whatever is on her mind. She'll also be quite a good complement to something that you lack."

"Oh really? And what is that, *Father*?"

"Humility, Liam," he replied matter-of-factly as he walked towards the door. "Oh, and Son, keep your hands off her."

The grin that was plastered on his face made me even more furious. So much for logical decisions!

Without hesitation, I shot Jimmy a text with Jamie's resumé and all her details demanding a thorough background check, my fingers angrily typing on the screen that took the punch of my sour mood.

That rage shot me up from my seat. I didn't intend to go after her until I saw her in the elevator, shrunk into the back wall, almost lost between the small crowd that swamped the space.

I lost it. I needed to know what the fuck was happening. No way Dad would hire someone for such an important project just to 'keep me grounded.'

"OUT!" I growled, "NOW!" Every single person in that elevator hustled to leave as they took in the danger coating my tone. "Not you." I pointed to Jamie, making her slowly retreat to her previous spot.

I hit the button to close the doors with such force I was amazed it didn't get stuck, isolating us from the prying eyes of every employee who witnessed my outburst.

Jamie raised her eyes to meet mine before quickly deflecting as she nervously gripped the metal bar behind her. I couldn't blame her, though. I knew what I looked like when I was flaring in rage. I cornered her against the wall, slowly closing the space between us until I was invading her personal space.

Fuck boundaries. She had obliterated them as soon as she stepped into my life.

My eyes were permanently set on her face which had been drained of all color into a caspery white. I tried to read her reaction, searching for the answers her words couldn't give me.

I placed my hands on either side of her body, barely touching her hands that still grasped that metal bar as if her life depended on it. I felt her slightly shaking, my overbearing closeness knocking down whatever brave wall she could have tried to put up. She lifted her eyes to face me again, but they quickly returned to admiring the floor.

She was right where I wanted her to be – stripped down to a primal instinct of survival.

"Look at me," I ordered roughly.

Jamie flinched at my harsh tone but didn't move otherwise. I needed to look into her eyes. Only they could tell me the truth I searched for.

"I said look at me," I grunted, capturing her chin between my fingers and forcing her to face me. I towered over her, leaning in and looking straight into her eyes, coming only inches apart from her face. I breathed what she expelled and inhaled her sweet scent once again.

Damn, she was pure trouble.

Without trying, she had yet again clouded my vision, making me doubt my own resolution. I couldn't keep my eyes from dropping to her plump parted lips.

Fuck, they drew me in like a moth to a fucking flame.

But I couldn't waiver. I came for answers, and I wouldn't leave without them.

Focus, Liam.

"If I were you, I'd think about my answers before I give them. Do you understand?" The threat was clear, both in my tone and my unwavering stare. I could feel the message was received as Jamie timidly nodded, but it still wasn't enough. "Use words, Miss Harden."

"I… I understand." She couldn't help the stutter that shook her tiny voice.

"Who put you up to this?" I asked, moving my hand from her chin to her throat. Her heart was pulsing harshly under my palm but kept a steady rhythm. "*This* cannot be a coincidence."

"No one. I... I don't know you or your father. I don't even understand what you mean." I watched her eyes intently as she spoke, noticing no dilation. She was being truthful, from what I could tell.

"How did you find me this morning?" I pressed further, tightening my grip on her throat, feeling her veins pulse furiously, but still, there were no changes in their pace. She was scared but not lying. Under the new pressure of my palm, Jamie released a breathy, almost undetectable moan that spoke straight to my cock. In a heartbeat, my intentions shifted under that heavenly sound. I wanted more of them. Louder and preferably laced with the sound of my name.

"I didn't. I swear. It *was* a coincidence. Can you please step away now?" She said with all the courage she had left in her, in a small voice that lacked confidence.

"You're shaking, Miss Harden. How should I take that?" I asked, keeping my gravelly tone laced with the anger I was feeling. Her deep brown eyes shut as tight as they could, making me question my tactics. "Are you scared of me?"

"What? No!" She snapped her eyes open, looking straight into mine. Her tone was firm for the first time since I stepped into the elevator.

The hand I had wrapped around her neck slid up, my thumb slowly caressing her bottom lip. "Then tell me, are you shaking because you're lying?" Jamie released the rail with her right hand, gripping my wrist instead. She wasn't pulling me away, she was steadying herself and keeping me in place.

I leaned further towards her, placing my lips on her ear, "Or is this the effect I have on you?" I finished. My lips grazing her ear lobe as I spoke.

"Liam," she exhaled. A softly moaned plea that escaped her mouth without permission.

Self fucking preservation just flew out the window at that sound. It was like water in a desert. The flood I didn't know I needed.

Jamie's head fell back, exposing her juicy neck to my eager lips. She shook her head in response. To what question, I didn't know.

"Words, Miss Harden."

"I'm not lying," she replied. Half-truths didn't suit my needs at the moment. I needed to hear it loud and clear.

"Tell me you're not shaking because I'm this close. Make me believe you." Jamie didn't reply. Instead, her eyes fluttered closed while a new shiver ran down her body. "Look into my eyes, Miss Harden, and tell me you aren't quaking with the need to be touched. To be kissed."

She opened her eyes again, facing me with a newly found confidence that dripped in unshaded lust.

"No, I'm not!" Her voice was steady, but her breathing picked up an unnatural pace, her pupils dilating until her eyes were almost completely black. All those tells were already enough to show me she was lying, but the cherry on top of the fucking cake was her tongue swiping across her bottom lip.

Caught ya.

"Liar. You licked your lips when I said 'kissed.' Were you imagining it?" I teased, my hand returning to her throat, feeling her skin erupt into millions of tiny goosebumps. "Try again, Miss Harden. This time make me believe you."

"How?"

"Easy. Tell me the truth."

She took a deep, steadying breath, preparing herself for the words she knew she couldn't contain, her mouth slightly opened in preparation.

"Say it," I pressed, too anxious to wait another second. "Tell me what you want."

"Kiss. Me." She mouthed, unable to verbalize her cravings. She was just as lost as I was, and I was only too eager to oblige.

"Good fucking girl."

I didn't need to be told twice.

Finally I took what I'd been craving since she bumped into me. It hadn't been all that long, but this desire was eating me up inside. I crashed my lips onto hers like raging thunder. Lust and fury mixed in a kiss I couldn't stop.

I picked her up, making her wrap her legs around me before slamming her against the opposite wall. My hands had a mind of their own, feeling every inch of her body before settling one on her ass and the other on her perky tit under her jacket that had been doing a poor job at hiding what was underneath.

It fucking fits to perfection.

Her soft, breathy moans filled the carriage in a language my eager cock was fluent in. There was absolutely nothing lost in translation. She was loving it just as much as I was.

I pressed my groin against her, making her feel how much she messed with me. Just how hard I was for her. I could bet her panties were soaked right through.

A louder moan escaped her mouth straight into mine as soon as she felt me, and right then, I knew I had hit the right spot. I bit on her lower lip, just enough pressure to mix the right amount of pain into this pleasure spell. She didn't wince. She took it like the fucking queen I knew she was, moving her whole body in unison with the best kiss I've ever had.

Her hips rolled and thrust in sync with mine while her fingers pulled on my hair. Nothing, not even air, fit between us.

Jamie was rocking against me while my ravishing kisses grew hungrier with each stroke over my needy cock. I craved to watch her face as she became undone in my arms. I craved to be buried so deep inside her that there was no telling where she ended and I began.

I wrapped my hand in her hair, yanking her head back to admire her swollen lips, almost bruised, glistening in a mix of both of us.

"Fuck," I groaned, unable to stay away for longer than a breath.

It was her who pulled me in this time, impatient to fuse our tongues again. All my senses were focused on pleasing her. Eating her. Riding her against this fucking wall.

Suddenly, Jamie pushed me off her, a rush of fresh air filling the space between us, making me realize the doors had opened and we had reached the ground floor.

The look of panic in her eyes was clear as she stared at me from a painful distance. Before I knew it, she was running out the door.

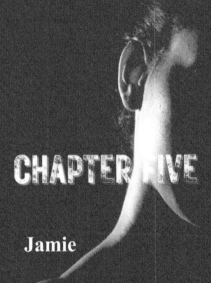

CHAPTER FIVE

Jamie

I got home in record time, propelled by pure shock and the nonstop string of 'what the hells' running through my mind in a loop.

Had I just dry-humped my boss?

Yes. Yes I had.

And somehow, despite all the wrongness that statement held, I could not find it in me to regret it. Today, at least. I was betting by Monday I'd have a different take on all this.

I needed a cold shower to calm all the intensely wired nerve endings in my body. Especially *the* nerve ending Liam had so expertly enticed.

I discarded all my clothes in a frenzied path to the bathroom, stepping under the water before it had time to warm enough not to cut my breath. Still, not even that was enough to have my mind detouring to something more appropriate.

I washed the rest of Liam's coffee off me, together with his fingerprints and heavenly scent, unfortunately, but the feel of him lingered.

I could still feel the tip of his fingers digging into the sensitive flesh of my throat, and I'd give an arm and a leg to have them there again. Digging much, much deeper this time around.

Liam had burned every working fuse in my brain, settling himself into it without needing permission. Was he a self-centered prick? I wasn't so sure anymore. He had changed from yin to yang in under a split second, and I couldn't decide what to think about him anymore.

When I saw him barging in that elevator, my anxiety peaked to a new high – his presence only adding to an already stressful situation.

My body reacted to the claustrophobic panic first, but soon enough, he had my mind focusing on something else entirely. His voice was like a beacon guiding me out of that pit of darkness. It was hypnotizing. His words enticing and unashamed.

How could a complete stranger have such an effect on me?

Somehow, restrictions of rights and wrongs were erased, and I was living in the moment, no strings binding me to any code of conduct. The closed space not causing any short circuits in my brain as it normally did. It was just him and me, the rest of the world be damned.

Every memory of that moment was imprinted in my brain and would certainly be haunting my dreams, panties and fantasies for weeks to come. Just as it was right now.

I couldn't stop them if I tried. My hands had a life of their own, moving towards the places I could only imagine Liam's would, sliding down my body, following the path of water.

Oh this is so, so wrong!

My eyes fluttered closed, and soon enough I was back in that elevator, pinned between the wall and Liam's hard body.

Starting at my bruised lips, just as he had, I caressed the tender spot he had sunk his teeth in, allowing my fingers to slowly glide down my body. They paused on my throat. On the exact same spot Liam's big, strong hand had been gently squeezing.

If I had any instinct of self-preservation, it should have kicked in at that moment. Yet instead of being scared of him squeezing the air out of me, there was a new rush of life and lust building from his stronghold.

I wanted more.

More pressure. More kisses. More dirty, dangerous words.

Could I even confess to that? No, not at all.

My fingers grazed my erect nipple, sending a jolt of pure pleasure soaring straight between my legs.

I was feeling the urge to do something I had never felt the need to do – touch myself.

I wasn't a prude, or so I'd like to think.

I'd had sex before.

Once.

Two awkward minutes that felt like eternity, half of which was spent opening and applying a condom. Fun memories, indeed. I had yet to find the craving to try it again, not to mention a proper man who could make it worth the embarrassment.

By the way I was reacting to my first-degree encounter with Mr. Tall, Dark, and Bipolar, I could finally see that the shitty experience was far from being my fault alone.

Still, I was questioning my sanity. How could things have gotten so out of hand?

Liam had set something on fire deep inside of me. A fire I didn't even know existed. I was trembling just thinking about the way he kissed me, and truth be said, I needed more.

From that small demonstration, I was sure sex with Liam would be different from the poor excuse of an experience I'd had. He surely looked like someone who had had plenty of it anyway. Putting the word "sex" in the same sentence as Liam's name had me dangling closer to an edge I couldn't define.

My mind was in dangerous territory, followed suit by my hands.

Before I knew it, I had sunk two fingers inside me, picturing green eyes staring into mine as he thrust in deep, long pumps that matched this perfect tempo.

"Good fucking girl."

His words rang on repeat inside my mind. It seemed degrading when I had read them in romance novels, but on his lips, they felt like a goad, pulling me into a heaven I had no idea even existed. They brought with them a strange sense of pride for being awarded with the title. Apparently, I yearned to be a good girl while being extremely naughty.

My fingers worked at a quicker speed each time he said them. My palm grazed my clit while my other hand pinched hard on my nipple. I couldn't picture Liam as a gentle lover. I imagined all that anger trapped inside him being spilled into every primal or emotion-driven thing he did in life. It didn't get more primal than sex.

Experience would be on his side, and I'd be all too willing to learn. But I tried not to imagine how many women he'd slept with already. The thought of his hands pleasing another was enough to twist my guts into something I could only guess was jealousy.

Fucked up much?

I paused those thoughts to chase after my release, focusing on the way Liam's tongue dominated mine. On the taste of his kisses. On the pressure of his hard shaft rubbing against me.

Soon enough, my breath was caught in my throat in those stilled seconds before the ultimate explosion. My head fell back, the water spray hitting me straight in the face while white spots invaded my vision. A loud moan escaped my throat as pleasure soared through my body.

I was quaking in ecstasy, courtesy of the dirty picture Liam had painted and two prying fingers that I never imagined could feel so damn good.

All too quickly, the pleasure had worn off, making way for a heavy conscience. Masturbating to the image of my bully boss was less than ideal. It held a yarn of wrongfulness I couldn't completely untangle even if I tried.

I finished the shower in automatic mode, my mind long lost to scenes of an embarrassing Monday morning, heightened by the memory of what I had just done. Flushed cheeks and inappropriate thoughts awaited me.

I curled into a fetal position in the middle of my bed, welcoming the cold breeze that cooled my still wet skin.

I had just masturbated to the thought of a stranger. To the thought of my boss. Whom I had only met today!

To add insult to injury, I felt jealous just imagining Liam with other women.

Jealous! Jea-lous!

How is that even possible?

Honesty was a damn trap, and acknowledging the rage and uneasiness that settled in my stomach at that thought didn't suit my needs at the moment.

Best I focus on the version of him I had bumped into. On the version he had shown inside that conference room.

Thoughts of Liam touching me, kissing me, sending me above seventh heaven had to be permanently banned. He had messed me up so badly that I couldn't even feel happy about getting my dream job. The duality of his actions, and mine at that, were nothing short of confusing.

Maybe this was all a game to try and get me to quit before I even started.

It won't work, Smartass.

I needed to focus on making the best out of this incredible opportunity Mr. Dornier had given me. Focus on making my dream come true and not lose it over something that should never have happened. It could only come back to bite me on the ass.

Besides, I won't do well as a trophy fuck.

Between today and Monday, I had the whole weekend to get him out from under my skin. I was starting a new life, one that didn't – No! Scratch that – couldn't, in any way, shape, or form, include Liam Dornier as anything but my boss.

Liam

Flashbacks of that interview had followed me through the weekend. Jamie Harden was a fresh and constant image I couldn't seem to shake. One that, as of tomorrow, would step into my closest circle.

I wasn't conscious of what that meant exactly. It was too easy for her to crawl under my skin. A part of me told me I should keep my distance while the other screamed for more of her.

She looked too familiar. Like a ghost from a recent past that I was trying hard to censor from every nightmare that dared to haunt me, night in and night out.

That was what I was holding on to.

The memories she brought back were dark and grim. Ones I'd do anything to erase.

> Any updates on that background check?

I texted Jimmy, finally giving in to my curiosity.

> Squeaky clean.

> Practically a nun.

He replied almost immediately. That last message made my lips spring into a dirty smirk. If only he knew how unholy she looked while I rubbed my hard cock against her pussy.

> That's hard to believe.

It wasn't. I was just fishing for a chip on that beautiful stranger's shoulder. Something that confirmed my suspicions of the danger I felt stinging my skin since I met her. Coming up with nothing bothered me more than if she was in the system for attempted murder.

> Address?

Old one was in some small town in Oregon.

> Okay. And now?

His vague reply made me feel Jimmy was trying to withhold information. I knew him all too well to recognize his tactics in avoiding disclosing information he thought would unnecessarily rile us up.

Changed three months ago to some shitty neighborhood in the Bronx.

It was clear there was something I wouldn't like in his answers.

> What shitty neighborhood?

The Bronx has so many.

He was definitely deflecting.

I dialed his number, my jaw clenching at the sound of every ring. It didn't take too many for him to answer.

"I knew you'd call."

"Then spit. Which one, Jimmy?" I grunted into the speaker. He knew by my tone to cut the bullshit.

"Tremont."

Fuck. Tremont was one of the most dangerous boroughs in New York. I hated everything about it with a passion. It didn't help that it was the stage of the worst nightmare I'd lived through. I hardly knew this girl, yet for some reason my gut twisted as I pictured her walking those streets. It was like the past repeating itself all over again!

"Any relation to Detroit?"

"Not that I could find."

There was a sudden flood of relief rushing through me that tipped my lips into a stupid grin. It *was* just the mother of all coincidences teamed up with my troubled mind playing tricks on me. If there was anything to find, Jimmy would have found it already.

"Send me a pin of the location." What was I doing? The urge to see her was a fucking unstoppable, moving force, unlike anything I'd ever felt before, and this was undoubtedly dumb as fuck.

"We have grocery store garbage to take out. Tomorrow." Fuck. Just like that, my smile vanished. Reality bringing my feet back to the damn ground.

"Shit. Fine."

"We need you at Dea Tacita tonight."

How could I have forgotten I was Midas? Only I didn't turn everything I touched into gold. I petrified it into fragile pillars of salt that crumbled under the pressure of an ill-fated man like me. I was cursed and couldn't force that fate upon anyone else.

Lately, everything I touched turned to ashes, and I couldn't bear the thought of seeing that goddess burn because of me.

Still, my thirst needed quenching, even if it only came from a distance.

"I'll be there. Send me her location," I insisted.

"Liam…" Jimmy's voice revealed his reticence, but I couldn't give a fuck about what he thought.

"Just pin the fucking location. I'll be at Dea Tacita later." I hung up the phone, holding it in an iron grip as I waited for her exact address.

I'd been fighting against the eagerness I felt for Monday to get here quickly. Admitting AD had just become all that more alluring with my father's latest recruitment was almost like swallowing razor blades and acid. But now that I wouldn't be there, it was clear as day that I had been looking forward to tomorrow.

I would be missing her first day at AD, and waiting until Tuesday to see her again was just too much.

I wanted to see what her reaction would be following the crazy shit that happened in that elevator.

"Oh, and Son, keep your hands off her." My father's words rang in my mind like a siren as I drove towards the address Jimmy had sent me. All it sounded like to me was a dare. But this *thing* I apparently had for her was more than the need to defy him.

There was more to her, and I needed to find out what and why I was being pulled in her direction.

I sat in my car in front of the worn-down apartment building, just waiting. It was a little three-story building, planted right next to a laundromat.

I didn't like the idea of her living here. I knew this part of town and it just wasn't suited for someone like her. She needed to move and she needed to do it fast.

I kept waiting, counting the brown bricks that made up the façade, inspecting every window for a sign of which was hers. There was little to no activity and time went by without Jamie showing her face.

As I counted down the minutes and hours, rationality slowly managed to kick my emotions into a corner. I was finally talking some sense into myself. How fucked up was it that I wanted to see her so badly that I drove across town just to get a glimpse?

She was nothing but a stranger. What was alluring was the *idea* of her. Something I had made her up to be in my mind. Nothing a good fuck with a hot piece of ass wouldn't change.

Because I don't run after women. She wouldn't change that.

It was time to leave. Disappointment lined my gut for not seeing her, and damn me if it wasn't the first time a woman made me feel that way.

I didn't like it. I didn't like it one little bit.

Shit. I need to leave before I fuck up further.

I pulled away from the curb with tire-squealing force, distraught and uneasy about leaving her here alone. I needed to do something about it, so I texted Jimmy again.

> I need a shadow up in Tremont, twenty-four seven. Find out who her landlord is and change the lock on her door. I want a spare. We'll find a way to get her out of this place, but before then, just get a guy here ASAP.

> Are you sure this is a wise thing to do?

> You're right.

Stephanie Amaral

> Buy the fucking building

> Just get it done and make sure she doesn't see him. I'm on my way to Dea Tacita now, he better be here within the hour.

CHAPTER SIX

Jamie

I wasn't ready to face the consequences of my hot-headed actions. That was the same as saying I wasn't ready to face Liam. What version of him would I get today?

It was Monday morning, the day I'd been dreading to the point of feeling sick.

I looked at myself in the mirror again before leaving the house. I chose discretion for my outfit today. Maybe blending in and flying under the radar would help me survive the wrath of the Greek God I now worked for. Simple, light makeup and high heels gave me a professional glow, but other than that, I was covered in bland black and white. Camo wouldn't work as well as what I had on. Right?

I'd just keep out of his way, try not to mess anything up and take the freaking stairs this time.

Infallible plan.

After gathering the rest of my stuff, I took another glance in the mirror, smoothed out my hair, and wiped a little smudge of mascara from under my eye.

Who am I kidding? Flying under the radar my ass.

I was fooling myself. I was trying harder than normal, putting way more effort into my appearance than I usually did.

Deep down I wanted Liam to find me appealing. I wanted him to look at me with that same fire I saw blazing in his eyes just before he whispered those words that did very, *very* wrong things to me — *"Good fucking girl."*

I mentally slapped myself. That was supposed to be degrading and cliché and diminishing. Why on Earth was it so damn alluring when he said it? I couldn't help but want to hear him say it to me again. But it was wrong. And it couldn't happen. I knew this. Why did I need to chant it over and over to try and make it stick? And why did I want him to like me so badly?

Questions, questions, and more questions. I was a mess.

I had spent the whole weekend either daydreaming about him or convincing myself how bad this situation was. I had no idea what to expect from Liam, but my mind was set on telling him that what happened last week was a weak moment, a big mistake that would not be happening again. Yet my body screamed "hell no" to all of the above.

Besides, why did I even think he would want it to happen again?

I was utterly confused. My body pulled me in one direction while my brain was set on the other. The right one, might I add.

I needed to set the record straight and tell him I was sorry if I made him think anything different, but I was emotionally – and physically – unavailable right now. Getting involved with someone like him could only bring me heartbreak and misery.

He didn't strike me as the relationship kind of guy and I surely wasn't made for flings. I was convinced that he could just as easily make me float on clouds as well as break me into pieces. I couldn't afford that. I was just now starting to mend again.

My head needed to be in the game, buried in work. That was the only way I could succeed and make a life for myself here. Far away from Jacksonville.

I shivered at the thought of going back. And this *thing* with my boss was a recipe for exactly that. A disaster in the making.

Problem was, what if he told me he wanted more of that elevator action? Would I be strong enough to say no? Did I even want to say no?

God! I'm so not ready to see Liam today.

My boss! He was my boss. My very handsome, unobtainable, far from my reach, out of my league, most-probably-a-play-boy, boss.

I sang those words all the way to AD like a mantra, reminding myself exactly who he was.

With a simple kiss, Liam had erased the infuriating first impression I had of him. I needed that back. Going back to hating him could bring me the power my will suddenly lacked.

I focused on our pre-elevator exchange.

'Don't worry, Sweetcheeks. At least now we all smell the coffee before the country girl on your clothes.' He was definitely a dick. *Smallville* my ass.

After forty-five minutes on the subway, replaying all the snarky remarks Liam threw my way, I had finally gotten some sense into my head. By the time I got to AD, I was fully bullet-proof. *I mean, Liam proof.*

Mrs. Parker was kind enough to show me around, introducing me to some of my new co-workers. AD was a huge enterprise, and there was absolutely no way I could keep up with all the names and roles she was throwing at me on a good day. Nevermind having my mind constantly diverting to someplace else. I was lost by the time she introduced me to the second Steven, after Rebecca and the other what's-her-name.

Finally, after what seemed like an eternity, we got to my desk. It sat in the huge bullpen, right in front of what Mrs. Parker told me to be Liam's office.

I noticed that sitting next to my keyboard was a brand new phone with a note on it.

"To replace your broken one." My heart fluttered as I took in the messy handwriting. There was no signature, yet I had no doubt who it was from.

It was a thoughtful gesture that affected me more than I'd like to admit. I couldn't have afforded anything like it, but its true value was in the thought behind it.

It told me Liam had been thinking about our fated encounter, and knowing I was in his thoughts messed with my resolve all over again.

Damn him.

I should probably thank him. No. I should probably give it back.

I stuffed the note in my pocket, looking up at the shut door in front of me, not being able to tell if Liam was on the other side of it or not.

But hours passed, and Liam was nowhere to be found. I should have felt relieved. It was much easier this way. Yet, somehow, I couldn't help but have mixed feelings about his absence. I couldn't understand the uneasiness swirling around in my stomach either.

I wasn't prepared to face him, but I was counting on it.

He was supposed to oversee my integration. Give me my assignments and guide me regarding the project I was going to work on. I knew nothing about the *Verten* building, so I lurked around the other people working around me, trying to figure out as much as I could.

But I felt lost and alone in this room filled with people. Like a little skiff adrift in a high, violent sea.

I sat at my desk for the rest of the morning, staring at the screen, thinking I had made a mistake by accepting this job. It was more than clear that Liam didn't want me here. He hadn't held back on that fact during the interview. And since he was my direct supervisor, it was easy enough for him to find ways to have me fired. Maybe I was just wasting time I didn't have.

By lunchtime, I was sitting in the corner of the cafeteria, alone, nibbling on a sandwich I didn't exactly feel like eating, while theories of Liam's absence swarmed my mind. This whole situation was making me feel uneasy. Like I was in deep trouble, just waiting for the painful consequences to catch up to me and bite me in the ass.

I was so deeply lost in thought I hadn't realized there was someone sitting in front of me.

"Hello there…" The voice of a girl around my age snapped me out of my daze while she waved her hand in front of my face. "Anybody home?"

"Oh! Hi, sorry. I wasn't quite here," I replied awkwardly, rubbing the back of my neck.

"Yeah, your mind left the building for a minute there and your body didn't get the memo," she chuckled, "You're Jamie, right? I'm Alison. Nice to meet you."

"Yes, I am. Nice to meet you, too." I smiled back at her, shaking her hand.

"Hard first day?"

"Something like that."

"Sorry to barge in on your thoughts, but apparently Mrs. Parker thinks I'm the bubbly welcome party of the herd." Her face lit up in a smile along with mine as her little joke made me feel somewhat lighter. "I still remember what it's like to be the new girl as if it was just a month ago. It was just a month ago." She whispered that last part, making my smile widen. "I thought you could use a friend. Plus, you're the only one here who still doesn't know I'm a little unhinged." The scrunch in her nose broke the final barrier of loom that had fallen over me.

"That would be great," I laughed. "I think I'll be accepting your offer. I can deal with unhinged."

"Perfect." Alison leaned closer, looking both ways as if to make sure no one would hear her. "Let me put you up to speed on the office gossip then. Katie from IT is definitely rolling around in the hay with Alex, Mr. Dornier's assistant. If you need a day off, the yogurts from the vending machine are almost always expired, so that's a safe excuse. And last but not least, Michelle, assistant to the AD stars and Liam's fan *numero uno?* Her boobs are as fake as polyester," she blurted before holding her silence and nodding with her eyes as wide as saucers, confirming all the above in a fake shocked expression.

We both burst out laughing at her theatrics, and just like that, my day got a whole lot better. She seemed friendly, and her candid face somehow made me feel I could trust her.

"Thank you, I needed that."

"No need to thank me. To be honest, I could use a friend, too. If you know someone willing to take the spot, let me know." Alison teased me with a wink.

We exchanged phone numbers and made plans for lunch for the rest of the week. Hopefully she was as trustworthy as she looked. Having a friend sounded amazing and could give me the sense of belonging I craved so much.

I was in better spirits as I left the cafeteria towards my baren desk. It didn't last long, though. As much as I tried focusing on something else, the shut door in front of my workspace pulled me right back to Liam.

Was he avoiding me, or was this just a coincidence? For someone who didn't believe in those, this one was pretty huge, considering the elephant in the elevator.

"Good afternoon, Miss Harden." Mr. Dornier stood in front of my desk, an annoyed eyebrow cocked upwards as his overpowering presence shook me to my core. I was so lost in thought I hadn't noticed him arriving. I scrambled to my feet, almost ready to salute, standing as straight as a cadet.

"Good afternoon, Mr. Dornier." I smiled as I swallowed the lump in my throat.

"Where's Liam?" His voice was low and charged with the gritty anger of a father ready to scold his son.

"I…hum… He's not here."

"I can see that, Miss Harden. Can you tell me where he is?" How the hell should I know? That was the impulsive reply I wanted to give. Instead I found myself on the defensive.

"I haven't seen him today, but from what I gathered, there was a last-minute preliminary meeting at the Department of Buildings."

Mr. Dornier crossed his arms in front of his chest, his expression telling me he wasn't buying my lie. He stared at me for a second too long, maybe waiting to see if I would back down from it.

"Sure," he finally replied. "How about you?"

"I'm still getting acquainted with the project and meeting everyone."

"Shouldn't you be with him at this *meeting*?"

"I wouldn't have been of any assistance. I don't know anything about the project yet. Besides, I'm still handling all the paperwork with Michelle for my contract."

Another long, hard look studied my face as I tried to find somewhere else to look besides straight into his sharp, steely eyes that held more questions than a police interrogation.

"Has he threatened you?"

"What? No!" Finally, there was no hesitation in my voice. "Why would you ask that?"

"Because I know my son. Please come to me if—"

"There you are, Adrian." A deep voice croaked from behind him, sending a shrill shiver down my spine.

Mr. Dornier turned to face the man, opening my line of vision towards him. I had seen him before. The eerie stranger sitting in the waiting room before the interview. Another shiver chilled my skin at the sight of his grin directed at me.

I couldn't forget this man even if I tried. He had this decadent look to him as if he was decomposing pre-mortem. Sinister and bone-chilling all around.

His ice blue eyes skimmed from my face to my waist where the table hid the rest of me, pausing on my chest for a moment too long. His gaze was greedy and consuming in all the wrong ways.

"Ah, Mr. Mercier. *Bienvenue.*" *Welcome.* Mr. Dornier's voice changed completely, accommodating his french accent more evidently. "Let's talk in my office."

Thankfully, the two men walked away, leaving me behind.

For a moment, my brain took a break from thinking about Liam, directing every cell into forgetting the ill feeling that stranger seemed to awaken in me every time we met.

But it was a short intermission. The shut door to an empty office right in front of me mocked my fluttering stomach every time my mind wandered to his kisses.

For another two days, I went home with depleted hope, only to wake up the next morning with a new reserve that I slowly lost through the course of yet another day of Liam's absence. Every time I asked Michelle if he was coming, she just shrugged and left me without an answer.

He was nowhere to be found, and with little to do without his orientation, I couldn't stop my mind from running wild. It had gotten so bad I was having fantasies about him while I sat at my desk looking at that damn door, which was not smart at all. How would I hold a straight face and not think about all the raw and nasty things my mind had him doing to me?

I had felt anxious about coming to work on Monday, fearing having to face him after humping him in the elevator. Somehow, this impasse was so much worse.

My anxiety had skyrocketed and each time a man walked in front of that door, my heart stopped for a second before I realized it wasn't him.

Yet time brought clarity. It wasn't fear of facing him that I felt. I was looking forward to it, and damn if that didn't make things all the more complicated.

It was as if my skin missed his touch and my lips needed his kisses. The more I forced myself to think I didn't want those things, the more I felt the exact opposite. The more upset I got at the prospect of not having them again.

Bad, bad sign.

These fantasies had fed the image of him to a point that the stars in my eyes were blinding. The signs of danger were evident, and I had to do everything in my power not to burn. At least I still had the good sense to know Liam wouldn't have given me a second thought. Not in that way, at least.

My phone lit with the perfect solution to my predicament. A reply to a submission I had made for another company before landing this job. They wanted to meet with me to settle the terms of my admission.

I traced the cracked screen with the tip of my finger, going back to the moment I broke it as I bumped into Liam. My gut twisted at the thought of leaving AD and never looking back, yet somehow it seemed like the best thing to do. My future here was already tainted anyway.

I had fallen under the spell of a man I met once. A man who had treated me like a piece of trash only to personally take me to heaven a few minutes after.

Clearly, I had issues.

I had to keep reminding myself that Liam didn't want me here. He had been perfectly clear about that during the interview. He hated my guts for some odd reason.

Fueled by that thought, I quickly wrote a reply, scheduling the meeting for the beginning of the week, reading it over and over as I fought to find the courage to hit the send button.

"Bring me a clean shirt." I heard the most alluring, hoarse voice grunting, pulling me away from my phone.

Liam stormed past, loosening his tie as he walked, shooting straight to his office with Michelle hot on his trail. His eyes set deadpan on mine before returning to the path ahead. His glower slashed right through me, searing any optimistic thought I could have about his arrival. No acknowledgment. No nod. Just a piercing, reproving look.

Michelle hustled to get the shirt, following him into his office, shutting the door behind her. Was he going to change in front of her?

I wasn't expecting the flood of envy that hit me like a freight train. I nervously chuckled to myself while my eyes were glued to that damn door.

Jealousy, anger, and revolt filled my lungs, every deep breath burning deep inside my chest. I hated this. It was irrational and senseless. Not to mention completely masochistic. That look alone told me exactly where I stood. The real Liam was the one I met on the street and in that conference room. The one that called me Sweetcheeks and Smallville, as opposed to the one that called me a good fucking girl.

'Liam's fan numero uno.' Alison's words came rushing back. Were they a thing? I tightly shut my eyes, cursing the uneasiness away. That thought shouldn't bother me as much as it did.

I definitely have to go.

Forever passed before Michelle left his office, directing a small see-you-tomorrow nod my way. Everyone had left already, and I was still stuck to my chair, rereading the email with my finger hovering over the send button.

My decision was made. I shot up from my seat, fueled by the insane rush of unwanted feelings, stopping right outside the door that had been taunting me for the last couple of days.

With a sharp inhale, I raised my hand to knock, but froze just before my knuckles hit the wood. He was so pissed, this was probably not the best time.

I'll just send him an email.

"Can I help you?" His low-tuned voice stopped me in my tracks just as I had turned to leave.

I squeezed my eyes shut, cussing his impeccable timing and taking a second too long to face him. I inhaled and exhaled heavily, gathering enough courage to slowly turn back around.

Liam had kept his tie off, the two top buttons of his shirt remaining open. My eyes glided down his torso, taking in the perfect fit of the white button-down against his toned body. He was rolling his sleeves as he crossed the threshold, hypnotizing me with the pornographic nudity of those forearms. I couldn't help but follow the blue line of the bulging vein running up his sleeve.

God! Even his arms were sinful. He looked absolutely divine. No wonder that blonde bimbo was drooling over him. I was, too.

"Miss Harden?" I thought I had seen a knowing grin on his face as my eyes roamed back up to settle on his.

"Oh... Hum. Do you have a minute, Mr. Dornier?" I finally blurted, my cheeks tinting red.

"Sure, please come in." Liam held the door completely open for me to pass, shutting it behind me even though there was no one left on the entire floor. It was like a trap I was oh-so-eager to be caught in. "I apologize for my absence. I had forgotten you were starting this week." I let that statement sink in, my eyes deeply buried in his, instinctively narrowing into thin slits. I knew it was a lie. He knew I caught it, too.

The man had given me a damn state-of-the-art brand new phone that I was sure had cost more than what I paid for rent. But if he was that desperate to show me he hadn't given me a second thought, I'd let him have it. I had come to put an end to this, after all. No need to dabble in the details.

"And by the way, it's Liam. Mr. Dornier around here is my father, not me," he coldly continued, breaking our stare as he pulled out his chair and sat down, motioning for me to do the same. I remained standing in front of his desk instead. I needed the metaphorical advantage on him at the moment.

"Yes, Sir."

"Jamie, no *Sir*. Just Liam." His voice had dropped an octave, and I couldn't help but shiver at the gravelly sound. But the words he used it for were far from pleasant. "You're not any different from anyone else in this company, so please call me Liam." There was no doubt the devil was out today. I just didn't have the same coffee stain to go with it.

"Sure, *Liam*." I accentuated his name with a tinge of the venom I felt creeping up my throat. His words stung more than I expected they ever could. "I wasn't expecting any kind of special treatment if that's what you're implying. What happened in that elevator was a huge mistake. But that's beside the point. I'm sure you'll be thrilled to hear that I'll be out of your way by the end of the week. I just came to tell you I'll be taking a job at another company starting next Monday. I'll thank your father for the opportunity, but I'm better off somewhere else, and you won't have to put up with me. It's a win for everyone."

There. It's done.

I almost made it to the door, but Liam grabbed my wrist, stopping my march.

"Jamie. That's not what I meant." He stood in front of me, blocking the way to the door. "You don't have to leave."

"I do. I just came here to tell you that you can start looking for a replacement. I don't understand why you dislike me so much, but I wouldn't like to have someone I can't stand imposed on me, either." I was shaking from his closeness, just like I was in that damn elevator.

"No, I mean I don't want you to go." He closed the gap further and I stopped breathing altogether. His fingers swiped against my forehead before he tucked a strand of hair behind my ear.

So fucking cliché but damn does it work.

I couldn't do this push and pull. I couldn't want something and fight against it. Could I?

"Jamie, I don't dislike you. I don't even know you. Yes, what happened in that elevator was a big mistake. I'm sorry for what I did. I think we can be perfectly civil despite that. If you can see past that lapse of judgment, so can I. I can promise I'll never do it again."

"I don't know." I wanted to say yes, but my brain was screaming otherwise.

"I thought you couldn't be trusted until I found out what you told my father. I know you covered for me, and you didn't have to do that." He smiled, and for the first time it reached his eyes. "It didn't work, though. He saw right through you, but it's the intention that counts." He chuckled, filling the room with that amazing sound and rendering me defenseless.

"He thought you had threatened me into it."

"Sounds like me," he teased. "Stay. I'm sure we'll find a way to work together and forget all about the day we met." At first my eyes were locked on his face as I pondered, slowly diverting to the floor as I shook my head in denial.

I'd get hurt. The fact he wanted to forget about that day was already tearing me up inside.

Liam cupped my cheek, stopping the negative movement and focusing my attention back on his face.

"Can you at least think about it?"

CHAPTER SEVEN

Jamie

I left the office with the promise that I would think about staying at AD.

I lied.

To say I was a confused mess was an understatement. Everything in me was screaming for me to leave. Every gut feeling, every logical thought, every past experience. Everything but that little piece of me that beat an inch off-center in my chest, and that piece alone was holding back my decision.

The way he said he didn't want me to leave replayed in my mind over and over, and I found myself doubting again.

This job was already slipping through my fingers even though I only started a couple of days ago. I should be focused on it. Doing my best to succeed and meet the expectations Mr. Dornier had for me. Instead, all I could think about was Liam, and most recently, Liam and Michelle in a closed-door office.

It was only a matter of time before I was invited to leave. It was best if I pulled the trigger first while I had a cushion to fall on.

As soon as I got home, I poured a glass of the only bottle of wine I owned. I'm not a drinker, but today I was looking for courage that didn't seem to surface. Maybe I'd find it at the bottom of this glass of red. If only my reflection on the rich liquid could tell me what to do, maybe she's braver and more determined.

I stared at the handwritten note Liam had left me, my chest tightening each time I read those simple words. How was I seeing more in that phrase than it truly said? I twisted and turned the damn thing, my resolve breaking further each time my eyes met those simple words.

Still, a decision needed to be made and I was on the fence, tipping to each side as I thought either with my head or my heart. But there was too much on the line, and the risk of losing it all was too great.

It only took a couple of sips to make me feel looser. Perks of hardly ever tasting the stuff. Looseness came hard and quick, haunted by another vision of Miss Blonde-McFake-Boobs locked up with Liam behind that damn door. Images of what they'd been doing inside crept under my skin, lodging an uneasy feeling straight in my gut. Again.

The notion that I was feeling jealous of a complete stranger clarified my doubts. This was not what I had come here for.

I scouted the email I'd written once more, downing the whole contents of the glass before finally hitting send. There was no turning back now.

As if on cue, my phone started ringing with an incoming call. No caller ID had me furrowing my brow.

"Hello?" I answered hesitantly. There was no sound on the other side of the line. I allowed a few seconds of silence, before repeating, "Hello?"

"Hi, Jamie." I had never spoken to him on the phone, yet all it took was a distant 'hi' for my gut to flutter.

"Hum, yes?"

"It's Liam. Liam Dornier," he clarified, as if I didn't know that already.

"Oh, hi." I played coy, "Is everything okay?" Why on earth would Liam be calling me at this time of the night?

"Hum, yes. Everything is fine." He sounded tense, something lurking behind his voice that I hadn't heard yet – uncertainty. "I got your number from AD's personnel files. I hope you don't mind." A moment of silence passed before he spoke again. "I know it's late, but I got a call from Verten's project supervisor. They'll be in New York tomorrow and want to meet at the construction site. It's the last meeting before they make their decision to trust us with the project or not. Would you be up for an update and brainstorming session tonight? We should at least include some of your energy-efficient ideas in the pitch."

"Well, hum... I'm not sure I should." I had just accepted a job at another company. Should I really be burying my nose deeper into this project?

"It's just for a couple of hours. I mean, if you're free."

"Why me, Liam? You have a team full of people who already know this project inside out." There's the courage I was looking for. I'm not sure what I wanted him to say. I wanted some kind of validation. Some kind of reply that would set me apart from all those people. I wanted him to say he wanted me there and no one else.

"You're my project manager. Remember? The green energy expert."

"Oh, right." I felt the blow to my ego hitting me straight in the gut. My chest deflated from all the hope it had gathered before he replied.

"At least until you hand in your resignation, that is. Before then, you're stuck with me." I couldn't help the flutters that flooded my gut. The imagery was too real and still too fresh to forget. "So, are you free, Miss Harden?"

The way he said my name hid a sinful promise of depravity, and just like that, my resolve crumbled.

"Y...yes, I'm free," I stuttered, as if overcome by a transe. "What time should I meet you at AD?"

"They're running security drills at AD tonight. No one outside of security staff is allowed in. We'll be meeting at my place." I gulped, swallowing the lump in my throat at the thought of going to his house.

Snap out of it. It's a team project. I'm sure there will be other people there.

Besides, how could I refuse without implying he had a hidden agenda and embarrassing myself completely? Still, I felt like I was walking straight into a trap, and somehow I couldn't find it in me to care even if it was.

The silence over the phone was deafening, contrasting with my loud thoughts. I hadn't realized I had yet to say a word after that little bomb of information. My hesitation, though? It spoke volumes as the silence grew.

"Jamie, it's *just* work. I made you a promise and I intend to keep it." The promise about not touching me. The one I so badly wanted him to break. "Send me your location and I'll get Carl to pick you up in ten minutes." His voice was final and commanding, leaving no room for discussion.

"I might need more than ten minutes. I wasn't exactly ready to leave the house." I'd taken all my makeup off, wearing nothing but underwear and an old oversized t-shirt. Not to mention my skin was buzzing with the heat of that glass of wine I had. I wasn't drunk. Just light-headed, but it had only just begun.

This was a bad idea. I shouldn't be walking into the lion's den in the first place. Nevermind doing it with a foggy mind and a loose mouth. What the hell was I thinking?

"Just throw on something comfortable. This might take some time. See you in a few minutes." Without giving me time to change my mind, Liam hung up and dread started filling my lungs as I realized what I had just agreed to.

I ran to my room, putting on a pair of jeans and a white t-shirt. I combed my hair into a messy bun and put on light makeup. There I was, trying extra hard again.

Ten minutes flew by, and soon enough, Carl was ringing my doorbell.

As soon as I was settled in the car, my hands started sweating as the reality of where I was headed hit me like a ton of bricks.

The drive was my only opportunity to ease my racing heart and get a grip, so I took what I had and silently talked myself off of the ledge. There was no way I could explain being this nervous to Liam without a white lie that would hardly be believable or telling him the embarrassing truth.

It was work. Nothing else.

"Miss Harden?" Carl called from the front seat, "We're here." I was so lost in thought I hadn't realized the car had stopped. "Mr. Dornier will buzz you up. Just press for 1052. The penthouse is on the tenth." *Of course it is.*

"Thank you, Carl."

The door to the luscious building was already open when I got to it. Without hesitating, I went in and made my way to the elevator. As I stepped into the confined space, I couldn't help but shiver. Elevators always made me nervous, and this one was no exception. Finally, the doors opened on the 10th floor, and I let out a heavy exhale, trying to calm down. I searched for apartment number 1052 and took a deep breath before knocking on the door.

I wasn't prepared for what I was about to see. No amount of mantra repeating on the way over could ever ready me for this.

Liam answered the door wearing only a pair of black sweatpants, with no shirt on.

No. Shirt! And holy sweet hardness, was he really an Adonis!

My eyes widened, and I felt my mouth slowly drop as I stared at this blessedly beautiful creature. He was like the perfected art piece of all the old Renaissance artists put together in one. A sculpted piece of ass that made me forget to breathe. *Jesus fucking Christ!*

Liam was absolutely gorgeous in every way.

My eyes burned from the sight of that defined V of muscles that ended in Sin City. Damn, they were begging to be scouted by my tongue, the wet path of saliva tracing a trail to see exactly where they ended. I knew my Hail Marys by heart, I could handle a little transgression.

The big bulge under his sweatpants left little to the imagination, my tongue darting across my lips at the sight. Big was exactly the right word to apply. Big cock and big trouble. Again, I wasn't a prude, but this was the first time I had craved having one in my mouth.

Look up, Jamie. Look up.

I focused on the ink adorning the right side of his torso, catching sight of the other tattoo running down his forearm. It was a phrase I couldn't decipher. Sexy and dangerous was everything I didn't know I liked.

"Good evening, Miss Harden," he said, snapping me out of my daze, my stare peeling off his abs to reluctantly settle on his jade eyes. The way he said my name was laced with bad intentions, and I reveled in the sound of it. The blush of being caught red handed was impossible to stop, my cheeks suddenly feeling as hot as the sun.

How long have I been staring? Coming here was a bad idea.

"G-Good evening, Liam," I stuttered, my eyes returning to his rock hard muscles that seemed to scream for me to gently stroke them.

"Oh, sorry. I just got out of the shower and thought it was the pizza guy," he said, turning to go get a shirt, leaving me rooted to my spot.

The view was premium, though. As he walked away, I couldn't help but notice how good his ass looked in those pants, my head querking to the side as I took his figure in. His back was perfectly toned with rippling muscles in places I didn't even know they existed. Two dimples just above his ass punctuated an image of perfection. For the second time today, I found myself drooling over my boss.

"Come on in and make yourself comfortable," Liam shouted as he disappeared further into his apartment.

I stepped inside and closed the door behind me. Glancing around, I realized that Liam's place was nothing like what I had expected. I had envisioned a luxurious penthouse overseeing Central Park, assuming that he and his family were extremely wealthy. However, the reality was much simpler. The apartment was situated in a less exclusive part of town, yet still spacious and well-appointed. Lean and clean, with an eclectic industrial feel to it.

Liam finally returned with a black t-shirt on that hugged his chiseled body. I preferred the previous version, yet I still had to force myself to look away.

"Again, I'm sorry. I thought you would call from downstairs. I wasn't expecting you to be here already. Would you like something to drink?" he asked, offering me a smile that melted me on the spot.

"Hum… Just water, please. Nothing else," I replied, smiling in return. I still felt the slight buzz from the glass of wine I had drank earlier.

"I'm sorry if I interrupted anything when I called," he said as he handed me the glass of water and sat on the couch opposite me.

"No, I haven't been here long enough to make plans or friends, to be honest," I admitted, taking a small sip trying to quench a thirst that called for a lot more than water. Apart from Alison, who was still a recent acquaintance I'd soon like to call my friend, I had no one else in this city.

"So, you're not from New York?" he inquired, his smile turning into a knowing grin.

"No," I chuckled. "You got it right at first sight. I arrived only three months ago. I'm originally from Jacksonville, Oregon."

"Smallville," he laughed. The sound pierced my gut and sent an electric current through my body. "That's far from home. What made you come all the way over to the east side?"

I smiled nervously, wondering how I could keep the conversation light when this was the topic.

"Where do I begin? I was looking for a new start, an opportunity like the one your father gave me, to be able to do what I loved, far away from prying eyes that don't usually cheer me on. I wanted to be independent and not shy away from being myself without the need to justify any of my choices, you know?" I tried to keep my smile, but I felt that it didn't quite reach my eyes. Liam saw right through it, and the air thickened with my discomfort.

"I do. I really do. Congratulations, then."

"For what?"

"Part one, at least, is achieved. You should be proud of that." Contrary to mine, Liam's smile was genuine, comforting, and easy enough to tame my anxiety as he didn't pry any further.

"Thank you. I'm extremely grateful. It's an amazing opportunity. I am a die-hard fan of your father's work, but I'm not sure it's my place. There's something that feels too heavy, too complicated." I couldn't find better words to say that without telling him he was complicating it for me. His presence, his existence alone was enough to occupy my mind without space for anything else since I first bumped into him. And if I was to make this work, I had to focus.

"I might be to blame there. I was a huge jerk."

"Yes, yes, you were," I laughed.

"I'm sorry I made your life harder. My animosity was misdirected. You were just an easy target, and I wrongly took out my anger on you. Contrary to what it might seem and what you think, I do like you." I couldn't help the blush from spreading to my cheeks again, my heart doing a small flip at the sound of that. "I'd hate to know you quit your dream job because of me. Because of how I treated you. Could you possibly find it in you to forgive me?"

"Mr. Dornier, if I didn't know any better, I'd think you were trying to convince me to stay," I said in a mocking tone, trying to lighten the mood.

"Maybe I am. Is it working?" he replied with a wicked grin as he took a gulp from the beer bottle he held in his hand.

Damn him, it was. But I couldn't waver, and there was no turning back. I had already accepted MG's offer, and I needed to tell him.

"I–"

"Let's blow Verten's mind with those ideas of yours, get you into this project as if you'd been designing it from day one. You'll see this is exactly the place where you should be," he interrupted me just as I was about to tell him I couldn't stay.

I pursed my lips, following his movement and taking another nervous sip out of my water, watching as his lips quirked into a soft smile that sparkled in his eyes. He looked different like this, like he wore his heart on his sleeve as a default, as opposed to the cold ruthlessness I had seen at AD.

We spent the next few hours discussing the project, studying the construction site, and going over all the details, with beer and pizza as company.

Liam's passion for his work was evident, but it was hard to focus on everything he was saying, try as I might. Devilish images of his perfectly chiseled abs kept popping into my mind, distracting me and taking me into dangerous grounds of a lust I had yet to experience. How could someone be so perfectly designed? I tried my best to hide my thoughts and pay attention, but it was difficult with him sitting so close to me that I could almost taste him.

I shouldn't have had those beers! I was feeling them on my knees, and worse than that, there was an alcohol and Liam-induced hum settling between my legs.

By the time we finished, we both slumped on the couch, tired. Liam had his head resting back on the headrest, his eyes closed, and a freshly opened beer in his hand.

"Liam?" I could feel my tongue dragging a little, my mind foggy but with a clarity that was frightening.

"Hum?" He sleepily replied.

"Why did you kiss me the other day?" I had lost my filter and brakes altogether. My sanity, too, as it seemed. Liam's eyes shot wide open, my question clearly catching him off guard.

"You asked me to, remember?" He answered after taking a large sip and gathering his thoughts.

"I did, but you coached me to it."

He flashed me a wicked smirk that did very wrong things to me. I squeezed my thighs together, trying to ease the need that had suddenly grown between them.

Mental note – never drink around Liam again. This was a dangerous road I was going down, but damn did I want to hear the answer to that question.

"Well, huh…" It was the first time I saw him nervous, and the implication only worsened my state. He cleared his throat and sat up straight, facing me. "I'm not sure what had me craving it more, seeing you half-naked in that bathroom or that sassy mouth of yours." Liam licked his lips while his eyes bore into mine as his words settled in, but quickly enough, he shook his head with a sharp inhale. "But like I said, my promise stands, and it won't ever happen again, Jamie. You can trust me on that."

Fuck! Right now I didn't want him to keep that promise. I wanted to feel his lips and his touch on me again. I wanted him to ease the fire blemishing between my thighs.

"Besides," he interrupted my thoughts, "I'm sure your boyfriend wouldn't appreciate it happening again."

It was clear he was fishing for information, and I was all too eager to clarify his doubts. "I don't have a boyfriend if that's what you want to know. I'm sorry I asked, but I needed to know. I've never had anyone kiss me like that before." Why on earth did I feel the need to share that?

"What? I'm not sure I can believe that!"

"Go ahead. It's the truth." Jack's out of the box now, might as well just go with the flow, even though the tide was high, rippling and pulling hazardously.

"Why wouldn't you have… Ohhhh!" Liam's eyes widened in shock as he scooted closer to me, his face barely an inch away from mine as he whispered, "Are you a virgin, Miss Harden?"

I couldn't believe he was asking me that question. And adding insult to injury, he was using the 'Miss Harden' spell that always hit me straight where it ached so good.

"I'm not sure that's an appropriate question, Mr. Dornier." I joked, pushing him back with my palm planted on his handsome face.

He laughed his way back to a less disturbing distance, "Humor me."

"No, I'm not. Happy? I've had sex once."

"Once? Well, well, well. Color me shocked. I would never have guessed you were soooo experienced." He mocked me while I stared at him in utter disbelief that I'd said that out loud.

Another mental note. No more alcohol. Ever.

"If I deconstruct that phrase, that means you lost your virginity, and that was it."

"How smart are you to infer that?" I mocked, trying to avoid the question I knew was coming.

"Why?" And there it was. *This is how I go. Death by embarrassment.*

"Isn't that a too personal conversation to be having with my boss, Mr. Dornier?" I was hoping that was enough to end the awkward prying into my non-existent sex life.

Liam's eyes squinted into sharp lines, his expression taking on a dark shade of mischief. "I've had my tongue shoved so far down your throat I could almost taste your breakfast. I know your boobs fit just right in my palm, and I can confidently say I made your panties soak right through your pants as you rubbed yourself against my cock. Some formalities have flown out the window by now, Miss Harden. Besides, I'm curious to know what happened to put off such a responsive little thing like you."

I could hear that tone of his in my bones, my blushing cheeks, and my needy pussy. Liam wasn't making things any easier for me, and despite telling me he would honor his promise not to kiss me again, apparently teasing me to death wasn't off the table entirely.

"I'm gonna need more alcohol if this is where the conversation is headed," I joked, waiting for him to relent, but he held his ground offering me the beer he held in his hand.

"Cheers," I said, downing the rest of the drink in search of a concealing veil for my embarrassment since I was opening this Pandora's box. "Okay, so… Prince Charmings, carriages, and white horses are never real, and neither are girls' expectations for the perfect first time. So, I uncomplicated things and just did it. Like when you have to rip off a band-aid." I shrugged, "I can't say it was exactly enjoyable. The whole two minutes of it were painful and awkward, and at the end of the day, the whole thing didn't exactly spark the desire to do it again," I blurted as quickly as I could, waiting for the backlash in his response.

"That sounds like everything sex should NOT be. You need someone to show you how it's really done. Only then can you know what you're truly missing out on." His devilish grin soaked me through as the possibilities behind his words sunk in. I had pictured him while I was in the shower the day we met and kissed in the elevator. My sorry excuse of a sex life, if I could even call it that, would be entirely different if Liam had been my first.

I swallowed the lump in my throat, trying to tame the permanent blush on my cheeks since this conversation began. I needed to throw a bucket of ice on it before I made him break that damn promise.

"Like I said, I haven't been here long enough. Maybe, in time, I'll find someone up to doing exactly that. Show me how it's done."

"Let me know when you do, will you? Find someone." *Damn, damn, damn. I bet you could.* I bit my tongue, forcing the words to retract while I simply nodded in reply to avoid them from slipping.

Breathe Jamie, breathe.

Even though the subject was embarrassing and too intimate for comfort, Liam didn't judge me. Whatever opinion he had about my actions, he kept to himself.

Contrary to my first impression, Liam was more approachable than what his appearance let on. Rich, gorgeous, and with his head deeply shoved up his ass. I was guessing that was a mask to deceive and scare away unwanted company.

Conversation ran way into the night, both of us sharing pieces of ourselves in an easy comfort that felt like we'd met in another lifetime.

"Hey there, Sleeping Beauty." I felt warm fingers stroking my arm in calm, soothing paths, up and down, while that husky voice woke me up from a deep slumber. I opened one eye to peep, making sure I wasn't dreaming, only to be graced with Liam's handsome face inches away from mine as he kneeled beside me. "We need to be at the site in about two hours."

"Oh my God!" I suddenly sprung up as reality sunk in, "What happened?"

"We fell asleep. You snore." Liam replied, a smile stretching from his crooked smirk.

"I do not!" I countered, frantically smoothing out my hair, which I was sure resembled a rat's nest.

I couldn't believe I had stayed the night. Nothing happened, but the walk of shame still awaited me, and I couldn't help but blush at the idea that whoever saw me would think…

"You look beautiful." Liam cut off my chain of thought, grabbing my hand and placing a coffee mug in it.

"I think your eyesight might still be hazy from those beers we had," I teased, taking a sip of my coffee before swiftly gathering my stuff, putting my shoes on, and searching for my phone under the couch. I had to hurry if I wanted to swing past home, take a shower, and change before heading back over to this side of town.

"I'm seeing you perfectly well. My eyesight has never been better." I smiled back at him as I found my phone, waving it in the air when I finally found it. "I can also see you're still using that old thing."

"Oh, yeah. Haven't had the chance to change."

"Sure," he mumbled. "Make sure you change to the new one today. That *thing* makes us look bad."

"I have to run. I'll meet you there, okay?" I shoved the phone into my purse, swinging the strap over my head as I headed for the door, Liam following behind me. "Oh, hum… and thank you. I had a great time last night. I missed having someone to talk to. I'll see you soon.

Bye." I kissed him and left his apartment, rummaging my bag for a comb.

The door shut behind me, freezing me in my tracks as I realized what I had just done. Horror settled in first. Shame and dread swiftly followed.

I had instinctively, stupidly, blindly, given my boss a goodbye peck on the lips.

CHAPTER EIGHT

Jamie

The meeting with Verten was a success, and they'd be crazy not to hand the project over to AD. Liam had worked his ass off to make it happen, and if my latest interaction with his father was any indication, I guess there was a lot more riding on the result of this particular meeting than he was letting on.

It was clear they didn't exactly see eye to eye, and judging by my own issues, I'd take every chance I got to prove my father wrong, too.

Liam had come to conquer and that was exactly what he did. I kept avoiding eye contact the whole time, but noticed how he thrived and dominated the whole scene. His dominance and unwavering confidence was as much of a turn on as his sculpted body and alluring eyes.

The lightness of last night had evaporated. I wasn't the only one playing the invisible game this morning. Liam had barely spared me a glance since I got to the construction site, flooding my gut with dread and my head with doubt. Was he mad at me for that stupid move?

He had insisted several times that he would not make the same mistake of kissing me again, and I had, without thinking, made him break that promise. I could feel the tension increasing as the meeting progressed, the distance between us growing wider than a damn canyon.

We parted ways with Verten's associates, agreeing on monthly meetings in case AD won the construction rights before walking back alone in deafening silence towards Liam's car. Still, not a word about the kiss.

He offered me a ride back to the office, and search as I might, my head was too cluttered with other stuff to find a proper reason to decline. I would have preferred to. My chest was filled with dread as I anxiously waited for him to address the damn elephant, and quite frankly, being in a tight space with Liam again was playing with me more than I'd like to admit.

If his apartment was less of a wealth statement than I was expecting, his car was the complete opposite. A long metal plaque on the side read 'Mercedes Maybach 6.' I'd never seen such a beautiful convertible in my life. It was modern yet somehow had a classic vibe, with a strange exuberant purity in its clean lines. A mixture of a Mustang and a Corvette in a deep midnight blue, with a stretched-out hood contrasting with a snow-white interior. Nothing short of extravagantly sensual.

Liam opened the car door for me, my annoyance spilling through the means of a raised eyebrow. "What? I'm a gentleman!" I could read between the lines – 'never kiss and tell' – but he was smooth enough to cover his bases with the double meaning.

Anxiety turned into frustration, which led to passive-aggression as we drove without so much as a whispered word between us. My blood was boiling over as my jaw hurt from clenching my teeth the whole damn ride. Finally, the silence was too much to take.

"Could you just say it already?" I blurted, tucking one leg under the other as I turned to confront him.

"Who said I had anything to say?" It was clear Liam was enjoying my agony. I could see it in his annoying grin. At least he wasn't mad as I had thought.

"You don't? You seriously want me to believe that? I know for a fact that either a reprimand or embarrassing and snarky comments have been running through your mind the whole morning. I can take it. Shoot."

"Jamie, I don't have anything to say. There is only one thing on my mind right now, and even though talking can be involved, it's certainly not mandatory." His voice had done that thing again when it dropped dangerously low, speaking straight to that part of me that hummed right back in response. I squirmed in my seat, my pussy rubbing into the leather as the small friction brought some instant relief, only increasing the need for more as soon as I stopped. He was messing with me and succeeding.

"Really? And what is that, Mr. Dornier?" Bluff called.

"Lunch." Liam smiled, another double meaning purposely hiding behind his words. "Will you give me the pleasure of your company?"

I huffed in annoyance again, this time with myself for knowing it was a trap but hoping it wasn't, nonetheless. "Whatever you say, *Boss*."

Liam exhaled a chuckle, his grin spreading all the way to his eyes before he breathed the single worst thing he could say to me, "Good girl."

I swallowed those words together with the lustful lump in my throat, wishing he was whispering them into my ear.

No, no, no, no, no!

I faced the road again, forcing myself to erase the sound of that from my mind permanently. Liam was a dangerous distraction I couldn't afford, not to mention he reeked of fuck-boy vibes. He'd do me good, only to do me so so so bad.

Not a freaking chance!

I'd lost track of where we were headed, and soon enough, Liam was pulling up into a private parking lot, darting out of the car, and opening the door for me again. He held out a hand, wrapping it around my fingers as he aided me in stepping out of the Mercedes, and instead of letting go, he placed my hand on his arm, guiding me toward the building.

I was all bubbles and butterflies inside. This felt too good to be true.

We stepped into the restaurant, and I was instantly enchanted by the atmosphere, my annoyance and apprehension completely dissipating at the entrancing sight before me. The lighting was warm and intimate, with golden chandeliers illuminating the space and small, low-hanging lamps providing a romantic and inviting glow in an otherwise dark room. The walls were a deep red, accentuated by the crisp white tablecloths and the plush, velvety chairs. The smell of delicious Italian cuisine wafted through the air, and I was immediately taken aback by how delectable it was.

"It's one of my favorites," Liam whispered behind me just as the waitress approached to show us to our table while he guided me with a hand dangerously placed on the small of my back. I couldn't help the shiver from running down my spine as soon as I felt his warm touch. "I hope you like Italian." Once more, his lips cooed against my ear, my panties flooding with need. *Oh God, how does he do that with just a whisper?*

I shook my head, focusing on the surroundings. I could hear the soft sound of opera in the background as we made our way towards the back of the restaurant, secluded, intimate, and private. I couldn't stop looking around, taking everything in. The attention to detail was impeccable. Every decoration had a purpose, from the intricate detailing on the ceiling to the delicate serving dishes on the table, all of it carefully chosen and combined to provide an unparalleled experience.

Liam pulled out my chair like the real gentlemen he had just stated he was, gracing me with a small smile once I took my seat.

"Liam! I'm delighted to see you here today. We weren't expecting your visit." The waitress gushed with an excited smile, her hand intimately resting on Liam's forearm while she bent down, showing off her cleavage almost enough for me to see through to her belly button.

"Good afternoon, Kayla. Could you bring us the menu, please, and a bottle of *Barolo?* Leave it to breathe a little while we wait for our order."

"A *Barolo?* Of course! A special occasion, I see." She replied, eyeing me up and down with a badly concealed disgusted expression.

"Something like that. The menus, please? Thank you." Liam said, dismissing her.

"What's a *Barolo*? I'm guessing it's wine, but what's so special about it?"

"It's shipped here directly from Italy, costs about a grand."

"WHAT?" I whisper-shouted in a concerned outrage. I was scraping to make ends meet, there was no way I could afford to pay for that. I shook my head continuously, "Liam… I huh–"

"Wipe that thought away. You are not even touching your wallet today. I invited you for lunch, it's my treat."

"I know you invited me, but I was thinking more along the lines of a food-truck lunch or hot dog stand. I… I can't afford this."

"Then just think it's AD's way of thanking us for nailing that meeting and sealing the deal."

"They haven't even decided yet."

"Don't worry, they'll decide before our food is here and then we can toast to it. Even if they don't, a celebration is still in order."

"Celebration for what?" The waitress was back, showing Liam the bottle of wine and receiving a small nod in return. "Liam, please, can we just leave?"

Pop.

"Oh my God, did she just uncork it? She did, didn't she?" I panicked, my head falling into my hands.

"Jamie, let's get one thing straight. When you're with me, you're taken care of, do you understand? Food truck or a high dine, it doesn't make a difference. Can I share this with you? Please?" Liam pried my hands from covering my eyes, making me meet his that pierced right through me, and I felt myself conceding before the words were even out of my mouth.

"Okay, fine. But can't we order tap water instead?" Liam laughed uncontrollably and I was caught in a spell watching him, admiring how beautiful this man was and how deep in trouble I already was.

"No chance in hell, Baby." It's an expression, I knew that. He meant nothing by it, but I couldn't help the tingles that soared through my skin as I heard him say it… *Baby.*

Kayla was suddenly back with the menu. I opened it but couldn't find it in me to actually read it. Instead, I was stuck watching and listening to Liam's exchange with the woman. She was overly friendly, a flirtatious tone in her voice matched by the twist of an ankle every time she spoke. Disguised touches to his arm, sometimes his shoulder, their words all muffling into Charlie Brown's teacher's voice as that irrational feeling seeped into me again. My stomach twisted into tight knots while my gut felt like a hole had taken over its space.

I'm jealous? Again?

Kayla bent down, whispering something in Liam's ear, and that ethereal sound of his laughter filled the room once again. That sound that I had only heard in the privacy of his house and then again just a moment ago, and wished I could bottle up and keep it for myself alone. Hearing him laugh like that with another woman was the push over the edge I didn't see coming.

"Now that the excessive flattery is over and unless you want to follow her out back and find a more intimate place where you can finish whatever just happened," I snorted as soon as Kayla left, the words leaving my mouth without permission while Liam's lips twisted into an amused smirk. "I'd like to talk about what I did this morning."

"Well then, talk." His face turned into an unreadable, blank expression, turning my previous assertiveness into uncertainty. I couldn't read what was going through his mind, and that was enough to make me feel uneasy, so I just cut straight to the chase.

"I just wanted to say that it was a meaningless impulse. I'm sorry. I didn't realize what I was doing, and I have no plausible explanation, either. But I'll be sure to avoid this kind of behavior in the future." I swallowed my pride and shame with a sip of the water the waitress had poured into my glass, glad that I had gotten it off my chest, but still expectant towards Liam's reply that was taking a beat too long to come.

"I didn't mention it because it didn't mean anything. The only thing I have to say is that I made you a promise, and I'm the kind of man who sticks to those. I won't kiss or touch you again. That's what you're worried about, right?" I didn't want to admit to that, but it was true, just not in the way he was implying it. "I don't have any interest in repeating my own mistakes. It's a sealed deal in my mind, Jamie. I will *never* do it again." His tone had taken a turn to the dark side now, the emphasis on the word "never" hit me like a punch in the gut, making it clear that he had no interest in me, and whatever I read between what I thought were blurred lines was nothing but a mistake.

That was exactly what I wanted, but I couldn't help the dejection that came with the rejection. Whatever fantasies I had about him were only exactly that. Fantasies. But the finality in his words slashed more than I'd expected.

I knew his type. Playboy vibes, with a different piece of ass on his arm every night for a non-negotiable one-night stand to scratch the itch and ease the edge. I couldn't be that girl. I couldn't *not* attach any strings to sex with Liam. He had kissed me *once,* and I was already feeling the tug on my heart. Liam didn't own it by any means, but I couldn't deny that something about him had caught me.

We would play, he would leave and I would bleed.

Just watching him study the menu was enough to have me all hot and bothered, dirty thoughts of him pushing me up against these blood-red walls and doing whatever he wanted to me flooding my brain without effort. We could put that thousand-dollar bottle of wine to a much better use. *Glasses are so overrated.* But I would want more, and he wouldn't spare me a second thought.

"Besides," Liam cut off my dangerous reverie, "I'm much more interested in talking about what you did last night than what you did this morning."

"Last night? What do you mean?" I was confused.

"Kayla." He called, leaving me hanging and agonizing over what he referred to. "Since Miss Harden hasn't taken a glance at her menu, I'll order for both of us. Ossobuco, please. And bring the wine." He barked the order and Kayla quickly scrambled away without a word.

"I don't understand what you mean. Nothing happened, right?"

"Wrong." His gaze pierced right through me. He was back to the Liam I bumped into a week ago, all dark, sharp edges and cutting words. "So I hear you accepted a job at MG Enterprise." It wasn't a question. It was a statement spit out with a venomous tone that chilled me to my core.

"How do you know about that?"

"I make it my business to know everything. You should remember that." His voice was deep, dark, and dangerous. Every note was as unsettling as the last, paired with words that seemed awfully like threats. The leisurely pace at which he buttered a piece of bread unmatching his tone. I stared at the gesture, unable to meet his eyes.

"It's truly the best thing to do."

"Why, Miss Harden? I thought we were getting along just fine. No animosity, no dangerous lines being crossed."

"It's just better this way, okay?"

"Tell me why."

I stayed silent, watching his hard features as he waited for my answer.

"You left my office saying you'd think about it. The forty-five minutes it took you to get home were all but enough to make that decision? You didn't mull over it too long, that makes me think that your decision was made, meaning you lied to me. Do you hate me *that* much that you can't fathom the thought of working with me?" I was frozen to my spot, not a blink or batter.

How could he not realize it was the exact opposite? That I couldn't focus with him around. That for the first time in my life, I wanted to get stuck in a damn elevator. With him.

My words were stuck in my throat, trying to find an answer that would both satisfy him while not telling him the truth. My eyes fell to my hands that laid on my lap, gripping the silky napkin, not being able to hold his smoldering gaze.

"I don't hate you," I finally replied in almost a whisper.

"It doesn't matter," he grunted, "You're not going."

"Yes, I am. It's done. If you're the kind of man that keeps your promises, you can certainly understand that I am, too. There's nothing you can do to make me stay."

"Oh, but there is, Miss Harden. Don't doubt me. You're not going anywhere." Was that another threat, because it damn well sounded like one. No, wait, it was a statement, no ifs there.

"What did you do?"

"Righted a wrong. As I said, MG is not a good fit for you."

"I'll be the judge of that."

"I don't know how else you want me to put this. But I'll be as clear as I can. You. Are not. Leaving. AD." He punctuated each word with a pause, forcing a smile at the end as the period.

"Liam…" I said, a weak threat underlining my tone. I didn't want to make a scene in the restaurant.

"I called Miles and told him he couldn't have you. That you're *mine*." His eyes bore into mine, the second meaning behind those words sinking into every inch of my skin, setting it ablaze. He let them sit out in the open, just long enough for me to feel their sweetness before correcting himself. "You work for *me*, Miss Harden. End of discussion."

"You did what?"

"MG Enterprise is not a good fit for you," Liam said, ignoring my question altogether. "You'll be underpaid and overworked. Besides, Miles is a misogynistic pig who doesn't know how to keep his hands to himself." Liam's hands balled into tight fists while his jaw clamped in rhythmic pulses as he mulled over his last statement. "No way he's putting his filthy hands on you."

"Is it common practice? The hands…" I was poking the bear, I knew it, but the anger rising in me needed an outlet.

"That was different."

"You don't own me, you know?"

"Kinda do." His nose scrunched in mockery as he spoke. "For five years, at least. That's what your contract states."

"I didn't sign any contract."

"Last night you did."

"You wouldn't…" I replied in disbelief.

"No, but you sure did. You were adamant about making the point that you wouldn't leave, so you made me print it, and you signed it. Imagine my surprise when I heard differently this morning."

"You trapped me into signing the contract?"

"Nope, all you. I have footage if you don't trust that I'm telling the truth."

"Footage?" Kayla came back with the wine, filling our glasses and pausing the conversation in the process, batting her eyelashes to Liam and I couldn't hold back the eye-roll.

"That's the kind of attitude that could get you into a lot of trouble," Liam said as she left.

"What?"

"The eye-roll," he replied before shaking his head and getting back on track. "Footage, yes. Surveillance cameras. You can check them if you want. I didn't force you to do anything. You were leaving because of what happened in that elevator. I told you there's no need to worry, it's in the past, Jamie. It was my mistake, and I couldn't have you paying for the dumb shit that I do. So now you can stay at your dream job and go back to hating me if you want."

"I told you I don't hate you."

"Your tone at the moment implies differently."

"I'm just… This is a big deal for me, Liam. I can't afford a thousand-dollar bottle of wine, or places like this. I ride the subway to work and I can barely make my rent payments on time. There's a lot riding on this job working out for me, and messing it up is just not an option."

"Then it's a good thing I prevented you from making a big mistake." If I were thinking clearly I'd say he was coming off as a controlling jerk, but I knew he was helping me. MG wasn't half as good as AD. And then there was that beating piece of me that tugged me in his direction at every pump.

Liam's phone buzzed, the screen lighting up with a new message, catching his attention. A big smile spread his lips making him square his shoulders and sit straighter, a relieved exhale coming out of his nose.

"So let's toast to you keeping the job of your dreams and not making the mistake of quitting. With a smile, Jamie." I raised my glass to clink with his, trying as hard as I could to smile. "An honest and wider smile, Miss Harden, cause AD just got the job, thanks to you."

"Alison!" I called out from the hallway towards her desk, ushering her into a more private spot. She worked two floors down where the interior design department was, and I was still new enough that I hardly recognized a face here. "I know you're not that busy, come over here!" Alison laughed silently and followed behind me.

We had gotten really close this past month, but somehow I hadn't found it in me to share anything about Liam. I didn't want people to think that I got any type of special treatment because of what happened, not that she would judge, but somehow I found myself doing it for her.

"I was deep in concentration, and you interrupted that. This better be worth it," she joked, not being able to hold back that naughty grin of hers.

"It's my birthday tomorrow, I was thinking maybe we could go out or something?"

"Tomorrow? You could have given me a little more notice. I would have thrown you a little party."

"No, no, no, no. No parties, please. I don't normally do anything for my birthday, I always feel a little depressed, to be honest, but I kinda need the distraction," I confessed. But drinks and a girl's night out sounded like just what I needed to get Liam off my mind, even for just one night.

"Well, there's this new club in town, I can get us in without a problem. We can go if you'd like. But, you'll have to tell me all about this guy you need to shake off."

"There's no guy." I replied as convincingly as I could.

"Sure, lie to my face, Miss Harden." I rolled my eyes at her, sighing in defeat.

"Okay, deal." I conceded holding my hands up in mock surrender. I could tell her about him and still keep his identity a secret.

"So it's a date."

"Sounds perfect. Now I just have to find something appropriate to wear." I had indulged in some online shopping after receiving my first paycheck from AD. Amazon was a good ally when it came to picking out stuff that would make me blush in a physical shop. Somehow I ended up buying a garter belt and stocking set that came with a lace babydoll and matching thong, all fit for a porn star. I loved it even though I had no practical use for the thing and no one to enjoy it with.

"Don't worry, we can meet after work today and go shopping for a birthday present and buy you something completely *in*-appropriate." We both laughed and for the first time, I found myself looking forward to my little birthday celebration.

It came at the perfect time, too. Being in a constant state of conflict with myself was exhausting and I needed a break. I couldn't deny how Liam affected me or how badly I wanted him. But he had been perfectly clear about our situation, and it was undoubtedly the best thing to do.

Never, as he had put it, was a long time, and I couldn't waste my life thinking about my boss in ways that I totally shouldn't. It wasn't going to happen and I needed to move on.

"Jamie, can you step into my office for a moment, please?" Liam called as soon as I arrived at my desk.

"Sure," I replied, a small nervous smile on my face.

I walked into his office, mindlessly leaving the door open, Liam's eyes swerving from me to the door and back, a dry smile etching the corners of his mouth.

"Don't worry, I won't bite," he reassured me, not knowing I'd much prefer he would. I was losing it, desperately needing to get a grip on myself. This obsession was starting to feel less than healthy. I closed the door before going to stand right in front of his desk.

"I'll be staying in later than usual today. The second Verten meeting is scheduled for tomorrow, and I could use your help with the prep."

I rubbed my sweaty hands, the uneasy feeling creeping up my spine. I shouldn't say no, but I needed time away from him, and the thought of the two of us alone at AD late at night gave me the type of jitters it definitely shouldn't.

"I can do it myself, there's no problem if you can't," Liam continued, catching on to my nervousness.

"I really hate to say no, but I kind of have a date Friday, and I need to get something to wear." It was out of my mouth before I could hold it. That simple statement had me looking like a superficial bimbo.

"Oh. A date!" His voice was drenched in surprise and something else I couldn't pin. "Sure, do whatever you need to do. I'll do the work myself. See you tomorrow."

"It's not a real date—"

"I don't need to know the details," Liam interrupted with a cold tone of indifference that hit me like a punch to the gut. "Keep your private life private." He got up and held the door open, motioning with his hand for me to leave while I took a second too long to react. I was struck by his words, rooted to my spot, trying to make sense of his reaction before Liam insisted again, "Do you mind?"

I crossed the threshold, my brows furrowed in confusion, searching his face for an answer to what the hell just happened. He closed the door right behind me and that was the last time I saw him today.

I thought we were past this, I had shared very private things with him at his request. Now he was back to wedging a distance between us with his dick-like attitude.

Why was my stomach so tight? I felt like I'd done something wrong and was about to suffer dire consequences because of it. I'd like to think it was because I had used the wrong words and told him I had a date. I did, but with Alison.

Never.

That word came back into my mind as I sunk into my chair, erasing the wishful thinking. He was pissed because I had denied him help, because I wasn't pulling my weight and he had to do it for me. It didn't help with the gut-wrenching feeling to acknowledge that, but going back into his office and taking it back wouldn't help either, so I stuck to the plan and went shopping with Alison.

I sat at my desk the next morning, completely lost in thought, while Steven, a colleague also working on the Verten project, talked beside me.

Just as he had promised, Liam hadn't touched or kissed me again. Five whole damn weeks had gone by since he did, and nothing. My craving to feel him again went from sizzling to an all-consuming fire I couldn't find a way to extinguish. I had to make an extra effort to focus when he was around, but all in all, I hadn't regretted staying at AD. Professionally that is.

To deny there was tension between us was being naive or trying to purposefully fog my own perception of reality. Some days it simply wasn't manageable and I found myself needing to take care of it as soon as I got home. If Liam felt the same, he was an expert in masking it. Nothing about him gave anything away besides a normal and comfortable professional relationship.

Things had been civil between us, and I found myself enjoying his company more and more as time went by. That made it even worse. My *thing* for him, which had yet to gain a name, meaning, or definition, was going from a purely physical fixation into something else. Something that scared me shitless.

It was too easy to be around him. Too easy to fall into comfortable conversation beyond work related topics. Too easy to get lost looking at him.

I felt his gaze on me, too, sometimes. Those alluring green eyes calling to me just as they were now. I glanced away from my screen to confirm that he was looking at me, and unlike all the other times, Liam wasn't budging today when I met his stare. He held steady, his expression turning broody and dark, reincarnating the first version of him I had met. He was a man full of layers, and this one was the most thrilling one of all.

He wore a mask that said "don't fuck with me" today, the danger lurking behind it evident on the sharp edges of the daggers shooting from his eyes towards me.

Towards me?

He held me pinned under his glower, never swerving as he stood up from behind his desk and stalked towards me. I couldn't help but shift in my seat, hesitant and expectant of what the hell that look meant.

There was a slow shiver slithering down my spine, creeping lower at each step he took, the pressure building in my gut as he reached his door and slammed it shut.

What the hell?

Something in me expected him to stomp over, grab my hand, take me to the service staircase, and pin me to the wall. I'd let him, no doubt in my mind.

"Jamie?" Steven called from beside me. He was hunched over me as he typed on my keyboard from behind. "Are you still with me?"

"Hum, yes, sure." I forced a smile, looking up at him, feeling guilty I hadn't heard a word he said before Michelle startled us, coming out of nowhere.

"I wouldn't go there if I were you, Honey. That's a hole you can never dig yourself out of. You won't like what you find there, either," she said, her smile just as fake as her boobs.

"No, we were just working," Steven quickly replied, backing away from me, completely missing what she was saying.

I narrowed my eyes at her, forcing a smile on my face, too, but not uttering a word.

"Jamie." Liam called from behind her, all three of us whipping our heads towards him as he marched down the hall. "Meeting at the Verten site. Now."

He didn't stop as he spoke, making me scramble to my feet, gather my stuff, and run after him, meeting him right in front of the last place we should be together right now.

The elevator.

CHAPTER NINE

Liam

Jamie Harden was a walking contradiction. She was reserved and shy at times, coming off as fragile, but then there was this fire in her that blasted everyone to a safe distance when she felt cornered against a wall. Figuratively and literally.

She had thrown the mother of all bombs at me yesterday. Something so small that had a corrosive effect I hadn't seen coming.

She was going on a fucking date!

A motherfucking date!

Why that filled me up with so much rage was beyond me. I could have torn my office into shreds as soon as I walked her out. But I couldn't show her how much it got to me, and it wouldn't have been a silent affair if I did.

I had made her a fucking promise. For her well-being, not mine, but fuck, did I want nothing more than to break it, and her, every way I knew how. She was leaving, and that concession seemed necessary at the time, but I was starting to regret it with every fiber of my being. I didn't want her to leave, but it shouldn't have been at the expense of letting her run loose in this world full of… *men*!

I thought it was what she wanted. What *I* wanted. Fuck, was I wrong.

Why do I even care? She sure doesn't.

Jamie was standing behind me. I could feel her uneasiness without even glancing over at her. The sight of what's-his-face hanging over her wrecked the final layer of restraint I had left in me. So she knew she got the dark side of me today.

"Did you get it?" I spoke as we walked into the elevator, the two of us alone in it once again. Damn, if these fucking walls could talk, they'd be singing a symphony of lust and stupidity right to my face, a tone of mockery underlining each spirited note.

"Get what?" Jamie asked. Her voice was small and weary as she stood beside me, watching the side of my face intensely as I locked my eyes straight ahead as if the stainless steel doors were more interesting than her.

"Something to wear to your date tonight."

"Hum, yeah. I did."

"Let's hope this meeting doesn't run late then. Prince Charming shouldn't be kept waiting." I was bitter. I could feel the acidity on my tongue as I spoke those words.

Jamie was about to counter, her mouth opening only to shut again as the doors dinged open, letting in a couple more people.

I had no idea what I was looking for with my provocation. Even if she wanted me as badly as I craved her, we still couldn't be together. It wasn't fair to her. My life was too messed up, too complicated to tangle her into a web she most probably couldn't handle.

We drove in silence to the construction site, avoiding each other the whole time we were there.

Once again, she had blown Verten's representatives' minds away, captivating them just as she had me. At least it wasn't Mr. Mercier attending today. I wasn't sure I could take his crap light-heartedly today as instructed by father dearest. I was unfit for ass-kissing on a good day. Today I'd tell him to fuck off without shying away from the crass language.

Soon enough, I was driving back to AD alone. Jamie had some bullshit excuse she threw at me, avoiding being in the same space as my moody ass. I couldn't help it. If only she knew how fucking enraged I was... but she couldn't. I was nothing to her and it should stay that way, I reasoned with myself over and over, hoping it would stick.

Yet reason held nothing over the bloodlust and punishment I was craving. Hers, of course.

I wanted to see if she'd crack, if she cared enough to react. To see her squirm and hurt for me, and I knew just the way to do it.

Yeah... reason was a word my dictionary didn't hold when it came to Jamie Harden.

I didn't care for mixing business with pleasure, meaning AD employees were out of the question – don't eat the meat where you earn your bread. I didn't date, fuck, or mingle with anyone from the office, even though my father thought I fucked every female who ever had a job here. It wasn't my fault they wanted to, but I didn't need that messy shit.

Michelle was the sole exception, and only because I had slept with her before she was hired. We occasionally still hooked up to get the edge off, an itch-and-scratch kind of situation. The deal was crystal for both of us, no mixed lines or misunderstandings.

And suddenly today I was feeling an itch I needed to have scratched.

It was petty as fuck. I knew that, yet I couldn't bring myself to care. I needed to make Jamie forget all about my hot-headed reaction to her date, and more than that, I wanted to see if she had a reaction to what I was about to do, too.

I needed to know if I was burning alone or if Jamie was standing right beside me.

The idea of someone else's dirty hands all over her had me craving destruction. I should find out who the lucky fucker was, make him pay for trying to take what could never be his.

There was this sickening image constantly wreaking havoc in my mind – candles, flowers, wine, all of it thrown at her in a fake parade of chivalry, just for a chance to get into her pants. I will be standing outside her door tonight making sure that doesn't happen.

I fought the urge to order Jimmy to send a shadow to her place. Mission? Scare off any dumb fuck who dared to step too close for comfort.

Fuck, fuck, fuck. Get a fucking grip! She's just some pussy you haven't tasted. Absolutely nothing else.

I tried repeating that in a loop. The forbidden fruit was always the sweetest, the grass was always greener on the other side, we always want what we can't have, bla bla fucking bla. Lies, all of it! She was so much more than that.

I bit my bottom lip, almost drawing blood as I sat behind my desk, watching as she settled into hers. I had that desk vacated for Jamie on purpose so I could watch her or shut the door when I couldn't handle it.

Jamie smiled at her phone as she tapped on the screen, probably texting her date, and that alone was enough for me to lose it.

"Michelle," I called out, walking towards my door, loosening my tie, and unbuttoning the two top stranglers of my shirt. I plastered a mischievous smile on my lips, waiting for her, watching as she sashayed her way over. She knew what that smile meant, and she was all for it. I didn't spare Jamie a single glance, yet I knew she was watching. I could feel the heat of her stare on me.

Michelle swayed her way over to my office as sexily as she could, just as all the other times. I greeted her with a devilish smile as she arrived at my door, closing it straight behind her.

We had done this a few times before. She was always up for it, too. Michelle let her hair fall loose from the all-professional updo she had going on, shaking her head, spreading all the strands for me to grab at will. I hesitated halfway and let my hand fall back to my side.

Michelle's hand ran the length of my chest, prying its way under my shirt as she opened it up, feeling every muscle while the other reached for my face.

She was hot as fuck. Everyone with eyes had to admit to that, yet today, all this, her hands, her hungry eyes, was doing absolutely nothing for me. She wasn't sparking the need to fuck her right here on my desk as she once had.

My mind was firmly set on the brunette on the other side of that closed door, the notion that she'd be doing this with some dumb-fuck tonight deflating any arousal still left in me.

FUCK. FOCUS!

Michelle's hand reached down between us to grip my cock, finding herself surprised to feel it soft. She stopped, her brows furrowed in confusion as she intently studied my face before stretching to kiss me. On instinct, I turned my face, and her kiss landed on my cheek. I thought I could do this, but something in me was screaming about how wrong it was.

"Liam?" Michelle asked. I could read between those lines. There was soft confusion on her face but what she really wanted to ask was "What the fuck?"

"What?" I grunted angrily, pulling her hands from my face and groin. Her lipstick had smudged all over her lips with the sudden graze on my cheek. On any other given Monday, that sight would have done it for me. I'd never have another normal fucking Monday in my life.

"Is everything okay?" *NO! Everything is not fucking okay. I can't even get off because of her. This has never happened before, how can everything fucking be okay?*

"Yes, fine," I replied instead. "I have work to do. You can go." I coldly dismissed her, Michelle's face twisting into a puzzled expression. "Today." I grunted as she took a little too long to follow through.

I'm a fucking idiot.

I watched her as she opened the door while fixing her hair and cleaning off what she could of her smudged lipstick. This had achieved absolutely nothing, so I turned towards my desk and let my body heavily fall onto the leather chair. My head sprung up as soon as I heard

Michelle's pissed-off voice, "What? Don't you have work to do? Mind your own business."

She finally left my office, the view now completely unobstructed. I was faced with wide brown eyes, a slightly ajar mouth, and the expression I was craving to see plastered on that angelic face.

Jamie was hurt, and fuck did I feel like shit in my own delight.

Jamie

Right then and there, I knew just how deep in trouble I was.

It was clear I had nothing to hold on to, if for some fucked up reason I still had my hopes up before.

From the looks of it, there was a very intimate reason why Michelle was Liam's fan "numero uno," as Alison had put it. They surely knew each other better than I had thought.

I fought back the urge to scream that came with the burning tears I didn't allow to fall. I had no right to feel this way. Liam wasn't my anything, I had no claim over him and no say in who he kissed, fucked, or loved.

Yet the visceral need to punch fake Barbie in the throat was more revealing than I'd like.

Liam, on the other hand, had proven to be exactly what I had made him out to be – a man whore.

Six o'clock had never taken longer to come, and to add insult to injury, Liam had kept his door wide open. I had no idea where we were going tonight, but the booze better be strong and flowing. I had memories to erase.

Alison had been out of reach the whole day, except for that embarrassing video she had sent wishing me a happy birthday. If only she knew how that was going. She was the only one, actually. Not even my father had called or texted me. He must have forgotten, as usual.

I looked up from the drawings sprawled all over my desk, Liam's green eyes meeting mine straight away. As I bore my gaze into them,

I decided I had had enough. I could regret it tomorrow, but tonight, I'd erase the shit out of him.

He was still staring right at me, and as soon as the clock turned six, I stormed out of the office, heading straight home before that conviction waivered.

I'd leave nothing to chance, deciding to pull that full lingerie set I bought on Amazon out of the box, paired with the slutty black dress I had bought yesterday with Alison, high heel boots that ended just above my knees, and a leather jacket.

I was dressed and made-up to kill tonight. My confidence needed the boost, and my bruised ego thanked me as I took my reflection in.

I wasn't worthy of his affection, that's what it said back to me, but today, I chose not to listen. I couldn't or I'd break.

Alison rang from downstairs. She was waiting for me, and suddenly my boost started to give in again, and I wished I was staying home instead. I closed my eyes, shook my head, and took in a sharp inhale, ignoring the derogatory thoughts.

"Damn girl, you look dirty hot." Alison practically shouted from the car while I made my way over towards her. I did feel sexy, but my mood certainly wasn't matching my outfit.

"You look reasonable, too, Alison. Who could have guessed you could look even slightly attractive," I teased her. Alison was an absolutely beautiful woman. She didn't need makeup, fake lashes, or fake boobs to turn heads everywhere she went. Tonight, though? She was ravishing, her green eyes sparkling in contrast with her devilishly sexy red dress, while her straight dark hair framed her face perfectly. She knew what she looked like and used it to her advantage.

"Shut up." She nudged me as I got in the car. "Let's get you wasted, shall we?"

"Maybe?" I hesitated.

"That's not the answer I was looking for. Getting you out of your own head tonight is my personal project. I can sense you need to have fun. Live a little, moral code be damned."

The image of Michelle stepping out of Liam's office with her lipstick all smudged around her lips came back, stomping all over my mood again, and I needed that to stop. I needed to find a way to put Liam out of my mind for good.

"I think you're right! Let's do this. Are there any hot guys in this club you're taking me to

CHAPTER TEN

Jamie

The club was absolutely incredible. The epitome of luxury and indulgence, packed to the brim with people in matching description.

Dea Tacita read the slick, backlit, metal plaque at the entrance. Exuberantly posh didn't quite cover the feel of this place. It was like I'd stepped into a different dimension made up of architectural finesse, good taste, and money. Lots and lots of money.

Alison had reserved us a table in the VIP section. She had told me she had connections here, and by the way we slipped past the long line at the entrance, her connections were damn good.

There was a bottle of *Dom Perignon* dipped in ice waiting for us on the table, with two flutes and a small birthday cake, the fake candles glowing a shimmering light in the darkened space.

"Happy birthday, Jamie." Alison hugged me, her gesture bringing tears to my eyes. "No, ma'am. None of that tonight. This is a fun night, we can leave the mushy crying for tomorrow."

We both stood closer to the tall table while a blonde woman opened the bottle of champagne, filling our glasses, before cutting the cake and serving it on golden plates.

Just as we toasted, a tall man stepped behind Alison, snaking his hand around her stomach before doing the same to me, pulling us flush against his body to whisper into our ears, "You pretty ladies want to do a line or two with us?"

He nudged towards the table next to ours, where a line of white powder was neatly stretched, and everything inside me froze at the sight. Alison tore out of his grasp, pulling me with her and stepping between us in a protective stance.

Her neck craned left and then right before she settled back down, her shoulders slumping from the stiff alert they had previously gained with an exhale of relief. Not even a second later, what seemed like an army of men crowded the space, the dirty blonde one in a black suit snatching my champagne glass from my hand and throwing the contents onto the pile of cocaine.

"Fuck, man. What the hell do you think you're doing?" The other guy protested at the loss of his goods.

His glacial blue eyes tore from the man's back to meet Alison's, a small nod and a sly smile towards her showing me they knew each other. He was intense and beyond handsome, intimidating and dashing in equal measures.

"No drugs in *this* club, Asshole. Boss's orders," he said with a shrug. The handsy druggy and his two friends were now being manhandled out of the club under his sharp inspection before he turned away and went back up the far stairs, knowing they'd be handled and escorted out, not a single word directed at us.

I was in a daze, trying to understand what the hell just happened, watching the stranger calmly walk away, turn back, and flash another smirk toward Alison.

"Oh… he likes you!" I teased, trying to ease the heavy mood.

"Max? Nah. He's like an older brother."

"That was a damn incestuous look then."

"Shut up." Alison swatted my arm before looking back towards where he had now disappeared to.

"That was a fast response time. How do you know him again?"

"Come." She took my hand, not bothering to respond, and led the way downstairs to the middle of the dance floor, the music getting louder with every step we took.

She pulled me towards one of the bars, pushing and squeezing through all the people obliviously dancing around us. She stopped in front of the sticky counter of the bar that sat in the middle of the club, with the sexy bartender behind it. Alison waved to get his attention, the man darting straight towards us once he caught sight of her.

She pulled him closer, whispering something in his ear before he turned to get whatever Alison ordered for us.

"Is he your connection?" I asked, noticing he was quick to leave the other patrons for us. "Or is Max?"

"Nope to both," she simply replied with no intention to elaborate while she mindlessly tapped on the counter to the beat of the music. Not even a minute later, the slender, hot bartender was returning with our drinks in hand.

Alison pulled out a twenty dollar bill from her clutch and locked eyes with me. I assumed she would be using it to pay for our drinks, but instead, she confidently slapped the money onto the counter and yelled over the loud music, "Twenty bucks says I can down this drink faster than you can," her mischievous grin spreading from ear to ear.

"Best out of three?" I replied, getting a little carried away, pulling out my own twenty to match her bet.

"Hey, Jack!" She called out to the bartender. "Can we get another four of these?" Alison asked, making me feel a twinge of doubt in the pit of my stomach as I looked at the tall glasses brimming with alcohol that had already been set before us. Jack, aka hot-booze-guy, returned shortly after, delivering two more drinks to each of us.

"Jack can ref for us. You're a cheater, I don't trust you." I chuckled, taking my chance to send Jack a little wink. He could very well be the fun I was looking for tonight.

Alison clutched her invisible pearls, feigning shock at my statement.

"I resent that! No head start for you, Birthday Girl." I laughed at her theatrics, already feeling lighter without a single drop of alcohol in my system. "Ready?"

"Set." I replied

"Go!" We shouted in unison before starting our little competition.

Alison downed the first two drinks as if they were water but slowed down on the third, allowing me to catch up. Just as I was about to finish my last, Alison opened her mouth wide and guzzled down the entire contents of her glass in one gulp as if there was a direct pipeline from her mouth to her stomach.

"It's a clean win." Jack reluctantly said as if he had taken my side, a fake pitiful look on his face.

With a small victory dance, Alison claimed her prize and stuffed the money into her cleavage, making me burst into a fit of laughter.

"Now to the good stuff," she said before turning back to Jack. "There's a bottle of *Havana Club Máximo* calling out to me. Serve us two and keep 'em coming. I hope you like rum, J, cause that's what's flowing tonight."

Fresh drinks in hand, we strutted out to the dance floor behind us, getting lost in the beat as we danced together. I was feeling the buzz of those drinks, even though Jack had been kind enough not to mix them as strongly as he could have. Still, I'm a lightweight when it comes to alcohol, and it wasn't long before inhibitions started to lift, my shoulders feeling lighter as if they had been weighing a ton.

"I have to pee," I shouted over the music, turning around and darting straight towards the corner of the club, not waiting for Alison's reply.

The line was never-ending, as it always was, so I slumped against the wall and pulled out my brand new phone, frowning at the memory of who got it for me. I knew I'd find myself regretting this tomorrow, but it was just stronger than me. My fingers moved of their own accord, not pausing for a read-through before they hit send.

> I hope fake barbie tasted like rainbows and unicorns.

It didn't even take half a minute for my phone to be buzzing with his reply.

> I'm sorry, what?

> Then again you should know by now. She seems like a regular.

> Is everything okay? Weren't you on a date?

> Everything is just perrrrrrfect. I should try it too.

> Does it work?

> What? You're not making any sense.

> You kissed Michelle. Did you fuck her too?

> Have you been drinking?

> Maybe. What's it to you?

> I'm coming to get you.

> I'll be coming, too. Just not with you.

> The only thing coming your way is an ass spanking if you keep this up.

My turn came up, so I pocketed my phone, ignoring Liam's last text, did my business, and headed to the bar where Jack was. I watched him for a minute, tossing bottles around like in the movies, serving a drink before he caught me from the corner of his eye.

I smiled as he came over, his black shirt showing just the right amount of flesh for me to know there were rippled muscles under there.

"Another rum?" He asked, already reaching for a glass.

"Sure. What time is your break?" I asked, being more forward than I normally was. But the thought of Liam kissing or maybe fucking Michelle had me tipping over an edge I've never crossed before.

"I can take one now." Jack flashed me a perfectly white smile, knowing exactly what I wanted.

"Good. Maybe we can dance a little."

He called out to his nearest colleague, telling him he was going on a break as he rushed to meet me. His hand rested low on the small of my back as we headed out to the dance floor. I was nervous, but not to the point I'd back down.

You cure a hangover with booze, so maybe I could cure this hard crush with another man. Guys did it all the time. Why did women have to be any different?

Stopping at a less crowded spot, I turned towards Jack, smiling devilishly as he draped his hands on my hips while mine dived into his longish hair just above his nape. Foreheads resting together, the glare we exchanged was flirty and did all the talking we needed.

Jack spun me around, pulling my ass flush against his crotch while his hands roamed my body as we both swayed to the sound of the deafening music. It was wrong, but I couldn't help it. I was imagining someone else behind me, and suddenly his touch turned all that more alluring. I reached behind and pulled his head closer, tilting mine to the side as he placed a kiss on my neck. His lips weren't ravishing enough, but they'd do the trick.

I took another large sip from the rum he had poured me, trying to muffle my thoughts a little more and live in the freaking moment.

I closed my eyes to concentrate, and soon enough the loud music was gone, the flashing lights dimmed, the movement around me stilled. *"Good fucking girl."*

My eyes flew open immediately as those words invaded my mind without permission, and I was in the exact same spot I was before, Jack's fingers digging deeper into my skin before they suddenly weren't. Not a palm, not a finger, not a breath.

I spun towards him, but instead, I was now facing the broad back of a man who definitely wasn't Jack, standing just an inch away from me. Taller. Bulkier. Sexier.

"Get your fucking hands off!" I felt that low growl in my gut, traveling south straight to my pussy before spreading to every part of my body. I clenched everything I had that had the ability to clench.

"Liam?" What the hell was he doing here? How did he know where I was? I thought he was bluffing.

Jack had regained his stance, starting for me again, his brows knit together with a burning fire in his eyes.

"Think straight, Jack. Don't do anything stupid. Walk. The fuck. Away. You don't want to die tonight."

Jack stopped, nose flaring before resignation took over his features, and he simply turned and left towards the bar. My mouth fell open. I was at a loss. Confusion, anger, resentment, all the above wrapped with a neat bow of 'what the fuck'.

"Did you just threaten to kill him?" My voice was high pitched, my indignation clear in that tone as I looked intently at Liam's broad shoulders, waiting for him to turn and finally face me.

He shrugged as if that was what a normal Friday night was about, throwing my exact words back at me, "Maybe. What's it to you?"

Liam had hell burning behind his eyes, his hair a rugged mess giving him that dangerous vibe I'd recognized in him that first day, his laid-back jeans and t-shirt far from his normal office attire, and with one long hard look, I was feeling myself ready to make a bad, bad decision.

Fuck he was beautiful. What was it about this man that had me melting with nothing but his presence?

I shook my head, focusing on what had just happened, bringing back the outrage I was feeling before, "What the fuck, Liam?"

"Was that your date?" He asked, but he wasn't expecting an answer. I could see that much in his eyes.

"That's none of your goddamn business."

"I'm guessing not." His tone was passive-aggressive, and I knew he was trying to etch under my skin however he could just to prove that he could. His eyes dropped to my feet, slowly climbing up as he took in every inch of me, his head cocking to the side once they landed on my exposed thighs. I watched as his tongue darted to his lips, sweeping a trail of wetness across as he finished his assessment, "Who's the fucker you've dressed like that for?"

"Again, none of your business. How did you get here so fast? What are you even doing here?"

"If you hadn't ignored your phone, you'd see I told you I was coming to get you."

"I'm off the clock, *Boss*. You don't get to dictate the rules in my personal life, too."

His jaw clenched a couple of times as he gravitated closer towards me, "Did he kiss you?" I stood there, forcing the blank expression to stay on my face, my eyes boring into his without uttering a word. "Did he?" Liam pressed, in a grunt that felt every little bit like possession.

"No." I simply clipped.

"Did you want him to?" I saw from the tic in his jaw and the murder in his eyes just how much those words cut on their way out, and I was enjoying it all too much.

"What if I did?" Liam's hand shot to his hair, his fingers wreaking havoc in his dark strands while all his muscles pumped in rage, pulling out a sarcastic laugh from my chest. "Jealousy doesn't suit you well," I simply stated, his eyes hardening even further at the impact of my words.

"It fucking suits you to perfection. Lets me know exactly where I stand."

"And where is that, Mr. Dornier?"

"On the wrong side of a fucking promise." He hissed right back at me, his face now as close as it could be to mine without touching it.

"Yours to keep and yours to break. I never asked you to make it." I was baiting him, treading a fine, hazardous line when I knew I shouldn't walk this walk, even though all I wanted right now was to feel his fingers on my throat again, his dirty words in my ear, and his hard cock between my legs.

"What are you saying, Jamie?"

I wasn't going to fall for that one. Seeing him squirm because of me was too damn delicious to pass on. I wanted more. I wanted him to break first this time. I wanted to sink my teeth so far into that wound that he'd be feeling me in his damn bones.

"Nothing. I'm just trying to have fun tonight, and you just scared my fun away. My father is miles away from here, and you're not it, so what the hell are you doing here?"

"Wishing you a happy fucking birthday."

"Noted. Thank you so very much." Sarcasm was dripping from my tongue, along with irritation, as I stood tall and faced him head on. "Now, I have someone waiting for me. Good night, Mr. Dornier."

"You're not going anywhere." Liam grabbed my wrist as I was about to leave him standing in the middle of the dance floor, dragging me towards the edge of the club.

"Get your hands off me." I pulled and tugged, trying to break free. Liam suddenly stopped, turning towards me, and in my frenzy to get out of his grasp, I crashed right into him, face and palm planted on his hard chest, trying my best not to spill the rest of my drink all over him.

Just like the first time, Liam wrapped an arm around my waist, holding me tight against him, but this time, I could feel it in his hold that he wasn't going to let go. I looked up, meeting his hypnotic gaze, all my walls crashing to piles of soft sand as he stared at me, too, his hot breath fanning my face.

"God, you're beautiful," I whispered, Liam's lips tugging upward in a sly smirk. "Shit! Did I say that out loud?"

"Yup."

"I take it back." I tore my gaze away, tipping my glass and downing the entire contents, a single drop escaping through the side of my mouth. I used my thumb to wipe it clean before taking it into my mouth and slowly sucking, my eyes suddenly captured by his, seeing just how much this little gesture messed with him.

Liam tightened his grasp around my waist, and I could feel him, really feel him. He was growing against me while each of his fingers sunk deeper into my flesh. He pulled my thumb out of my mouth after erasing his uncontrolled expression. His whole face was an ode to lust that, in a split second, turned thirsty for punishment.

"I'm trying to keep a fucking promise here, Jamie. I can't do it if you keep acting like this!" Liam was beyond pissed, yelling straight to my face. Maybe if I were sober I'd be flinching at his tone, but I wasn't, and I was craving that punishment just as much as he was. "Don't provoke me."

And just like that, Liam released me. The coldness of that gesture made every bit of me boil inside. He was turning away again, but I knew it was the last thing he wanted to do. That I wanted him to do.

I couldn't help the smirk from spreading across my lips as I realized just how hard I could get to him, too. The lack of inhibition that came with being a little drunk took away the perception of hazard, too. The lifeline between my brain and decorum was unplugged, and I was more than ready to take the plunge.

"I found him!" I shouted towards him.

"What?" He turned back in confusion, not knowing what I was talking about.

"You asked me to tell you if I found the right guy to show me how it's really done, remember? Sex…" If Liam was angry before, he just took a sharp left to the psychotic lane now.

It took him only two long, hard strides, and he was up in my face again, the vein on his forehead bulging in anger, "YOU DON'T EVEN FUCKING KNOW THE GUY!"

I had no idea where all this courage came from, but I grabbed a handful of his hair right at the base of his neck and tightened my grip to get his attention, pulling him down towards me so I could reach his ear to whisper, "Not him. You."

I pulled back to assess the damage and take in his expression, eager to see his reaction to my words, but there was none. Instead, he pulled me into him again, placing his lips on my ear so that he only had to whisper to be heard.

"What are you saying, Miss Harden? I need proper words. No half sentences waiting for me to fill in the blanks. If you want something, ask for it."

"Show me how it's done, Liam. Show me exactly what I'm missing."

"Still not enough."

I swallowed hard, pushing the shyness and embarrassment aside, allowing the alcohol to do its job and release me from bullshit conventions and finally say what I'd been craving for over a damn month, "I want… I want you to fuck me."

CHAPTER ELEVEN

Liam

Fuck my life!

Jamie was tearing me right down the middle with her words. My promise was hanging by a damn thread, and she had just cut the last feeble string.

I had been forcing myself to think straight and put her well-being first, but apparently, I'm a selfish fucker that could only think about kissing her and making her mine once and for all.

Without a proper reply to her demand, I took the glass from her hand and put it on the counter. I grabbed her wrist and pulled her behind me towards the back of the club, until we were in a dark corner close to an emergency exit.

I pushed her against the wall, giving her no escape besides the sole getaway I was about to whisper into her ear. The last opportunity she would have to back out because I couldn't see myself holding off for the sake of a high road I couldn't even see anymore.

The irony of this dichotomy, her being trapped between my body and the damn wall as I gave her permission to take those words back, was like a sadistic self-inflicted pain.

She was so close, so ripe for the taking, so sinful in her scent I could almost fucking taste it, yet I was a simple nod away from setting her free.

"Don't play with me, Jamie. I am not in a state where you can say things like that and expect me not to act on it." I could see the heat of her body rise to her face and settle fiercely into her eyes.

"Good. Because I'm waiting, and you shouldn't keep a lady waiting." There wasn't an ounce of question in her stare. No uncertainty as she held my gaze and worded my demise.

She wants this. She wants ME.

There was a predatory rumble in my chest before I unleashed him. The Liam I was taming into an unbearable submission every time I was around Jamie. My lips settled on hers with an unmatched hunger, my tongue immediately spreading her lips to savor every inch of her as I held her face between my hands. Maybe in this iron grip she couldn't flee. Maybe in my hold she couldn't leave. Maybe in my arms she would finally be mine.

These lips.

I was ravaging her without mercy, because that was exactly who I was. A merciless prick who's soul had been sold to the devil long ago. Now? He was making good on that deal, flashing an angel before me, requiring the savagest of sacrifices. If there was a choice before, right now I couldn't see it.

She tasted like rum and heartbreak. Menace and solace. Guilt and cherry lipstick.

I inched my thigh between her legs, pressing into her pussy while my hands pushed her ass further into me. I made her grind that sweet cunt against me, relishing in the breathy moan she released into my mouth.

"Ride it, Miss Harden. You're gonna come for me before we leave this club."

Jamie's eyes darted open, her head turning from one side to the other, watching the crowd in front of us, and I knew exactly what she was thinking. I grabbed her jaw, forcing her to look at me again, my leg pressing into her further while my other hand squeezed her ass harder.

"Don't worry about the people. Focus on me. No one will know." She swallowed hard at my words, still not convinced.

I placed another bruising kiss on those sexy lips of hers, biting her bottom one harder for effect. I was so lost in her I could eat her in the middle of this club just so every fucker in this damn place knew who she belonged to.

I grabbed her hand and ran it along my crotch, "This is what you do to me. Can you feel that? How hard I am for you?"

Jamie nodded, her cheeks flushed, but she should know by now that I need words.

"I can't hear your nods, Miss Harden. I need proper words," I whispered straight against her ear before kissing the tender skin of her neck, nibbling and licking to my heart's content.

"Yes. I feel it," she replied, her voice throaty and unsteady as she stretched her neck to give me better access.

"Show me how badly you want it." I bit down on her neck, pressing my thigh further against her pussy, "Ride my leg and come for me. After that, I'm taking you home and showing you exactly what you're missing out on. Exactly how much my hard cock wants you, too."

I pulled back to look into her eyes, her lip so tightly tucked between her teeth I could swear she would draw blood any second now. I pulled it out with my thumb before setting my lips on hers again in a kiss so deep I could taste her soul.

My leg rocked against her, and soon enough she was riding me on her own, my hands now freely feeling every inch of her I could reach.

"That's it, Miss Harden, chase it." I grunted into her ear, her head falling back against the wall. The sight of her was pure Heaven, and I'd burn in Hell for the wreckage I was about to cause.

The thought of what I was about to sentence her to loosened my grip on her, my thigh pulling back an inch, my conscience pulling me out of the lust-induced trance for just a second.

"No, please. I'm close," Jamie moaned, her words hitting me like a bullseye, right in that egotistical part of me that wanted her all to myself. Fuck the consequences.

I pulled her closer to me, my fingers digging into her flesh, my mouth fucking hers with my tongue, my leg punishing and unrelenting. I edged her like that before pulling back from her mouth so I could watch her fall apart.

Da Vinci, Botticelli, Klimt, all those fuckers knew nothing about art and perfection. This was it. Jamie Harden coming undone in my arms. I couldn't take my eyes away from her, watching every second of her ascension.

"That's it. Come for me, like a good fucking girl."

It was as if I'd poured the last ounce of gasoline into her raging fire. Her mouth fell open in a silent plea for release before her eyes shut as tight as they would go, her body stilled in that last moment before ultimate pleasure.

I rubbed my thigh against her clit again, the last movement needed to push her over that delicious edge before watching her fall. The bliss on her features was enough to have me craving my own release. But I needed to wait. Being inside her garnered that honor and many more.

Jamie came hard, her nails digging luscious holes into my back and arm as she held onto me for dear life until she couldn't anymore. Her knees gave out from under her, giving me the pleasure of holding her up after that sensational fall.

She looked up into my eyes, hers holding a truth that slashed at something inside me. Something I thought I didn't have.

"Fuck, you're beautiful," I murmured, swiping a strand of hair from her face. "Now let's go destroy you."

I took her hand and pulled her out of the club, waiting for Carl to pick us up.

Out here she was vulnerable. Where the darkness and deafening music of the club brought a strange sense of privacy, out here in the open, under the beam of the street lamp, Jamie shone in all her exquisiteness and her shyness, too.

I pulled her to me, her body clashing against mine as I confirmed once again if this was what she really wanted. "You can still back out."

"I don't want to." Her voice was steady, and the determination behind it just made me want her all the more.

Taking her face in my hands, I placed another one of those hungry kisses on her lips, only this time, despite its passionate start, it took a sharp left into something that tugged at the stone inside my chest.

It was a strange feeling, a new swirl inside me that burned and sizzled me to life. I pulled back, looking into her eyes, confirming if she'd felt it, too. How could I tell?

Jamie spun her head to the black SUV that slowly came to a stop beside us, cutting off my assessment and the moment. Carl and his impeccable fucking timing.

I opened the door for her, watching as she made her way inside, her dress riding up her thighs and exposing a garter that hit my crotch like lightning. Fuck, I'd never been this hard in my entire life.

I stalked in after her, asking Carl to drop us off at my apartment before mouthing a clear "behave" towards Jamie. I couldn't hold back if she unleashed that fire in this small space, and fucking her in the backseat of a car, with Carl in the front seat, didn't seem like the way to go about this.

It was a quick ride that seemed to last a freaking lifetime. The notion that Jamie was inexperienced, practically a virgin if we rely on the thirty-second rule, was extra present in my mind as I watched her. She was looking out the window, her fingers intertwined with mine, resting on the leather seat.

This girl is trouble.

I needed to reel in that feeling. Turn this into what it was supposed to be in the first place. Just. Sex.

Tugging on her hand to get her attention, I leaned in to whisper, "I'm going to make you come so hard, you won't even remember your own name. But mine? Mine will be branded on every inch of you." I watch her cheeks tint red, her eyes sparkling with the need to kiss me.

Instead, her lips moved in a silent warning, throwing my words back at me, "Behave."

My hard cock strained against my pants. The sheer sight of her and the thought of what was about to happen had me with an unrelenting hard-on since I held her up against that wall.

Jamie's eyes dropped to my crotch, her chest rising and falling at a more rapid pace as she took in the bulge in my pants.

I was about to explode. Thank fuck we were pulling up in front of my building. Grabbing Jamie's hand, I guided her out of the car, thanking Carl before slamming the door harder than was warranted, watching as he drove off.

I closed the space between us, taking out all that pent-up tension in a kiss that aimed to consume her, but yet again, whatever damn pixie dust she had turned on me. I found myself being burnt by her, craving more of her taste each time I kissed her. Craving more than what I should want from her.

The devil was indeed a cruel fucker. Dangling my ultimate vice before me in a sinful package with an even more sinful persona, knowing I'd be her doom.

I grabbed her ass with both my hands, pressing my erection into her, fuck the world around us and their prying eyes. I needed to hear her reassuring words that took the guilt away, even if only for the night.

"Tell me you want me, Miss Harden." My voice was a low-tuned command, her body shivering upon impact.

"I want you," she exhaled in a whisper.

"No. Tell me you want *me*." I clarified, grabbing her ass a little tighter for effect.

"I want you, *Liam*." My name on her lips came out like a delicacy I couldn't wait to swallow. I wanted to hear it over and over and over again. Whispered. Screamed. Shouted to the fucking four corners of the Earth.

My hands had their own will, roaming around every inch of her as we made our way up the elevator to the tenth floor.

"I never thought I'd develop a *thing* for elevators," I whispered against her lips, pausing my assault on her mouth for a second. She'd tensed up as soon as the doors shut, and I was starting to pick up on a pattern. Was it me or the tight space?

I wanted her relaxed, or at least tensed up for another reason, so I pressed her hand against my cock again, hoping the feeling would pull her back to us.

"That's all for you. Are you gonna take it like a good fucking girl?"

"Yes," she moaned, "Aren't we there yet?"

As if on queue, the elevator dinged open, the both of us darting straight to my door.

This was it. I was finally going to taste Heaven.

I opened the door, holding it out for her to get in, then shutting it behind me, Jamie's purse and jacket now adorning the floor. She was just as eager as I was. I couldn't wait to rip her clothes off, taste her sweet pussy, and watch her come undone again and again until she couldn't take it anymore.

That's what that selfish fucker who took her virginity should have done. Ladies fucking first.

I tossed my key on the entrance table, missing miserably but not giving a fuck, and before I could join her, I heard it. "WHAT THE HELL!"

Jamie's voice was loud, strained, and outraged.

I took the couple of steps necessary to get to her, but she was turning my way again, marching for the door. Jamie stormed right past me, fury escaping her every fucking pore.

"I can't believe I thought doing this with you was a good idea."

I wasn't understanding until behind her came the flash of blonde. Michelle was standing completely naked in the middle of my damn living room.

Fuck, fuck, fuck.

"I have no idea what the fuck you think you're doing, but by the time I'm back, you better not be here." I berated her just before storming out my door after Jamie.

But as soon as I got to the sidewalk, she was gone. No trace of her besides the twist in my gut and the anger in my chest.

Jamie

There had been a day, not so long ago, when I finally realized I had nothing else to lose. That there was no lower than the low I'd hit.

I was wrong.

This was my new low, and there *was* something I still stood to lose.

The last of my dignity.

I held onto the tears that burned my eyes, not allowing a single drop to fall until it was safe. The sky, though? It was coming down like I wished I could.

The image of Michelle, butt-naked, standing in the middle of Liam's living room, haunted me all the way home. It had no subtitles, though. I couldn't allow any words or thoughts to accompany that image until I was home.

Instead, I watched the lights pass by in a blur, a two-drop race on the window momentarily distracting me into a less dark place. Thankfully, the Uber driver kept to himself, not making unnecessary small talk, or I simply hadn't registered if he had tried.

As soon as I saw the Laundromat next door to my apartment, my heart sped up. I knew the inevitable was coming any second now.

My heart was right.

I didn't even make it to the top of the entrance stairs before the tears were free and rapidly falling. I steadied myself with a hand against the glass door as I cried, the sobs shaking my shoulders with violence.

A wave of nausea hit me at the same time, each new sob making it worse. I ran all the way up to my apartment. I couldn't trust my stomach not to turn. How this affected me so much was beyond me. It was just a hookup, just sex. Right?

There were no promises of exclusivity, no promises of anything at all. Liam wasn't mine in any way. I had no claim over him. So why the hell was I feeling like he had betrayed me?

My *thing* for Liam – I refused to give it a name or definition – was worse than I'd thought. I was hurt and nothing had happened between us yet. There was a line I shouldn't have crossed, and yet I couldn't even see it anymore.

I burst into my apartment, straight to the bathroom, emptying my stomach into the toilet. A mix of too much alcohol and too much emotion making me hurl without relief.

You're ridiculous! How could you ever think that a man like Liam would ever be with someone like you? You're worthless. Not even good enough to be a meaningless one-night stand.

I knew where those words came from, and I couldn't stop myself from feeling each one deep in my bones and believing them like an unshakable truth.

Today, they were.

My father was right. I could try to disguise it all I wanted, but sooner or later the truth would prevail, and Liam would see me for who I really am. A worthless fraud.

I cried harder at that realization. I had fought long and hard against it, but I couldn't hold up my sword anymore.

Suddenly, there was a hand holding my hair back, his scent hitting my senses like a ton of bricks, making me heave even harder.

The humiliation apparently wasn't over.

"Please leave," I said, my voice weak and hoarse, my vision blurred by tears and shattered illusions.

"No." He simply replied, his warm hand settling on my back, rubbing soothing circles. It felt so damn good, which only made it feel like sandpaper on an open wound.

Fuck, I was completely damaged.

I took my time composing myself before I felt ready to face him. As ready as one could feel, at least.

"Please leave me alone," I finally pleaded as I stood up.

"I'm not leaving, Jamie. I don't think you should be alone right now."

"I shouldn't be with *you* right now," I snapped, darting past him towards the entrance.

I held the front door open, a hand gesturing for him to leave, watching as Liam just stood there, taking in the mess that I was. The tears hadn't relented, rendering my actions weaker than I'd wish them to be.

Liam slowly stalked towards the door, and I thought that at least he had the heart to do as I'd asked. But no.

He placed his hands on the door and closed it, turning the key to lock it as many times as it went. "I'm not leaving you. Go lie down, I'll make you some tea and bring it to you."

I closed my eyes tightly, tears still falling despite them being shut, my head shaking in a loop.

"I'd be much better alone right now than I am with you here. Please, just this once, do as I ask." I tried my damnedest to hold back the tears and failed gloriously. I covered my face with my hands, the sobs returning without grace.

Why was he haunting me? Couldn't he just leave me in my embarrassment alone? He had humiliated me enough already.

"Liam, please. I'm begging you… leave me alone," I sobbed, my voice laced with an emotion I absolutely shouldn't be feeling, "Today, tomorrow, and every day after that."

"I am not going until you're feeling better and until I've at least tried to explain myself."

I huffed mid-sentence, turning towards my room, not finding the strength in me to carry on fighting him. I was drained.

There was no use in shutting my bedroom door, he'd either knock it down or convince me he would so that I'd open it. Or maybe I wanted it open.

Completely. Fucked. Up.

Climbing onto my bed, not bothering to pull back the covers, I curled into a ball, crying the remaining tears into the pillow, trying to imagine in what scenario what I walked into was okay.

Fuck, I was weak.

Soon enough, Liam was setting the cup of tea on my nightstand, taking a seat on the edge of the bed.

"This will soothe your stomach," he stated, as if he knew anything. He didn't understand that only an indiscernible part of me feeling sick could be healed with a cup of tea. What really needed mending sat further north, broken in more pieces than I cared to admit.

How could I like him so much? He was still practically a stranger, and yet that meant nothing against the heavy weight of these feelings.

I breathed into the pillow a couple of times, steadying myself and finally managing to stop the tears. Remaining curled up in a fetal position, I tried as best I could to regulate these illogical feelings, deciding to rationalize my reaction but coming up empty at every turn.

"I didn't know she was there. I didn't invite her over." Liam's voice was calm in comparison to the tempest in my mind.

"You don't owe me any explanations," I said in the flattest voice I could muster.

"Of course I do. Do you really think I would have someone waiting at my apartment, *naked*, when I was on my way there with you? How sick do you think I am?"

"And yet there she was. You just needed to secure a fuck buddy for the night."

"That couldn't be further from the truth."

"It doesn't matter. As you can see, I'm feeling better already. You can leave." I lied, holding all my emotions back, hoping he would finally cave and leave me alone. Liam didn't move a single inch.

"I keep a key at the office. That's got to be how she got in." He explained as if I'd asked the question plaguing my mind.

"I don't care." I lied.

"You clearly do, Jamie. And I'd seriously be disappointed if you didn't." What the hell did that mean? "But in reality you have no reason to be upset."

"Oh, sure." My voice was acidic, the perplexion from his statement unmasked, "You are absolutely right. I almost gave myself a reason, but technically, I don't have one." Tears burned my eyes again, but fuck if I was going to let him see me like that again.

I shouldn't blame him, because as he'd expertly pointed out, he had done nothing wrong.

"Don't twist my words. You know full well that's not what I meant."

I didn't dignify that with a response. I needed to get my head straight, and with him sitting hardly five feet away from me, that was an impossible mission. So I fell into an eerie silence, staring into nothing.

"JAMIE!" Liam practically growled after it got too heavy for him, "Can you please talk to me?"

He did not get the right to be angry. I'd used all my strength to keep it together for five miserable minutes, but now I simply couldn't anymore. I sprung up, sitting on the bed, facing him head-on. I needed to look into his eyes if I was going to spill my heart out.

"What the hell do you want me to say? What do you want to hear, Liam? Huh? Do you want to hear me say that I'm broken inside? Is that not obvious? That I was looking forward to something happening again since that day in the elevator? Is that what you want to know? That I haven't been able to take you off my mind and that I died inside when I saw you kissing Michelle in your office? And now she magically appears inside your apartment when something's about to happen between us. NAKED! With a fucking KEY." I shouted before settling down in resignation. "She has a fucking key, Liam. Is that better? Knowing I'm so fucked up and craving a kind of attention I've never had before, that I'm all caught up by someone I met a month ago? And my boss, to make matters worse!" I quieted for a minute, my voice lowering to just above a whisper. "And still, you are completely right. I have no reason to be mad at you or anyone else, for that matter. No. Reason. At all. Happy?"

A new sea of tears flooded my eyes, running down my cheeks without permission.

"Now can you leave?" I managed to squeeze out before falling back onto my pillow, covering my face while I cried harder than before.

I felt the mattress ease without his weight, but soon enough, it dipped again, right behind me, Liam's arms forcing me into a hug that felt both like Heaven and Hell. I fought him first, Liam's hold only intensifying to keep me there.

I finally gave in, sobs shaking me as he held me tighter. I had no right to feel this way. I shouldn't have these feelings for him. I shouldn't have any at all. But reason held nothing to what simply was.

And now he knew.

He soothed me back to calmness, a different, more comfortable silence filling the space around us.

Liam must have thought I was asleep. I didn't know the meaning behind his confession. His voice was low, pained, and whispered against my hair. "You have no idea how undeserving I am of you."

CHAPTER TWELVE

Jamie

The morning wasn't gentle in its clarity. I'd never felt more disposable than last night.

When I woke up, I knew I was alone. The spot behind me where Liam had been lying was still warm and smelled like him. He had stayed longer than I had silently gambled with myself.

Still, he left without saying a word. If he knew last night that he would sneak out without facing me, he could have done me that courtesy when I asked.

His words pounded in my brain like a jackhammer, "You have no idea how undeserving I am of you." I had no clue what that was supposed to mean. Was he admitting guilt for what happened last night?

He had seemed honest when he said he had no idea Michelle was there, and I wanted to believe him so badly because although I shouldn't, I still wanted to forgive him, find a reasonable explanation, and pick up where we left off.

Somehow, I was sensing that none of that would be happening.

I picked up my phone, naively wishing there was a message from Liam there, but there was nothing besides Alison's reply to the message I'd hurriedly sent her last night saying I was heading out.

Even though it killed me to admit, my stomach dropped and my heart pained a little. While a part of me expected Liam to run after I had admitted my feelings for him, the other part hoped he felt something similar and that my first step would encourage him to take one, too.

By Sunday evening, it was clear my hopes would die on that bridge.

I had taken advantage of the weekend, using half of it to wallow and the other half to brush it off, pulling myself together as well as I knew how to. I couldn't let myself be a mess on Monday. It was bad enough as it was.

Monday morning came quicker than I'd like, and my ego and heart were still bruised.

I hid it under a fake smile and a ton of makeup that did its job of concealing the dark circles and puffy eyes. There was no such remedy for my soul.

The way I saw it, I only had two options: ride or get off the damn horse. So, I was going to make that decision today based on my interaction with Liam. I had to know if I was just an easy fuck or if there was space for more. After all, Michelle had been standing naked in Liam's apartment, a sure fuck to end his evening, and still, he spent the night with me, fully clothed, not trying to push his way into my pants after what happened.

I wore something eye-catching, hoping it would work as an incentive, strutting into AD as confidently as possible under that last piece of logic. I ignored the daggers directed my way in Michelle's glower, settling in my desk earlier than normal.

As much as I had talked myself into having an ounce of confidence, I still couldn't bring myself to start this conversation with Liam, so I waited for him to come to me.

I watched him work, and unlike other days, I hadn't felt his eyes on me once. By lunchtime, my ego was shattered together with any hope I still had left. Not a word, not a look, not a signal. Nothing. It was as if we hardly knew each other.

Finally, just before I headed down to meet Alison for lunch, he crept up behind me as I studied the 3D model of the *Verten* building.

"Jamie, I need you to print the ground floor's floor plan. Leave it on my desk before you head out for lunch." Liam's voice was cold, no hint of emotion in it. Just a blunt, barked-out order as if nothing ever happened. "Oh, and we have a meeting at the DOB tomorrow at 10 a.m. sharp. Maybe meet me there."

My gut twisted as I turned and took him in. Damn handsome and alluring as always, and there was no remorse, no heated look, no sympathy or warmth. Stone-cold eyes and an empty expression.

Fuck, he looked like my father!

"Sure thing, Boss," I replied shortly, my disappointment dripping onto those words even though I tried as hard as I could to hold it back.

I expected at least to see some kind of reaction, even if he quickly buried it as he usually did, but there was nothing but a blank poker face. There was a different edge to him today as if he had stepped back on that high horse he galloped in on when I first met him. The lurking danger behind those pools of green was there, too. Maybe it was his tone or the scowl he wore today like a permanent fixture.

Without another word, Liam turned on his heels and left, and I just stood there watching him march away, my eyes glued to each step he took, feeling the distance grow deep inside me.

We are surrounded by people, there's no way he would address the issue in front of everyone.

I tried keeping my morale up, finding excuses and giving it until the end of the day before finally making up my mind. Yet, the rest of the day went by and Liam didn't seem to care at all, so I stayed until everyone else had left, convincing myself Liam couldn't talk to me with AD bustling with employees.

Inhaling all the courage I needed, I got up from my desk, gathering my stuff and walked towards Liam's office. He had his head hanging over some paperwork he was dealing with, completely oblivious to my presence.

"It's past seven, I'll be heading home. Do you need anything else before I leave?" I tried giving him a last chance.

"No. You can go." He replied in the same detached voice, his eyes never lifting to set on mine.

"Really? You have nothing to say to me? Nothing at all?"

Liam slowly lifted his head, a veil of what seemed like annoyance taking over his features as he looked at me.

"Nothing at all."

"Okay, then. I guess I'll see you tomorrow." My voice had taken a turn, too. Liam didn't reply, keeping busy with those damn papers making me feel stupid for standing there a minute too long, gathering my stupidity before leaving.

What on Earth was I thinking?

He didn't have feelings for me. I was just an easy fuck that didn't happen, and that suddenly wasn't worth the struggle anymore.

What did you even think would happen? Huh? That he would fall madly in love with you? That will never happen! You're just not good enough, and you never will be. He's a Dornier, for Christ's sake, and you are a nobody!

I admonished myself all the way home, completely devastated, dropping onto my couch in tears as soon as I was in the safety of my apartment. Somewhere during this last month, I'd given Liam the power to make me feel small, worthless, and unwanted. Something only one other person in my life ever could. My father.

I was long past a crush. Liam had my heart in his hand, and he squeezed it into a pulp without mercy. To make it worse, he knew exactly what he was doing, and still, I hadn't found any emotion in his eyes as he did it. That night, I cried myself to sleep, curled on the couch, feeling completely deflated.

I didn't want to feel this way. I'd been fighting against these feelings, brushing them off as a severe case of infatuation with an overly attractive man in a position of power. It was absolutely none of that.

It wasn't the power that held me captive. It was Liam for all he was. I'd like him just the same if he wasn't the son of AD's CEO.

The morning sun dragged my eyes open while the mother of all headaches pounded in my head. My body was aching from sleeping scrunched into a ball on my small couch. At least now the package matched the contents.

I grabbed my phone from the floor where it had fallen, realizing it was dead. Everything seemed to be matching my energy today. I stretched and struggled to get up, heading to the kitchen to check the time. It felt like I still had an hour or two to sleep.

"Fuck, 11:45!" I shouted, scurrying to the bathroom for a quick shower. I should have been at AD at 9. I'm never late. How the hell could I have let this happen? This was a major fuck up, especially since I should have been at the DOB for the meeting at 10.

I stepped under the water, scrubbing myself clean in record time. As soon as I turned off the water, I heard someone slamming on my door. Big, loud, practically continuous thuds.

Wrapping the towel around me, I ran to the door to see what the hell was happening, but before I could get there, it swung open, a very angered Liam barging inside, his phone attached to his ear. He stopped in his tracks as soon as he saw me, his eyes taking me and my small towel in from head to toe.

Liam looked like hell in such a glorious way that I had to clench my thighs to stop the tingling. His normally impeccable tie was loose and skewed, his hair a sexy tousled mess, his eyes dark and dangerous under a furrowed brow that wrinkled his forehead. His suit jacket was gone, along with all his decorum and serenity.

"What the fuck do you think you're doing?" Liam closed the gap between us, practically growling to my face, pinning me between his glower and my inability to move as he stood merely an inch away.

"I beg your pardon?"

"Why the fuck aren't you at work?" He spat. Furious wasn't even the right word to describe his state. There could be fire coming out of his flared nostrils, his face tinted red under his golden complexion. "I've been calling you for over a fucking hour!"

"My phone died and I overslept," I explained, not taming my tone so it matched his, watching as Liam took off to roam my apartment, checking every corner. "How the hell did you get inside my apartment?"

Liam simply waved me off with his hand, finishing up his search for God knows what before coming to stand right in front of me again, another grunted demand through gritted teeth, "You could have fucking called."

He stood there staring at me, waiting for my reply. Liam was so close I could almost taste his cologne. But there was a hint of something else, too. Bourbon, maybe?

"Have you been drinking?" I asked, not masking my concern.

"You could have called." He repeated, his voice closer to normal but not losing the accusatory tone.

"I told you my phone is dead," I replied, watching as he turned away, his hand wreaking havoc through his already disheveled hair. "What do you care? What are you even doing here?"

"I couldn't get a hold of you. I was worried something had happened."

Yesterday he couldn't even find the decency to say goodbye, and today he's all worked up because I hadn't shown up for work? Fuck that! I couldn't keep up with this bipolarity.

"Well, as you can see, I am just fine! I don't think it's standard procedure for the boss to check on their employees when they don't show up for work. You can leave now. Thank you so much for the concern, *Boss*."

I walked towards the door, opening it wider and motioning for him to leave. Liam followed closely behind me, taking one last look at me from the floor up, lingering on my still-wet thighs, his head shaking left and right before he walked past me, stopping just outside my door.

I tried to shut it behind him, but Liam held the door from slamming in his face, "I'll be downstairs waiting for you in my car."

"Don't. I won't be going in today. I'm not feeling well. Have a good day, Mr. Dornier." I slammed the door, leaving absolutely no room for him to protest.

Despite being angry at him, I couldn't help but spy on his reaction. I knew he'd be pissed. Liam Dornier was not used to getting a no for an answer.

I watched him scrambling for something to say but ultimately deciding he had no comeback. His heavy, angry footsteps resonated through the hall as he disappeared. When he was out of sight, I exhaled in relief, leaning against my door.

Why did he act all cold and distant only to burst into a fit of rage thinking something had happened to me? That's a reaction someone who cared would have, right?

What was with the searching? Was he worried I had someone over? A man, maybe?

If he did care, if he did have feelings for me, why wasn't he honest about them? Had I not been clear in my confession?

I had nothing but questions. But this miscommunication deal was getting really old, really fast.

Despite what I told Liam, I was going to work. I just needed space and boundaries.

The forty-five-minute train ride was hardly enough to get him off my mind. But then again, did such a thing exist?

As I settled in my desk, staring at that damn door of his, I decided I'd wait for everyone to leave tonight, again, so I could finally label whatever this is between us.

He clearly wasn't ready to jump off the horse, and neither was I. We just couldn't expect each other to sit there and wait for the other to make a move. So, I'll take the reins and settle this once and for all.

Liam huffed and nodded in disapproval, pissed that I was sitting at my desk, contrary to what I'd told him. And if that hadn't given me the clue he didn't like what I'd done, the door to his office slamming shut left no doubt at all.

I allowed him space for the rest of the afternoon as I rehearsed my speech in the reflection of my computer screen.

CHAPTER THIRTEEN

Jamie

I watched in disgust as Michelle swayed her way over to Liam's office at ten past six. The same exact routine every day, yet somehow, today her swing had less of an attitude. I couldn't help but wonder what Liam had said to her after I left them alone in his apartment.

Had he berated her? Had he called a rain check? Was trespassing not reason enough for termination? I guess not.

Even so, I bet he could just hint at a blow job, and she wouldn't hesitate to drop to her knees and oblige. How many other times had they done exactly that in his office?

I had bile rising to my throat at that image, and for some reason, try as I might, it wouldn't leave me alone.

The floor was completely empty as I waited for Michelle to head out, too, allowing a few more minutes to pass to be sure no one else lingered around. I inhaled deeply, hoping it would infuse me with the courage I seemed to be losing at each passing second.

Feeding off the anger of seeing her flirt with him again, I stood up and marched right up to Liam's door, pushing it open without even knocking. Liam was right on the other side, pulling the door open, ready to head home.

His eyes rolled as he saw me, his hand brushing over his chin in annoyance as he released the door knob. He walked back inside, threw his jacket onto his chair, and leaned against his desk, waiting for me to speak, arms crossed over his chest.

His guarded stance did nothing to ease me, the fury in his eyes piercing right through me, making me second-guess what I came here to do in the first place. But then Michelle's bare fucking ass came into my mind once more, and I was firm in my mission again.

"Can we talk?" I started, trying to break that anger into small chunks so I could chew on each reason for him to be acting this way separately. If he looked on the edge of madness this morning, he had definitely tipped over now.

"What do you want, Jamie?" His tone was harsh, but for some reason, it wasn't enough to deter me. I closed the door behind me, coming to stand in front of him, crossing my arms in front of my chest, mimicking his body language.

"I didn't see you being this arrogant to Michelle just a minute ago. To what do I owe the special treatment?" I accused.

"She doesn't get on my every nerve like you do."

"Oh! Shouldn't I be the one pissed off here? If I recall correctly, I was the one who found someone naked waiting for you in your apartment when you had your tongue shoved down *my* throat."

"I told you I didn't know she was going to be there."

"Right. And for some stupid reason, I believed you."

"I don't have the habit of lying, Jamie. If I said I didn't know she was there, it's the fucking truth." His tone was dipped in all shades of pissed, fueling me further.

"But I still get the cold shoulder and not even a word about it from you after Friday night." I couldn't help my own anger from seeping into my words, "You slept in my damn bed and left without a word in the morning."

"Today is not a good day for this," Liam said, heading for the door, ready to dismiss me. But I'd come this far, and I wouldn't find the courage to do this again, so it was either today or never.

I stopped his advances, my hand landing on his chest, making Liam pause barely a foot away from me.

"Jamie, I told you today is not a good day for this conversation." There was anger under his breath, mixed with the same scent of bourbon I'd sensed earlier. His eyes settled on mine in a warning.

"Why?" I pushed.

"Because I'm not the best version of myself today."

"I'll take it if it's an honest one."

"Don't push, Jamie." It was a warning that sounded more like a goad.

I did exactly what he told me not to. I pushed him back with the hand I still had on his chest. Liam caught my wrist, pulling me flush against him, his mouth hovering an inch away from my lips while his eyes were so deeply buried in mine that I felt them stripping my soul.

"I pushed, and now what?" I dared to taunt.

"And now I'm taking every damn thing you have to give."

With that, he crashed his lips onto mine, his free hand grabbing my ass to pull me closer. His kiss was harsh, urgent, and hungry. Small but hard enough bites punishing me for my insistence.

Liam ravished my lips without mercy, walking me backwards until the back of my thighs hit his desk, his hands just as hungry as his tongue.

"I could have been gentle. I could have been caring." He said between kisses, both his hands fisting my hair tightly. "But today, I'm none of those things, and I warned you. You just had to push, didn't you?" He kissed me again, harsher this time, "Tell me to stop, Jamie, or I'll ruin you."

"No." I panted into his mouth. "I want you, *Liam*. Please don't stop. Don't hold back." I accentuated his name, remembering how he had asked me to say it. No vague words. Whether or not I would come to regret this moment was an issue for later. Right now I wanted him to take exactly as he said he would.

"I can't. Believe me, I've fucking tried."

Liam sat me on his desk, pulling my skirt up to my waist, spreading my legs, and placing himself between them, never breaking the kiss that had set both of us on fire.

"Goddammit, Jamie." He pushed his erection into me, his forehead resting against mine as he watched his cock grinding against my pussy, "Can you feel that? Can you feel how hard I am for you?"

I nodded, knowing full well I'd pay for it. He took my lips again, biting down on the bottom one, making me wince, his cock still rubbing against me, erasing the pain straight away.

"Words, Miss Harden."

Liam grabbed the edges of my blouse, pulling in opposite directions, the buttons flying all over. He didn't bother to take it off. He just pulled my bra down, my boobs spilling over the edge, revealing my hardened nipples.

He pinched one between his fingers, a rush of pleasurable pain soaring straight to my core.

"Oh, God! I feel it." I panted, "It's not enough. I need more, Liam." I wasn't above begging at this point. This exact moment was too long overdue to have my pride standing in its way. "Please."

Liam shook his head no repeatedly, his face a mask of both lust and anger, some sort of battle being raged in his head.

"Fucking selfish." I thought I heard him mutter to himself, one of the sides winning the war before he kissed me again, his hand tangling in my hair and yanking me back as he conquered my mouth with his tongue.

His lips wreaked havoc against my neck, my skin erupting into goosebumps all over as he covered me in hot, wet kisses. If this wasn't Heaven, I had no idea what was.

Feeling him, his need for me, his rapture, didn't hold a candle to every fantasy I had of this very moment.

Liam reached down, pulling one of my nipples into his mouth, sucking and biting, a new string of stars making way into my vision as he did.

Without warning, Liam pulled back, a full step back, leaving me seated on his desk, legs wide open, my skirt around my waist, and my boobs overflowing the top of my bra.

The heat of his haze on me had me twisting in what I couldn't figure to be embarrassment or pure lust. I felt exposed and indecent, but at the same time, his look was so ravenous, I felt pride and longing right alongside it.

Dirty, in all the bad and good that word held.

"Look at you. Ripped to shreds on my desk, begging to be fucked." Liam's tongue swept across his lips as he took me in, his eyes roaming my body at a slow, agonizing pace. I held my breath, waiting to understand if that was judgment or praise.

God, I hope it's praise.

I shifted, my hand crossing my chest to conceal my exposed breasts.

"Don't hide from me." Liam pulled my hand away, holding my cheek in his other hand, forcing my gaze to settle on his, "Don't you ever hide from me."

He placed my hand on the edge of the desk behind my back, pulled my skirt up higher around my waist, slid my thong off, and spread my knees further before taking another step back to look at me.

My breaths were shallow. I was getting nervous and anxious. I wanted his lips on me, not only his eyes. I was done with the visual feasting, I'd done it every single day since we met. Right now, I needed his hands, his mouth, his dick.

"Fucking exquisite." The words were like a symphony, my body arching as they hit my ears, beckoning him to touch me, "Now beg me again."

His hand rubbed the bulge in his pants, up and down, teasing me to say what he wanted to hear. Liam's fingers gripped his swollen cock, showing me exactly what I'd be getting if I said the right words. Thick and hard, just for me.

"I need you inside me, Liam. Please." It was a moan, a whisper, an indecent plea I'd never imagined to voice. "Please fuck me."

I could hardly get the words out before he was on me again. His lips and hands had a new urgency to them, kissing and gripping everything he could.

Liam reached towards his jacket, pulling a condom out of his wallet and ripping the packet open with his teeth. I've always heard you shouldn't do that, but I was too eager to have him stretch me to say anything.

"Pull my cock out." He commanded in that dark tone that did very strange things to my insides. I quickly did as he said, pulling his pants and boxers down as best I could from this position, my eyes widening when I took in the perfection of the tall and thick cock in front of me.

There was a bead of pre-cum already on his tip, my tongue swiping across my lips as if I was tasting it on them.

What does it taste like?

I'd never given a blow job before. Fuck, I'd never had my pussy eaten, either. How would that feel? Is it something people normally do?

"Not today, Beautiful." Liam said, noticing my gesture, "Today my cock needs to claim you or I'll break everything in this fucking office."

Liam handed me the condom, "Put it on me." I focused as hard as I could, trying not to make a fool of myself by doing it wrong. He held the base of his dick while I rolled the condom over it, my heart beating in my ears at the anticipation of having it inside me.

I looked up, and Liam had a wicked grin on his face, his bottom lip tucked between his teeth, and a scary fire burning in his eyes.

He reached behind me, swiping his hand over the desk, sending everything that was on top of it flying to the ground before curling his arm around my waist and pulling me to him. I pushed my hips up, searching for his hard cock, desperate to have him fill me.

"So fucking wet." Liam practically chanted, the back of his fingers tracing my pussy as he pumped his cock in his fist. The head of his dick followed, tracing a line from my entrance to my clit. The warmth sent a rush of blood straight to my pussy, a new ache I never knew was possible. It was as if I'd been stranded in a desert, and his hard erection was all the water I needed.

"Please, Liam," I begged again, hoping he would push inside me, finally being rewarded with the wide crown of his cock stretching my almost virgin pussy.

"Shit." He roared. "I can't hold back from destroying this beautiful cunt. Not today. Fuck, Jamie, what have you done?"

His hand came up to my hair again, yanking it back just as he thrust all the way inside me, pulling a whimper from my chest.

"Shh, you can take it, Beautiful. Every last inch of me." He stopped balls deep inside me, holding me so close to him there was no telling where I ended and he began. He stilled for a moment, allowing me to catch my breath and bearings, the pain slowly subsiding as he stroked my hair.

"You'll have to stop pulsing around my cock if I'm supposed to hold off."

"I... I can't help it."

"I know, Baby. I know. But I can't stay like this, or I'll come before I fucking move."

Liam pressed his palm between my boobs, pushing me down onto the desk, his hard cock still deeply buried inside me. His hand stayed there, steadying me while he started to pump in small strokes first, that grew longer and harsher with each one. I tried to swallow my moans, too embarrassed to let go, but some of them were simply pulled out of me without permission.

I watched him, my eyes firmly set on his face while his were set on the place where we were both joined together.

"Fuck, your tight little pussy is pulling me in every time I pull out."

"Hm... Jesus." I couldn't form a single sentence that would make sense right now. I felt full to the brim, and still I couldn't keep from wanting more. Liam's thrusts were nearing violent and uncontrolled, shoving me into the desk every time he pushed back inside me.

"I'm a bastard. I shouldn't be fucking you like this, but I can't control it."

His hand traveled up my chest, resting on my throat, still keeping me in place while squeezing just a little.

Up until this moment, I had no idea what real pleasure was. Having my pussy this full, his words, the friction, that damn hand on my throat, it was all so intense I was close to exploding.

"This pussy was made for me. Tell me no one else will ever have it." I couldn't properly register the words or say any of my own, but the possessive tone in them sent new shivers of bliss up my spine, "Tell me." He demanded, squeezing tighter.

"I huh... Oh God!" I moaned, feeling the first ripples of my release tearing their way through me.

"Jesus, you're gone." Liam pumped harder, his free hand rubbing my clit in circles that sent me straight to Heaven. My back arched, I was balancing on my ass and head on this desk while pleasure tore me to pieces, Liam's unrelenting thrusts shoving me right over that edge.

Liam's groan filled the room, his orgasm taking over him just as mine had subsided. I watched him come, a sense of pride filling my chest at the notion that I'd done that. That I had made him soar in bliss.

With a last shove inside me, Liam collapsed onto my body, his nose inhaling deeply in the crook of my neck.

"Fuck." I heard him murmur, only this time the word wasn't laced with the lechery I'd heard in it earlier.

Liam pulled out of me, the whole atmosphere around us dropping to a coldness I wouldn't imagine could follow such fire.

I slowly got up, my gut twisting into an untieable knot, pulling my skirt and bra to their place and covering my chest with what was left of my blouse. Liam had his back to me, discarding the used condom, I supposed, and buttoning his pants back in place.

I couldn't shake the sense of dread that filled my lungs as he turned to face me, his expression far from the lightness it should hold after such an intimate moment. He'd dipped back into Hell, only this time, I felt like I had been the one to push him down.

I swallowed the massive lump that was lodged in my throat as he faced me, waiting for the words that would confirm my gut feeling–this had been a fucking mistake, and I was about to be hung up on his trophy-fuck wall.

"This can't happen again, Jamie." Exactly as expected, only that sentence slashed deeper than I'd ever imagined.

"Why?" I had no idea why it mattered, nothing he'd say would wipe this feeling away. Dirty came back to my mind, but only the bad half of it. The half that made me feel like a slut.

"It just can't. Leave it at that."

"So you fuck me, and I'm not entitled to at least a half-assed explanation?" My pain was masked with anger, but I wouldn't allow him to see me shatter. Not again.

"You're not right for me, okay?" Translation–I wasn't good enough.

I can't believe what I'm hearing.

I swallowed back the tears that started forming in my eyes and nodded once, "Okay."

Resisting the urge to say more or feel more, I turned around and walked out of his office, holding my head high until it was safe to let go.

I think I just made the biggest mistake of my life.

CHAPTER FOURTEEN

Liam

Asshole.

Selfish fuck.

Self-centered prick.

None of those came even close to describing me right now. How could I have done that?

This morning, something switched inside me when Jamie didn't show up for work. Something that scared the living crap out of me. I thought something had happened to her. That she was in trouble, or danger, or worse. That she'd packed up and left after the fuck up on Friday night.

It didn't happen, but the possibility was definitely real now.

I had forced myself not to park outside her apartment during the weekend like I'd done all the others since I'd met her. Give her some space and try to take her off my mind in the process.

I didn't. I couldn't.

So I checked my phone a million and one times for the tracker I'd put in hers. It hadn't moved all weekend from the same shitty apartment in Tremont that I was so eager to get her out of. She was probably still recovering from the clusterfuck that was the end of a promising night.

A big fucking mistake avoided by that lunatic, Michelle.

But when she didn't show, I kicked myself in the balls for giving her space.

Space and privacy are fucking overrated.

Thinking something had happened was just the icing on top of the fucking guilt cake. So saying I was out of my damn mind when I couldn't get ahold of her was being conservative, to say the least.

With her phone off, I couldn't trace her, so saying I'd gone to Hell to make another pact with the devil in exchange for her safety was not an exaggeration in the slightest.

I was halfway into alerting the fucking cavalry before I got to her apartment and found her barely covered by a skimpy towel that did nothing to hide her curves. Instead of relief, I felt anger, which only fueled the lust that still soared through my veins since the club.

The taste of her lips still lingered on my tongue, the image of her face as she came around my cock was the only thing I saw when I closed my fucking eyes. She was all I could think about.

That *thing* inside me? That thing was a scary notion that she had made her way and settled in a place in my chest that she had no business being in.

I couldn't harbor feelings like these.

I had no right to. I didn't deserve having them, never mind actually having them be requited.

There was more than lust in her eyes, I'd seen it. Felt it in her kiss just outside Dea Tacita. There were stakes higher than a simple fuck for her. Fuck, for me, too.

And there were so many reasons I shouldn't have given in. Jamie would fall so hard and break so bad. But there I was, nonetheless, losing a battle I didn't want to fight in the first place.

I had held off on pulling that towel off of her in her apartment and claiming her right there, punishing her for making me go crazy thinking she was in danger.

Her defiance when she slammed the door in my face, showing up after she said she wouldn't just so she didn't have to step foot in my car, had me thinking she was finally doing what was best for her. Pushing me away once and for all.

Fuck, was I wrong.

She knew what she was doing when she pushed my buttons. She knew I was threading a fine line between restraint and unleashing a hell neither of us could control.

Being inside her felt like home. It was where I belonged, and again my chest ached with that damn feeling that had no business to be poking at my heart.

This was bad for her. *I* was bad for her.

There was something about her that had all my fucking self-control reduced to ash. All it took was a push. First Jack, with his filthy hands all over her, and now her, with her little hand practically daring me to snap.

I fucked her with a foreign need before dismissing her as if she was nothing.

God, was she beautiful writhing beneath me. There wasn't a sight on this Earth as mesmerizing as Jamie with my cock buried inside her.

This wasn't what I wanted. If I had the luxury to ever have it my way, I would want to erase any other man from her life. Her first time wasn't hard to top from the description.

Knowing there had been someone else before me made me want to burn this office to the ground. I'd fuck her over and over until he wasn't even a memory. Cock lobotomy.

But I couldn't allow it to happen again. I couldn't allow her to step into my shadows.

I waited for her to leave my office before I took my frustration out on everything I could set my hands on in this damn place. I was used to destruction, but I couldn't bear to see the wreckage on her face.

She'd trusted me with the highest honor of all, and now? Now it seemed I used her for her untouched pussy. Wanting nothing but to corrupt her, only to kick her out on the street with the idea that she wasn't good enough for a fucker like me.

More like the opposite.

I'm the one drenched in sin.

My own shadow hides from me.

I couldn't dare to drown her in my darkness. Could I?

Fuck! I was so far gone I was trying to find an angle where this, where us, wasn't a bad idea.

Even plagues in the minds of purists were a purge. From their perspective, even death had an upside. I could twist this any way I wanted to justify my actions, yet the outcome would always be the same. And that ill fate, I couldn't force upon her.

Getting her to hate me would be a smart thing to do. Maybe I was even halfway to it already. It was an easy way to push her away. I couldn't trust myself to stay clear out of my own will.

"You're not right for me, okay?"

Those words felt like razor blades on my tongue, the devastation in her eyes, the acid that kept the wound from healing.

I'm a selfish son of a bitch that should have let her go without tainting her light with my darkness.

Now? I'm stuck in a loop, trying to shove my depravity into a spectrum of color where it didn't belong. Jamie was light, love, and life, yellow, red, and green. My shades didn't even have a gradient. They were all black—complete absence of light.

Jamie

The night I had sex with Liam was the last time I was allowing myself to cry over him. He turned out to be a disguised version of my father, telling me that I wasn't good enough for him.

He could have called me a fucking whore and given me a stack of bills and it would have hurt less.

The first thing that came to mind was leaving AD, but I couldn't. The offer over at MG Enterprise was long gone, and I'd been a dummy not to take it when it was up for grabs.

Besides, my father knew I had landed my dream job, and it filled me with pride that I could prove him wrong. Now all I could hear was his toneless voice saying he'd see me when I fucked it up.

I guess that would be now.

Somehow, going back to Jacksonville seemed like the short end of the stick as opposed to going back to AD to face Liam with my tail between my legs, like the not-good-enough-girl I was.

All I needed was to refocus, get my head buried far enough into the job, and dismiss everything else. With that plan set and locked into my brain, I cried myself to sleep again, promising this would be the last time.

My efforts to forget my dire decision-making were shattered all night long. Each time I moved, I felt the ache between my legs. I still felt him everywhere and probably still would for a couple more days.

This small physical pain didn't hold a candle to the torment racking through my soul, yet it was a harsh reminder every time I succeeded in pushing those thoughts away.

Without much sleep, I got to AD earlier than ever, deciding to clutter my mind with the *Verten* project. The next meeting was just around the corner and I had to be prepared to make my pitch so bulletproof that it would resist even the blast that was Liam's presence.

Years of degrading words were hard to erase, and before I knew it, I was falling back into that dark pit of emotional abuse as I worked on auto-pilot.

I'm not classy enough.

I'm not from a wealthy family.

I'm not talented enough.

I'm nothing. Nobody. Not good enough.

Not. Fucking. Right.

There was anger in my thoughts, too, curled around the pain. I gripped the pencil tighter, the tip breaking at the exact moment Liam came into sight. Of course he looked like a fucking gift from the Gods.

My eyes locked with his, the pain in my chest crippling my senses. I forced myself to tear my gaze away, averting my eyes back to the stack of floor plans on top of my desk.

What are you? Stupid?

"Good morning, Jamie." Liam was standing right in front of my desk, his voice calm and low. There was pity in it, just as I'd seen in his eyes when he saw me. I didn't need that shit. The only thing I needed was to be left alone.

"Good morning, Sir," I replied between gritted teeth, not bothering to lift my eyes back to him.

Liam lingered there, looking at me, waiting for fuck knows what while I pretended he wasn't there. As soon as he turned on his heels and barricaded himself in his office, I sprung from my seat, shooting Alison a text saying I was coming down, and stormed out.

Good. I have an invite to give you.

I had no idea what she meant. Alison saw me coming before I called her, her smile vanishing from her face as soon as she took in my blood-shot, puffy eyes. Alison grabbed my hand and pulled me towards a window, far from the commotion of the center bullpen.

"Hey? What happened? What's wrong?" Her arms were tightly wrapped around me, my tears freely falling onto her shoulder.

Pathetic. There goes the last-time promise.

I let myself soak in her comfort before pulling back and cleaning my tears with the back of my hand.

"Is this about that guy you say doesn't exist?"

I nodded, clearing my throat before speaking, "I'm done. He said I wasn't right for him, so I'm done." I admitted, leaving out all the compromising details that would only make me look even more stupid. Who even falls for their boss anymore?

Alison sighed heavily, pulling me into another hug, rubbing my back in soothing circles, and somehow pulling more pained words from me, "I'm not going to grovel to make someone like me. He clearly doesn't care about me, so I need to shut it off, too. I need to stop caring." I pulled away to look into her eyes, "How do I stop caring?"

"I don't think that's how it works, Babe."

"Shit." I covered my face with my hands, embarrassed to have been so naive.

"Ice cream and a depressing chick flick at your house at 9. I think that's the standard first step."

I nodded in agreement before remembering her text.

"You said you had something for me?" I tried redirecting the conversation so I could at least compose myself before I had to get back to my desk.

"Oh, don't worry. It's nothing."

"No. Come on. Gimme."

"It's not an actual paper invite. It's my birthday this Saturday, and my parents, mostly my mom, are organizing a dinner party back at the house. It will be another one of her pathetic excuses to try and set me up with some son of a friend of a friend. It would be so much easier to endure with you there. But I totally understand if you're not up for it."

I wasn't exactly jumping up and down at the idea, but there was no way I'd deny her that. The smile on her face was plastered like a mask, concealing the real meaning behind her invitation. She needed me just as much as I needed her right now.

"Of course I'm coming. Goes without saying." She hugged me, trying to tone down her excitement for my sake.

I avoided Liam as much as possible for the rest of the day, counting down the seconds before I could get away from here.

Every time my eyes landed on him, I felt more humiliated and ashamed, reduced to a fraction of myself as I shrunk into my own body. I was an expert at it. Soon enough, I would make myself so small I would be invisible.

The moment that damn clock hit 6 p.m. I flew out of the office, not bothering to stop by the boss's office like I did every evening since I started working at this damn place.

I went straight home, only stopping at the store for two depressingly large buckets of ice cream and a bottle of vodka. I was thinking ice cream alone wouldn't cut it.

When Alison arrived, it was a welcomed reprieve from the murky thoughts replaying in my mind. My pride was hurt, my already non-existent ego shattered to pieces. I was angry, but Liam wasn't the recipient. I was.

I'd been stupid enough to think that a fuck boy like Liam would settle for someone like me.

"What are we watching?" I asked.

"The Notebook," Alison replied, sinking into the couch.

"I think I'm failing to see the effectiveness of this plan."

Wasn't watching an excessively romantic movie just like rubbing salt in my already painful wound?

"Tell me about this dinner party," I asked, stirring our attention away from the TV after a while. Even though Ryan Gosling was good eye candy, I just wasn't in the mood to focus on that.

"It's always this huge deal to my mother. She throws these huge parties to celebrate my birthday. I'm the only one who lets her anymore. It's mainly just family, a few of my family's friends and associates. You will kind of be the only one I've invited myself." Alison confessed, trying to make it a smaller deal than what I realized it actually was for her.

"And why is that?" I gave her a small sympathetic smile.

"Don't look at me like that. It's just that there are very few people I actually trust. I'm not a crowd of friends kind of girl. Less is more, right? Besides my brothers, you're… kind of it."

As if to swallow that piece of uncomfortable information, Alison stuck her spoon in the ice cream bucket, pulling out a huge chunk, not thinking twice before shoving it into her mouth. She was rewarded with an instant brain freeze while I fell back laughing at her antics, her face contorting while her mouth, still filled with ice cream, ran wild with cusses better suited for a sailor.

I felt light for the first time since last week, thanks to the one person I'd found I could rely on. I finally managed to stop laughing, looking straight into her eyes while I pulled her hand into mine, "I wouldn't miss it for the world."

CHAPTER FIFTEEN

Jamie

Keeping to the normal version of myself around Liam was getting harder by the day, so I welcomed the weekend like never before.

I had been trying my damnedest to avoid him altogether, cursing under my breath each time I couldn't. We stuck with being civil and discussed nothing besides work. All other topics were completely banned, and I somehow found it easier to cope that way. My rug was already so full of crap underneath, just a little more dirt wouldn't do it any harm.

That damn door to his office was a constant, haunting reminder of what had happened. I found myself lost in thought more often than I'd like to admit as I stared at it. It was still better than the times Liam left it open and I felt his eyes burning into me.

They always held pity in them, and instead of disappointment, that brought out anger in me. That was an emotion I despised. I have never needed anyone's pity in my life. I wasn't about to start now.

I'd made some dumb, rushed decisions in the last few days, making a total mess of my own head in the process, and having to look at his damn handsome face day in and day out only made matters worse.

Why couldn't he just look like shit? At least I wouldn't be star-struck every time he walked by or spoke to me. How could I stand my ground against that?

I couldn't, but I damn well tried.

There was no way I was stooping lower and allowing Liam to see just how deeply what he said affected me. I had allowed myself to cry and wallow about it, but no more. I couldn't let him see how much power he held over me.

Pathetic – my name would come up as a synonym in a Thesaurus.

Keeping this mask up, perfectly placed with a fucking smile like a cherry on top, was damn hard, so the reprieve of the weekend was very welcomed. Two days was short, but I'd take any break from him I could at the moment.

Alison's birthday party came as the perfect excuse to get out of my own head. Even though I wasn't exactly a social butterfly and I knew that mingling with people I'd never met would come at the expense of a huge slice of my monthly socializing quota, I was looking forward to it.

I was still nervous, though.

If anything, at least I'd be there for Alison. She had become a constant presence in my life, a rock I could lean on at every given turn. I wouldn't miss this for the world. She deserved as much.

We had found common ground in many things, but one of them was definitely having a very limited friend list. Which, in regards to Alison, was strange. She was not an awkward introvert like me. Quite the opposite, she was fun, outgoing, reliable, and such a good friend. It was hard to understand why she only had me.

I felt there was a story there somewhere, but she'd looked so uncomfortable talking about it, I just left it alone for now. Still, I was glad I could be there to celebrate this with her and her family. It made me feel a part of something somehow. That definitely was a first for me.

Exhaling deeply, I took another glance at my reflection, finally deciding that I looked alright. I'd picked out a bottle-green dress that fell just above my knees with a low cut back, which Alison approved. It had no cleavage, but I was already showing enough skin on my back to make it quite a statement.

For the first time this week, I'd gotten some sleep last night, the bags and dark circles under my eyes fading a little. Concealer also went a long way in making me look less like the dead.

Hopping into the Uber I'd called, I finally replied to Alison's texts saying I was on my way. I let my thoughts wander a little during the ride, mentally slapping myself every time they landed on Liam. Tonight was not the night for that. Tonight I would try to be open, meet new people, and have fun for a change.

Maybe even the awkwardness would help keep my head free of Liam and his damn handsome face for a few hours.

As I arrived at the address Alison had given me, I was astounded by the masterpiece before me. The driveway alone was big enough to fit at least ten cars, and the mansion that sat atop the hill was breathtakingly beautiful. I stepped out of the car and took in the grandeur of the place.

It looked unsettlingly familiar, too.

The façade was built out of concrete, floor-to-ceiling windows, and steel panels. The front garden was simple but so beautiful, towered by high trees that looked a century old. The strategic lighting that glowed together with the setting sun painted the scene in hues of shimmering gold cut from a fairytale dream.

I texted Alison, letting her know I had arrived, watching as a few other guests made their way inside the glorious architectural wonder. Just a few seconds later, my phone was buzzing with her reply.

Come on in. Your name is on the list. I'll meet you in the foyer.

"I know you." A deep voice startled me from Alison's instructions, making me turn around to find the blond guy with icy blue eyes from the club. "You were at the club with Miss Battaglia."

"I'm sorry, who?"

"Alison. You were at Dea Tacita with Alison. Come, I'll take you inside." I offered him a small smile and walked beside him towards the entrance. "I'm Max, by the way." He said, holding out his hand for me to shake.

"Nice to meet you, Max. I'm Jamie Harden." I remembered him. He was the man with the piercing, searing-hot look towards Alison. She had brushed it off as nothing, yet here he was, walking me right into the house without having to mutter a word to the guy holding the guest list by the door.

I spun on my heels, taking in the exquisite space. The curling staircase to the top floor, the double-height ceiling with its grand crystal chandelier, a damn Salvador Dalí hanging next to an unmistakable Pollock.

I'd set foot into a different dimension with a cool flute of pink champagne in hand that a waiter had handed me as soon as I was through the door.

"You're finally here!" Alison almost squealed from behind me, hugging me before I could catch my bearings.

"Are those real?" I had to ask.

"Yeah." She replied nonchalantly, not acknowledging my shock, "I'm so happy you made it."

"I said I would. Max escorted me inside." I said with a small nod towards him and a smile that said thank you, looking for her reaction. I felt there was something there between them, but none of them gave a hint of anything away.

"Thanks, Max." She waved him off, "Come, let me introduce you to everyone. But first, a real drink. That pink champagne tastes like moldy rose petals."

I laughed and let Alison drag me through the house, straight to where they'd set up a bar.

"You didn't tell me you had one of those houses fit for a luxury design magazine."

"That's because I don't. It's my parents'. Well, actually, my mom's, to be more accurate. She got it in the divorce settlement. The mention of it still rubs my father the wrong way, so just leave it out of the conversation."

"Got it."

It was clear there was a lot about Alison I didn't know, but there was one thing I did. Right now she was all I had, and I was grateful to have met her that day. I looked around us, noticing the elegance of each guest. The men wore fine suits, dark and somber, while the women looked primed to the nines. Haute couture, I was sure, and the contrast with my little green dress was blinding.

"You mentioned a dinner party, Alison, not a gala."

"You look stunning, J." She said, noticing my sudden embarrassment towards my skimpy dress as I took in the finesse around me. "Perfect enough that maybe I can pin one of my mom's setups on you." She teased, trying to lighten the mood.

"Don't hold your breath on that one. You know I'm not exactly looking to mess up my life any further."

"I know, just promise me you'll try to have a nice time? Maybe take your head off of things, you know…" Alison's voice trailed off as she craned her neck before almost shouting in my ear. "MATT!" She called out, waving her hand above the crowd, "I want you to meet my brother."

Oh God, here we go!

When I turned toward the person she was calling, my eyes were immediately stuck. I couldn't get in a blink if I tried.

This perfect specimen of a man was walking towards us; tall, dark, and my God was he handsome. I swallowed dryly, gripping Alison's hand tighter in anticipation.

I had a feeling I'd seen him before, only I couldn't picture where. He was strikingly similar to Alison's grandfather, whom we'd met on our way to the bar. Maybe that was where I was finding the similarities. No, I decided after staring a little longer.

After the first impact of his perfect face, I noticed the regal posture of his walk, as if he owned the room and every single soul in it. People scurried to make way for him to pass, the unobstructed view allowing me to take all of him in. Broad muscles hid under the fine fabric of the bespoke suit he wore, adding power to his already undeniable mystique. His dark hair and perfectly trimmed beard contrasted with eyes the color of cold steel.

I couldn't help but shiver once they set on me. Dark despite their lightness, calculating and bone-chilling, if I was to be kind.

"Happy Birthday, *Principessa.*" He reached over to Alison, pulling her into a deep but tender hug that spoke volumes about their connection. Alison's pride in her brother was unmasked as I watched them exchange affection and a couple of private jokes before his attention came to settle on me.

"Aren't you going to introduce us?" He asked, his eyes deeply buried in mine.

"Of course. Matt, this is my friend Jamie Harden. Jamie, this is my oldest brother Matt." Alison beamed.

Matt nodded, narrowing his eyes for some reason before his features changed, and he placed his hand on the small of my back, his fingers brushing against my bare skin as he placed a kiss on my flushed cheek. The intensity of him made me shiver. His presence alone was overbearing yet so alluring it was scary.

"Nice to meet you, *Miss Harden.*" His voice was low and sultry, his lips grazing my ear as he said those words.

Holy shit!

I swallowed the lump in my throat, noticing the innuendo in his voice that hadn't rendered me indifferent. What was it with the 'Miss Harden' crap that made me tremble right down to my core?

Liam's intentions were always wicked when he called me that, and somehow, Matt's tone was dripping in just as much mischief.

"N...Nice to meet you, too, Matt." I steadied my voice as much as possible before replying. His Lord and Commander vibe rattled me right to my bones.

"Give me a sec, Mom's calling. Matt, can you keep Jamie company for a minute, please?"

"It would be my pleasure." He smiled with a cocked eyebrow directed my way.

Alison left me standing there alone with her brother, at a loss for words. I was still too caught up in his magnificence to be coherent. He was definitely ripped and toned in all the right places, the buttons of his shirt struggling to remain fastened under the force of his muscles.

I couldn't stop staring, not only because he was damn attractive but because of the sense that I knew this man from somewhere.

"Alison never told me she had such a beautiful friend." I blushed and tried my best to seem composed and not totally bewitched. His gray eyes were like shards of steel slashing through me.

"Thank you. She never mentioned that she had a brother."

"Well, it looks like I'm not worth being mentioned," Matt replied, faking disappointment.

"I don't think you really believe that."

"What I believe doesn't matter. What you think is what I want to hear." Oh lord! He didn't even bother to ease into it. Instinctively my eyes darted to the floor, not wanting him to see how nervous he made me. "Maybe you could be my date for the rest of the evening?"

"Quite forward, aren't you?" I was stunned by his bluntness.

"I know what I want when I see it. I'm just honest about it."

Matt stepped closer, his tongue darting across his lips while he tucked a strand of hair behind my ear, his finger lingering to caress my cheek.

All this felt wrong somehow, but his honesty was refreshing, and my thin self-esteem was loving the attention. Besides, Matt's spell was as strong as they get, his direct approach left no room for doubt or misinterpretation. I tried to ease the anxiety growing in my gut. It wasn't like I was cheating. Liam didn't want me, he said so himself. But why did it still feel that way?

"I'm sorry if I'm coming on too strong, but you look absolutely ravishing in that dress. I couldn't help it even if I wanted to." He confessed, his bare fingers tracing my spine up and down. My cheeks couldn't handle the heat anymore, the weight of his gaze forcing me to admire the wooden floor again.

"She does, doesn't she?" I heard, coming from behind me. A low and menacing grunt that made Matt look up, a grin plastered on his face. I spun on my heels so quickly that I almost missed a step. I'd recognize that voice even if I had earplugs. It settled straight in my gut each time I heard it.

"Liam," Matt said with that grin growing into a full smile. I was beyond surprised to see him here.

His expression was wild, dangerous, and as alluring as ever. It spoke right to the deepest, most intimate parts of me, and I couldn't help the tingle that settled between my legs at the sight.

After everything that happened, my treacherous body still reacted this way to his presence. If I closed my eyes, I could still feel his touch, missing the feeling of his lips all over me.

Liam's tone suggested possessiveness, like he was pissing on his territory and for Matt to peel his hands from me. It had the exact opposite effect. Instead of single digits, Matt had his whole hand now resting on my naked back, his fingers under the side hem of my dress.

I looked up at him as he started caressing my skin again, taking in the vile grin that stretched his lips once he registered the goosebumps his touch and Liam's stare had elicited all over my body.

Both of them stood there in a staring match, Liam's nose flaring while Matt's serenity was unnerving, yet he was the first to break the silence.

"Where are my manners? Let me introduce you two. Liam, this is Jamie Harden, my date tonight." Matt said, his chest swelling at his choice of words while I couldn't help but wince. But the worst was still to come. My ears and nerves were not prepared. "Miss Harden, this is Liam Dornier, my little brother."

CHAPTER SIXTEEN

Liam

Royalty had thrown up inside the house and forgotten to clean up after itself.

There wasn't an inch in this place that hadn't been prepped and luxed up to entertain the parade of vultures. All of them ready to pounce on the opportunity to mingle at one of Teresa Battaglia's soirées.

Mom was always eager to fill this enormous house with life now that the three of us had our own places and moved out. She'd taken it from my father out of spite in a messy divorce settlement that went on for what seemed like forever. This mansion was one of his hidden, most prized projects and possessions. It screamed Adrian Dornier in every detail.

Even despite all the animosity between the two, my mother had always kept the details of their fall out to herself, never involving any one of her three kids. Still, I knew my baby sister had witnessed the worst of it.

My baby sister who wasn't, theoretically, such a baby anymore. She was turning twenty-five today, but she'd always be our little princess no matter how old she turned.

She still allowed my mother to throw these huge parties in her honor since Matt and I had cut her off long ago, sacrificing our hypothetical weddings to appease her distress and make peace with the party planner addict that was Teresa Battaglia.

That was one of her love languages.

I made my way into the house, a flute of pink champagne being immediately thrust into my hand as I looked for the birthday girl. As always, Alison and I would endure this first part of her party so we could go out after and have the real fun until the crack of dawn.

It wasn't easy to find her in this sea of people that cluttered the house, but I soon managed to catch her just a few feet away from the makeshift bar in the corner of the family room.

"Happy birthday, *Principessa*." Alison jumped at the sound of my voice, her arms immediately squeezing the air out of me as she wrapped them around my neck.

"Thank you." She squealed, "I'm so happy you're here. Mom's been trying to set me up with the Kennedy's younger son all night. I swear, if I have to listen to another speech about old bones and pottery, I'm gonna stick my fist in his mouth. Someone needs to tell him the world can only handle one Ross Geller and he's been cast already."

I couldn't help the laughter from bursting out of me, earning a swat on the arm from the little brat in front of me.

"Are we still up for later tonight?"

"Of course. It's tradition. We might have company, though, if you don't mind."

"The Kennedy's younger son?" I chuckled.

"Hell, no!" Alison almost shouted, "Jamie, she works at AD, too."

Jamie? Fuck!

Alison gestured towards the bar, my eyes catching on her perfect form, her bare back turned to me, covered by Matt's hand. It hung low, barely on the limit before the curve of her ass. He whispered something in her ear, making her avert her gaze to the floor.

Why the fuck did he have his hands all over her?

"You don't mind, do you?" Alison asked again, her voice pulling me from the sight before me for a mere second.

"No." I quickly replied before cutting through the crowd straight at them, each step closer, heavier on the ground.

There was a sudden heat rising through my core as anger burned everything in its path inside me. Jealousy was reserved for weak men, yet here I fucking was, languishing in it like a pig in dry mud.

"...you look absolutely ravishing in that dress. I couldn't help it even if I wanted to." I heard him saying.

Damn! I loved my brother, but right now I wanted to rip his fucking arm off and beat him with it. Each muscle in my body was a mass of wrath, my hands clenched tightly into fists as my nails dug into my palms.

"She does, doesn't she?" I spat out between gritted teeth. My tone was dark and full of menace, clear for anyone to hear. My brother knew fairly well what he was doing and that his paws were set on something that belonged to me.

Only... she didn't.

Despite my tone, Matt made no move to peel himself off her, making me wonder if he knew who she was or was just playing dumb.

I took in her shocked expression, her full, plump lips parting as she acknowledged my presence. It was clear to see that she had no idea I was Alison's brother, and going by the panic on her face, I was the last person she expected to see here tonight.

"Where are my manners? Let me introduce you two. Liam, this is Jamie Harden, my date tonight." Matt paused, allowing that little information to sink in before continuing, "Miss Harden, this is Liam Dornier, my little brother."

"There's no need for introductions. We are well acquainted with each other." I hissed, my eyes settled on Matt's.

My dearest brother didn't lose that shit-eating grin he had on his face, pulling Jamie against his side, looking down into her eyes, making sure their faces hung inches apart for my viewing pleasure.

"You don't say? I had no idea. There's still a lot to find out about this beauty." He smiled, knowing I'd see right through his words. He did know who she was. At least in the version I'd painted for him when I told him all about the woman who'd stolen my every thought.

He made a point to keep touching her, pushing the limit further each time. I was close to an explosive eruption, wanting nothing more than to yank her from his arms and kiss her in front of every damn person in this room so they all knew who those lips belonged to.

"A word?" I demanded, my voice strangled in fury and bitterness. Matt followed behind me before I stopped a few feet away, out of listening range.

"What the fuck do you think you're doing?" I roared.

"Proving a point."

"What?"

"You are not some reverse version of Midas, Liam." Matt berated me, some kind of lesson being taught in the most twisted of ways. "You will not fuck up everything you touch. This girl, she's different from the others, I can tell. But you won't let yourself go there because you're a fucking coward."

"Oh so now you believe in love and shit?" I'd never thought of my brother as a hypocrite, but here he was, lecturing me on something he'd sworn off.

"I've never *not* believed in it. It might not be in the cards for me, but it doesn't mean you and Alison can't live a happy, normal life."

"Sure, because everything about our life is fucking normal."

"Just don't be a dick and take the win when it hits you in the damn face."

"I will not pull her into this, and neither will you. Do you hear me? Now, back. The fuck. Off." I punctuated each word to make it as clear as I could without a drawing.

"You think you can just walk away?"

"Damn right."

"Fine. I'll prove you wrong then."

Jamie

If looks could kill, both Matt and I would be stone-cold by now. Liam's glare would be shooting daggers if it was loaded.

I watched as the two men pulled away to a safe distance, purposely leaving their backs to me so I couldn't make out a single word they said.

If this was going to be my night, I needed another drink.

After collecting another one of those pink champagne flutes from a passing waiter, I sauntered back to the foyer. Looking at beautiful things had a calming effect unless that beautiful thing was Liam. I parked in front of the Dalí, its surrealism matching the one of my current predicament.

It was less disturbing than his normal pieces, but still messy and raw, just like all the emotions running through me. This night was definitely going to persist in my memory for eternity. Pun very much intended.

There was no lying to myself. I knew it was wrong, but that didn't change the fact that I enjoyed watching the way Liam was seething. There were only a few times when his words weren't controlled and carefully chosen, so forgive me if I relished in the fact that he was jealous to see me with another man.

"There you are!" Matt spoke straight into my ear, his hand resuming to what I figured to be his favorite spot. "I thought you had run out on me."

I should have.

"Just taking in the beauty in this piece. Shouldn't this be hanging at a museum somewhere?"

"Not that one. That piece is personal. Salvador was a close friend of my grandfather's. That woman blended in the sky?" Matt stood behind me, his full body pressed against mine while his lips rested on my ear as he pointed towards the canvas, "That was my grandmother."

"Why is she wearing two rings on her necklace?" That particular part of the painting was more prominent than the rest, the huge ring standing out with its bright tones of gold against the darker colors around it.

"That's somewhat of a family tradition, running for many generations now. Our initials are engraved in it, and the patriarch of the family is expected to gift it to the love of his life. My grandfather gave that ring to her as soon as he knew she was it. Which just so happened to be the first time they met."

"Wow. He moved fast." I couldn't help but notice some resemblance. "And the other one? There are two rings there."

"Let's just say she was a very courted woman."

"She's holding a gun bigger than her. She looks like a force of nature."

"Yeah, she was fierce." There was admiration and longing in his voice, a soft tone coming out of such a rough man.

"She was beautiful."

"Salvador, my grandfather, and another handful of men thought so, too." He whispered before spinning me around to face him, "Imagine if they saw you."

Smooth. How he spun that around was a lesson in mastery pick-up lingo. I had no response other than a deep blush that settled on my cheeks.

"Come, let's get back to the party." He offered, seeing that my words were lost.

While Alison was busy greeting her guests, Matt paraded me around the room, his strong hand caressing my skin in a permanent touch. I could feel Liam's gaze on us, his glower burning a hole in the back of my skull.

To say his reaction was confusing was an understatement. He was pissed to see me with someone else, yet he was the one who had pushed me away. I'm not good enough for him.

So I can't have you, but I can't have anyone else, either?

Fuck that!

I was not about to get it on with his brother, but what I knew to be certain was a long way from what I was willing to let Liam believe.

"Can I get you a real drink? That champagne tastes like a flower shop." I couldn't help but laugh, noticing the similar remark Alison had made earlier. Apples and their trees, right?

"What am I missing?" Speaking of the devil, Alison cooed from behind me, her lips spread into a wide smile, her eyebrows doing a bouncy dance referring to the intimate proximity she caught me and Matt in.

"I was about to get Jamie a proper drink. Do you want one?"

"Yes, please. Rum. The good stuff." Matt looked at me, silently asking for my choice of poison.

"Same." I quickly said, waiting for him to leave so I could have a moment alone with Alison, but Matt blew that chance, grabbing her hand and pulling her along with him.

I was alone again, fidgeting with my fingers, not knowing what to do with myself. It was short-lasting, though.

"I can see you're having fun." Again Liam startled me, his low, husky voice right next to my ear. I almost lost my balance as I turned to him, Liam's hand coming to rest on my ribs, steadying my stance. Our eyes locked on each other. Deep and unsettling, as always.

He kept his hand on me, slowly gliding backwards until he reached my skin, the tip of his finger tracing my spine past the end of my dress, stopping right before he reached my underwear, all while looking straight into my eyes.

His stare was so intense that he had me pinned under his hypnotic green orbs, incapable of tearing away. It was like our first encounter all over again, only this time I knew what I was up against. My throat contracted, trying to swallow the lump while my chest heaved heavier with each passing second.

Liam's gaze dropped down, a smirk twisting his lips as he took in my hardened nipples, perfectly visible under the thin fabric of my dress as a direct result of his warm hand traveling my body.

He trapped his bottom lip between his teeth, and I knew he was reigning his lust in, too, his eyes growing darker along with his expression. He was doing this on purpose, threading me along to see my reaction to him, to confirm that he still stood on the pedestal I'd placed him on, and I fell right for it.

I closed my eyes, breaking his spell with a deep exhale, trying to regain control by allowing his cutting words back into my mind.

"You're not right for me, okay?"

I harshly removed his hand from my body, anger consuming me after his attempt to manipulate me.

"Fun? Yes, I am. What's wrong with that? Apparently, Matt thinks I might just be right for him. No harm in seeing where that goes." I spat out, the vindictive thirst in me not minding how wrong that sounded.

"You can't…"

"I can't what, Liam? Huh? Have anyone else? You don't want me, you've thrown me in the trash, remember? You have absolutely no say in it." I cut him off, blurting my pain and fury into those words.

Liam's hand quickly ran up my neck, under my hair, fisting a handful and making sure my eyes were set on his again.

"I never said I didn't want you." He gritted, his face coming closer to mine with each word, making sure they wouldn't fall in the space between us. "You have no idea how much I want to fucking kiss you right now. Get you out of here so that none of these fuckers can feast their eyes on you in that dress. I want nothing more than to rip it off your body and force you to come over and over again until you black out, your throat burning from screaming my name at the top of your lungs." His words dripped with venom, his eyes blazing in an unrestrained fire. Liam leaned in, inhaling sharply along the silky skin of my neck, yanking on my hair for better access, "I fucking hate that you already smell like someone else but me."

"Is that jealousy, Mr. Dornier?" My stomach fluttered at his actions, but I couldn't forget what he said and how cold he was when he said it.

"No, Miss Harden. It's grounds for murder."

"Too little too late, Liam. Words mean nothing to me anymore." I harshly replied, resentment coating my words as I tried to guard what was still left of my heart, my hand peeling his off my hair.

Each breath I took stung like a million wasps in my chest, not enough air reaching my lungs, as I turned away from him with every ounce of strength left in my body. Alison was coming back from the bar, Matt trailing behind her, our drinks in his hand.

I seized Alison's wrist, pulling her harshly along with me, cutting through the crowd, only stopping once we were outside, the cool evening's breeze finally allowing me to breathe.

"Jamie? What's wrong? What happened?" She urged me.

The truth was strangling me and blocking all my airways. I looked at her, my eyes boring into her face without a single blink, holding my silence for a while, much to her despair.

"Jamie Harden, tell me what's wrong right now!"

"It's Liam, Alison." The words finally tumbled from my mouth, "It's been Liam all along."

Alison just stood there, looking at me, her face blank of any expression that would hint at what she was thinking. Now that I knew he was her brother, I was afraid this would mess with our friendship in some way. Her prolonged silence started to freak me out, I needed to know how she felt about it.

"Can you please just say something?" I whisper-shouted.

"I should have figured." She simply replied, her eyes averting to the floor, her lips falling into a thin line.

"What do you mean? Oh, God! Alison, please don't be mad at me."

"I'm not mad. Not at all. It's just that Liam is… complicated. I don't want to see you hurt. And now I've shoved Matt onto you, too. Shit, I'm so sorry. I had no idea."

"I swear to God I didn't know Liam was your brother."

"I know you didn't. I didn't exactly come clean regarding who my family is. People tend to get close because of who I'm related to. Trying to climb the ladder, you know? So it's something I try to keep to myself. I'm sorry." She confessed, and I finally understood why such an amazing person had such a limited friend list.

"Alison, you don't need to apologize for that. I couldn't care less who you're related to. I just couldn't bear the thought of losing you because I have a thing for your brother."

"A thing?"

"I don't have a name for it, and I'd rather leave it without one. It's too messy."

"Yeah, I understand, and I just added gas to that fire. I don't know how to make Matt back off. He's not keen on following orders. Besides, they're both quite persuasive and adamant regarding what they want. And I use those expressions loosely."

"I don't give a shit about what they want. I'm not getting any deeper into this clusterfuck than what I already am."

"Let's hope you have the choice—" Alison said before one of the waitresses interrupted.

"Dinner will be served in five minutes. If you wouldn't mind taking your designated seats."

"It will be okay." Alison encouraged, pulling me into a hug before we stepped back inside, "We'll figure this out."

I scanned the crowd that was now moving into the enormous hall where impeccably decorated tables were set, searching for Liam, but he was nowhere to be found. Matt was just a few steps away, though, waiting for us, a broad white smile welcoming us back.

As soon as I was within arms reach, Matt pulled me into his rock-hard body, his arm curling around my waist. My hand landed on his muscled chest, trying to absorb the impact while he leaned over my ear, my skin tingling under the warmth of his breath.

"I'd prefer to have you sitting on my lap, but since my mother imposes certain etiquette rules, I've arranged for you to be sitting right next to me at dinner."

Why wasn't I pushing him off me? First, it felt good to be wanted for once, and by a man like Matt, nonetheless. Second, I was hell-bent on calling Liam's bluff. I wanted to know exactly what he meant by "grounds for murder," as he had phrased it.

"Straight for the kill," I muttered under my breath, more to myself as a comparison between Liam's push and pull and his brother's unapologetic bluntness, but Matt heard it anyway.

"Not tonight. We're still here as opposed to naked in my bed."

I grabbed one of the drinks from his hand and gulped it down in one go. My head should be clear for this, but my senses surely needed to be numbed.

"Woah, calm down there, tiger." Matt chuckled, taking the empty glass from my hand. "Do I make you that nervous?"

"No, sorry. Just had a bad week at work." I dismissed, erasing any flirty edge possible.

"That bad, huh? What do you do for a living? It seems like your boss is sucking the life out of you." I paused at that last part. It almost seemed like he was inside my damn mind.

"I'm an architect. I work at AD. What about you?"

"Oh, so do you work with Al or with Liam?" Matt asked, not bothering to answer my question.

"With Liam. What about you?" I asked again.

"With neither." He chuckled, "So, how does my little brother treat you back at the office? Is he, by any chance, the reason you had a shitty week?"

Jack-fucking-pot.

"No." I lied, "And I'm not answering any other question before you answer mine."

"You want to know what I do for a living? That's quite a tedious topic." Matt avoided my question again.

"I didn't come in for interrogation, and seeing that you're looking for a one-sided conversation, I guess you should find someone else to question. Nice to meet you, Matt." I turned to leave, but Matt grabbed my hand, slightly pulling me back.

"Okay, okay. Fair enough. I own a couple of businesses." He finally answered, his eyes rolling in what seemed annoyance or boredom.

"That wasn't so hard, was it? So you're the only sibling that didn't follow into the family business."

"Let's just say I followed another side of the family business." I cocked an eyebrow, confused by his answer, but Matt wasn't about to elaborate as he cut me off before I could ask, "I think dinner is served. Shall we go?"

With a hand settled on the small of my back, Matt led me towards our table, pulling out my chair as a true gentleman before taking his seat beside me. Alison sunk into her place right in front of me, her eyebrows almost rising into her hairline as she tried to gesture to my right without being obvious.

I looked towards her motion, being met with those green eyes that took my breath away. Of course Liam would be sitting right next to me.

Talk about being trapped between a sword and a shield!

I locked eyes with Alison, focusing on her while trying to forget I was seated between Matt and Liam. Dinner got served, and if someone were to ask what it was, I couldn't give a straight answer since all my focus was set on trying to survive this nightmare.

Liam brushed his fingers up my arm, bringing my attention to his darkened eyes before he placed a feather-light kiss on my shoulder.

Color me shocked. I was sure he'd had enough of this game when he disappeared, and especially when he hadn't muttered a word during the entire dinner.

"I've been watching you." He whispered, his voice rough and low, settling right where it shouldn't.

"What?"

"I've been watching you, trying to figure out if you decided to forgo the whole underwear set tonight. I know there's no bra under that dress. Did you come without a thong, too?" Liam's warm hand settled on my thigh, a small gasp threatening to escape my parted lips, both in surprise and the exhilarating current that simple gesture sent up my spine.

His hand started to travel up my leg, steadily climbing under my dress at an excruciatingly slow pace that fed my need for more.

My heart slammed against my chest, filling my ears with nothing else but the pump of rushing blood. I parted my legs for him, Liam's grin growing at my instinctive reaction.

"What are you–" My voice trailed off as he reached that spot between my thighs right before my pussy.

"Just checking for myself." I swallowed dryly, anticipation making me burn under his touch.

"Aren't you going to taste your dessert?" Matt asked from the other side, a devilish smile on his handsome face, making me spin my head towards him. I tried to hide the blush on my cheeks and the lust in my eyes.

"Oh, umm…of course." I hadn't even noticed it being placed in front of me.

Liam didn't stop his advances, his fingers drawing dangerously close to exactly where I wanted them. This felt like a dangerous game, but fuck I just couldn't make him stop.

I tried my best to conceal my heavy pants and heaving chest from Matt's glare, a rush of adrenaline and lust taking over every inch of my body. I closed my legs, trying to squeeze them together, but Liam had other ideas. His hand hastily held my leg in place before hooking his foot around mine so I had no choice but to stay as I was.

"You'll find it delicious." Matt pressed once I had made no move to try the delicacy in front of me.

Shakingly, I picked up my spoon under his attentive stare while Liam bore his fingers into my flesh, pushing my thong aside without so much as brushing against my skin. I scooped a chunk of the pannacotta and shoved it in my mouth.

As soon as I closed my lips around the spoon, Liam slid a finger inside me, his palm pressing firmly against my clit. It was perfectly timed, a deep moan escaping my chest from the delicious intrusion.

Matt looked at me, surprised by the sound I had just made, and I felt the need to disguise it under words that were hard to articulate.

"Oh God…it's s…so good." My voice was strained, a failed attempt to mask the pleasure that Liam's pumping fingers were bringing me. My eyes were tightly shut as I savored the dessert together with the exquisite torture Liam's digits delivered with each thrust, trying my damnest to keep quiet and discrete.

"You've got a little on your lip," Matt said, making me turn to look at him, opening my eyes to see a wide smile spreading his lips. Did he know? No. He couldn't.

I licked my lips trying to clean them, apparently failing.

Matt held my jaw in his firm hand, turning my face to him again, "Here, let me do it." Before I knew it, his lips were devouring mine.

His tongue swung across my lip and rushed inside my mouth in such a swift move I had no chance to stop it. My mind was in a fogged haze from Liam's touch, I couldn't help but release another moan straight into Matt's mouth.

It was all so fast, there was nothing I could have done to stop it.

Liam pulled his fingers out of me, pushed back his chair with a screech, and threw his napkin on the table.

In the blink of an eye, Liam was crouched down next to Matt, discreetly jamming a fork into his thigh, deep enough that it stood on its own.

Matt winced, and a low growl rumbled in his chest, but other than that, he didn't even react.

"Touch her again, and you die." His grunted words had a shiver running down my spine.

I had never heard Liam's voice so laced with hate and fury. And directed at his brother, of all people.

He stood back up and fixed his jacket before turning around and disappearing through the double doors of the hall, leaving me to feel like the worst person on Earth.

Because I am.

CHAPTER SEVENTEEN

Liam

"Another," I grunted to Lilly, Dea Tacita's bar manager, seeing her disapproval plastered all over her face. "Keep your judgment for your real customers. The ones who can't have your job *and* your head in the same night."

"Sure thing, boss," She mumbled, not masking the acidity in her tone, "I'm just not sure *Signore* Matteo would approve of me not saying anything."

"Fuck *Signore* Matteo!" I practically spat. "If he doesn't know I'm here getting shit-faced, he doesn't know me at all."

I was waiting for Alison at the club, sitting in my brother's chair, in the office that reigned over Dea Tacita like God from the fucking sky.

No, no.

This was as far away from Heaven as one could get. This was Sin City—like the devil from his stone throne in the depths of Hell sounded more appropriate.

I couldn't have run faster from that fucking table. When I saw Matt savoring Jamie's mouth, when I heard her moaning against his lips, I couldn't take it anymore.

There was no choice but to leave. The alternative was too bloody and unsuitable for my baby sister's birthday celebration. How I managed to be so objective in that moment was beyond me.

I yanked my hand from inside of her straight away, and Jamie swung her head my way, shooting what looked like an apologetic and confused look. I didn't care. The damage was done.

Matt was proving a point, I was aware. Still, I had to remind myself over and over that it wasn't real. But this rabid feeling in my chest that yearned for my fist to punch a hole in his face was too telling of my own feelings. Feelings that bothered me to be feeling.

I hadn't asked for this. I didn't want them. But fuck, I wanted *her*.

That fork in his leg? It was a kind concession because he was my brother.

Lilly poured me another drink. Was it the tenth? Fifteenth? I had lost count. But it slid down my throat with the same ease as all the others and did nothing to appease the burn in the pit of my stomach.

I had scanned the line of people waiting to get into Dea Tacita. There were over a dozen women who would have caught my eye any other day. They would be easy fucks, uncomplicated, and with zero strings. No phone call the next morning, no sleepovers, no tears, no names. Impersonal as fuck, but the itch would have been scratched, and my life made easier.

Why I was craving the clusterfuck that Jamie would mean was out of my spectrum of understanding.

She could be like Michelle.

I had tried that line of thought, only Michelle never meant anything. We had slept together before she started at AD and occasionally did because it was convenient. There were no blurred lines there. She knew what the deal was from the start.

Jamie didn't fall in that category. She had one of her own, where no other women had ever come close to.

I'd be happy to hold her while she slept, as I did last week, with my dick neatly tucked in my pants.

That was definitely a first. Liam Battaglia, craving to cuddle. Shoot me now!

"One more," I demanded, and this time Lilly didn't protest, pouring me another shot, still not holding onto her tongue.

"Whatever you need, you won't find it at the bottom of that glass. You've tried seven times already." She'd been with us for a long time now. We knew she was trustworthy, and the familiarity gave her the nerve to try and stretch her boundaries at each given turn. Or maybe that was because Matt had fucked her a couple of times and she thought she was entitled.

"Bartender psychology, Lilly? Really?"

"Whatever works." She replied, her hand sliding up my arm and across my shoulders as she came to stand behind the chair, her palms squeezing my tense shoulders.

"Do you have a five-foot-four brunette named Jamie Harden that holds the universe in her eyes when she looks at my brother lying around here somewhere?" Alison asked, strutting into my brother's office, *alone* thank fuck. Lilly's hands froze, her advances being stopped by the fiery little lady who had been born without boundaries. "No? Then I don't think you have anything that will work, Lilly."

I shot her a warning glare, being met with the same one directed at me.

"You can go," Alison said, waiting for Lilly to leave and shut the door behind her, leaning onto the edge of the desk before speaking again, her arms crossed in front of her chest and a scowl settled on her face. "What are you doing?"

"Getting drunk. I thought you'd be smarter. You could have inferred that."

"Don't be an ass to me, Liam. I see right through you. You'll be trying to piss me off so I can leave you to wallow in your damn misery alone so that I don't spoon-feed you the truth that you don't want to swallow. You're out of luck. I know you too well to let your sharp tongue affect me."

I wave her off, pouring another glass, which Alison snatched from the table between us, tipping the entire contents down her throat.

"Ugh, disgusting." She grunted after swallowing, her face contorted from the taste.

"Then don't drink it. That was for me, anyway." I snatched the glass back from her hand, refilling it.

"I'll drink every one you pour until you stop being a jerk and talk to me."

Alison started for the glass again, but I swept it off the table, downing the whole drink and slamming the glass back onto the table, leaving my hand wrapped around it for safekeeping.

"There's nothing to talk about, Alison." I wanted her to drop it. I could feel all the anger crawling up my throat again. All I came here for was to drown it in booze, and Alison was getting in the way.

"Like hell, there isn't. Jamie told me everything. I know what's been going on."

"You don't know a thing." I pushed back again.

"I know Jamie's obsessed with you. Can't you see that?"

"Nope. She seemed pretty ecstatic to have Matt's tongue shoved down her throat!" Those sour words had every muscle in my body tense up again, balled masses of unreleased fury craving a target to destroy.

"Don't be a dick! You know that's not true."

"I don't care, Alison." I shot her a glare, my voice dropping an octave, but she still wasn't backing down. My baby sister wasn't done handing my ass to me, and no amount of warning tactics would make her back off.

"Then why did you fire Jack?" She asked, her eyes never leaving mine, daring me to lie to her.

"Who the fuck is Jack?" I asked nonchalantly, pouring another shot and drinking it straight after.

"You know well enough who Jack is. He was one of your best bartenders and you still fired him. Why was that, I wonder?"

"He had his fucking hands on something that didn't belong to him," I growled, the glass in my hand shattering into a million pieces as I slammed it onto the table.

"What the hell, Liam? Are you trying to hurt yourself?" Alison yelled, springing from her seat, shaking my hands clean from all the glass.

"I'm okay," I grunted, pulling my hands away.

"She's struck a chord in there, too. I know it. Why don't you let yourself have this?"

"Alison, I don't want to talk about it." I exhaled deeply with my eyes shut, my thumb and index pressing down on them, trying to shake those thoughts off and push Jamie to the back of my mind, as far from the surface as possible.

"If you're wondering if they left together, the answer is no. She went home. *Alone.*" I sat back, leaning against the chair, trying to seem unfazed. "I saw her poking her finger into his chest before she left. She's been hurting over you and your push and pull. I didn't know it was you at first, but it all makes sense now. The hot and cold she spoke about. You deserve to be happy, too, Liam."

"Let's not talk about me. It's your birthday, let's focus on that."

"No!" She stood, her foot pounding on the ground like a toddler having a tantrum. "You can be really obtuse sometimes. Don't you see she's completely head over heels for you?"

I took the bottle to my mouth, tipping my head back, letting the liquid slide directly down my throat, wishing it would numb me and the feeling of hope growing inside me at Alison's words.

"Liam–"

"I'm going home." I cut her off, standing and placing a kiss on her forehead, "I'm sorry your night turned out like this. I'll make it up to you."

"It's okay. Just think about what I said. Please?"

"Will you get home okay?" I said, purposely ignoring her question. "I can ask Carl to take you. Let me send him a text."

"I'll get home fine." She replied, placing a hand over mine that held my phone, pushing it down. "I don't need a chaperone. Besides, Carl is taking you, one of the other guys can take your car to your place." She snatched my keys from the desk, "No way you're driving after what I suppose you've had to drink."

"Fine. Don't get in trouble." I relent, placing another kiss on her head before leaving.

Normally I'd be doing this drive back home with a sure fuck on my arm. Kicking in the door with some hot chick I found at the club clawing at my back.

Tonight the eerie silence in my apartment just made all my fucking thoughts excruciatingly louder than I could handle.

How the fuck did I get myself into this shit?

"Fuck!" I grunted in anger. I'd left my phone at Dea Tacita, meaning I couldn't even check on her location.

I couldn't stop thinking about Jamie, her moans filling the air as I watched her writhe beneath me, taking me like a goddess while I slammed into her again and again. And even with those images flashing in my mind, I would still settle for the opportunity to hold her against my chest while she cried over a dumb fuck like me.

I laid down on my bed only to get up again and go to the couch, which also didn't have the desired effect, so I found myself pacing from the living room to the kitchen, breathing heavily as if I'd been running for miles. I was trying to avoid the urge that was taking over me to know where she was and with whom.

I trusted my sister and wouldn't doubt her words, but I still needed the visual confirmation that Jamie hadn't run for comfort into another man's arms. Who? Fuck if I knew.

I couldn't fucking stay here and keep wondering, so I yanked my jacket from the rack and grabbed my keys, ready for another night of sitting under her window in the solitude of my car.

No.

I had to talk to her. I had no idea what I needed to say, but there was something constricting my airways that I needed to set free. Hopefully I'll have it figured out by the time I get to Tremont.

As soon as I closed the door behind me I looked down the hallway, and my fucking heart skipped a damn beat.

Jamie was standing right there. She had stopped in her tracks, looking at me, her eyes wide, glistening in what I could only identify as fear. Jamie stared at me for a minute, her mouth opened to speak but nothing came out before her gaze averted downwards as if her words had fallen to the ground.

She held her hands in one another, rubbing her palms together nervously. She looked up again, taking an unsure step forward as if gaining traction for her small voice to reach me.

"I'm sorry." She said. She was anxious and shaking, but those words came out undoubtably steady. She meant it. "Can you please give me a minute?"

I carried on looking at her for a few more seconds before stepping back and opening the door to my apartment again, motioning for her to go in.

Jamie walked past me, unsteady steps as she made her way into my apartment. I couldn't help but close my eyes, inhaling deeply and reveling in the sweet scent at her passage, but that damn image of my brother's hands all over her didn't leave me alone.

I closed the door behind me with a gentle click, watching her shaky figure as she scrambled her mind for the words she came here to say.

As if a tidal wave hit her, Jamie frantically started to speak, "I'm so sorry, Liam. I wasn't expecting anything like–"

Grabbing her wrist, I pulled her towards the bathroom without saying a single word, cutting off whatever she was saying.

"Liam? What are you doing?" Her voice trembled in fear as she spoke, but I couldn't have this conversation while she reeked of another man.

I switched the water on and pushed her into the walk-in shower, soaking her under the spray, clothes and all. Jamie's breath hitched in her throat as the cold water hit her, her mouth falling open, gasping for air that struggled to come.

That smell needed to come off. The only scent she'd be wearing was mine.

Before she could protest, I stepped into the shower, too, standing an inch away from her, my towering figure protecting her from the cold water as it drenched me instead.

Jamie looked up into my eyes, my face dripping ice-cold water onto hers. I stared into her eyes for a moment, noticing the redness in them. She had been crying.

That notion stabbed at my heart, making me bite down on my tongue in punishment. I had done that.

Fuck she was beautiful in her vulnerability. The water had stripped us both, leaving only bare bones and honesty behind.

I couldn't hold it any longer. With fury in my veins and something I couldn't name in my chest, I kissed her. Water mingled with our need to consume each other as Jamie kissed me back with as much passion as I was kissing her. She tasted like damn sunshine and rainbows on a rainy day. Those clouds needed to scatter and I knew I was the one who had put them there.

"I'm sorry." She repeated, her plump lips a little swollen from the force of our kiss. "I liked seeing the way you reacted to your brother being around me, and I didn't stop him because of it. Seeing even a tiny hint of jealousy in your eyes just told me that I meant something to you. That's all I wanted. To mean something to you. It was wrong, I know. Very, very wrong. I didn't even consider your feelings, and I truly never expected it to escalate the way it did." She blurted, almost without taking a breath. She moved her eyes back down again, looking ashamed as she continued, "I know I don't deserve your forgiveness. I was selfish, I only thought about what seeing you angry meant to me. I never even stopped to think if I was hurting you or what the hell I was doing. And with your own brother! I'm so stupid! I don't know how I could be so…" Her words were lost again, maybe from the lack of a reaction from me. Her hope was fleeting as she stopped her rant with a final statement, "I'm sorry."

Jamie tried to push past me, but my feet were like concrete blocks on the floor. I placed a hand on her stomach, pushing her back to the spot she was in before, under me.

Her eyes shot up to mine, waiting for me to speak. I searched her eyes, trying to find any hint of dishonesty but finding none.

They shone with unshed tears and candidness.

Jamie struggled to keep those tears in place and not let them fall while I studied her face and rummaged my brain for the words I'd left my apartment to say.

"I'm sorry, too." I finally broke the silence, earning a shocked glare from her while her body broke into a constant shiver.

"What? You didn't do anything, why are you apologizing?"

"I'm sorry because I wasn't honest with you. I'm sorry I made you feel that you meant nothing after you'd given yourself to me." I stepped forward, making her back up towards the wall. "I'm sorry for leaving you alone the other morning. I'm sorry for letting you think I kissed Michelle and being happy to see you jealous. I didn't do it. I couldn't because of you. I'm sorry for not being able to leave you. And mostly, I'm sorry for lying to myself about the way I feel about you." I finished, closing the gap between us with each sentence until I was merely an inch away, her back hitting the wall once I was done.

Slowly, I bent down again and captured her lips in the most heartfelt kiss I've ever given.

Jamie inhaled deeply as soon as our lips met, her chest filling with the unexpected gesture. She was the heaven I'd otherwise never get to taste.

Breaking the kiss, I leaned my forehead onto hers and laced our fingers, my chest imploding with the need to hear her say she was mine.

"Tell me you forgive me, Jamie. Tell me you want me because, *fuck* I want you with every fiber of my being." I kissed her again with a different urgency this time, nibbling on her bottom lip before pleading again. "Tell me you're mine."

CHAPTER EIGHTEEN

Jamie

"I'm yours."

All the turbulence in my mind quelled once Liam's lips settled on mine.

There was a different intensity in his touch tonight, a different weight in his kiss. It held more than just lust, even though it didn't lack desire. This kiss had passion charged with relief, with possession, with a deep connection that claimed every piece of my soul.

On my way over to his apartment I had played out all the possible outcomes of our conversation. From him not wanting to hear a word out of my mouth and shutting the door in my face or facing a Liam with a blank expression that denied being bothered by everything that happened tonight. This scenario most certainly wasn't on the list.

He kissed me like I've never been kissed before. It was so much more than our lips touching. It was like his soul was pulling mine into a heartfelt hug that promised never to let go.

Soft, slow, and lingering, yet harsh and burning at the same time. It made me buzz with exhilaration and, at the same time, gave me a peace I don't ever remember feeling.

Liam held my face in place while his lips took over mine again and again, his tongue probing into my mouth with a softness that melted every part of my being.

"Stay." He whispered against my lips between demanding pecks that tasted like devotion. "Stay with me tonight."

Liam rested his forehead against mine, the water cascading down his back, his green eyes boring into me. It was a soul search that tore down barriers and shattered any illusion I ever had that I could resist my feelings for this man. The warmth I thought I saw in his eyes made me not care for the consequences.

He was fire and I was more than willing to get burned, hurt as it might, the heat and beauty of its embers were more than worthy.

I wrapped my arms around his neck, pulling him closer for another kiss in a silent reply to his demand. Unlike all the other times, I found that his request held no second intention. And I was right.

He shut the water off and handed me a towel so I could dry off, bringing me some sweats of his to change. He waited for me in his room, standing from the bed once I came out of the bathroom. He was already fully clothed, his hair still messy and damp.

Liam pulled me towards the living room, his hand tightly wrapped around mine, only stopping once we reached the couch in the dimly lit space. He laid down, pulling me onto him, my body fitting perfectly on his.

He stroked my hair with one hand while the other held me against him, my head resting on his muscled chest, his steady heartbeat soothing mine that raced with joy.

This was where I belonged, enveloped in his arms, drenched in his scent, covered in him.

I finally felt safe.

I finally felt at home.

"Tell me you'll still be here in the morning," Liam whispered against my hair, soft kisses showering me with affection.

"There's nowhere else I'd rather be." Never had truer words left my mouth. I sank further into him, allowing myself to relax into his caresses until I finally fell asleep.

What I had done had no excuse. I simply wasn't thinking. It was stupid, immature, and selfish. I wasn't expecting Matt to kiss me, though. It had caught me off guard for how fucked up it was. As soon as I pulled back and looked at Liam, he was seething and had every right to be.

Despite being built like a rock, I should have punched Matt in the face right there, but I was rooted to my spot, frozen in shock.

I was too focused on making Liam jealous that I hadn't pushed Matt back enough for him to get the proper message. It felt too good to know that Liam was watching and that having another man's hands on me made him angry. It told me I mattered to him. I didn't even care about the way it would make him feel.

The look of disgust Liam shot me before he stormed out slashed right through my heart, tearing me into pieces. I never want him to look at me that way again. I felt dirty and small, and just that look was enough to have my mind back in Jacksonville where it had no business to be in after all the work it took to tear it from my being.

Coming clean about how I felt about him was a risk, but it was the only way. I could see that now. The possibility of losing my job was real, but I didn't care. Losing Liam weighed more on my scale.

So being here, wrapped in Liam's arms, feeling him finally let go and stop pushing me away was like walking on clouds. I was in Heaven.

I woke up alone, curled on his couch with a blanket over me, the morning sun shining brightly through those huge windows. I sprung up, panic filling my lungs, searching the space for Liam, feeling the dismay increase every time I turned and didn't find him.

"Are you looking for me?" His deep voice came from behind me, my heart finally slowing to a normal rate. Until I turned around and took him in.

Liam stood there shirtless, low hanging sweats leaving very little to the imagination, a striking V of muscles leading down towards a bulge I had had the pleasure of experiencing.

I was struck by his perfection, my mouth falling ajar at the image before me. Ripped muscles clenched as he rubbed a towel against his wet hair, each mass straining as he moved.

Just as the first time I saw him without a shirt, I noticed the tattoo running the length of his torso, just under his arm. A woman and a skull, both with a butterfly on their mouths, an infinity loop holding them together. I never thought I'd find tattoos attractive, but damn he looked good with the ink.

This man was sculpted in pure sin, drawn with allure, and painted in divinity.

Just like the first time I had seen him like this, my eyes dropped to his pronounced bulge, my throat immediately being invaded by a massive lump.

Holy Father, how many, many sins were running through my mind.

"You can take a *warm* shower when you stop staring if you want." Liam interrupted my reverie, pulling my eyes back to his face, his lips twisted in a grin.

I picked up the closest pillow and threw it at him, my cheeks deeply blushed from being caught admiring him. He dodged it and in two massive steps, he was pulling me up into a playful hug, tickling me and covering me in small kisses while I squirmed in his hold.

"If you keep wiggling against me like that, you'll have a lot more to stare at in a second." I stopped, leaning my back against him, wanting to feel him completely. Liam buried his nose in the crook of my neck, inhaling deeply while the playful air suddenly turned thick and serious. "This was the best night of my life."

It was a vulnerable confession whispered against my sensitive skin, his words drenched in a meaning that made my heart and stomach flutter. Absolutely nothing had happened, and yet everything had changed.

"I couldn't agree more," I replied once the knot in my throat allowed me to speak.

"Come on. Time to shower, Miss Harden. I left clothes out for you on my bed and a towel in the bathroom. How does bacon and eggs sound for breakfast?"

I turned around, locking my arms around his neck, looking deep into his beautiful eyes, my face lighting up with a smile, happiness overflowing from every pore.

"You sound absolutely perfect."

I had never felt love before. I had just never had it in my life.

If someone were to ask me, I couldn't tell them what it felt like. Its smell, its taste, the feeling and warmth was all new to me, and it was now tied to the man currently making me breakfast as I showered in his bathroom.

I had always imagined love to be in the little things. Your favorite cake baking in the oven when you come home from school. A soothing hug of comfort when you're feeling down. The smell of bacon and eggs someone was cooking you for breakfast. The warmth and security of knowing you are accepted and wanted because someone who loved you did those things for you out of love.

I had never had that.

Affection was never an emotion my father harvested towards me. There was only deception and disdain in his eyes. I learned to see myself as he did.

He blamed me for my mother's death, and in a way, I did, too. He never found it in his heart to forgive me even though I was nothing but a helpless baby.

There was always someone else taking care of me. How he paid those bills was still a mystery to this day. But somehow those women never stuck around for long. They stopped showing up as soon as I learned how to make my own cereal when I was six.

I did everything I could to keep out of his way. I avoided being in the same space as him like the plague. He never had a kind word to say, and that was on a good day. Being locked up in a closet for the whole night, or even for the entire weekend, was a kind reprieve from the basement of the drug store he worked at.

His words of unworthiness still haunted me as I hadn't learned how to free myself from measuring my worth by his standards. They still affected me. They tore me to pieces and made me wish every day that I had a different life. Or none at all.

So being here today, accepting the fact that maybe I deserve happiness, was an enormous step. I felt wanted and accepted, safe in Liam's arms, even after the stupid shit I did last night.

I locked all those feelings in their little box, drying off before sauntering into the living room, watching Liam as he finished up breakfast. He was humming and swaying to the sound of the music playing on his speaker, and again, I was stuck staring and feeling. *Feeling* so, so much.

Liam met me with a smile as soon as he sensed my presence. It illuminated his face, his eyes shining brighter than stars.

"I like my clothes a lot better on you." He teased, his eyes raking over my body from head to toe, stepping closer towards me as he took my figure in. Hooking an arm around my waist, Liam pulled me into his grasp, swaying me along with him to the uplifting tune.

How this was my life was beyond me. Happiness that didn't fit in my little body wasn't something I was used to.

I let my lips find his, our kiss immediately deepening as Liam's hands roamed freely down my body, a palm squeezing my ass while pushing my hips firmly against his groin. My body's reaction to him was instant, the heat of his touch setting me ablaze.

"Are you that hungry?" Liam pulled back after my stomach growled in contempt, the emptiness and the smell of breakfast pausing his advances.

"The smell of burning bacon always gets me going." I chuckled, watching as Liam ran to the oven, trying to save it. His laughter filled the space while he turned towards me with a plate filled with charcoaled pieces of bacon.

"Bacon a *la Vesuvio*. My specialty." He said, laughing harder, and I couldn't help but join. "Take a seat while I fix us some bacon we can actually digest."

We sat in a comfortable silence, having breakfast together, with a familiarity that made it seem we had been doing this forever.

It was strange seeing Liam so carefree as if last night had unlocked something in him. But it was a side of him I was enjoying seeing.

I watched him munch on his food, my eyes permanently locked on him, studying his tattoo. The woman and the skull with the butterfly over their mouths, wondering what on Earth it meant. I noticed one more running the length of his arm. A phrase scribbled in cursive handwriting that I couldn't figure out.

"Checking me out again, Miss Harden?" Liam's eyes held amusement, that sly grin back on his perfect face, the one that made me blush for being caught again. There was no denying it, though.

"It's hard not to when you're walking around like *that*!" I gestured to the lack of a shirt.

"Should I throw something on?"

"Don't bother on my account. I'm pretty pleased with the view as it is." I confessed before hiding behind my coffee cup, taking a slow sip. "I was actually admiring your tattoos. They're beautiful. What does it say?"

"*Perdonare sì dimenticare mai.* It means 'Forgive yes, forget never.*"

"Is there a story behind it?"

"Something like that," Liam said, his eyes displaying something like discomfort.

"Who is she?" I dared to ask the question I feared the answer to. I was hoping it didn't represent anyone real, anyone important enough to have marked on your skin for life. What other parts of him had that woman scarred, too?

"How good is your knowledge of Roman Mythology?"

"Roman mythology?" Everything ancient was absolutely my jam. Egyptian, Greek, or Roman, but this one didn't ring any bells. "Is she a Goddess? I don't remember ever seeing that image."

"Dea Tacita." He said, his accent thick with an Italian curl to it.

"Like the club?"

"Like the club." He repeated. Now it made sense why Alison said she had connections there. But why would that name hold so much significance?

Now I was even more confused. As if noticing the questions building in my head, Liam clarified, "Goddess of the Dead. Silensor of the unworthy. And yes, we own the club."

"I've never heard of her. I always preferred Greek mythology, anyway. But why a Roman Goddess? Does it have a meaning?"

"You prefer the Greeks? Really? I take that as an insult, Miss Harden." He replied, faking outrage.

"What? Why?" I was utterly lost.

"Because we Italians take our heritage very seriously. And liking the Greeks above us is a serious offense."

"Italian? I thought you were French. Your father is as French as they come, and so is your last name."

"Yes, my father is French, but my mother is very much Italian."

I had seen her yesterday at the party, but I didn't get to meet her, and Alison sure never spoke a word about it. "They met in the south of France, in Cannes, when my mother was on vacation after a short pass through Italy to visit some relatives."

"I had absolutely no idea. I take it back, I think I've changed my mind. Italian is becoming my new go-to flavor." I smiled mischievously, "But why a Goddess of the dead?" I was intrigued by the option. There were so many powerful figures to choose from in mythology, why would he have picked a lesser-known and dark deity?

"It's a long story. Maybe some other day I'll tell you about it." There was a new discomfort to his posture, his voice dipping into a graver tone while his pecs flexed rhythmically. Liam avoided my gaze while he fiddled with the scrambled eggs on his plate, showing an uneasiness atypical of the self-assured man sitting in front of me.

I wanted to ask about the words written on his arm, but now definitely wasn't the right time.

We both fell silent, and unlike before, this one was charged with a different energy, making me feel as if I had stepped too close into his space, pushing a boundary that he didn't want anyone to be touching, nevermind trying to poke a hole in like I was doing. So I did the only thing possible. I let it go and deflected.

"Would you... umm... maybe like to grab some lunch with me today?"

"I have plans already." He replied with a tone I didn't exactly care for.

"Oh, umm, sure. I'll just wash these and head home." My shaky voice managed to say as I stood up, grabbing my plate. I was assuming things, and if embarrassment could kill, I'd be good and buried.

"The plan is to lock you inside this apartment all the way until Sunday night. You, Miss Harden, will not be leaving this place anytime soon." I balled up my napkin and threw it at his chest, a smile of relief spreading my lips.

"You're an asshole, did you know that?"

"Is that a yes?"

"I'll think about it." I faked a flat tone and walked away with the dishes, placing them in the sink to start washing them. Liam's arms snaked around my waist, his lips brushing against the sensitive flesh just below my ear.

"Think about it? You need to think about it?" He teased, his teeth slowly sinking into my skin. "Let me show you what I think about you having to think about it."

Liam scooped a handful of water, splashing it right in my face, his unrelenting laughter echoing through the entire kitchen while I tried to catch my breath. My face dripped cold water onto my shirt, drenching it right through.

I turned towards him, my eyes narrowing into thin slits, the word 'revenge' running through my mind.

"You seem pretty happy about what you just did. Let me see that smug face now." I aimed the muzzle right at him, not giving a damn if I got everything wet.

All is fair in love and war.

Liam battled against the water jet, finally getting a hold of it, directing it my way. We were a matching set of wet, breathless messes, laughing so hard it was difficult to draw in oxygen.

The huge puddle on the floor made him slip, and I couldn't hold back the even louder giggles that left my mouth. He sat there chuckling, wet strands of hair framing his face, extending his hand in a request for help to stand.

As soon as I placed my hand in his, I felt a strong pull, making me fall right on top of him. Liam rolled us around, my back landing right in that puddle while he spread my legs and placed himself between them.

If I was wet before, I was completely drenched now. The white t-shirt he had lent me was now transparent, my nipples hardened by the cold water and the notion that Liam was pressed up against me.

Suddenly, he lost his smile, his eyes darting down my body while he held my hands above my head.

"My clothes definitely look better on you." His voice was low, hitting right on the sweet spot where I felt him hardening against me.

Liam's lips hovered over mine for what seemed like an eternity, just a breath away, teasing me with their closeness, making me crave that kiss more with each passing second. He stared deep into my eyes as if he was committing this moment to memory, a long pause drenched in an intensity I couldn't dare to decipher.

He captured my lips in a soft kiss, his eyes fluttering closed as he savored my lips as if it were the last time. And all of a sudden, it was over.

"This might just be the best memory I have in this kitchen," he whispered against me before hungrily taking my lips in his again.

Lust and passion weren't enough to describe it. He consumed me with every stroke of his tongue, every thrust of his hips, every inch of my body his roaming hand covered.

Electric currents soared through my skin as Liam pressed his hard cock further into me, his hand traveling up the hem of my drenched t-shirt. Every digit that touched me made me shiver in delight, craving more of this new addiction.

He suddenly broke the kiss again before his hand reached my breast. The heavy pants escaping his mouth told me he needed all his self-control and then some to be able to stop where this was heading.

He took a few moments to gather his breath, swallowing dryly and shutting his eyes tightly before he was able to speak.

"We should get you out of those wet clothes before you get sick." He said, standing up and helping me to my feet. I looked at him puzzled, not understanding why he felt the need to stop things from taking the course they obviously were.

He saw the uneasiness in my eyes and cupped my cheek, holding my face in place.

"We need to talk before anything else happens. I don't want to repeat my mistakes."

Stephanie Amaral

Art by Xavier Guzman

CHAPTER NINETEEN

Liam

I ate every delicious moan that came from Jamie's lips, and each new one made my hunger for her grow wilder. My wet clothes clinging to her body had sent me overboard, but I needed to control my impulses. And *damn* was it hard.

I wanted to claim her right there, take my time savoring this incredible creature that was trapped beneath me, her pleading eyes glazed with lust, a weakness that damn near had me breaking my own resolution. Again.

I was never this weak to keep my word, but promises were like pillars made of sand when it came to being away from her.

But there was no way I could falter this time. I knew I was lost when I felt like someone had sunk their fist in my chest and pulled out my heart in one swift move as soon as I saw Matt's tongue down her throat. Wanting to kill my own brother was enough to tell me that this girl wasn't just a fresh piece of ass I wanted to fuck and chuck.

I wanted more, and with Jamie I wanted it all.

For that to happen, she had to meet the real me. There were things she needed to know before I took her forever. My demons were dark and I couldn't keep them under the rug forever. More so, Jamie deserves honesty.

I was all in, and once I realized that, a huge weight lifted from my shoulders. My shield came tumbling down. Better yet, *she* had smashed it into pieces, and I could finally be myself with the woman who'd reached a part of me I thought was dead.

I didn't want to take advantage of her even though my cock pleaded to be buried so deep inside her that her body would mold to my shape. I didn't want her to get into something she knew nothing about. So I slammed my foot on the brakes using all the strength I could harvest.

The confusion was clear in her eyes since my words weren't matching the hard erection I'd been pushing into her while I kissed her on my kitchen floor.

Last night, while having her nested in my arms, I had played out what I'd say to her over and over, how I'd explain who and what I was, but there was no version of this conversation that could ever sound good.

In every one of those versions, I saw Jamie running for the hills.

I set out another t-shirt and a pair of sweatpants for her to wear and left the room to give Jamie some privacy. After about ten minutes she still hadn't come out.

"Hey, are you okay in there?" I asked, knocking on the door.

"Yeah. I'm fine. You can come in if you want."

"My bones are feeling the cold wa–" I walked in, my words being cut by the sight before me. Jamie was lying on my bed, stomach against the mattress, her ass barely covered by the dry t-shirt I had given her.

My cock couldn't help but twitch. Cold or not, it was growing hard because of her. Every ounce of strength in my body was used to tear my gaze away from the perfection of her skin. Pink, tight, ripe for a good hand print to be marked as a reminder of who she now belonged to.

It would be a suitable punishment for the agony she was teasing me into. It was a test, and by the sigh she released as I walked right past her, I had failed miserably.

Her eyes were set on me, watching as I pulled on a dry pair of underwear and sweats, only to follow me as I walked to the bathroom to change.

Denying her was like a poison spreading through my veins, but until I opened my personal Pandora's box to her, this was necessary. I could have just blurted it out, but I was a selfish fucker, and I wanted to have at least today with her.

One damn day to enjoy her before wrecking it without the possibility of amendment.

When I came out of the bathroom, Jamie was sitting on the edge of the bed, a worried expression knitting her brows together while her thumbs fumbled with each other.

"Come." I simply said, my hand stretched out for her to take.

Jamie looked up at me, her questions and reticence flashing in her eyes before she stood to her feet and placed her hand in mine like a feather. She wasn't sure of that decision, and it was clear in the lightness of her grasp.

We walked towards the living room with our fingers intertwined, her hand fitting in mine as if it had been made exactly for me.

I sat on the couch, but Jamie didn't follow. She stood there hesitating, looking at the other end where she had been sitting the very first time she came here.

"Not a chance," I grunted possessively, knowing she was thinking about putting some distance between us. I pulled on her hand hard enough to have her stumbling right to the place I wanted her in. Right next to me, her skin touching mine, her side glued to me as if we were a single item. "This is your place."

"But…" Jamie searched for words she didn't have. The questions were there, I saw them, but she didn't know exactly what to ask.

I didn't try to word them for her. I still wasn't ready to answer them. I needed to take everything I could, feed off of her for today. My fear of losing her to my truth was all too real, and I needed a sample of my addiction that could at least live on in my memory.

I buried my nose in the crook of her neck, inhaling her until my lungs couldn't take anymore.

"Liam," her voice was small and shaky.

"Hmm?" I merely hummed, my senses completely inebriated by her scent.

"Is everything okay? Did I do something I shouldn't have?"

"No, not at all."

"Then please tell me what's going on." She pressed, her eyes brimming with uncertainty. I couldn't delay it anymore. Jamie was just a breath away from pulling away anyhow.

"Okay," I finally conceded. "But you have to promise to hear me out before you run."

Jamie

Liam was pushing me away again.

Even though his touch said the exact opposite, he was keeping me at arm's length, in a limbo between belonging and merely being.

He brushed it off each time I asked, saying he needed to tell me things before we moved forward, but that was as much info as he was willing to give about his strange behavior. A couple of hours had gone by and I was still in the dark, battling with my thoughts, but finally, it felt like he was ready to open up.

"Why would I run?" I asked, confused.

"Because I'm not the person you think I am. And what I'm about to tell you will change how you see me forever. It will change your feelings, too."

"You're making me nervous, Liam. Can you please just spit it out?"

What on Earth could be so bad that my feelings for him would change? There was nothing I could think of that would make me want to step away from this. From him.

My stomach twisted in both fear and anticipation of what he was about to tell me. Liam studied my face, holding his peace while I was growing increasingly nervous.

"I'm trying to find the right words. The ones that might not freak you out as much."

"Right. I've never known you to filter your words, so maybe it's a question of trust. I understand if you don't trust me enough to tell me what this big thing is. Maybe we should just leave things as they are." I got up from the couch, my body chilling in the spots where it had been snuggled against his skin. "Call me whenever you think I'm worthy."

There was no denying the resentment drenching my words. I started collecting my stuff, trying to swallow the tears that threatened to fall.

Adding to everything he had said to me before, I was getting pissed and hurt by the web he tangled around me so I couldn't reach him.

From that mysterious one-liner he left me sleeping with when he said he didn't deserve me to telling me I wasn't right for him, yet still being jealous of other men, I was as confused as ever.

"Jamie," Liam practically growled as he stood up, his tone pinning me in place. "Please sit down. Let me just figure out how I'm going to say this. Please?" He shot me a soft, pleading look, never averting as I slowly sat back down on the couch across from him.

"Okay, so... AD is not the only business my family owns." He started.

"I know, your brother told me as much, half an hour into meeting me." There was accusation in my tone. In just over a couple of hours, Matt had told me more about him than I knew about Liam.

"For him, the truth doesn't sting. I'm the one in for a loss here." Liam sighed, his body slumping onto the couch as his head fell into his hands. "We own a few businesses around town, strategically located. Bars, clubs and restaurants. At the moment, Dea Tacita is our base of operations."

"Dea Tacita, like your tattoo?"

"Like my tattoo. It's the club Alison took you to on your birthday."

"Oh, that's how you knew where I was. You were there already."

"Something like that, yeah." There was a smirk in his tone even though his face didn't show it, but he continued before I could dig further. "I help run the business. It's been in the family for several generations, still back in Italy. We grew up in the lifestyle and inherited our position from our Grandfather. He's still the head of the family but will soon be retiring." Liam paused, gauging my reaction. I hung on every word he said, trying to take it all in and understand how it affected us.

"Okay, so you have other work besides AD. What's the big deal?"

"The business I help run is not exactly the clubs and restaurants. Those are legit businesses that also work as territorial landmarks for the other part."

"Right." I thought I was starting to understand what Liam was trying to say, but still I sat there saying nothing else.

Liam abruptly stood up and marched into his bedroom, returning just a few seconds later. A clicking sound followed his heavy footsteps making me turn back to see what it was.

My eyes bulged from their sockets as I took in the shiny metal of the black gun Liam was expertly dismembering. With a loud thud, he slammed the gun on the wooden table between us, standing straight with his hands on his hips just staring at me. My heart picked up its pace to an unnatural beat, the blood in my ears louder than words, if there were any spoken in that moment.

"Do you get what I'm trying to say now?" Liam's voice was strained with frustration, apprehension swimming around his words, too.

"I… I think I do." I stuttered in disbelief.

"Say it." He demanded. I swallowed dryly, my eyes burning from the tears I tried to hold back. "SAY IT!" He shouted, my whole body trembling at the sound.

I shook my head in denial, not wanting to hear the word that had just burned my newly found happiness into ashes.

"I'm Italian, I have more money than I can spend, I have an image of death engraved in my body, I managed that gun as if it were a part of me, and I knew where you lived before you filled out the company's form." His tone was harsh and cold, accusatory in some strange way. "*Mafia*, Jamie. You can say it. I'm a part of it as much as it is a part of me. My whole life is drenched in sin, and you?" Liam kneeled in front of me, taking my now tear-stained face in his hands and forcing me to look into his eyes, his voice lowering to a hushed whisper. "You are the only light in my darkness, Jamie."

I shut my eyes as tightly as they would go, more tears falling down my cheeks. With the pad of his thumbs, Liam wiped them away, bringing his lips to kiss mine that didn't respond to his kiss like they had always done.

Liam pulled back, his hands falling onto his legs, his head hanging in disappointment from my reaction. I was stone cold, shock taking over my body.

"You are free to go." He muttered under his breath, the quiver in his voice piercing me right in the middle of my chest.

Despite the relief his words brought to me at first, I couldn't find it in me to move. Every part of me screamed in a need to hug the defeated man kneeling on the floor in front of me while my conscience told me to run and never look back.

Instead, I stayed and pried further into a darkness I had no business plunging into.

"You've killed people." I wasn't sure if it was a question or an affirmation. Liam's face grew pale at my bluntness, and I knew the answer was yes.

"Matt is the one running everything right now. My job is to make sure the rules are followed. I'm an enforcer."

"You have." I insisted, the image of Liam's bloody hands bringing more tears to my eyes, which I couldn't stop from falling freely.

"Yes, I have."

My heart stopped at his confirmation, a long, painful pause before sobs shook my body uncontrollably. I took my face in my hands, trying to hide from his eyes, but Liam pulled me to him, trapping me in his arms, soothing me with his scent and soft kisses.

I lost track of time as I cried in the embrace of a killer, my imagination running wild with scenes of violence that were all so familiar I could smell them.

"You're okay," Liam whispered on and on, trying to calm me back into a state where I could register his words again. "You're okay."

After what seemed like an eternity, I had settled after the shock, tears still falling from my eyes like raindrops, but my storm wasn't raging as hard. Liam tilted my head up with his finger hooked under my chin, forcing me to face him. His eyes were red, his expression pained and tortured, and I fought the urge to kiss all of it away. I couldn't, right? How could I care for him still?

"I would never hurt you," Liam finally broke the silence. "You know that, right?"

I simply nodded. My voice was trapped in my throat with the truth to that question, and I just couldn't dare to say it. I've been hurt before by people who should love me and protect me. It was an instinctive reaction driven by experience.

"You have fear in your eyes, Jamie. I know you are lying to me."

I buried my head in his chest again, shielding myself from his knowing gaze, inhaling him once more before I left, not knowing if I was ever coming back.

Liam had been right. I was thinking about running. But the only thing making me want to flee was my conscience. How could I be okay with this? How could his revelations not have changed how much I feel for him?

I'm broken, and until now, Liam was the only one close enough to piece me together. I wanted him so badly, yet I didn't know how I could ever take him now.

CHAPTER TWENTY

Jamie

It took me two weeks to be able to say the damn word.
Mafia.
Ma-fi-a.
I couldn't help the chill that ran freely down my spine each time the imagery and the word collided in my brain. The first time it slipped from my tongue was like I was losing a piece of me along with it.

Never in my wildest dreams could I have ever guessed that would be the big secret Liam was struggling to share. Matt had lifted that veil at Alison's birthday party, and I was just too blind to see it for what it was.

I had tried to tie the image I had of Liam to what I assumed being in the Mafia was, and I simply couldn't. Picturing his perfect hands stained in blood was too unreal to be true.

Right?

But it wasn't. This was who he was, and more than his confession, what fazed me the most was my reaction to his revelation.

None.

Nothing.

Absolutely fucking NADA!

Nothing changed about how I felt. I should have been repulsed and scared and intimidated. But the only urge running through my body as I saw Liam expose himself to me was to hug him. Kiss away his fear of losing me. Love him until he had no doubt he deserved to be loved just as much as I did.

Instead, I left after asking Liam for time and space to wrap my head around everything. He did exactly as I asked. Still, despite going out of his way to keep at a distance during the day, he would send me a text every single night wishing me sweet dreams. No questions, no demands. Just a reminder that I was on his mind every night. As if the fresh red rose he left on my doorstep every day didn't do that job well enough.

Right and wrong were waging a war in the comfort of my conscience, my moral compass falling from its high horse every time *he* won the rigged battle.

How could I be okay with this? How was I not packing my bags and leaving without a trace? How sick and twisted did I have to be for nothing about his gruesome reality to so much as dent the fire that burned inside me for this man?

I was in love with a damn hitman. An enforcer, as he had put it, and the only thing I could think about was the way his lips fit perfectly in mine. The way the heat of his body balanced out the ice in my heart. The way his demons could take my soul to Hell, and I wouldn't mind the one-way ticket, as long as it was a double.

Him and me.

Me and him.

The rest of it all be damned.

I can't be in my right mind. A sane person wouldn't accept this.

Two weeks had passed and he still hadn't spoken about it, or us. He respected me enough not to push.

I was too wrapped up in labeling myself for not minding who or what he was that I had shut everyone out. And yet nothing I told myself soothed me.

> I know.

I texted Alison. Nothing beyond those two words came out, and I was hitting send before I had time to think this through again. I needed to talk to someone who understood. But no one besides her ever could.

She had texted me a few times during the last two weeks, checking in and making sure I was okay. I hadn't found it in me to reply because I didn't know exactly how to. My brain was eating away at my conscience, or was it the other way around?

Either way, I had no truthful answer to such a simple question. Soon, my phone buzzed with her reply.

> I know you do. Liam told me.
> Are you ready to talk about it?

I stared at the screen for a while, debating what I would say, ask, scream. I wasn't sure if I was ready to verbalize my doubts or concerns, mainly because not even I knew what those were. Maybe Alison could shine a light on all this. After all, she was smack in the center of it all. She would know how to stop it from haunting my conscience.

> I think I am. Can we meet for lunch?

> Of course. I'll wait for you in the lobby at 1.

I exhaled deeply before glancing up at that stupid door, finding it open today, Liam's eyes boring into me. His lips quirked in a small smile as soon as I caught him staring, and it was enough to melt my soul and blend it with my heart.

I tore away, focusing on the pile of paperwork in front of me, but before I could erase him from my mind, his scent was hitting my senses like a train wreck. Liam was standing in front of my desk, hands buried in his slacks, his hair a disheveled mess, calling for my fingers to tame it back into place.

He wore that dire expression that turned my resolve into a pile of sand, green eyes slashing at my will like sharp knives. I tried to turn down the pace of my racing heart by painting his hands in crimson, splattering his shiny shoes with blood and his white shirt with sin.

Nothing. Not even the faintest of fears ran through my body. My pulse steady in its gallop as it always was when Liam was close.

Again, not fear, something else that pulled at the strings in my chest like a helpless puppet in the hands of its master. *Him,* the thief of hearts who had mine caged for life, standing right in front of me.

My breath hitched in my chest as my hands gripped the armrests of my chair. Liam's gaze hardened as he noticed, his eyes averting from mine in reprieve.

"Umm…" Liam cleared his throat, his eyes still stuck on the desk between us, "Our monthly meeting with Verten was canceled. They'll be hosting their annual fundraiser this weekend. It's in LA. We've both been invited. I understand there's a faint possibility you might even consider going, but let me know if you do."

Yes was on the tip of my tongue, but I didn't budge. Liam stood there for a couple of seconds, waiting for an answer as he intently watched my white-knuckled grip before turning those eyes to my face. They followed the lump I swallowed, my lips still sealed with my reticence.

Somehow it felt my answer was about a lot more than just this trip, and before talking to Alison, I wasn't ready to take that plunge just yet.

A sharp exhale left Liam's nose as he turned his back to me and walked back to his office, shutting the door behind him.

Whatever he read in my reaction hurt him, I saw it in his eyes. That look gutted me, but I needed my ducks to be in a neat row before I could move on.

I ran down and paced the lobby until Alison arrived, mentally going through what I thought our conversation would go like, drawing a blank as soon as I saw her coming out of the elevator.

We walked in silence to a nearby diner, taking a seat in the most secluded booth available.

"Spit it out." Alison said, breaking the ice with a sledgehammer.

"I... How?" That was the only thing that came out.

"Eloquent," she mocked, returning a long lost smile to my face. "But I'm going to need you to elaborate on that."

I held the bridge of my nose between my fingers, exhaling deeply before my words came tumbling out directly from my brain without a filter. "I don't care. How can I not care? How can I be okay with knowing that Liam has killed people? I know he has, yet it hasn't changed how I feel about him. It hasn't changed the fact that I feel the safest I've ever felt in my life when I'm with him. It should have changed everything, but it didn't. What kind of person does it make me when I don't find it in me to care?" My tone was hushed for obvious reasons, but even so, it didn't lack frustration, guilt, and impatience.

I'd been bouncing between two versions of myself for two weeks, finding that this ball always wanted to land in his court.

"The kind that loves and wants to be loved." Alison simply stated. "Do you really mind falling in love with the devil? So long as he loves you as much as he loves Hell, I really don't see any problem. Besides, Liam isn't all that. He's conflicted. A wolf, sure, but the skin doesn't suit him. But neither does the sheep's. My brother is lost between what he is and what he thinks he *should* be, just like you are balancing now between what you feel and what you *should* feel. Some things are born with you, you don't get to choose," I knew all about that. "And in our case, there's no opt-in or out button we can click. This is who my family is, and has been since its genesis. Labeling it as right or wrong? That highly depends on the agenda."

213

"What do you mean?"

"There's this notion of righteousness that's shoved down our throats from the moment we draw our first breath. Tell me, what comes to mind when you think about justice?"

"Well… umm, police, court, judges. I don't know."

"Exactly. All the high figures that should be monitoring the scale of equality and justice. Yet those are the first pawns to fall under the veil of corruption. Hardly any keep their own agenda from interfering with their jobs. How many innocent people have lost their lives because of it? Bribes, rape, theft, drug dealing, turning a blind eye, or actively meddling to achieve the result that benefits them the most. They do it all and get away with it just because they are on the 'right' side of the law. Does that seem like justice? Raging wars against other countries for self-interest, sending our own to kill innocent people and die far away from home, from their loved ones. Is that just? They hide behind a façade of justice and virtue. At least we admit to what we do, which doesn't necessarily mean it's always bad. We are guided by values like respect, loyalty, family, and truth. We protect our own in this fucked up world. I'm not saying we are the example of goodness, but we are also not the only bad guys. There's a whole gray area you should consider. This notion of what's right is what's holding you back from being happy. Why are you letting others dictate how you should be feeling?"

Alison's voice was unwavering, her reasoning making a whole lot of sense to me, or maybe I was just dying to find an out. "Why are you looking for a definition for yourself? Why can't you just be Jamie who's in love with Liam?"

Jamie who's in love with Liam.

Hearing those words out loud was like a gust of fresh air hitting me straight in the face. I wasn't the one saying them, but still, having the truth that was strangling me thrown into the world like that felt liberating somehow.

A thrilling shiver ran through my body at the possibilities brought by admitting to that truth.

"Are you afraid of him?"

"What?"

"Are you afraid of my brother?"

"No!" I firmly stated, my reply laced with indignance.

"Do you think he would ever harm you? Because I strongly believe that he would kill anyone who tried hurting you without so much as a second thought. I'd sit on the bleachers and cheer him the fuck on." Alison said, squeezing my hand in reassurance while my brain was stuck on that word she added in that sentence without flinching.

"It's hard for me to imagine Liam doing that. Killing someone." It came out like acid that burned its way up my throat, making me take back the two steps forward the L word had made me take towards accepting my feelings.

"Everyone is capable of killing under the right circumstance, Jamie." I found it hard to believe and even accept. "Maybe one day he can tell you who those people were and settle that heart of yours. If you give him the chance, that is."

"You're in it, too?"

"It's our heritage, Jamie. A part of who we are. But I'm not *in it*. Not like my brothers." Alison admitted. "They do their best to keep me in the dark. Some things bother me, too. I just love them too much to make those things bigger than what I feel for them." Her candid smile was blinding, the love she felt for her brothers was pure and all-conquering. "Family is everything for us. To me, you are family now, too, whether you decide to admit that you love a criminal or not."

I gave her a small smile in return for her warm words, but the lump in my throat just wouldn't budge.

"A criminal…"

"That's all you got from what I said?"

"No, of course not."

"Let me ask you this: you do realize that Liam will not stay single forever, right? And that if you choose to ignore what your heart is telling you, he will one day find someone and settle. How do you feel about that image? My brother, married to another woman?"

Bile rose to my mouth, followed by anger and a swamping sadness that tore my heart to pieces.

I'm that woman. No one else. ME.

Alison was stuck in a loop of nods, her smile telling me she could read my mind in that moment, her green eyes glistening in victory.

"Exactly. You don't know her and you already want to rip her to pieces. You love him. Don't lie to me or yourself."

"I do. I love him." I smiled back, my heart settling a little, finding that what he did had no relevance towards how I felt for him. My heart knew who it beat for. "It will take time to get used to the idea."

"I know. Whatever you decide, just put him out of his misery. He's been a bigger pain than usual, and we both know my brother can be a real dick."

I couldn't help but join her in her laughter before squaring my shoulders and setting my mind on where to go from here.

I still wasn't a hundred percent fine with all of it, and it would take a lot more than two weeks and a pep talk to get me there, but somehow my heart felt more at ease.

I'd need time to be comfortable with this new reality. Maybe knowing more about the business and their lives could help. Maybe Liam could help me understand it better.

We walked back to AD, our conversation taking a sharp left into lightness. Before heading up, I hugged Alison, thanking her for lunch and for the clarity she was able to provide me.

Once I got to my desk, I saw Liam's office door was still closed. I inhaled deeply, summoning all my courage to face him, gently knocking on the door before opening it.

"Do you have a minute?" I asked, immediately being met by a smile and a small nod.

"Of course."

I closed the door behind me, showing him I was okay with being alone and isolated with him.

Liam got up from his chair, only stepping out into the open space, not making a move to close the gap between us. Every single move he made was carefully thought through, not wanting to freak me out.

"I'm sorry it took me so long to come talk to you. It was just a lot of information I wasn't expecting." I said, my eyes traveling from his to the floor and back, as I rubbed my thumb in the palm of my hand. Liam didn't speak, making me feel even more uneasy. "I just wanted to let you know that I'll be going to LA with you if you still want me to."

"Of course I do." He quickly replied. "Are you sure you're fine with being alone with me?"

"What? Why wouldn't I be?"

"Jamie, you were shaking when you left my apartment." He said without tearing his gaze from mine, a worried expression knitting his brows together.

"I know. I'm sorry. It's just that… I was caught off guard."

"I know, I'm not trying to push you. I told you that you would run, that you would think less of me." He said, defeat clear in his voice as he turned his back to me going back to his seat.

"Liam…" I called, slowly motioning towards him. "I'm… I'm not running. I'm right here." I opened my arms, showing him my feet were rooted in place, waiting for him.

He spun his head in my direction as soon as my words hit him. I had merely finished a blink and Liam was an inch away from me. An inch away from my lips, his hand hovering on each side of my face but not touching me. I could feel his heavy, warm breaths on my face while his eyes bore into my soul, looking for a sign of uncertainty.

"Are you sure?" He exhaled.

I could feel his need to touch me, to hold me tight to his chest, but still, he waited for my reply.

"I am."

As soon as my words left my mouth, Liam held my face in his hands and crushed his lips to mine in an earth-shattering kiss, pouring all his need and urgency into it and reassuring my heart that *this* was exactly where I belonged.

CHAPTER TWENTY ONE

Liam

J amie, *my* Jamie Harden, had accepted my shadows.

There was an angel with Dornier as his last name looking down on us from Heaven, and I was sure he had a hand in that.

Having her sitting in the car on our way to the airport was the only thing thrilling about this trip to LA.

It would take time for her to feel a hundred percent at ease with it all, or me, for that matter. That much was clear in the way she was clasping the strap of her handbag against her chest, sitting so far away from me I thought she might blend into the car's door.

Carl glanced at me through the rearview mirror, wary of the tense atmosphere that had filled the SUV since we picked Jamie up at her apartment.

She had barely looked at me, her whole body language screaming panic. I knew there was a chance that Jamie would be afraid of me, but knowing and seeing were two very different things. My heart was squeezed into a pulp watching as her chest rose and fell in an abnormal rhythm.

My presence was doing that to her. The realization hurt far more than all the damn bullets I'd taken in my life.

At least the drive to the airport was short and she'd be free from being stuck in such a tight space with the killer that made her shake like a leaf.

I had personally booked our flights and separate hotel rooms, thinking that giving Jamie space was the best choice at this point. I wanted her to feel comfortable around me. Safe. Yet by the looks of it, there was still a long road ahead of us.

Our jet stayed grounded, and so did my shadows, Mike and Jimmy, much to Matt's disagreement. I didn't need to stress Jamie out further with the guys tailing behind me everywhere I went. The middle ground was settled by having Carl with us until we were on the plane, the flight manifest scanned meticulously, and a gun waiting for me on the other side. Courtesy of Vincenzo Massimo, future Don of the California *famiglia*.

That was already more than enough.

Flashing signs of our true nature before Jamie's eyes seemed premature and, truthfully, a recipe for disaster. My reality was still new and tender to her, and I figured that easing her into our lifestyle would be more fruitful than shoving it down her throat now that she knew the truth.

It was a risk. Calculated and necessary, but still a risk.

New York was safe. It was ours to rule.

Going outside of our domain was always a sticky deal, especially alone. Matt had made sure to inform Don Massimo that someone in the high ranks of our family was traveling to LA for a couple of days on business unrelated to the Mafia. He would have done it even if I didn't need him to provide me with a weapon.

It was a mere courtesy to avoid future misconceptions. One we would be appreciative to see returned if the roles were reversed. There was no bad blood between us and the Massimos, so Jamie's safety was assured. Mine? That was secondary.

There was unspoken tension between that prick Mercier and me. I could smell a weasel from a mile away, but his stench was disguised by prime connections and hundred-dollar bills.

Still, I was looking forward to mingling with him as much as I was to be stepping on horse shit.

There was something about that living cadaver that pushed every one of my buttons, and by knowing so, dear Dad had been sure to lecture me about the importance of maintaining a good relationship with the fucker.

So the only thing good about going to LA was this gorgeous creature sitting beside me, avoiding my gaze at all cost.

"You can still stay if you want," I said, watching her knee bounce while we waited to board in the airport's VIP lounge. "I understand if you're not ready."

"N-No. I'm fine." Jamie replied, a small but extremely fake smile on her perfect lips. "I'm just not a fan of airplanes. I've only flown once, but I'd hand over a kidney if I never had to get on a plane again."

"It's only a five-hour flight, I can hold your hand the whole way if it will make you feel better." I smiled, trying to lighten the mood and gauge her reaction to the brush of my skin on hers.

She didn't flinch as I covered her hand with mine, her tight grip on the armrest subsiding, even if just a little.

"So… it's not exactly like we read in books," Jamie said, shaking her shoulders as if she was trying to get rid of the tension that stiffened her whole body and breaking the silence that had settled between us.

"What isn't?"

"In books, men… umm," She hesitated. "Men like *you* have private planes and secret landing strips off the grid."

I looked at her in question, her face turning a more vivid shade of red in contrast to the pale complexion she'd been sporting since she set foot in the car.

"I might have been reading a couple of novels about, umm, gangsters and stuff."

The laughter left my body before I could hold it back, every piece of my shattered hope being suddenly glued back together with that confession.

"What?" She indignantly asked, lightly swatting at my arm. "I needed to know that there could be a happy ending for girls like me with men like you."

Jamie averted her gaze downwards in embarrassment, but I wasn't having it. I hooked my index finger under her chin making her look right into my eyes, almost getting lost in the genuine sweetness of hers.

She was finding her own way back to me. Using whatever she had at her disposal to fight her fears.

"That's a tricky question. I don't own fate, and my life is built on hazard and sin, condemned by default. Happy ever afters aren't written on undeserving pages, Jamie. I'll settle for the stolen moments I can get."

It was the truth, but only half a reply. I was trying to tame my cravings for her sake, not to come on too strongly and scare her away. I trembled at the thought of having such an angel drenched in the danger that was our life, of forcing my fate upon her.

Jamie noticed my non-answer, her polite side smile giving her disappointment away. I had to say something reconciling, pull her towards me again.

"And you are far from being a girl, Jamie. Don't belittle yourself. You're a woman with all the glory that word holds. And my God, what a woman!" I tucked a strand of hair behind her ear, my thumb caressing her cheek.

This time her smile was wider, stained with a deep blush and a new sparkle in her eyes. It was short-lived, though.

"Boss, it's time to board. One of the Massimo men will see that you get some steel on you as soon as you land." Carl said, oblivious to his misstep, while Jamie swallowed a new lump that had formed in her throat at the sound of his words, her hand returning to its tight grip on the chair.

For every brick I knocked down on her wall, a whole damn bailey grew, reinforced with a pit and no bridge. Fuck.

"Thanks, Carl. We'll be right in." I let him walk away before turning back to Jamie, picking up our previous subject in an attempt to reel her in again. "To answer your question, those novels of yours might have gotten a couple things right. I just thought you'd feel more comfortable with other people around instead of stuck in my jet alone with me."

"I'm okay with being alone with you, Liam." Her voice was small and far from convincing. Jamie disregarded the fact that I had just told her we owned a jet, showing me that contrary to many of the women I'd been with in my life, status and wealth meant nothing to her.

She was as real as they got, which only made her reaction sting harder.

"I doubt that. See?" I replied, peeling her fingers from gripping the chair. "You're still afraid."

"It's just that I don't–"

"You don't like airplanes." I interrupted her, the hope she'd built before crumbling to dust. As true as it might be, I couldn't help but feel she was hiding behind her fear of flying. "I'll give you all the space you need, Jamie. I'll give you time to wrap your head around my reality or set you free if you'd prefer, but I need honesty."

We hadn't kissed since Jamie came to my office a couple days ago, and somehow now there was this huge space between us that just made it awkward.

I felt her pulling away from me while her words said the opposite. The mixed signals were driving me insane. We abided by a code of honor, one where honesty and truthfulness played a central role, so having Jamie hiding her true feelings was grinding on my nerves.

"This is your seat, Mr. Dornier, and your assistant's is by the window." The flight attendant said, stopping Jamie in her tracks as she made her way further down towards the tail of the plane.

The woman's hand lingered on my arm for longer than warranted, dragging her fingers up in a trail Jamie's eyes followed. All the way from my elbow to my shoulder. "I'll be at your service, Sir. *Whatever* you need."

The suggestion in her tone and choice of words was clear, Jamie's eyebrows shooting up into her hairline as she heard the blonde woman. My eyes were stranded on Jamie's, her frown as dire as looking down the barrel of a gun.

"First class, Liam? This must have cost a fortune! We would have been just fine in coach. Maybe the *service* wouldn't be so *personalized*, but it would have been fine. For me, at least." Jamie didn't hide her disgust, talking through clenched teeth. I wasn't sure her words expressed what really bothered her.

"Jamie, I told you the only reason we didn't bring the jet was so you wouldn't be overwhelmed. I'm taking a huge risk as it is. Money is of no consequence. Besides, AD pays for all this."

"A little much for your *assistant*." She huffed and took her seat by the window, turning her face away from me.

Her annoyance didn't take away from her anxiety as she sat there folded into herself, her arms constantly covering her chest in a protective stance. Her eyes darted all around her several times as if she was looking for a way out.

We were about to hit the runway and there was no way out now, so I tried easing her mind by making trivial conversation.

"What color is your gown for the gala tonight?"

"Shit!" Jamie cussed, her eyes wide and her hand covering her mouth. "I left it at home. Shit, shit, shit."

I quickly shot Alison a text asking her to have the hotel pick up a few dresses and set them up in Jamie's room. I knew she'd have me covered.

"Done. You'll have a couple to choose from when we get to the hotel."

"That was easy." She spat, her voice dripping in venom and taking me by complete surprise. "It's as if you've done it several times before."

"What?"

"I don't need to travel in first class, Liam. I don't need you to buy me expensive phones and dresses. I'm sure you're used to doing that with your *lady friends*, but you can't buy me." Her tone was clipped, the anger simmering under her surface making her cheeks blush in anger. What the hell got into her?

"Woah, woah. I was just trying to help. I never thought I could buy you! Where did you even get that idea?" I replied, my hands up in surrender.

"I'm not all your other hookups. So don't treat me like one."

"I really don't understand where this is coming from, and I don't appreciate those stereotyped conclusions you're jumping to. If you have any questions, just ask me. Don't assume anything about stuff you know nothing about."

We avoided each other for the rest of the flight, Jamie keeping to the book she was reading on her phone while I got some work done and out of the way.

I tried hard not to flaunt our lifestyle in front of her, toning everything down for her sake. Still, she thought I was flashing cash in front of her to try and buy her affection. She got it all wrong. Her assumptions hit a spot in my chest, drilling a hole that bled all my caution and thoughtfulness.

Fuck it!

No need to be taking unnecessary risks if it's not having the desired effect.

As soon as we got to LA, I canceled the plane tickets back to New York and asked Alison to send the jet and make it available until Wednesday, even though I was foreseeing that this trip would be as long as it necessarily had to be and not a second longer.

One of Don Massimo's men was in the limo that awaited our arrival as planned, and I made sure Jamie saw the whole exchange. If she wanted me, she had to accept the whole package. The good, the bad, and everything in between.

We still haven't spoken a word since our little fight, and with every minute that passed, I got angrier at what she tried to imply. The limo ride was filled with awkward silences and avoidance, grating on my nerves even further.

I had done everything I could to accommodate her, make her feel comfortable around me. How had that evolved into her thinking that I was trying to buy her affection?

"I'm sorry, but the limo was already booked, too." I spat, my voice dripping in acidic sarcasm. "I booked us rooms in the Waldorf. If you think that's too much, feel free to stay wherever you please. The gala is at the Ritz at seven. I guess I'll see you there."

I was bitter as fuck. I'd give her the fucking world if she asked, but implying that I needed to buy her affection hurt like a motherfucker.

Still, I bit my tongue and tried offering a white flag, "I'll happily escort you if you don't think that would be treating you like my other *lady friends*. I'll be leaving at a quarter to seven and not a minute later."

I got out of the car, not waiting for her, darting straight to the reception where the key card to my room was already waiting for me. I dared one last glance towards her just as the elevator doors closed, her face a mask of regret.

Jamie Harden was my damn demise. She messed with me in ways no other person could. Her words stung because they came from her. How could she think so little of me? Was *I* not enough? Did my value only lie in the wealth and status my family was known for?

Fuck that!

I went straight to the bathroom when I got to my suite. Splashing some water on my face could maybe help clear away the frustration. I looked up, taking a glance at my reflection as water ran down my face, but instead, in its place, all I saw was blood. Blood of an innocent girl who had died in my arms not so long ago.

I closed my eyes, trying to clear my vision, and in the darkness, I saw Jamie in my arms, my hands drenched in her blood as I tried to kiss her back to life.

Agony spread through me like wildfire, my eyes flying wide open in an attempt to erase that fucking vision. Again I was met with my reflection in the mirror. I punched it again and again, my fist colliding with the glass with bone-crushing force, shattering the damn thing into pieces.

Who was I kidding? I didn't deserve happiness. I didn't deserve Jamie.

My hands gripped the vanity as I tried to calm my ragged breathing, a red flow of blood staining the white marble.

How could such an angel care for a monster like me? My darkness would drown her light until it was nothing but a dim memory of who she used to be.

I didn't want that for her.

I got myself cleaned up, wrapping my hand in gauze from the first aid kit before getting dressed and heading down to the bar. I'd wait for her, as I had told her, and break whatever we had, or didn't have, off.

"Bourbon," I grunted to the bartender, handing him my key so he could charge it to my room. "Tell reception to add a broken mirror on it, too."

"Rough day?" A woman in a red, low-cut dress asked from beside me, motioning to my hand after hearing my words. It was the blonde flight attendant from earlier.

"Rough life." I simply replied before tipping the entire drink down my throat in one go, motioning for a refill.

"How can such a handsome man not have all his needs catered for?" Her hand brushed over mine, a featherlight touch trailing the bandage. My eyes followed her movement for a second, thinking how damn easy it would be to take her to my room and fuck her. The invitation was clear, but I wasn't interested in the slightest. She pushed further after a lack of a reply, "I'll have whatever you're having if you order for me."

"I'm sorry, but I'll be leaving in a couple of minutes."

"I'm free later tonight. We could meet here. I'll hold you to that... *drink* then." She insisted, shifting forward so I could have a clear view down her cleavage.

"I've got company already. But thank you."

"It seems like your company hasn't been treating you right. I'll just leave you my phone number here, and you can call me if you change your mind." She said while scribbling on a napkin.

"Liam, I don't think this lady speaks English properly," Jamie said from behind me, my lips involuntarily stretching into a smirk before I turned around to face her. "Let's see if she understands it better this way."

Jamie moved to stand between my legs, her hands sliding up my chest, coming to rest on my shoulders before her lips met mine in a slow kiss that breathed possession. Under her touch, my demons came to a still, reality shrinking to a detail as Jamie took her place in the center of my universe.

Our audience had disappeared when Jamie pulled away while I sat there still stunned by her boldness.

"Can I still take you up on that offer to escort me?" She asked, a pink, natural blush rising to her cheeks.

"It's my pleasure," I replied, standing and offering my hand for her to take. I twirled her around, allowing my eyes to roam her body, taking in the goddess before me. "You look absolutely incredible."

"Thank you." Her voice was small and shy, her lashes batting a million times in a row. She'd taken the compliment, but I was sure she noticed my tone was off.

I wasn't lying, I never do. But I had caged my decision in a diamond drawer, one that Jamie had just shattered to pieces with a feather kiss and a black silk dress.

I was at war with myself, and I couldn't let my heart win this time around.

"I'm sorry, Liam," Jamie said just before entering the limo, turning back to me, coming to stand just a whisper away from me, her hand smoothing out the lapel of my black tux. "I didn't mean to imply that you were trying to buy my affection. I was just caught up thinking how many women you'd bought dresses and fancy gifts for. It seemed so natural to you, like you'd done it so many times before, it was nothing but a reflex now. I hated feeling like I'm just another one of them."

Fuck. *A damn feather!* A damn fucking feather kiss slayed my resolve without the possibility of resurrection.

I cupped her cheek, looking deep into her eyes until I'd reached her soul. I needed her to feel my words there, carve them into the core of her essence until she believed me. "You, Miss Harden, are very far from being one of them."

CHAPTER TWENTY TWO

Jamie

I f regret could kill, I'd be as good as gone by now.

I'd choke if I bit my tongue after what I said to Liam on that damn airplane, but it was like there was a mixture of things running through my veins that I couldn't properly process.

Fear and jealousy combining in a stupid need to pick a fight with him.

Something. Anything that could take my brain off being inside that flying coffin. Anything that could poke at the man I yearned for, trying to figure out how he'd react.

After all, there had only been one man in my life. The one who was supposed to love me unconditionally, and yet, all my life he had done the exact opposite.

There'd been no violence in Liam's reaction, no bloodlust in his eyes despite the derogatory remarks I'd made. And despite having my stomach in a tight knot because of the fight and feeling that Liam was pulling away from me, there was a foreign sense of relief running through my body.

I was safe with him. My mind had told me that again and again, but somehow, my past was a ghost that still lingered.

I had five hours of peace to think, and each passing minute of Liam's silence was weighing heavier on my heart. It was clear that despite *what* he was, I was undoubtedly his.

So arriving at the hotel and seeing he had booked separate rooms was a blow I wasn't expecting. The icing on the cake? Liam turned his back to me, marching to the reception area and leaving me alone. Dropping the gentlemanly gestures was completely out of character for him, showing me just how hard my words had hit.

There were dresses spread out on the massive bed once I got to my room, accessories and shoes to go with all of them. Right in the middle, there was a small box and an envelope.

I hope you love the dresses the way I'm sure my brother will love to peel them off you.
And if you're still having doubts, there's a little gift from me to get you through the trip alone.
Love you, girl.
Alison

I smiled to myself as I read her words, a sigh of relief escaping my mouth knowing that she was the one behind Liam's solution to my predicament.

I picked up the red box, tugging on the exaggerated bow to open it. My eyes bulged as I saw what was inside, a fit of laughter filling my heart with lightness. There was a small pink bullet vibrator lying on top of a lacy black set of lingerie.

Revealing and sexy, a perfect match for the black silk dress on top of the pile.

I got dressed with a renewed resolve burning beneath my skin – I wasn't going to allow Liam to pull away. Living a loveless life was living a slow death. I was choosing happiness even if it came at the cost of future heartbreak.

When we got to the Ritz, everything looked like it came out of a fashion magazine. The décor, the setting, the people. Everything.

I thought I would feel misplaced, but Liam could make even the aridness of the moon feel like home. He kept touching me discreetly, whispering the names and positions of the people we met in my ear. His lips would sometimes purposely graze my skin, making me shiver under his warm breath.

There was always the comfort of his hand guiding me, on my back, on my waist, or on my hand. But still, there hadn't been even so much as a whisper that didn't relate to work.

Finger food danced its way through the large hall, followed by tall, crystal glasses of French champagne that was a little too bitter for my palate.

Everywhere I looked there were women dressed in haute couture, the high price tags evident on their perfect form and manicured nails. They were either models or lived like one. Not a hair out of place, their makeup as flawless as their noses.

I felt less.

How was it that the most handsome man in the whole room had *me* hanging on his arm when there was so much better to choose from?

My self-deprecation was cut short when a waiter stopped in front of us, a glass of something *not* bubbly placed in the center of his tray. "Your drink, Mr. Dornier."

"Thank you," Liam replied, taking the glass from the tray and handing it to me. "I believe that's what you were drinking with Alison at the club. You seemed to like it." I smiled at his thoughtfulness, taking a sip from the glass. "I like to see your nose all scrunched, but there's no need to endure when you can appreciate."

"You're absolutely right, Mr. Dornier. Could you maybe do the same? Appreciate, I mean." Liam looked at me puzzled, not sure what I meant. "Would you give me the pleasure of this dance?"

Liam's lips spread into a blinding white smile, stretching out his hand in a silent request to take mine. But before I could take it, Liam's eyes diverted over my shoulder, the cheerful glint giving way to something I couldn't quite describe. Something I'd seen on his face only twice.

Bloodlust.

His shadows were pulling him under, fear making my body erupt into goosebumps. As an instinct, I turned around to see the source of the sudden change, the sinister stranger from the waiting room and his crooked smile chilling me down to my bones.

I heard Liam inhale sharply, and when I turned to him to avoid the man, his face had changed again. Now all I could see was a fake smile and a posture of forced formality.

"Mr. Mercier," Liam greeted, his voice morphing to accommodate a hard, professional tone that hid the demons I'd seen just a second ago. "Thank you for your invitation."

They shook hands vigorously, Liam's jaw pulsing to the beat of his heart.

"This is Miss Jamie Harden. She's the reason *Verten's* project is as green as you'd requested it to be. Jamie, this is Mr. Mercier, Verten's CEO."

Fuck. Me!

This sinister creature before me had shivers running down my spine in a loop. He was thinner than I remembered him to be, his ice-blue eyes sunken deep into their purple sockets. He took my hand in his, placing a kiss on my knuckles, the clammy touch of his fingers on my skin churning my stomach in disgust.

I had no idea why I reacted this way to him. There had been nothing but caution and alert in my brain ever since I'd seen him sitting in that waiting room at AD.

"It's an absolute pleasure to meet you, Miss Harden. My men had spoken about the beauty of one of your collaborators, Liam, but their tales were far from reality. You are as breathtaking as this red rose, Miss Harden." He took the flower from his lapel, handing it to me.

"The pleasure is mine, Mr. Mercier," I replied, reminding myself that I needed to be as professional and polite as I could. But there was no easing my discomfort around this man.

"No work tonight, Liam. Please have a good time." He smiled, making me hold back the shiver that grew at the nape of my neck. "I will be seeing you soon, Miss Harden. Maybe for a dance?"

Liam's glower was fixated on me, taking a big gulp out of his glass of champagne while Mr. Mercier held my hand and made me twirl around as if we were dancing.

"I'm going to need something stronger," Liam grunted as soon as Mr. Mercier left, pulling me along with him to the bar. "Fucking asshole." He said with his jaw tightly clenched, his hand coming down onto the bar's marble countertop like a sledgehammer.

I covered his clenched fist with my hand, plastering the most honest smile I could on my face. "Forget him." I paused, watching as my touch slowly brought him back into the light. I wanted to ask why he got so worked up, but that would send him back to his murky shades.

"I'd still like to dance with you, though," I said instead, my finger drawing circles on his skin while Liam poured a full glass of liquor down his throat.

He paused for a moment, reigning in his sour mood before replying with a smile, "Your wish is my command, Miss Harden."

Liam led me to the dance floor, pulling me into his hard chest once he'd chosen our spot. His vice-like grip on my waist was commanding, possessive in its claim. Everything around us vanished as his scent invaded my senses, his closeness sending me into overdrive.

I leaned my head on his chest and simply inhaled, trying to imprint this exact feeling in every fiber of my being.

"I think I'm at a loss," He whispered, his lips grazing my hair while he spoke into my ear. "There are no words to describe how exquisite you look tonight." He paused for my reaction, but I was too high on him to reply. "I saw you looking at them, your eyes saddening as they walked past. You are blind to your worth, Miss Harden. No one, not one single soul in this room holds a candle to your beauty."

Liam spun me on my heels, pulling me into him once more, purposely making me collide against his hard muscles. His green eyes stared into mine while the hand he had on my back glided down, settling on the chaste edge before the curve of my ass.

"Fucking exquisite." He growled an inch away from my mouth, his fingers sinking into my skin.

A burning heat grew between my legs at the sound, my grip on his shoulder tightening in response. There was unchained lust in his eyes, his lips coming to settle on my ear again to deliver more torture straight into my brain.

"Do you have any idea how many men in this room would kill to take my place? I can feel their eyes on you right now as your hips buck in search of my erection. But not a single one knows how sweet you taste. No one but me." It was involuntary, but now that he mentioned it, I was extra wary of my movements and fuck was he right. Liam pushed into me in response, more teasing on the tip of his tongue. "Can you feel it? This is what you do to me, Miss Harden. And tonight, I'm craving punishment. You weren't very nice to me, now were you?"

Jesus fucking Christ! What was he doing to me?

My thong was soaked right through, and I couldn't help the moan that escaped my lips when he punctuated that sentence with a stinging bite on my ear. He heard me. I could feel his smirk against me.

"Behave, Miss Harden. Or we might have to cut this fucking party short." His voice was drenched in lust, unholy promises filling the tight space between our heating bodies.

"Who's stopping you?" I dared him, my face tilting up to meet his gaze defiantly.

"May I cut in? I'm eager to get my dance with this beautiful young lady." Mr. Mercier interrupted us just like a cold bucket of ice poured down my head.

Liam grasped my hand tighter, not ready to let go, if he ever was.

"I'd love to, Mr. Mercier. But I was actually telling Liam that my poor feet needed a rest. Fashion can be a high form of torture." I tried to dismiss him as politely as I could, but he was relentless. I couldn't risk offending the man who could make or break the deal we had just recently secured. I'd seen Liam work tirelessly on it, there was no way I was jeopardizing it now.

"Nonsense. I'm sure you can endure it a little longer just for this dance."

I looked at Liam, shooting him an apologetic look as I pulled my hand from his.

"Well, if you insist." I relented, swallowing dryly as I placed my hand in his.

I could feel Liam's raging eyes following our every move. Somehow that storm behind his green irises made me feel safe. There was absolutely no way he would allow any boundaries to be crossed.

Finally, what seemed like the longest song in the history of music came to an end, and Mr. Mercier accompanied me to where Liam was standing, another glass of what I supposed was bourbon in his hand.

"I hope your stay is long enough for me to take you to dinner tomorrow night, Miss Harden. From what I reckon, you're available, aren't you?" Mr. Mercier said as soon as we were in Liam's hearing range. I shot a surprised glare towards Liam who most certainly heard every word the man said.

"Well, Miss Harden, are you? Available?" Liam asked, an intrigued expression in his eyes.

"I… umm… I'd like to think I'm already spoken for, Mr. Mercier. Sorry to disappoint you, but I will have to respectfully decline." I managed to reply, holding Liam's gaze as I spoke. The slight smirk that tipped the corners of his lips filled me with relief and the need to get the hell out of this place as soon as possible.

"You'd like to think? Undefinition in a relationship is never a good sign. A man of good character and in his right mind would have put a ring on that pretty finger of yours. Who on earth would risk having such a perfect little thing like you running loose in this world? I'd say the boy doesn't know what he's doing. Or maybe what you need is a man."

"The boy is all the man she needs," Liam grunted, his voice descending to the depths of Hell as his arm snaked around my waist, pulling me into him possessively.

"Oh, I see." Mr. Mercier replied, motioning with his index finger between us. "It's not words that make a man, *boy*. It's actions. Take what's yours, or someone else will. I'll see you in New York in a couple of months. Liam, send my regards to your father, please." His snicker was sickening, his lingering gaze repulsive.

As he walked away I could finally feel myself loosen up, only to tense up again when I saw the way Liam was looking at me.

"You *think?*"

I simply shrugged in response, not knowing exactly what to say. We hadn't spoken about our relationship. Did we even have one? I wasn't sure.

Liam grabbed my waist, pulling me into his chest, holding me harshly against him with one hand as he settled his lips against my ear again, the lightness of his touch from before disappearing completely. I shivered again, not in fear but pure thrill and delight. His menacing voice doing very wrong things to me.

"You can be damn sure you are. Let's get you out of here, I'm fucking tired of sharing."

CHAPTER TWENTY THREE

Liam

My hand was itching and twitching, craving the feel of cold steel and a trigger on the edge of my index finger. There were already images of myself coating the damn bullet with my saliva dancing around in my mind so that it would poison him quicker than it took for him to bleed out from it.

To say I couldn't bear watching Jamie dancing in that fucker's arms was an understatement. Seething didn't even come close to the state I was in as I watched them glide around the dance floor.

So getting the fuck out of there was my top priority. Bathing Jamie in me was a close second.

I led her through the party, my hand on the small of her back, not stopping for anyone, taking her straight to the safety of the limo that was already waiting outside. We drove back in silence with our fingers intertwined. That was the lifeline of peace I needed to reel me back from the depths of my direness. I was listing all the things I wanted to do to Jamie once we got to the hotel, if she'd let me get close enough, as I watched the city go by in a blur through the window. Suddenly, I was being pulled out of depravity by my phone buzzing with a text from Matt.

> We need to talk. Call me ASAP. The Commission is meeting tomorrow.

I turned the screen down, ignoring him. That specific topic had me on edge, but I couldn't give in to it tonight. I didn't want to know what the damn peace proposition was because something in me told me it would come at my expense.

Once we got to the hotel, I accompanied Jamie to her room, the lingering thoughts about what Matt wanted to tell me pulling me back to reality each step we took.

Who was I kidding?

I was a lost cause, and I couldn't force that fate upon another. I couldn't condemn Jamie to a life of death and corruption. I couldn't drown her with my constant shadows.

She would be consumed.

Too easily consumed.

The danger that lurked in every corner of my life, of me, was too great and too final to expose such an angel to.

Jamie opened the door to her room, leaving it wide for me to follow. I watched as she sat on the chair, fiddling with her necklace, oblivious to the invisible line at the threshold that kept me from following her. I was debating if I could or even should cross it. I wouldn't leave without a piece of her soul if I did.

"It's late, we have an early flight tomorrow morning. You should get some sleep." I said, my hands balancing me on the door frame, my brain keeping me outside while my body pulled me in.

"Oh, umm... okay." There was painful resignation in her voice. My rejection slashing her to the point where she couldn't even look at me. "See you tomorrow." She finished, her voice struggling not to break.

Fuck, fuck, fuck.

That was a sound I couldn't bear to hear. It tore reason to shreds, propelling my feet towards her to burn every feeling of pain she ever had into ashes and distant memories.

There were tears behind her eyes, I could see them in her reflection in the mirror as I got close. I was the fucker who had put them there. She was finally taking me, accepting every damn thing that I was, and again I was pulling back.

But did I have any other choice? What pain would be greater? Today's or the one down the road after she'd had a taste of my poison?

My mind wasn't in sync with my body, and my hand was now pulling her hair away from her neck, giving way for my mouth to settle on her skin.

I wanted nothing more than to carve my teeth into her flesh. Mark her, claim her as mine for every damn soul to see she was taken by a sinner.

But Jamie was too pure to be stained that way. Too tender.

I tasted her skin, my lips tracing small kisses all the way from her shoulder to her neck and up towards her ear.

Send me away, Jamie.

The words wouldn't budge from the tip of my tongue, especially now that I was having a mouthful of her. I pulled her earlobe into my mouth, slowly sinking my teeth into it, my fingers tightening their grip around her arms as I steadied her.

Jamie's shallow breaths were a whisper against my cock. I could feel each and every stifled moan as if they were being released right onto it. My hunger grew wilder at her willingness and my hand wrapped around her hair, pulling on it for better access to every sensitive spot.

I was ravenous, feasting on her between full, opened-mouth kisses and firm bites. I needed to consume her, inhale her, claim her. *This* would never be enough.

I kept her hair in a tight grasp while my other hand glided to squeeze her full tit, pinching on her hardened nipple that craved attention through the silk of her dress.

I kissed every inch of her skin until I grabbed her jaw and finally captured her lips with mine, in a hungry, passionate, and shamelessly harsh kiss.

She kissed me back, craving as much of my darkness as I did of her light. Moans of pleasure left her throat as my tongue took over hers, desperate for more at each passing second.

Fuck. me.

I pulled back to look into her eyes, but when I opened mine, I was met with my own reflection in the damn mirror. My vision was blurred with the same image I'd seen in my suite before punching the glass to pieces. Blood and destruction sliding down the jagged edges.

Panic coursed through me as I fought to keep a calm expression before her.

This was madness!

I stood straight, trying my damndest to ignore Jamie's pants, steadying myself before pulling away.

"Have a good night, Miss Harden," I said in the calmest tone I could, my heart punching hard into my chest.

With that, I bit down on my tongue in punishment, turned away, and left.

Jamie

What the hell was that?

He just left me panting alone in my room, just like that!

I squeezed my legs together in a failed attempt to ease the throbbing he'd left me to deal with. The pressure just made it worse and I knew there was no chance of it going away on its own.

Liam's kisses were always knee-weakening, but that one? It was unlike anything I'd ever experienced. There was possession in that kiss, as if he was informing every cell in my body that he had claimed me.

Who knew that I could get this worked up with only a few kisses and bites on my neck? It was so insanely intense, I was still trying to figure where he had gotten the strength to stop from.

Why is he doing this? Why is he holding back?

My mind was in a frenzy, trying to find the reason why Liam was pulling back again while my body still felt every searing touch of his on my skin. One of them had to give, and my mind quickly surrendered to the ache soaring between my legs.

I turned on the water, thinking a cold shower could help with my predicament, hoping that it would so I could at least get some rest.

For some reason, he was controlling his impulses, and for the first time since he had told me he was in the Mafia, I wanted him to lose control. That alone was a good indicator that my trust in him was back to where it used to be.

Stepping under the cold water, I stood still, waiting for the ease that never came, and before I knew it, my hands were trailing the path that his had just a few minutes ago.

They weren't even remotely as pleasurable as Liam's had been, but there was nothing else I could do right now besides settle for my own fingers.

My hand slid down my stomach, settling between my legs, drawing hard circles on my clit, the first impact immediately having my back arch in delight. My clit was already swollen before the friction, Liam's kisses winding me into a state of desperation.

A moan rippled its way through my throat while my fingers pried into me, the heel of my hand now rubbing exactly where it ached. I closed my eyes and thought of him, of how rough he was, of those damn words I hadn't heard from his mouth for so long but hadn't ceased to haunt my dreams – *good fucking girl.*

That's what I wanted to be, so, so badly. *His* good fucking girl.

I steadied myself against the shower's wall, my hand pumping faster as I hunched into a position that would have brought me shame to see myself in if it weren't for him. I'm not this person, I've never been. I don't even know if I could get off like this. But somehow, Liam did *things* to me.

Damn him for being thoughtful and booking separate rooms. Damn him for not pressuring me. Damn him for leaving.

My skin was stone cold, a shiver pulling me out of my thoughts. I cut the water and got dried up before marching into the room with Alison's gift on my mind. Maybe that could help me get the release I needed now.

I pulled the pink bullet out of the box, washed it, and made myself comfortable on the bed. As soon as I placed it on my clit, my soul almost left my body.

Fuck.me!

My heart rate instantly rose, and I could feel it hammering heavily against my chest. My flushed cheeks throbbed with every new circle I drew on my clit, my mouth falling open as every muscle in my body contracted.

Suddenly, my phone buzzed with a new text, pulling my focus away. I tried to ignore it but another one came in.

> Meet me in the lobby at 8 tomorrow. We have an early flight.

> Sweet dreams, Miss Harden.

"Sweet dreams? Sweet dreams?" I said to myself, my voice high with indignance. "How am I supposed to have sweet dreams when you've done this to me?" I shout to my phone, falling back onto the pillows with a thud.

I thought we would only be leaving in a couple of days. Had something happened? I considered not replying, he deserved to be ignored after leaving me in this state and then interrupting my little private session. But instead I decided that I shouldn't be suffering alone, and Liam needed a little taste of his own poison.

> Sleep won't be coming easy tonight. Do you have any idea of the state you've left me in?

No, I don't. But I'd like you to tell me.

> I can't right now. I'm busy fixing this throb you left between my legs.

I was blushing just thinking about Liam reading my words. But somehow the safety of the screen made me bolder than I'd ever thought I could be. I see those three dots taunting me as I waited for his reply, grinning to myself as soon as it appeared on the screen.

Fixing? What the fuck do you mean, fixing?

> I don't really know how to describe it. Maybe I should come to your room and just show you.

Fuck, Jamie!

Penthouse suite.

I'll give you 2 minutes to get here before I come get you.

I bounced to my feet, leaving the room with nothing on but an oversized t-shirt and a pair of short shorts. No time for underwear. I wouldn't be needing it, after all.

The anticipation had my toes curling and my skin tingling as I scurried through the hotel as quickly as I could.

Liam was leaning against the top of the door frame when I got to his room, no shirt on while his slacks hugged his legs and groin in a perfect fit. His muscles clenched in masses, pulsing with each step I took closer. Damn this man was sexy! My breath was caught in my throat as soon as my eyes landed on his perfect skin.

His hair was a mess and his eyes were wild, swimming with dark promises of lust. I couldn't wait to have his hands on me, chasing all this pent-up need away with every kiss.

"It took you long enough." Liam taunted as I made my way past the threshold, merely stepping aside for me to enter. His gaze followed my steps, the smirk on my face unable to be erased.

Liam, on the other hand, had a scowl on his brow, the lurk of danger more than noticeable on his features. Instead of threatening, it was sending thrilling jolts of electricity down my spine.

The door banged heavily behind me, and before I could take the grandness of his suite in, Liam wrapped his arm around my waist and pulled me back.

My hands were held above my head, a deadly grip and a matching glare pinning me against the entrance wall. My body screamed for more connection, arching and searching for him, but Liam kept his body at a safe distance. His hand was the only thing touching my skin, holding my wrists like a vice.

His lips wandered over my face, hovering but never touching, teasingly close, awakening my body to an unprecedented need. From my lips, to my neck, to my ear. Not a graze, not a touch. I could feel his warm breath brushing against my skin, making me urge for him to kiss me. Take me. Devour me.

"What are you doing here, Miss Harden?" He whispered, his voice lowered to a husky tone right against my ear.

"I…I came to get what I need." I stuttered, my body overriding my brain with desire.

"And what is it that you need, Miss Harden?"

My name felt like a heavenly sin on his lips, the same ones that insisted on not touching me as I needed them to.

My back arched off the wall again, trying to reach him, my body calling out to him in a deafening plea for more.

"I need you, Liam." My reply was steady and confident, almost an exhaled cry.

A smirk covered his face, the glint in his eyes telling me that was exactly the answer he wanted to hear.

"Good fucking girl!"

The moan that came out of my mouth was uncontrollable, as if those words had been whispered right against my pussy.

Liam finally pressed himself against me, his chest warm on my painfully hardened nipples. He pushed his big cock into me, showing me just how ready he was to take me. I released another moan when he parted my legs with his, pressing his cock on my throbbing sex before he captured my lips in an earth-shattering kiss.

His tongue stroked my lips, demanding entrance, and I immediately conceded, surrendering my mouth to his will.

Those strong hands of his traveled down the side of my body, harsh and needy, coming to rest on my ass, grabbing it with such force I was sure I'd be bruised tomorrow. I couldn't find it in me to care. Seeing Liam this hungry for me only fueled my desire further.

I squirmed under his hold, wanting to touch him, grab him, pull him closer to me, but Liam wasn't relenting. His free hand glided from my ass to the front of my body, between us, resting his fingers on my needy pussy, just the thin layer of my shorts separating him from my skin. A hard circle drawn on my clit made me moan right into his mouth, Liam's lips quirking into a smile against my lips.

"You like that, Miss Harden?"

All I could do was shake my head in a vigorous "no." I needed so much more than what he was giving me.

"No? Maybe this is better." His hand was now sliding down the hem of my shorts, landing straight on my bare skin. His eyes shot open in surprise, finding nothing in his way. "Fuck, Jamie. You have nothing under this."

In a swift move, I was in the air, my legs wrapping around his toned body while my hands flew to grab his neck.

Liam held me tightly against him, taking me over to his massive poster bed, placing me on the mattress. He took a step back, his eyes traveling the length of my body.

"What?"

"Just taking in the image of you in my bed. Nothing has ever looked so amazing." I couldn't help the smile that lit me up from the inside, his words warming every inch of me. "Now, how on Earth can we top that?"

"Will this work?" I said before taking off my t-shirt, my nipples hardening even further from the cool air.

"I'm not sure it's enough." Liam's gaze was smoldering, burning my skin with his stare alone.

"Maybe this will do it," I replied, sliding my shorts down my legs and throwing the fabric at him. He caught it mid-air, taking it to his nose and inhaling sharply.

"Fuck!" He groaned, tossing the shorts behind him, as he rested his hands on my knees. "What's an image without a flavor to go with it? The scent alone tells me I'm in for the feast of my life."

Liam's fingers sank into my skin, pressing on each of my knees to open them, exposing me to him completely. There was nothing to hide me, the lights were on, no clothes, and Liam had a clear, uninterrupted view of every inch of my body. Somehow, I wasn't concerned or ashamed. My skin burned with need for him as I couldn't wait to feel his touch on every inch his eyes had scanned.

Liam placed a knee on the mattress between my legs, one hand placed right next to my head, holding him up. His free hand settled on my clit, drawing circles with his fingers while his eyes bore into mine. Without a warning, he plunged two digits inside me, withdrawing only to come up and tease my clit some more before going back to bury them inside again.

My back arched on repeat as I squirmed under his touch, wanting more, but he kept his assault slow and teasing.

Liam pulled his finger from inside me harshly, bringing them to his lips and sucking every drop of my arousal from his skin.

"Sweet and fucking tempting. I need more." With a grunt, he pushed off me, hooking his hands under my knees and pulling my ass towards the edge of the bed as he kneeled on the floor.

His eyes were now level with my bare pussy, just a few inches away from touching me, his ragged breaths fanning my sensitive skin.

"You are so fucking beautiful, Jamie. Tell me you're mine. All mine."

Before I could speak, Liam's lips latched onto my clit, a wave of pleasure soaring through my body. My back was off the bed in an arch of bliss, each flick of his tongue bringing me more pleasure than the last.

"I'm yours." I moaned, breathless but firm, the words coming from deep inside my heart, "I'm all yours." It was the truth, unwavering and unshakable. I was his in every way I could be and in every way he wanted me.

My hands were knotted in Liam's hair, pulling him into me while his tongue darted in and out of me. I tugged hard on his strands, making him stop his assault on my pussy.

"I need more, Liam. I need you inside me." My plea was hushed, almost as if I couldn't dare to say the words, but I did. I wanted to feel him inside me again, completely naked this time, how it should have been the first time around.

Liam pulled back, rising to his feet to take off his slacks and boxers. I let my eyes take in every inch of his perfect body, from his abs to his tattoos, from his wild dark hair to his erection standing tall and magnificent. There was nothing closer to perfection than him.

Liam held his thick cock in his hand, his fingers gripping it like a vice as he pumped it from the base to the tip, his eyes ablaze and set on mine the entire time.

He slowly took his place between my legs again, the head of his cock set right at my entrance without pushing in. I instinctively shut my eyes, waiting for the sting as Liam pushed inside me, but it never came.

"Open your eyes, Beautiful. I want you to look at me." One after the other, I do, my legs shaking as much as I tried to steady them. "I won't be the bastard I was the last time, I promise. This should be enjoyable for both of us. Tell me if it's sore. and I'll stop immediately."

I had no idea why all of a sudden I was this anxious. I inhaled deeply, trying to steady myself as much as possible, giving Liam a small nod to continue.

Liam grazed his warm cock from my slit to my clit, taking his time to help me ease up, only poking at my entrance each time he reached it again. He kissed me, his urgency calming into something solemn as he repeated his motion again and again.

I felt him sinking into me, deeper each time, only to withdraw and glide his shaft along my wet pussy before slowly stretching me again. Another inch surrendering to him, accommodating him as if I had been made for this man. No pain this time, only pleasure and a new sense of fulfillment.

"That wasn't so hard was it?" He pulled back from my lips, grinding himself against me, his mound rubbing against my clit. "I'm buried inside you, Baby, and it's the best fucking feeling in this world."

"Oh my God." I moaned as he pumped in short strokes, making sure to graze my clit each time he did. There was no pain this time, just pure bliss.

"I was made for you, Jamie. Look how damn well I fit inside you. Are you okay?"

"I'm perfect," I managed to reply, his eyes never leaving mine, making sure I wasn't holding back. I was more than perfect. I was feeling complete for the first time.

Liam slowly started thrusting into me in steady, calm motions first, grinding his hips every time he was deeply buried inside me. My mouth fell open, small pants growing into moans of pleasure. I'd been picturing this for so long I was worried I would ruin it.

His thrusts increased, getting deeper and faster as he stared, plunging harder into me at my request, and I couldn't contain the gasps and moans anymore. Uncontrolled and wild.

"Liam... Oh God!" I tried telling him that I was close, but it was getting harder to speak, coherently even worse.

"Don't hold back, Jamie. Come for me, hard and fucking beautiful," Liam encouraged, his voice taking on a commanding tone that had me shivering. He took one of my nipples in his mouth, sucking hard on it before sinking his teeth into my skin, and that was all it took to send me over the edge. "Sing my name, Baby. I want to hear your pleasure."

"LIAAAMMM!" I moaned out loud in a desperate plea for release, making him plunge hard, his shaft all out and then all in, hitting all the right spots as I come undone.

"That's my fucking good girl. Taking my cock like the greedy girl you are." I felt him throbbing inside me as I came down from my climax, the room filling with the sound of his loud groan. I watched him come, his muscles tensing into masses before relaxing completely.

My body was shaking with the intense waves of pleasure that left my core and spread to every inch of my body. Liam captured my lips as if it were the first and last time he ever could, a kiss so deep it stroked my soul. He collapsed over me, the weight of his body feeling like Heaven.

We lay there for a while, catching our breaths, and I couldn't help the huge smile I had plastered on my face.

Liam held me to him, placing feather-light kisses everywhere he could reach.

"Can we sleep like this?" I asked, not ready for him to pull out of me.

"Of course, let me just take care of you first."

Liam sauntered to the bathroom, returning with a damp towel, cleaning his cum that had leaked out of me with a nurturing care I wasn't expecting. After a second, he was back, pulling me to my side and taking his place behind me as his cock found its way inside me again.

We lay there in comfortable silence, my heart filling with the memory of what just happened.

"I'm glad you could wait," I said, my voice heavy with regret.

Liam pulled my back further into him, his cock buried to the hilt, but there was no movement, no attempt for a second round. It was closeness we were both searching for, connection and vulnerability. All those things that could be so dangerous to admit to felt easy with him and I never wanted it to change.

"I'm glad you came back." He confessed, and my heart fluttered, showing me just how lost in him I was. This was more than just sex. This was more than possession. It was something I couldn't dare to say.

CHAPTER TWENTY FOUR

Jamie

I was tucked in Liam's arms when I woke up in the middle of the night. We had both fallen asleep peacefully after experiencing what I would consider to be the most wonderful moment of my life.

He strengthened his hold on me as I turned over in bed, keeping me firmly pressed against his warm body. It felt like Heaven – his scent, his touch, his strength, and most of all, this need he had, even in his sleep, to hold me in his arms.

I could feel the hardening of his cock against my naked body. Somewhere during the night it had slipped out of me. My core became lighter as a new flame rose inside of me, hardening my nipples and making my clit pulse with a new rush of desire. Liam was fast asleep, and gathering all the courage I found in me, I rolled him onto his back and gently eased my body over his, straddling him beneath me.

My heart was racing from all the lust and adrenaline in my system, anxiety increasing with each passing second.

I placed his erection at my entrance, holding it firmly by the base as I slid onto him. Again, there was no pain, instead only the most amazing feeling of pleasure that flooded every inch of my body. Liam reached for my hips, his hands running over my thighs, his fingers digging into my skin. He had a firm grip on my hip, helping me settle completely onto him.

"Jesus fuck." He groaned, fueling my resolve. "I've never been so happy to be woken up in the middle of the night."

"I'm so sorry to wake you." I teased, seeing that he didn't mind one bit to be missing out on an hour of rest.

"Mafia men don't sleep, Miss Harden. Even if I was in a coma, this perfect pussy of yours would have me waking up from the dead. Fuuuuuck!" He groaned again as I pulled up, only to thrust all the way down again.

Liam's hands were in a frenzy trying to touch all of me, small jolts of electricity igniting my skin wherever his fingers trailed. My head fell back in ecstasy while my mouth opened involuntarily, small exhaled moans escaping with every deep thrust.

Liam wrapped his big hand around my totally exposed neck, squeezing just a little, enough to intensify every ounce of pleasure running through me.

Sitting up, he held me tightly against his hard chest, kissing my neck before capturing my lips in a harsh, primal kiss. My whole body was his, my soul completely surrendered to him as I reveled in our lovemaking.

Never in a million years could I have imagined I would enjoy this kind of vulnerability as much as I was. I knew, in that very moment, that my heart belonged to him and that it would break me into unmendable pieces if he didn't feel the same way.

I was aware that whatever this was, it was all too fresh and new for me to be feeling this way. We barely knew each other. But I just knew.

In a swift move, Liam picked me up, laying my back on the bed and regaining control. From our first encounter, it was clear to me that he was used to being the one calling the shots. It sure wouldn't be any different when it came to sex. I wasn't complaining, though. The way he commanded and controlled the situation made me burn hotter with desire. I never thought I'd like to be manhandled, but damn, I did.

His dominating nature served me and my lust just perfectly. His every touch was full of need, trailing every part of my body, making pleasure erupt from my every pore.

He placed his body between my legs, drawing a path of wet, hungry kisses down my chest and stomach until his head was buried between my legs, assaulting my throbbing clit with kisses, licks, and nibbles.

My eyes immediately rolled to the back of my head at the feeling of his wet, warm tongue dipping into me. My breath quickened again, making my chest heave erratically as I started to drop into the pit of my climax.

"Liam…. I…I.. won't be able to hold…if you… JESUS" I tried saying, between each breath I managed to take.

Liam didn't seem to care and remained in place, plunging two fingers deep inside me, twisting up and rubbing my most sensitive spot. I shut my eyes tightly, feeling an overwhelming sensation growing in my core, clenching my muscles and making me hold my breath before finally releasing in a heavenly orgasm. My body was shaking and jolting with every powerful wave of ecstasy as I moaned and gasped and exhaled in the mighty apex of bliss.

I finally managed to open my eyes and look down at Liam, still placed between my thighs with a huge grin on his face. I couldn't help the blush that tainted my cheeks under his examining gaze, covering my face with a pillow.

Liam pulled it away, capturing my mouth in a hungry kiss, silently telling me he wasn't finished with me yet. He grabbed my waist and spun me around, my stomach flat on the mattress before he pulled on my hips, pinning my ass up.

I looked back at him and gave him a small, consenting nod that I knew he was waiting for. He then buried his hard shaft deep inside me, making my eyes widen. With every thrust, Liam's movements got more erratic, more urgent. He held me firmly in place, one hand rough on my hip while the other fisted my hair in a tight knot, pulling back.

Pain mingled with pleasure, all my senses heightened by the tip of his touch.

Liam's groans became louder. Quicker. More. My body vibrating every time those primal sounds landed on my ears. My pleasure growing in response to everything he was doing to my body.

Fuck, I could hear him coming before he actually was.

With one last deep push, we both came, his hot cum filling me up to the brim.

Slowly, Liam let go of the grip on my hair, holding my hips in place as he started to pull out of me. I tried to move forward, but he held me there, ass in the air as he kneeled behind me, his eyes intensely glued on my pussy.

"I want to see us. Your cum mixed with mine before I get you a towel to clean up."

Another blazing hot blush covered my cheeks, embarrassment flooding me at the image he had painted in my head.

"Fucking beautiful." I heard him saying before his fingers swiped against my entrance, pushing our cum back inside me. "I'm a part of you now. At least until you've pushed out every last one of my boys."

I couldn't help but laugh, the movement making more gushes of cum come out of me while Liam frantically fought to push it all back in.

"Stop laughing, you're spoiling perfectly good swimmers."

I laughed louder, slumping forward and pulling him along with me.

I have never felt peace like this. Like what I felt when his arms were wrapped so protectively around me. I was in the safest place in the world, and no one could burst this bubble.

"You're amazing, do you know that?" Liam whispered, his fingers slowly stroking my skin.

"I feel amazing when I'm with you," I confessed. "Can we stay here for a couple more days before going back to reality?"

"We have somewhere to be tomorrow, but we can push our return to New York a few days forward after that."

"Where are we going?" I curiously asked, resting my chin on his broad chest.

"It's a surprise. And you're not convincing me to spoil it. You'll see when we get there." He teased with a devilish smile on his face. "Oh, and we'll be traveling like the gangsters in those books of yours. The jet will be fueled and ready first thing in the morning."

My heart grew heavy with the memory of how I had reacted during the flight over. I was going to be a mess again in the tight space of the plane, but this time I'd try to calm down before lashing out in jealousy, fear, or all the above.

"I'm sorry I overreacted. Whenever I picture you with someone else, I just feel a burning anguish growing inside me. And I know you've been around. I thought that buying dresses and jewelry and first-class tickets and stuff like that was something you would normally do for one of them. It just seemed so natural to you, I guessed it was something you did often."

"Yes, I have been around. Just meaningless hookups, like scratching an itch. Nothing like this." He smiled, his gaze deeply buried in mine. "Never anything like this."

"Like this... and what is *this*?" I couldn't help but ask.

"It's whatever you want it to be. I don't want to push you into anything, but I'd like to think that you're mine. *All* mine. Just mine." Each word that left his mouth more serious than the previous one. My lips crashed onto his in a passionate kiss after he had just verbalized my desires.

"Does that mean you'll also be mine? All mine? Just mine?" I asked, perfectly echoing his previous words, unknowingly holding my breath for his answer.

"I already am." His reply was unwavering, coming in hand with a smile so big it illuminated his entire face. I kissed him passionately again, sealing our deal.

When morning came, I woke up with a trail of Liam's kisses down my naked back, small goosebumps erupting all over my body.

"Good morning, Gorgeous." Liam greeted once my eyes were open. "I had the hotel staff pack your bags and bring them here. You can shower and change before we go."

I sleepily opened my eyes, seeing that Liam was wearing nothing but a low-hanging towel around his waist, his hair wet and dripping onto me. My face must have shown my disappointment as he burst out laughing.

"Don't worry, we'll have plenty of time to shower together. Right now we have to hurry up and get to the jet before nine." He said, planting a tender kiss on my forehead.

Without inhibition, I got out of bed, completely naked, letting the sheet slide down my body, walking to the bathroom as seductively as I knew how to, turning only when I arrived at the door.

"Pitty. I kind of felt like round three in the shower was a good idea." I teased, licking my lips before closing the bathroom door, leaving Liam with a graphic idea of what I had in mind.

The hot water helped me relax my taut and sore muscles from last night. It was a good feeling, a good sore. But I welcomed the relief anyway.

I quickly got dressed casually, seeing that Liam was in a pair of dark jeans and a white t-shirt. I asked him again where we were going, but still, he refused to tell me.

I was dumbstruck when we got to the airstrip and saw that we were, in fact, stepping into a luxurious jet that was waiting *just* for us.

Liam greeted the staff, showing me to our seats. Charcoal carpet covered the floor, accentuating the white leather seats and wooden tables and details.

It smelled like luxury and power, impeccable taste and opulence.

Still, it could be covered in gold and even that wouldn't take away from the anxiety already growing in the pit of my stomach, my chest tightening as if the weight of the world was suddenly pressing on it.

Liam locked his fingers with mine while we were taking off, rubbing small, soothing circles on the back of my hand. Once we were high in the sky, the pilot started to speak, providing us some information about the flight.

"The sky is clear, no turbulence ahead, shortening our flight to about four and a half hours. The weather in Jacksonville..."

My ears blocked. My vision blurred. My heart stopped beating all together.

JACKSONVILLE???

There was a panic attack coming on. Hard and fast. I couldn't get the air in or out fast enough. An acute pain shooting through my chest.

Breathe.

I couldn't be going back home with Liam.

Breathe, Jamie

He couldn't meet my father.

Breathe.

A disaster was about to happen.

Breathe.

Holy, holy, holy, fuck!

CHAPTER TWENTY FIVE

Jamie

God, please let this be a nightmare.
On the count of three, I'll open my eyes and we'll be back in bed, warm and snuggled together.

But when I opened my eyes, we were still in the damn jet, and this was *not* the worst of dreams.

My lungs screamed for air that didn't come, while my eyes welled up with tears that I fought desperately to keep from falling. My heart was ready to jump out through my throat as I kept thinking about the disaster that was about to happen.

We were on our way to Jacksonville.

My hands were shaking as if the pilot had turned the temperature to polar-freezing but I was as hot as the surface of the sun, sweat beading on my forehead.

Jacksonville was my Vegas: what happened there, stayed there. I had banished the past from my new life in order to carry on. Nothing good ever came from falling down that pit.

But now my worlds were about to collide. Past and present. The ugly face of my true self rearing its head to the only person I couldn't bear to disappoint.

I'd been standing my ground as much as I knew how to, morphing into the strong person I've always thought I should be. The person Liam thought I was. And for some part, I had succeeded in being *her*, the woman I had imagined I could be far away from there. Away from him. All that was about to be exposed by my harsh reality.

Maybe he'll behave since I'm with someone else.

Maybe he's changed.

Maybe, just... maybe.

I felt Liam's eyes on me before even looking up, and when I did, his eyebrows were hunched together in concern.

His lips moved quickly, his eyes darting all around my face, but I couldn't register the words.

Panic had taken over my body, the only sound drumming in my ears was the one of my own blood rushing in despair.

He's going to see. He's going to know how weak I am.

The contrast between who he is and who I am has never been clearer. He's in the damn mafia. He's all about strength and power, while I'm a weakling.

"JAMIE!" Liam shouted, his hands on my shoulders, shaking me out of my haze. The gesture broke the hold I had on my tears that were now free-falling down my cheeks. I didn't have the strength to hold them back anymore. "Why are you shaking? What's wrong? Tell me."

The concern was clear in his demanding words, but try as I might, I couldn't speak. I was frozen.

Allowing Liam to see what I'd endured was opening a box that I had been trying to seal shut my whole life. It wasn't just about the vulnerability of having him know about the abuse, it was more about the consequences. He would never see me in the same light after I'd brought him into my darkness. He wouldn't want me anymore.

I was weak while what he needed was strength. Someone who didn't need to be saved. Someone who wouldn't take from his power just by being by his side.

Behind a great man is always a great woman.

That wasn't me. I wasn't the woman a man like Liam needed.

Liam pushed two pills into my hand and a bottle of water into the other one, ushering me to take them. I obliged before curling into his chest without saying a word.

Liam held me, his hand drawing soothing circles on my back until I fell asleep.

There was no escaping my past. It was clear that even if we turned around now, Liam wouldn't settle for a half-assed explanation for my reaction.

Was it even fair that he had taken such a huge risk in opening up to me, telling me who he really was, while I hid behind a false façade? Logically I knew it wasn't, but I couldn't fathom telling him the truth.

I was too scared that he would think I wasn't worthy of his affection, too broken to be loved.

Before my eyes fluttered open, I felt everything around me still. No noise or turbulence, no vibration from the plane's engines. Nothing.

I was still nestled in Liam's arms, but the airplane had landed.

"How are you feeling?" Liam asked as he noticed me waking up.

"Where are we?" I asked instead of answering his previous question.

"Jacksonville." His voice was pained, as if he had figured it out and regretted bringing me here. "We can leave in about two hours."

I felt relief flooding me as I heard his words, but at the same time, I knew that hiding wasn't going to do me any good now. This wasn't just going away, and Liam would for sure want to know what the hell happened.

Besides, I'd tried talking about what my father did to me, but the very few people I opened up to seemed to never believe me.

I sunk deeper into his hold, absorbing every ounce of his affection. I tried to control my emotions the best I could. Whatever medication he had given me brought me a peace and clarity that made me think clearer.

I could see that Liam had a million questions just swimming around in his mind, but he was holding them back for now.

"No. We should go." I ended up saying, his expression cautious as he nodded and helped me out of my seat.

Once we were off the plane and in the car, Liam finally broke the silence.

"It's clear that you're not happy to be back home. I'm sorry. I thought that it would be a nice surprise. It's been a couple of months since the last time you've been home. I just thought you could be homesick." There was disappointment in his face, mixed with regret. He had no way of knowing that this place couldn't feel further from home. New York had been a better home to me than Jacksonville ever was. But the thought behind his gesture was sweet, and I hadn't acknowledged that.

Liam had shared his secrets with me, completely placing his life in my hands. There was no way he could be sure I wouldn't go to the police with all the information he had given me. His life was literally on the line, and he still did it anyway.

He deserved to know, even if it hurt.

If, after all, Liam decided that I wasn't suitable for him, then maybe it just wasn't meant to be. A new flow of tears ran down my face at that thought, my mind racing with all the ways he would dump me.

Just take me back to New York first. Please.

"You shouldn't be apologizing. How could you have known? It's just… hard, having you here, seeing my ugly past." My tears were free, falling without restraint.

"There's absolutely nothing I can see here that will make me think less of you." With the pad of his thumb, Liam wiped my tears away, lingering to caress my cheek in a comforting gesture that made my heart flutter.

His eyes bore into mine, stripping my soul to its bare bones, his eyes filled with tenderness and something I could only pray could be love. Liam reached down towards me and placed a slow and loving kiss on my lips, my heart warming and speeding up with just that kiss alone.

It was timed perfectly, because before he pulled back, the car was stopping right in front of my childhood house.

"Shall we?" Liam asked before helping me out of the car, his hand steadying me as my legs trembled in a new rush of panic. I didn't miss him tucking a gun inside the back of his pants, even though he tried his best to conceal it. It was evident that my state had raised some of his red flags.

I latched onto his hand, trying to draw strength from the rock beside me.

Liam held his head up, his chest filled with the courage that I lacked, and before I knew it, we had climbed those steps and he was harshly knocking on the door.

I held my breath, hoping that my father was having one of his good days. Not that he treated me all that well on those days, but it wasn't as bad.

My palms were clammy, and my heart slammed against my ribcage as if it were trying to escape my chest. Without hesitation, Liam knocked a second time, stronger than the first, my anxiety skyrocketing every time his knuckles hit that wooden panel.

Right as I was about to pull him away, relieved that Frank wasn't home, my father opened the door and I was completely lost for words.

"Oh great, it's you." He grunted, his tone emphasizing the disappointment of seeing me standing at his doorstep. "What the hell are you doing back here? Fucked up that fancy job you got already? That must be some kind of record, even for a useless piece of shit like you." He had turned inside, walking down the hall as he spoke, leaving the door open for us to follow at our own discretion.

Liam looked at me, his mouth slightly open in surprise from that warm welcome.

"No, I haven't fucked it up. This is my boss, Liam Dornier. Liam, this is my father, Frank." I replied in a shaky voice, following him into the kitchen with Liam tailing close behind me.

I dared a glance towards him, his face was a mask of darkness and high alert. Liam glanced around, studying his surroundings carefully but never losing sight of me.

"So tell me, to what do I owe the absolute pleasure of your visit?" My father asked, his tone dripping in unmasked sarcasm.

"We had a business meeting in LA, and Liam thought I could be missing home." Those words tasted like acid even though I was merely stating facts.

"You shouldn't have bothered." His reply was directed at Liam, who had yet to say a single word. I would be lying if I said I wasn't worried about what was going through his mind.

"I can see that." Liam finally spoke, his words being spat with disdain in a low voice that didn't hide his scorn. His hand came to rest on the small of my back, his figure towering over me in a protective stance.

"So, it's Liam, right? I see your company does some serious charity work. Does it bring any tax benefits?" He was talking about me, and I could hear the low growl rumbling in Liam's chest as my father spoke.

"No tax benefits, but sometimes we're able to give some deserving people a shiny new pair of shoes." My father scrunched his nose, not understanding the connection. I was a little lost myself, but somehow I got the feeling that Liam wasn't speaking about AD. His hand tightened the hold around me, pulling me further into his side. "Let's call it charity to mankind."

My father waved Liam off, looking at him as if he was on acid, not understanding a single word he said.

"Oh, now I see. You are still working at that fancy job you bragged about because you're fucking your boss. Smart girl!"

From the corner of my eyes, I could see Liam's jaw clenching in a rhythm, matching the pace of his muscles. I intertwined my fingers in his, giving his hand a squeeze in a futile attempt to calm him down. His face had taken a sharp turn into an eerie serenity now, sending a fearful shiver down my spine. I knew this wouldn't play out well.

"You should wash your fucking mouth with bleach before you speak about Jamie." Liam spat between gritted teeth.

"You'll have your fun and then move on. That's the only thing she's good for. You'll see. That murderous little bitch doesn't deserve the time of d–" I barely blinked, and Liam had let go of me, lunging towards the knife stand on the counter, drawing one and pinning my father against the cupboards. Liam's hand was wrapped around my father's throat, the blade pressed against the feeble skin above his Adam's apple. There was blood already. Just a drizzle, but enough to drain my father's face of all color. Liam wasn't joking, and he knew it.

"Call her that one more time and I fucking swear I will fucking kill you right here." Liam grunted, his rage dripping out with every word. "Make my fucking day."

"LIAM, STOP." I cried out, despair making my hands shake like a damn leaf. "It's not worth it."

"Your tongue isn't so sharp now, is it? Come on, you fucking coward. Give me just a small reason to shred your throat right here." I'd never seen Liam like this. It was clear in his bulging eyes and flexing jaw muscles that he would do exactly what he said.

I knew this part of him, but seeing it still came as a shock. I was scared he would crack at any second by the way he was seething. I didn't want him to have my father's death on his conscience, and I sure didn't want to have it on mine.

"Liam, please. Look at me!" I called again, trying to steer him away from his anger and his focus on my father.

"You're a useless fucking son of a bitch. How can someone treat his own daughter like that? You don't deserve to breathe the same air that she does." Both the knife and his hold on my father's throat tighten, and I see more blood seeping from underneath the sharp blade. "APOLOGIZE! She's your fucking daughter!" Liam's shouts shook the walls, my father's face contorting in pain before resolve hit his features.

"She's a mistake." He croaked through ragged breaths. "She shouldn't have been born!" I had heard those words every damn day of

266

my life, and still they stung like a swarm of bees attacking me in unison.

Liam's knuckles turned whiter as he tightened his grip on my father's throat even further.

"LIAM!" I screamed again, desperate to save his soul more than my father's life.

"APOLOGIZE TO YOUR DAUGHTER, YOU SON OF A BITCH." Liam roared to my father's face, rage punctuating each word while spit hit my father's skin.

"I'M NOT HER FATHER."

There was a pause. We all froze.

Liam released his hold and my father fell to the ground with a loud thud, gasping for air while he held onto his bleeding throat.

"I'm not your fucking father. You were a mistake that your mother should have taken care of right from the beginning. And you? You took her from me. You killed her!" He viciously spat, his voice hoarse, stealing the air from my lungs with his confession. "It's fucking liberating to finally say it. I'm not your fucking father. You're a bastard. An unwanted fucking bastard."

I tried to inhale, but air didn't reach my lungs.

I need air.

I turned around and ran outside, trying to pull the much-needed oxygen in through gasps, but it simply wasn't reaching my burning lungs.

I bumped into Liam's men on the way out, only stopping once I was in the middle of the front lawn.

He's not my father? How? Why?

My vision blurred, and darkness slowly invaded my sight. I feel my knees going weak before they give in and fail under me. The world went silent and dark right before I hit the ground.

CHAPTER TWENTY SIX

Jamie

10 years ago

I was in the dark again.

My nails scraping on wood, praying someone would hear me. But no one ever did.

As the years went by, I should have become used to this. Used to being locked in tight spaces that would quickly run out of breathing air. Some days I wished it did, and I would just fade into a sound sleep that took all the pain away.

I had screamed my lungs out, and my throat was burning and raw from my despair, but not even then did he come for me.

How long it took before I saw the light of day again depended on the space he used. He would never cross that line and risk being caught for murder. I had come to that realization when I was eight or maybe nine. I mourned that strange moral line every minute I spent in these closed spaces.

Even now, at fifteen, I had no clue what his trigger was. The only pattern I found was that, around my birthday, it got significantly worse.

"Please stop."

"No. Not the closet, please."

"I'll shut up. Please don't lock me in the trunk."

And the one that hurt the most, "No, Daddy, please. I'll be good, I promise I'll be good."

But there was no way I could ever be good in his eyes, no matter the size of my halo.

One day I'll get out of this box. One day I'll erase this version of myself and be a new Jamie. One day I'll have someone who loves me and maybe find a way to love myself, too.

CHAPTER TWENTY SEVEN

Liam

I couldn't believe what I was witnessing.

This world was filled with assholes, but that fucker put most of them to shame.

When I saw Jamie running, my immediate instinct was to follow her. I knew she would be broken, and I wanted to help her pick up the pieces and mend her. Fuck, I'd do it alone if she wasn't capable. I wanted to be that for her.

I was there when she crumbled, catching her right at the last second, just before her body hit the concrete. I sat there on the ground, holding her unconscious in my arms, rocking her gently, and kissing her pale face until she came back to me.

"Wake up, Baby, please. I'm here." I whispered, swiping her hair away from her face. "No one will ever hurt you again. Come back to me, Baby."

Slowly, Jamie opened her eyes, and I picked her up and took her to the car. I placed her into the passenger's seat and buckled her in before stepping behind the wheel and driving her straight to our hotel.

While she was out, I had instructed Jimmy and Mike to stay behind and pull the truth from that fucker. Jamie would eventually want answers, and when she did, I'd have them ready for her. There was no way I would allow her to ever deal with that sorry excuse of a human being ever again.

My men would force it out of him if he held back, and if he didn't break, they had *carte blanche* to break him and dispose of the remains once they had what we needed. Either way, he didn't get to live. That fucker was a waste of space and oxygen.

Why, who, and where. That was probably all she would need to know once she was ready for the truth.

Never in my wildest dreams could I have imagined that that was what awaited us. Jamie's reaction was warranted, and I couldn't help but wonder if she had endured that kind of abuse her whole life and if there was more I still didn't know.

Family was a pillar in my life, the absolute best thing in this world. I'd die for mine, as well as kill. In a fucking heartbeat.

Meaning that witnessing that fucker mistreat *my* woman messed with me in the most primal of ways.

We had been in our room for over half an hour and Jamie was still in the same position – sitting in the middle of the bed, her shaking arms hugging her knees to her chest while her skin was soaking in tears.

I gave her the space I thought she needed to process the information, deciding not to speak or ask her anything for the time being.

There were a million and one fucking questions running through my mind, but I knew now wasn't the time. Jamie was lost in the universe of her own thoughts, hardly blinking as the tears fell freely down her face.

I paced back and forth, trying to ease the wrath that coursed through my body, fighting the need to go back and finish that fucker off. The world would be a better place without him. But still, beating him to death was too good for him. He deserved a lifetime of torture and constant punishment for what he put this beautiful creature through.

Coming clean to Jamie was one of the hardest things I'd ever done in my life. There were so many things that could have gone wrong. My life was most literally in her hands, and I could have dealt with any consequence of my actions. But worse than the risk of her going to the police, or even our enemies, was the possibility of her hating me. That would have been more lethal than anything else.

I had promised to control myself in her presence. Never show her the violence that tainted my life. But today I couldn't help myself. The bloodlust was a fucking moving force that gripped me by the balls.

I craved that fucker's screams. I fed off of each gasp for air. I wanted nothing more than to drain the life out of him slowly and painfully.

I couldn't bear listening to that mother fucker abusing *my* woman. I couldn't bear seeing her suffer. And I was the one who pushed her into it again.

Guilt was running through my veins like a fucking poison.

I couldn't come close to imagining what Jamie had gone through her whole life. Now I finally understood why her job at AD and her life in New York were so precious to her. It meant being away from her old life, being free from a lifetime of abuse, inflicted by the person who should love her the most in this fucked up world. That was what AD meant to her.

And to think I had almost fucked that up for her.

There was no way I was allowing anyone to ever hurt her again.

I stopped pacing, noticing that the room had suddenly gone silent. Her small cries had quieted, her breathing had finally evened out.

Jamie had stopped crying and her body was steady, no more shaking. Her expression was still pained, her normal light dimmed down to overcast shadows. There was something in her eyes that resembled hope or closure, I couldn't be sure.

I calmly walked towards the bed, sitting on the edge.

"Jamie," I called, cupping her cheek until she was looking into my eyes.

"I'm okay." She said with a small voice.

"Are you sure? You can talk to me. I'm here for you." I assured her. There was no place on Earth I'd rather be than right here, trying to mend the broken pieces of an angel.

"Liam, I didn't want you to find out like this. I'm sorry."

"There's nothing to be sorry about. Why are you apologizing for something you didn't do?"

"I was weak, Liam. I know that. I never did anything to stop it. I just let him do that to me every single day and never fought back. I'm not the strong person you thought I was. I'm a fraud. You need someone strong, someone who can stand their ground in your world."

"What? You are the only person I need beside me." I reassured her, making her meet my gaze once more. "You left this. You stood up for yourself and went after what you needed and wanted. You got out. Now that I know this about you, I can't even begin to tell you how proud I am of you. How could you have endured this your whole life and still become this amazing person?"

I took her lips in mine, hoping that she could feel the truth in every word I had spoken through that kiss.

Jamie's eyes lingered shut for a while after I pulled back, inhaling sharply as if conjuring courage before she spoke again. "Do you remember that night on my birthday when Michelle was at your apartment?"

"I do. I had never been so disappointed to see a naked woman in my apartment before." I tried to lighten the mood with a small joke.

"You came to my apartment and took care of me. You stayed even after I sent you away. Held me when all I needed was a shoulder to cry on. That was the first time I felt cared for in my whole life." She confessed, her eyes not meeting mine as if she was ashamed of her own words, keeping her gaze on the mattress as she continued. "That was the night I fell in love with you."

Jamie

There was a battle raging inside me.

I should be devastated by that revelation. I should be crying my heart out knowing that Frank wasn't my father after all. That my life was a lie.

But instead, the only thing I could bring myself to feel was relief. And guilty for feeling relieved. Just like I felt guilty for not caring that Liam was in the mafia and all the things that were inherently attached to that by definition.

Alison's words came rushing back into my head about preconceptions of right and wrong.

I couldn't fight this feeling, it was too strong to suppress or ignore.

I was relieved to know that the only person I thought should love me unconditionally and never had wasn't that person after all.

Relieved to know that Frank's hateful words were never about me. They were nothing but a reflection of what he felt about himself.

Relieved to know that I was not what he had made me to believe, and glad that by some miracle, I didn't allow his abuse to define my life.

Frank *not* being my father lifted a weight I carried since the moment I drew my first breath.

For a moment, I thought I would be afraid of Liam after what I saw him do. After the unhinged look in his eyes, the rage in his body, the anger in his voice, and the violence of his actions.

Liam didn't care for the life that was draining out under the pressure of his fingers. There was no remorse in his eyes. But to my surprise, Liam made me feel what I never thought possible.

I felt safe, cared for, and most of all, loved.

When I heard Liam saying that *I* was the only person he needed beside him, I just allowed my emotions to take over and told him exactly how I felt. It seemed like today was my day of truths.

"I'm sorry. It's stupid, and too soon, and a very strange moment to tell you this, but I've never had that before. I've never had someone hug me while I cried. Snuggle with me the whole night while I was hurting. You did all that. And today, you did it again. I mean… I think

I'm just trying to say thank you." I blurted, my cheeks flushed in embarrassment while I stared at the white sheet and drew nervous circles on it with my index finger.

Liam grabbed my wrist and pulled me onto his lap until I was straddling him. He held my face in his hands and kissed me. His lips worshiped mine slowly in a passionate kiss that melted my soul and fired up my heart, making me sink deeper into his touch.

The kiss grew wilder before he pulled back, resting his forehead on mine as his lips curled into a blindingly perfect smile.

"You fell in love with me…" He taunted, his smile widening as he said it, lighting up his beautiful green eyes.

"I hum… I…" His words and his deep gaze made me blush and stutter. Liam put his index finger on my lips in a gesture for me to stop talking.

Liam looked into my eyes, still holding that big smile, and swiped a loose strand of hair behind my ear before making my whole world crumble at his feet.

"And *I* love you, Jamie Harden."

It was cliché, but my heart skipped a couple of beats as I heard those words, my stomach fluttering while my throat blocked in joy.

How could this be my life? Liam loved me, too.

I wrapped my arms around his neck and hugged him, pushing his back onto the bed, an immense feeling of happiness flooding my every pore.

This was the safest place in the world to be, cradled in Liam's arms. I nestled against his side, his arm around my body while his fingers drew circles on my skin.

We stayed like that for a while, in a comfortable silence that breathed devotion, before Liam spoke. "Are you okay, Baby?" His voice was soft, treading carefully not to burst this perfect bubble.

"I am. I really think I am. I'm relieved he isn't my father. He never loved me, never cared for me, so knowing that he isn't my father comes as a relief somehow. It all makes sense now. My mother fell in love with someone else, and I'm the living reminder of it. She died giving birth to me, and he still loved her despite everything. That only makes him hate me more."

"Don't try to understand his actions, Jamie. There's no good enough reason to do that to a child. Never mind your own daughter." Liam was trying as hard as he could to keep his temper at bay, his hand balling my t-shirt into his fist.

"I'm not. What I'm saying is that now it doesn't hurt as much, if that makes sense."

I felt free somehow. Lighter and less bruised.

"What you saw wasn't even the worst of it. He used to lock me in the basement or in the closet for days on end."

"Fucking asshole!" He growled, my bones rattling by his enraged tone alone. I pulled up and kissed him softly, trying to calm him down. Somehow, for the first time, I could finally speak about it without shame, without guilt. Liam had infused me with courage and love, and I knew that there would be no judgment.

"That's where my fear of closed spaces comes from."

"It figures." There was pain in his expression, running just as wild as the anger that burned behind those green eyes of his.

"That's why I was shaking before you attacked me in the elevator at AD the day we met."

"Fuck! I'm so sorry, Jamie. I'm such an asshole."

"No. You most definitely are not. That was the best elevator ride of my life. I have dreamed about it and you every night since." He chuckled lightly, the darkness in his eyes clearing just a little. "What?"

Liam pulled me onto his body, my legs straddling him while my arms caged him beneath me. "You loved me then?"

"Well, maybe I did," I replied with a sneaky smile.

"I loved you then, too. I just couldn't make sense of it."

I smiled wider at his confession. A kind of smile that came from deep inside my heart and spread to my whole body. Threading my fingers through his dark hair, I leaned down and kissed him with all the passion and love I could put in a kiss. It started off slow but quickly grew wilder.

Liam's hands glided down my body, grasping my ass and pulling me into him, making me feel just how much I affected him.

"This is what you do to me, Miss Harden. Every single time since I first laid eyes on you."

Liam's phone rang, cutting off the tension that was building, but it was a different ringtone than I was used to hearing from his calls. By the way Liam sprung up from the bed, he knew exactly who was calling.

I watched him walk across the room and answer. "Hi, Matt. What's up?" Liam's voice was etched with annoyance even though it was his own brother calling. "Can't this wait?"

He fell silent, and I watched as his features darkened again, his jaw clenched in a tight bite. "I'll be back in a couple of days." It was clear on his face that Matt didn't agree with that, Liam's face growing even more tense. "Fine. I'll be there tomorrow after lunch."

Without another word, Liam hung up and threw the phone onto the bed. I wasn't about to pry even though I was curious about what was so urgent that required Liam's presence back in New York, so instead,I simply smiled.

But Liam wasn't having it. He let his body fall onto the mattress in a slump, his weight making the whole bed jiggle.

"We still have tonight," I said, trying to ease him up, swapping my disappointment for hope. I wasn't ready to go back to reality. I needed more time alone with Liam, more time in our little bubble that we had still barely entered. But Liam's expression didn't change. "Anything serious?"

"It's just business that needs my attention right away. I'm sorry, Love." Apparently my attempts to sound light were feeble. He had seen right through me.

What would it mean for us to be back to reality? Would Liam want to be discreet, keep whatever this was just between the two of us? Or be open?

I wasn't sure what was the best approach. When you're in a good place and show it, it's so much easier for anyone to screw it up.

Not to forget that Liam still was, in fact, my boss. How much gossip will that particular detail render at AD?

"I'll need to head straight to Dea Tacita once we arrive." His voice was heavy, matching his frown and his heavy steps as he got up and made his way to the bar set in the other corner of the suite and poured himself a drink. Not even a second later, the whole thing was gone, spilled down his throat in one single gulp.

"It's okay," I reassured, making my way towards him, snaking my arms around his waist and hugging him from behind. "It's not a big deal. I can get an Uber when we arrive."

As I finished that sentence, Liam turned around, his hand sliding across my lower back, right on the edge of decency. He held me tightly against him, my head resting on his muscled chest.

"What if I took you on a date tonight? A real one."

"Hm, I'm not sure. Convince me."

Liam spun me around before pulling me into him again, my ass tightly snuggled against his crotch. With one hand cupping my pussy while the other harshly grabbed my boob, he whispered, "I'm parading you as mine tonight, Miss Harden, and when I'm done with that, I'm eating this pussy for dessert."

CHAPTER TWENTY EIGHT

Jamie

"Y ou look ravishing, Miss Harden," Liam said as I came down the stairs to meet him in the lobby. We'd gotten ready separately, trying to mimic what an actual date would be like.

Liam's teasing had heated me up inside, so I'd chosen the sexiest outfit I had in my suitcase. The same little black dress I had worn on my birthday paired with stilettos and a skimpy black thong underneath.

Liam waited for me at the bottom of the stairs, his hand stretched out for me to take. He was devouring me with his eyes, practically undressing me with his gaze, his green orbs turning darker the closer I got. His stare made me feel sexy as I swayed my way over towards him. There was an unusual confidence under my strut, all because of the way Liam looked at me.

"So fucking ravishing." He groaned in my ear as soon as I was in his arms, that low husky voice of his sending delightful shivers down my spine. My knees trembled under that tone and my pussy desperately craved his attention.

"Is this too much?" I gave him the full view with a little twirl, making sure to slow down when my back was to him, showing off how tight the dress was around my ass.

"It's perfect. I'm a good fighter, I can take out any fucker that dares to drool over what's mine. Besides, my gun is loaded and ready to go."

His possessiveness was exhilarating, and not even the mention of his weapon cooled the heat that pooled between my legs.

"You look quite dashing yourself, Mr. Dornier." Liam was wearing a black suit, tailored to his fit body, paired with a white dress shirt and no tie. I let my eyes roam his figure as I praised him, tucking my bottom lip between my teeth, the image of his sculpted muscles under the layers of clothes making my mouth water.

"Let's get this date out of the way, shall we? I'm suddenly desperate to have you in my bed again." He grunted, untucking my lip from the iron clasp of my teeth with the pad of his thumb.

With a hand on the small of my back, Liam steered me towards the car where the two men I'd seen yesterday were waiting. They had caution etched into their features, but I felt them soften as soon as we approached, even though not an inch of their scowls gave in.

They both slid into the front seats while Liam held the back door open for me before stepping inside the car beside me. I was in a vehicle filled to the brim with mafia men, yet, until this day, I'd never felt safer in my life.

The drive was short and charged with a lustful energy that wouldn't give. Side glances and chaste touches were all Liam was giving me, together with a calm façade that didn't match the erratic beat of my heart whenever his thumb came full circle around the back of my hand.

All I saw in those glances was the disguised craving for more. Candid smiles that bit back on all the sordid desires, tamed to give me this moment of pure romance. Was I projecting? Most probably.

There was something about the wait, about the expectation of what was to come. The anticipation was burning on both ends of my fuse. I couldn't wait to see what happened when both sparks met in the middle.

Liam had booked us a table at a fine dining restaurant. One where I couldn't dare to check out the price list. Chandeliers ornated the ceiling while simple yet exquisite dinnerware covered the tables with glamor.

My eyes bulged as I took in the exquisite decor. My head snapping right and left, taking it all in, just like the poor unaccustomed-to-wealth girl that I was.

"Liam," I called, my grasp on his arm suddenly pulling back.

He stopped in his regal stride, knowing exactly where my hesitance came from, turning to face me. "None of that tonight. We are on a date, Miss Harden. I'm a gentleman, the kind that doesn't do halfsies. Better start getting used to it."

He sealed the discussion with a kiss to my lips that told me there was no argument and that nothing I said would make him change his mind.

I nodded once and let him lead us behind the maitre d' as he directed us to our table. Liam pulled out my chair like the gentleman he was, fixing me with a massive smile as I took my seat, melting me right on the spot.

The waitress came to take our order, and I couldn't help but feel like I was reliving this exact moment. A dejá vu kind of thing, one that had left a bitter taste in my mouth. I'd lived out this very scene before.

The woman taking our order was practically drooling over Liam, her lashes batting towards him faster than my damn heart.

Jealousy crept up my spine watching Liam politely smile back at her as they spoke, discussing the wine list and taking forever to choose a damn bottle. My fingers balled my napkin in my fist, leaving hard wrinkles on the pristine fabric that would probably never again be ironed out.

She placed her hand on Liam's shoulder as she faked her laugh, taking the opportunity to feel for herself how well he filled out that damn suit.

The daggers that shot from my eyes towards them were sharp and cutting, and I didn't even bother to disguise them.

"I think a *Chateau Lafite* is a good choice, if my wife agrees," Liam said as soon as he noticed my frown. His devilish grin spread across his face while I raised an eyebrow at the sound of those words. The waitress's eyes widened, and she scrambled away with her flirty tail tucked between her legs, only returning to fill our glasses and bring our food.

I'd never seen myself as one of those jealous girlfriends who couldn't stand seeing any woman merely talking to her man, but it just seemed that everywhere I went with Liam, there was always some tramp dying for him to get in their pants.

"I hope you find the restaurant suitable for our first date, Miss Harden"

"It's quite alright." I wave it off, my annoyance clear in my petulance. "The staff needs better manners, though."

"Jealousy suits you, Love. But there's no need for it. I'm yours, Baby. There's no woman on this earth that can so much as hold a candle to my girlfriend." My heart skipped a beat, easing my frustration, even if just a little.

My heart swelled with pride at that definition. *Girlfriend.* There was just a different ring to it when Liam said it out loud. Possession and claim draped over the word, but there was pride in his tone, too, and that was something I don't recall anyone ever feeling towards me.

We ate and chatted without a care in the world, the comfort between us ran as deep as if we'd been doing this together our whole lives. I could be myself with Liam and the same applied to him. This lighter side of him wasn't something he showed often or to just about anyone, so seeing it came with a sense that I was privileged to witness this shade of him.

"Tell me something about yourself that I don't already know," I asked, watching as Liam's eyebrow raised in question. "It's a date, we are supposed to get to know each other."

"You already know pretty much everything there is to know about me, even the parts you shouldn't. But I can see there's something specific hiding behind that question."

"Well, I'm just intrigued. You said you're Italian, yet your last name is French. I know your father is French. There's no faking an accent like his. That leaves your family on your mother's side."

"Correct. Is there a question in there somewhere?"

I laughed, noticing that all the above were facts. I was trying to find my own questions, but I wasn't sure where exactly to start.

"What Mafia are we talking? Italian? Is there such thing as a French Mafia? I guess you couldn't use Dornier as your Mafia name so as not to tarnish AD's business, or is AD a façade? Who's the leader?" I whispered in a frenzy, forgetting to stop so Liam could answer. He laughed at my onslaught, taking a sip of his wine before replying.

"It's Italian Mafia. No, AD is not a façade. My father hates everything about the business with a passion. We use my Grandfather's name, and he's the Don, or what you referred to as leader, while Matt is his second in command, or *sottocapo*. Did I get them all?" His tone was playful as he stretched a finger each time he replied to a question, counting them out.

"Almost, but no. What's the name you go by then?"

"Battaglia." He took a sip of his wine as if he was washing his mouth after that revelation. I mimicked his movements but licked my lips after the rich liquid made its way down my throat.

"Battaglia." I repeated, trying to replicate the Italian accent he'd used, the word coating my tongue like velvet lust. "It's sexy. Suits you like a second skin."

Liam's jaw clenched, his features darkening, even if just a shade, before he quickly changed the subject back to me. "What about you? Tell me something about you that I don't know."

Bingo. Right where I want you.

I was expecting him to throw my question back at me. I took his hand and placed my closed fist in it, releasing the thong I'd wiggled out of during our conversation and closing his hand around it.

"I'm not wearing any underwear," I whispered, my eyes bored into his. I didn't want to lose a second of his reaction. His eyes darkened first, while his tongue swiped across his bottom lip second, before a wicked grin spread his lips.

"Play nice, Miss Harden." He warned in an exhilarating sing-song that was drenched in danger. Liam took his clenched fist to his nose, inhaling deeply while his eyes closed in delight. "Smells like dessert."

That hoarse voice of his had stepped down into a low tone that messed with everything inside me. The lingering promise behind his words making me tingle in all the right places.

"Should we take it to go?" I urged.

"For fucking sure," Liam replied, motioning for the check. It was clear that with that single little push, he was ready to go just about as much as I was.

"Meet you up front, Mr. *Battaglia*." I made sure to emphasize his name as I stood up and straightened my dress, my hands slowly traveling down my body. "I'm going to freshen up before we go."

I could feel Liam's eyes on me as I walked away towards the restroom, adding an extra sway to my ass for his viewing pleasure. Wetness was already pooling between my legs as the expectation of what was to come made my clit tingle in anticipation.

Liam had made sure to give me space after everything that happened at my father's. At Frank's, I mean. So I thought that an incentive wouldn't hurt to show him that I was okay.

The bathroom was empty and just as luxurious as the rest of the place. The large mirror behind the vanities made it look even bigger than what it already was. I splashed some water on my cheeks, my hand damping some coolness on my neck.

I was giddy, as if it was the first time we were about to have sex. It didn't make sense, but I felt the anxiety anyway. Maybe it was the build-up, the notion that it was definitely happening, the desire firing up inside me.

Before I could decide on the meaning for my nervousness, the door to the bathroom burst open, only to shut with double the violence. I spun towards it, my heart racing in a different way now, not slowing even after seeing who it was.

"Liam," I called out in half relief, half surprise. He had that dangerous look in his eyes again, making me shiver right down to my core.

"You don't think you can tempt the beast and not be punished for it, do you?" He marched towards me, reaching me in under two wide strides and spinning me so that my back was against his front.

He continued to walk forward, his erection pushing into my ass and forcing me to move at his will until my thighs hit the sink.

"I told you to play nice, Miss Harden. What should I do to such a bad girl like you?"

"Oh God." I moaned in reply, his hand gripping my breast with force while his teeth sunk into my neck. "Someone might see us."

"Imagine how jealous they will be. This is what you get for being naughty." He groaned into my ear, and before I knew it, my dress was scrunched around my waist, his fingers tracing my dripping slit from behind. "Is this all for me?"

I watched him take his fingers to his mouth and suck on them before a rumble resounded from his chest. It was like a switch had been flicked in his mind. He kicked my feet apart and pulled out his hard cock, slamming into me without restraint.

I couldn't hold the half gasp, half moan that ripped through my throat, my hand landing on the mirror in front of us in a feeble attempt to steady myself.

"You can't expect to call to the darkest side of me and not pay the price." Liam pulled all the way out before plunging into me again, the force of it making my thighs hit the marble. "Say it again." Another punishing thrust.

"Mr. Battaglia." I gasped between his relentless assaults. My body trembled with excitement, all my muscles taut with the thrill of what was happening.

"This is what you fucking do to me, Miss Harden. You drive me completely insane. How could I wait to get home when you're already dripping wet for me, hum?"

"Oh my God, Liam."

"Turn around." He pulled out and spun me around before lifting me onto the sink and sliding inside me again. "Your dress barely covers your ass, and you decide to walk around the damn restaurant with no underwear?"

His thrusts were harder than before, pulling me towards him each time, my body colliding into his with brutal force. It was meant as punishment, but my body was taking it like a damn prize. There was heat rising from my core to my chest. The fact that anyone could simply walk in on us and catch us having sex was nearly inflammatory.

I let my head fall back in delight as I took his wrath, but Liam wasn't having it. His hand grasped my jaw, pulling my eyes back onto his before his lips crashed onto mine like thunder in a harsh and greedy kiss.

My body burned everywhere he touched and pained everywhere he didn't. My chest heaved with my rapid, uncontrolled breathing as Liam fucked me with abandon.

Liam bit down on my lip as he pushed into me again, my eyes rolling to the back of my head in pure pleasure. He was a man possessed - possessing me and claiming each piece of me for himself. Something about this primal side of Liam lit a fire in me, daring me to talk back. I let the weight of my body be held by one hand while the other reached for his hair, fisting it, followed by a tug.

"Your turn. Say it again. Who am I?"

A growl rumbled from his chest, settling right on my clit, making it throb in excitement. "You're my girlfriend. You're fucking mine, Jamie."

Liam's thrusts became more frantic, quicker and more desperate. He was almost over the hill, pulling me along with him. With one last strong thrust, he made both of us come, our bodies trembling under the rush of pleasure.

"Mine," He groaned as he coated me with his cum, my legs trembling as each pump intensified the pleasure soaring through my body. My whole body shook with the electric current that drove through my veins as I pulsed around him.

"Yours," I whispered, my forehead resting against his as we both caught our breath. It was incredible how, with Liam, soft and sweet did it just as much as quick and hard. I was always craving his touch, to get lost in his kisses, to revel in our intimacy, whatever shape or form that took on.

"The things you make me do, Miss Harden." He teased as he pulled out before helping me to my feet and grabbing a handful of paper towels.

"I think I need to misbehave more often, Mr. Battaglia."

"That was tame, Jamie. Next time you won't get off so easily." It was supposed to be a warning, but somehow, all my brain could register was the thrilling goad behind his words.

Bring it on, Mr. Battaglia.

Art by Xavier Guzman

CHAPTER TWENTY NINE

Jamie

Liam held a tumbler of bourbon in one hand while the other was gripping the armrest of the jet's seat since take off. A little over two hours in, and he had yet to utter a word. His jaw was tense, clenching in rhythmic pulses as something rummaged around his brain that clearly had him tipping into the shadows that lurked in his mind.

I was sure it was related to the reason Matt had called on him to be back in New York ASAP. Was it related to the Mafia? I was almost sure since Liam had dodged every question or conversation about it.

My finger worked in circles on the back of his hand, adopting a calm and soothing rhythm that still did nothing to pull him from the darkness. I watched as the direness etched in his features grew as we got closer to home. Shades of murk clouding his otherwise perfect face.

I had demons lurking in the corner of my mind, too. The uncertainty of what *this* would look like once we were back to our lives was eating at me inside, still holding on for dear life to the hope that when our little happy bubble burst, it wouldn't be as bloody as I somehow felt it was going to be.

I'd only had Liam to myself for a couple days, and I was greedy for more. I didn't want to share him with his life, his business, or even with AD. I wanted more of the dreamy reality we had in LA. Just the two of us, away from everyone and everything that could somehow break this.

I looked up at Liam again, his brows furrowed into a knot of worry that twisted my gut and shattered my heart. Scurrying through last night's conversation, I tried my best to find a light topic that could maybe distract him from whatever wrinkled his perfect complexion. So I set my tone to candy-sweet as I plastered a smile on my face before pulling him out of his trance.

"Mr. Battaglia," I called, waiting for him to look at me. He seemed to have enjoyed hearing me call him that last night, even though right now my tone wasn't drenched in covet as it had been the night before. "Can I ask you another one of my intruding questions?"

"Of course," Liam replied, a light chuckle escaping his chest and immediately changing his semblance.

I fixed myself on the seat before asking, the movement granting me another smile that didn't quite meet his eyes. "From what my books imply, Italians have a strong sense of pride in their legacy. Why don't you or your brother and sister have more Italian-based names?"

"Is Matteo not Italian enough for you?"

"Well, okay, maybe it is. But Liam isn't, and definitely not Alison, either."

"Like I told you yesterday, my father nurtures a special hate for all things Mafia-related. Starting with anything my Grandfather could hold dear. When Matt was born, the big and famous Adrian Dornier was still making a name for himself, mostly traveling around the world, and he was hardly ever around. Let's just say that my mother won round one and managed to stamp her heritage on my brother, from his name all the way down to his DNA. Matt breathes this stuff as if it were the oxygen in his lungs. But when it came to me and Alison, my father was adamant about drawing a different path for our lives, even choosing our names himself. Liam and Alison, French-influenced, of course." He paused, taking a sip from the third refill of bourbon in his hand. "Didn't do him much good, though. I was still brought up and raised as a mafioso. It seems like he wasn't around as much as he thought he was. Even so, he still managed to rub off on our interests in some way. Both Alison and I still followed in his footsteps, although I do think Alison did it to please him more than herself. Matt, though? He was already a lost cause to Dad."

There were hints of heavy issues in his words. Still, my intention wasn't to drench him further into the darkness but to bring him back to the light.

"Thus Matt being in charge."

"Partly. It's in his blood. Matt doesn't exist without the Mafia side, they don't dissociate. It's who he is. He just loves the whole thing."

"What about you?" I bit my tongue as soon as the words left my mouth, and the tension that returned to Liam's face told me I had stepped exactly where I didn't mean to.

He downed the whole content of the glass before inhaling deeply to reply. "I used to." It was an admission that I saw cut deep. Liam watched my face, wary of any negative reactions, but I was free of judgment in this conversation. All I wanted was to know him, understand him, love him as he was.

"What changed?" I dared to ask.

Liam's green irises bored into me in silence for a while as he chose his words carefully. Suddenly I felt stupid to be picking at a scab that seemed to be better off left alone.

"Something happened about a week before I met you. It changed me." I wanted to pry further, but if Liam felt the need to leave it hanging in the air between us, it was because it wasn't the right time for him to tell me. It bothered him deeply, that much was clear.

His fingers were back to digging into the leather seat while he gestured to the flight attendant for a refill. Maybe someday he'll trust me enough to tell me about it.

"Does Alison also work with you and Matt?" I found myself changing the subject, eager to fill a silence that was far from comfortable.

"No. We try as hard as we can to leave her out of it. Just as I tried to stay away from you."

"What? Why?"

"This life comes with hazard attached to the leg like a fucking leach, Jamie. Those books of yours? They romanticize what they shouldn't. You shouldn't want me. You weren't supposed to come back after I told you what I was."

"Is that what you want?" My voice was broken, suddenly feeling that Liam was pushing away again.

"Fuck, no. But that just makes me even more of a selfish son of a bitch. I want you so bad that it fucking hurts. The criminal in me doesn't give a damn about consequences, but the part of me that bleeds for you? That part is petrified of the day that this life will bring you harm."

Liam

"How was LA?" Matt asked from behind the curtain of smoke he had just puffed into the air. His expression was heavy, his eyes shaded by a darkness that told me whatever business he needed me for wasn't going to be of my liking.

More so, he was sitting on one of the brown leather couches in his office at Dea Tacita, waiting for me. Not behind his desk, on the couch. That detail alone told me that more than business, this was personal.

"Better than New York," I replied, my tone clipped as I plumped onto the couch opposite from him. I didn't mask the bitterness I was feeling. I was still wound up about being forced to cut the trip short.

"So I've gathered. I hope she was worth the risk you took by traveling solo." There was a scold in there somewhere, but I couldn't bring myself to give a fuck.

I was blinded by an emotion I'd yet to experience in my life, something that turned smart decisions into stupid impulses. Those still left a sly smile plastered on my face each time her face popped into my brain.

"Damn right, she is." My words were dry, but the grin plastered on my face spoke much louder.

"Fuck. You're a goner."

"Proudly so. She knows everything, Matt. I told her, and she still came back. She still found it in her heart to fucking come back." It was still unbelievable to me. How could such an angel accept a darkness that would surely stain her wings in crimson? "I'm happy when I'm with her. When was the last time I said that word? When I was ten?"

"You love her?" Matt's eyes were softer, holding something resembling pity.

"I do."

"Jesus fuck." He leaned forward, his fingers cradling his temples as he shook his head left and right in some sort of denial I didn't understand. "You just made this so much harder."

"What are you talking about?" I demanded, leaning forward in a match of his position, supporting my elbows on my legs.

"The Amatos decided what they want in exchange for keeping the peace." My eyes fluttered closed in preparation for whatever blow was about to come my way.

"Spit." I finally said, half ready for whatever was weighing so heavily on his shoulders, while the other half dreaded the sentence I knew was coming.

"They want you to marry Enzo Amato's niece, Francesca, tying the families together." My heart sank to the pit of my stomach and my blood ran cold in my veins. I couldn't fucking believe this was happening.

"FUCK NO!" I roared, springing up from the couch in protest.

The Amato Family controlled Detroit's territory, and Enzo Amato was their undisputed Don.

By blood you enter by fucking blood you leave.

My Omertá hung heavy on my shoulders ever since that dreadful day a couple of months ago. The one that stole my life away from my grip as I still waited for my sentence.

The wait was over, this was it.

Not even my grandfather, the mighty Giancarlo Battaglia, could save me from this one.

Only a week shy from meeting Jamie, I had met a girl in a white dress at one of the 7-Elevens we provided protection for up in Tremont. We started talking in one of the back aisles, flirting, setting a date for me to take her out, when out of fucking nowhere, a group of masked kids came in to rob the place.

Three came right in through the front door while the other two came from the back. I was alone with her and completely surrounded.

I fought them off as best I could, taking their blows as if they were throwing feathers instead of punches. My gun was on the floor, taken from its holster as soon as they got to me. They didn't seem like experienced criminals, but they weren't stupid either, and leaving me with a gun would have been a huge mistake.

Three to one wasn't good odds, but I tried anyway. When the other two were added against me, it took less than a minute before my face was scrunched against the dirty, tiled floor, the barrel of a gun snuggly pressed against the back of my skull.

If I closed my eyes, I could still see the image of the dirty soles of the Chucks that pressed my cheek into the slimy floor.

My fate was sealed, right then and there, until the girl in white charged at them with a bottle of booze in a feeble attempt to get them off me long enough for me to escape my certain death.

Several shots rang in a row, half my damn magazine emptied into the beautiful creature who had dared to try and save the devil. One of the thugs had picked up my gun and aimed to kill.

Three damn shots to the chest.

The silence that followed was deafening, only to be broken by the shattering of the bottle she held in her hand seconds before her body hit the ground.

293

Two seconds too late, Jimmy and Mike came running into the place, the five boys escaping through the back door. I hustled up and nestled her slim body in my arms, trying to stop the flow of blood that left her chest in torrents.

She died in my arms, staining me, my soul, and my conscience with her blood.

Only, I had no idea that that girl was Amelia Amato, Enzo's only daughter. She was killed with my gun, on my watch, in my fucking territory.

The whole robbery was a stunt the owner pulled, trying to lower the price he paid us for our services. All the security cameras had miraculously malfunctioned at that time, leaving me without proof of what actually happened.

The Amato family blamed me. I would, too. In fact, I did and still do blame myself.

They thought I was the one who killed her.

Thankfully, my grandfather is an old shark, a respected Don in the Mafia's extended *famiglia*, and before the Amatos could finish me off, he decided to convey The Commission and have them rule over my fate.

This consortium of mafiosos, called The Commission, was composed of the five most influential Dons on this side of the pond, who regulated the Italian underworld. Both my grandfather and Enzo Amato were on it, which somehow ended up playing in my favor for at least some time.

That is how peace was kept between the different *Coscas* in the *Cosa Nostra*. Five old men dealing the cards as if they were either light bringers or the damn Grim Reaper.

Rules didn't matter when you were the Lord of the fucking food chain. They can flip it with less than a snap of their fingers. Kings to peasants in nothing but a blink.

The rules are theirs to make and theirs to break. That's what power means.

Lords of the Commission.

That was what we called them.

My life was ripped from my bare hands that day, and now they have come to take the little that was left. They were taking the best part of it.

My Jamie.

It took a moment for Matt's words to truly sink in, but when they did, I was far gone, beyond feral, beyond fucking insane. I had just barely tasted the sweetness of happiness with Jamie, only to be left with a sour taste in my mouth.

In the space of a sentence, I had gone from thoughts of forever with the woman I love, to being certain she would never be mine.

A switch inside my mind had flipped. In the midst and havoc of my rage, I hadn't even noticed the destruction I'd already bestowed upon Matt's office until he grabbed me from behind and shouted into my ear.

"There's nothing we can do about it." He repeated as Mike and Jimmy helped him pin me back onto the couch. "Breathe, Liam."

I did as he said.

In through the nose, out through the mouth.

Repeat.

In through the nose, out through the mouth.

The fog in my mind was far from clearing, but the killer in me was fighting for the front row in my mind, and he always came with a bone-chilling coldness.

There was a part of me that I always fought, the part that eclipsed all light still left inside me, but right now, my light had been threatened to be put out forever.

My hands were drenched in sin, to the point of no return, each body piling higher on my unaffected conscience, but hers weighed like a fucking cinder block.

I willed my rage to simmer down to just below the surface, underlining my thin skin. I needed it to consume me, burn me like wildfire so that I could find a fucking solution as soon as possible.

I didn't feel guilty for those five pricks I sent six feet under only a week after it all happened. I only felt guilty for the pieces of my soul that died along with them.

Those feelings, that dark place, my own personal inferno was where I needed to be right now. My head deeply focused and in the game.

"They can't do this," I growled back, my demeanor changing to an unsettling calmness while my heart broke to never be mended.

"They already have. The Commission has agreed. You'll marry in a couple of months. That's how long you have with Jamie. You know it has to end once you marry Francesca."

I pulled my arms free from Mike and Jimmy's grasp, folding over myself and holding my head in my hands in total despair. How was I going to tell Jamie? How was she not going to hate me after this?

After everything that happened these past few days, I hated knowing I was going to break her heart again.

I couldn't hold on to this for two damn months, but I needed time to figure out a solution. I couldn't lie and say that slaughtering them all hadn't been the first thing to cross my mind. But *they* were figures too easily replaced. The Lords of the Commission were an entity far greater than the people who stood in the circle. They would never die simply because *they* were every fucking Mafiosi they represented.

Still, if there was even the slightest chance for me to avoid going through with this marriage, I would take it, no matter the cost.

Not being with Jamie killed me, and knowing that by not having her I would be handing her over to someone else killed me even more.

I stood back up and paced the length of the huge floor-to-ceiling window that overlooked Dea Tacita, my brain running wild on different scenarios, but none of them fit the predicament.

Jamie… I closed my eyes, letting her sweet scent invade my memory as I inhaled deeply as if she was standing right in front of me.

"What the fuck am I going to do, Matt? Huh? I can't get married!"

I wasn't finding any immediate solution. If The Commission had ruled, there was no fucking way out besides inside of a damn body bag. The problem was that no one could ever predict who would be inside it.

I couldn't risk it.

The alliance this marriage would forge between us and the Amatos served them more than it did us. They were a powerful *cosca*, but the Battaglias still casted a fucking gigantic shadow over their little family.

Having our name associated with theirs would raise their status tenfold, giving them more power than they had ever seen. Translation – they would do anything in their grasp to ensure that this fucking marriage happened.

"Liam, there's no way around this. You have to tell her. You have to end it. Because if you don't, for your sake and hers, I will." Matt coldly said. He wasn't trying to be an ass, as much as those words seemed exactly like it. I knew what he meant. And fuck, he was right.

"She'll hate me forever and beyond." I exhaled, closing my eyes and falling back onto the couch in defeat.

"Perfect. That means she'll stay away and stay safe. She knows too much already."

I never thought of it that way when I told her about us. What she knew, even if it was close to nothing, was still enough to paint a damn target on her back, and knowing that I cared for her would just magnify the fucking bullseye.

"I have to bring her here. Every single soldier, associate, or ally of ours needs to remember her face if, for any reason, shit hits the fucking fan." I was telling him, a mere courtesy, not asking for permission. I had to make sure she was safe. Always.

"Okay, do whatever you think you have to do, but tell her. And do it fast before the whole situation gets out of hand."

"Does anyone else know about this? Does Alison know?" I asked. Alison and Jamie had grown close, and I was afraid Alison wouldn't manage to watch her friend get burnt and try to do something stupid, like warn her. Her heart would be in the right place, but the clusterfuck that could ensue was unpredictable.

"No. Only you, me, and Pops." He meant our grandfather, of course.

I sighed in relief. I had to be the one to tell her.

I texted Jamie, telling her Carl would pick her up for a late dinner. Again, it wasn't a question. I needed to feed off her sunshine one last time before I buried the sun for good.

At least I could have one more night with her, one last chance to say goodbye.

This will haunt me for the rest of my life.

I finally found her. Finally found the one who eases my soul and warms my heart, and there was nothing I could do to keep her. I had been greedy to think I could.

Life and it's fucked up lessons.

CHAPTER THIRTY

Jamie

I thought I said after work," I chuckled as Alison strutted into my apartment and practically threw herself onto my couch.

"You did." She replied nonchalantly, fixing the pillows around her and rearranging herself until she was buried in throws and cushions. "I kinda needed a break, so it was perfect timing."

Even though her father was the CEO, Alison never slacked. She worked harder and longer hours than everyone in the office. Still, whenever I called, she was there within the minute.

Our flight had landed past lunchtime, and Liam had Carl bring me home instead of AD before they headed straight to the club.

"Come on, spill. I want to hear all about the fairytale that put that stupid happy smile on your face." She teased, pushing me to smile harder at the memory of everything that happened. Even finding out that Frank wasn't my father came as a not-so-bad moment. I was free because of it. Free from his torture and his abuse. Free from the thought that I was such a bad human that not even my father could find it in him to love me.

I told her everything. From the gala to that creep, Mercier. From the awful flight to the exquisiteness of the dresses she ordered for me. From Frank's confession to Liam's caring thought of taking me home.

"He said he loved me, Alison." I cooed, my heart melting at the sound of my own words. "Turns out he cares for me, too."

"Oh my God, Jamie. I'm so happy for you both." She jumped up and hugged me, crushing my bones with the sincerity of her joy in that tight grasp. "He means it, J. Liam wouldn't say that if he didn't truly mean it."

"I think so, too. I mean, I felt it in the way he kissed me and looked at me, you know? I didn't want to think too much of it because I was scared to be heartbroken if he didn't. But the way he kisses me makes me feel it in my bones."

"Ew. Cute, but ew." She joked. "I'd totally be down for the dirty talk if we weren't discussing my brother. I'd need a lobotomy after that kind of detail."

"You are the best part of coming back, did you know that? I'd gladly stay away from reality a little longer."

"Well, both of your lives are here. If you were able to make my stubborn brother admit that he is also worthy of love, you can do anything, Babe. You're glued to him for life now." The normally light and bubbly Alison was nowhere to be found as she spoke. The seriousness in her tone made me feel every one of those words more intensely.

I couldn't help but smile at her. Somehow forever didn't seem daunting at all once Liam was in the equation.

There was nothing but happiness running through my veins. A new sense of belonging I could have never described before for lack of experience.

I had an amazing friend who celebrated my victories and helped me in troubled times. I had the job of my dreams. And the icing on the cake was that I now had a boyfriend I loved, who looked at me as if I was the best thing in his life.

I was exactly where I was supposed to be. My past? If it hadn't happened exactly how it did, I wouldn't be here today. As hard as it had been, I couldn't find an ounce of regret or resentment in me.

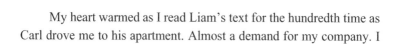

My heart warmed as I read Liam's text for the hundredth time as Carl drove me to his apartment. Almost a demand for my company. I was only too happy to oblige.

Alison had left my apartment earlier, mumbling something about a date she didn't really want to go on before shoving the red rose she found on my doorstep in my hand and faking nausea for the sweetness behind the gesture.

My palms were sweaty, the giddiness I felt in the restaurant last night returning to my gut as if I were meeting Liam for the first time ever. But I knew what it was. My body was calling to his, and I knew exactly what was about to happen. I shivered in delight at the thought, my mind trying to decide how I'd prefer him to be tonight – sweet or rough.

There were two sides to Liam, just like a shiny coin. Just like night and day. I'd discovered I liked the moon just as much as the sun.

The answer was right before me as soon as I walked down the hallway to his apartment.

I stopped in my tracks immediately when I saw him, halting my thoughts together with my breathing and any remaining ability to speak.

Liam was standing at his door waiting for me. He had nothing on besides a dangerously low-hanging pair of jeans, the button suggestively popped open.

His hands were up on the door frame, stretching his body out, his muscles tensing into masses of perfection. His black hair was wet and messy, only adding to the allure of the mouth-watering picture before me. But it was his eyes that gave me the answer I sought. Dark, shady, and dead-hungry eyes watched my every movement like a predator watches his prey.

It wasn't hard to figure out what was for dinner.

Me.

I was. And I had absolutely no objection to it.

Without a word, Liam stepped aside and extended his arm in a silent invitation for me to enter his lair. The door slammed shut behind me a second before Liam's arm wrapped around my waist. Before I could blink, I was pinned against the door, his lips a mere whisper away from mine, fanning my face with his hot, heaving breath.

I looked into those pools of green and saw raw need. A lust charged with something else I couldn't decipher.

We stood there for a moment, just searching each other's soul, our breaths and hearts evening out and pulsing in sync. Liam towered over me, his arm caging me against the door while his other hand sunk each one of its digits into the flesh of my hip.

This intensity, this closeness would have scared me a few months ago, but then those dirty words of his came tumbling into my mind, and I was all but ready to combust. *Good fucking girl.*

Liam bit his bottom lip harshly, drawing a sharp inhale through his nose before unleashing his wrath in a mindblowing kiss.

It was harsh, dominant, and lustful, but filled with a kind of need that ignited my heart. The hand he had on my hip pulled me closer to him as his mouth ravished mine without control. The other had slipped into my hair, fisting it to deepen our kiss.

I was already a messy pile of lust, and all the man had to do was kiss me.

My feet left the ground as Liam picked me up, wrapping my legs around his waist, pushing his already hard cock into me.

He took me to the couch, pulling off my top and bra before we had a chance to get there, almost ripping them off my body. His hard, warm chest grazed my nipples as he held me closer, my body morphing into his as if it belonged to it.

Liam laid on top of me, frantically and urgently kissing every part of my body while slipping off my pants and underwear, followed by his own. There was no playing tonight, there was a different urge to him, an obsessive need to be inside of me, like he had been dying of thirst and I was the oasis in his desert.

He buried himself deep inside me with one swift move, a pleasurable moan escaping my mouth as I adjusted to his thickness.

"I'm sorry." Liam stopped, his chest heaving in heavy pants, his eyes shut as tight as they could go as he rested his forehead against mine.

"No, no. Don't apologize. It's okay, it doesn't hurt." There was pain, but the kind that mingled with pleasure in an ultimately blissful sensation.

After studying my face for honesty, Liam started moving slowly but vigorously, holding my knees up and wide while he hit every sensitive spot inside me. I heard myself moaning with every hard plunge, but there was nothing I could do to hold them back.

Hard kisses and bites covered my neck in goosebumps, intensifying every electrified feeling running through my body.

His big hand skimmed the side of my body, holding firmly on my ass as he increased his pace, ramming hard into me. This, him, everything about us was utter bliss.

Liam held me down, my knees an inch from touching my chest, while he watched his cock drive in and out of me in a frenzy, helping me ride on the most raw, primal, and intense high of my life.

"Oh God, Liam!" I moaned in a voice that didn't sound like mine as what seemed like a ball of fire was about to explode inside me. I sunk my nails into his back, trying to bring him closer, needing just a little more friction on my clit before I came undone.

My back arched, my head fell back, and my eyes rolled as I hungrily met every thrust of his with my own.

One.

Two.

Three.

That was all it took. Three hard pumps and I was falling.

Liam's warmth coated me inside, a loud groan rumbling from his chest with the last deep thrust before he stilled, deeply buried inside me.

His body fell heavily onto mine while my body still quaked beneath him in my own ecstasy.

Liam had his nose buried in the crook of my neck, inhaling my intensely aroused scent. I smelled like him, like our intimacy, like raw and possessive sex.

But it was more than that. It was heavy in emotion, drenched in a passion that came from a place of love.

"Fuck, Jamie. You have no idea how much I love you." Liam confessed in a desperate exhale.

"Keep sending me those red roses every morning, and maybe one day I might believe you," I joked, his body tensing at my words.

"What roses?" He asked, pulling back from my neck.

"The ones you've been leaving on my doorstep. Come on, don't pretend you know nothing about it."

"I *don't* know anything about it." He pulled out of me, looking straight at my face, waiting for me to elaborate, but there was nothing more I could say. I had thought they were from him. "I didn't leave any roses on your doorstep, Jamie. Do these come with notes?"

"No, nothing. Just a red rose outside my door. I thought it was you."

Liam paused for a moment too long, an uncomfortable silence settling in the air.

"You're coming with me to Dea Tacita tomorrow after work." Liam finally said in a clipped tone with no room for discussion.

"O-kay... Any specific reason?" I asked, finding the shift in subject strange.

"I want you to know the place and the people who work for me, and I want them to know you, too." I smiled at that. He was willing to be with me in front of his employees. "I want them to know who they should die to protect if it comes to it."

"What?" That last part startled me.

"It's just protocol." Something told me he was being dismissive, but I relented anyway.

"Sure, no problem. I'll be there."

The tension had stolen the moment, so I got up and followed the scent of pizza, bringing the box to the couch where we eat buck naked. Soon enough, we were back to the start. I didn't get to finish my last piece before Liam yanked it from my hand and started kissing me all over. It was clear that, for him, the night had only just begun.

We made love again on the floor, and then again on the counter, and still again on the bed until I couldn't take it anymore. I was completely spent, my muscles aching all around, my pussy raw and hypersensitive from his unrelenting hunger.

We met at Dea Tacita before dinner. Liam showed me around the place and introduced me to everyone. Mainly big, bulky, angry-looking men. I already knew Mike, Carl, and Jimmy, but there were probably another twelve or fifteen men there, not counting the ones prepping the bar for opening time. Max, Alison's friend, was there, too, flashing me a small smile in acknowledgment.

I met every one of them, and as per Liam's instructions, I tried my best to memorize their faces. It was just too much, too fast, but he was adamant and kept pushing me to remember.

I sat down on Matt's chair in his big, manly office on the top floor. There was a huge floor-to-ceiling window overseeing the dance floor. And right there, it clicked. Liam had seen me from this window on my birthday. He knew exactly where I was, except when I went to the bathroom since the hallway was tucked away in the corner.

I was ready to tease him about it, but when I spun the chair to face him, Liam had a hard expression on his face. There was something bothering him, probably since yesterday.

Not that I didn't like the dominating handler he turned into every time he was troubled. But there was something serious poking at him.

"Jamie, I want you to listen to me carefully now." He turned the chair further towards him, lowering himself to my eye level "Whenever you feel that you are in danger, I want you to come here. Even if it's just a strange feeling that you might not be safe. This is where you run to. Each one of these men will protect you. Do you understand?"

"Why would I be in dan-…"

"I asked you if you understood what I said." He cut me off, his tone dead serious, and dipped in a darkness that chilled my bones.

"Geez, yes, I understand. What's going on, Liam?"

"Nothing. You know the dangers from my line of business. I want you to know that you always have a safe place to run to if you need one."

There was definitely something up, but I also knew this was not the time to push for answers.

"I can't stay with you tonight. Carl will take you home, and Jimmy will stay the night, standing outside your door."

"Absolutely not."

"It wasn't a question, Jamie. Someone has been leaving red roses on your damn doorstep. Do you know how easy it is to get inside your apartment?"

"No." I reluctantly answered.

"Let's just say that I've seen you sleep more times than you can count, and up until right now, you had no fucking idea."

"What? How?"

"I had a key made and swapped out yours. As simple as that. Jimmy stays."

I glared at him in disbelief before nodding, accepting his non-request.

Carl drove us to Tremont as agreed, and Jimmy stood guard outside my door. It was hard to sleep when my mind was running wild, both because of Liam's confession and the fact that maybe someone was following me. Who could be leaving those damn roses that made me smile every morning?

After a ton of effort, I finally managed to fall asleep, still pissed that Liam had stalked me that way. My dreams were a blank, though, and I woke up with the same burning revolt I was cuddled with last night.

The morning went by in a blur as I avoided Liam. Whatever I needed to say to him had to wait for privacy. But there was a piece of my mind I needed to give him. How could he have done that? Violated my privacy that way?

Around lunchtime, I was waiting for the elevator to meet Alison for lunch when *Mr. Night Stalker* walked towards me, and somehow, as a damn miracle, whatever resentment lived in me simply melted at the sight of this heavenly man.

"Are we going?" Alison said from behind me as she stepped out of the elevator. My eyebrow raised in a question I didn't need to voice, her answer seeming like she lived inside my head. "I was hungry, and you were taking too long."

"I'm coming with you," Liam informed as he strutted towards us as if he was on a damn catwalk. I tried to hold on to my anger, but it was near impossible with the nonstop fluttering in my heart in response to his bright smile.

"Liam?" Michelle called as he walked in front of her desk. "There's someone on the phone for you."

"Tell them I'm out. Take a message." He dismissed, his eyes permanently fixed on mine.

"She says it's urgent."

"I said take a message, Michelle." His annoyed tone was firmer this time, but still, she didn't relent.

"It's your fiancé."

CHAPTER THIRTY ONE

Jamie

*F*iancé.

His fiancé?

No. It couldn't be.

I looked at Michelle, waiting for her to correct her words, hoping for some kind of misunderstanding or misinterpretation. Maybe it was a strange code they used in the Mafia that had a completely different meaning than what the word itself entailed.

Something. It has to be something besides what I heard.

But Michelle's features were as tied up in confusion as mine. So I focused my gaze back on Liam, his brows furrowed in a panicked knot, his hands stretched out towards me, his palms flat in a universal gesture that meant 'calm down.'

Calm down? How could I calm the fuck down?

That look and gesture were all it took for me to know that there was no mistake. No secret code.

It *was* his fiancé.

With that single look, I knew it was true.

It's your Fiancé!

It's your Fiancé!

It's your Fiancé!

It's your Fiancé!

Michelle's words were an echo ringing unrelentingly in my ears so loud it made me flinch. They bounced around in my brain, refusing to sink into understanding.

With every painfully sour breath I took, my heart sank deeper into my chest.

My knees grew weaker.

My soul died further.

My body was frozen, incapable of any reaction. I just stood there without so much as a blink, feeling the life drain from my face. The realization that Liam had played me sinking into my pores like acid. How could I have fallen head over heels for him? How had I been tricked into overlooking what I saw in him the first time we met?

I'd give my life up just for the chance to be with him. I had finally found a meaning for my existence. I was finally complete. Fucking happy.

And now?

Nothing.

There was a void spreading through my body, like when darkness etched its shadows at nightfall. Poisoning and consuming every damn thing in its path. Agony came after the emptiness, filling every crack and crevice, wrapping my heart in a grip that cut my breath off.

My shoulders sank with the weight of disbelief while my feet seemed to be glued to the damn floor. I couldn't move. My brain screamed for me to get out of here, but the sharp stab smack center in my chest was simply crippling.

Fire burned in my throat from tears begging to fall, but I couldn't. I couldn't fall apart here. He would win if he saw me break.

My core trembled, a building pressure rising and irradiating everywhere. I was a time bomb on the verge of explosion.

Liam took a step towards me, his hands still stretched out, reaching for me now. As he moved forward, I took a step back, almost bumping into Alison.

"NO," I warned, my voice low but steady.

I turned back and marched straight into the elevator, angrily pressing on the button to close the damn doors. I didn't stop jamming my finger into it, even after the doors had closed and I was safely alone inside this fucking death box.

I stumbled back until my back hit the wall, welcoming the sharp pain I felt after harshly banging the back of my skull against it. Any pain that could muffle the one eating at me inside was a welcomed reprieve.

I had fought the tears, but I couldn't hold the dam any longer. A loud shriek left my mouth, and I exploded into tears. The panic of being in a small, closed space was completely overridden by the abyss of helplessness I was falling into.

The time it would take to reach the ground floor wouldn't be enough to pull myself together, so despite my innate fear, I pushed the stop button, giving myself more time to cry my heart out.

My knees gave out from beneath me, and I crumbled to the ground, my body shaking in waves of sadness and despair. There was no stopping the tears.

I knew that they would come for me soon, and all I needed at this moment was the grace of solitude. My phone was ringing without a pause, calls from both Liam and Alison pulling me out of my stupor. I rejected each call, only to have my phone ringing again. I took that small moment of clarity to call an Uber and get out of here, switching my phone off as soon as I was tucked into the back seat of the car.

I knew I wouldn't be free from them at home, but at least I would be in my own space, shielded from the stares of strangers or co-workers.

The driver was kind enough not to ask. Aside from a curt 'Are you okay, Madame,' he kept his eyes on the road and his thoughts to himself while I stared out the window with unrelenting tears falling down my cheeks.

How could he have done this? How could he have said he loved me if he was engaged? Was it all a game to him? Getting me to relent, to fall for him only to destroy me right after?

The answers to those questions didn't matter at all because they wouldn't change the fact that the love of my life was engaged to another woman. They wouldn't change the fact that I'd be scarred for life after being deceived this way.

I took the stairs up to my apartment in pairs, eager to bury my face in a pillow and scream until I passed out. Maybe unconscious, I wouldn't feel as unworthy, dumb, and gullible as I do now.

Stupid little girl. How could you ever think that a man like Liam would settle for a nobody like you?

Taking the last two steps, I practically ran to my door only to find it wide open. My heart pounded harshly against my rib cage as I tried to scout the visible space inside my apartment without actually entering.

Red roses.

My mind was on the warning Liam had given me about running to Dea Tacita if I ever felt threatened. Instead, my eyes swerved to the doorstep, and seeing that there was no rose there, I took a wary step forward and then another until I was standing in the middle of my living room.

And there he was. Just standing there looking at me.

Only a day ago, I'd say there was pain behind his green eyes, but today, I couldn't be so certain. It had all been an act. A show to make me fall, only to humiliate me and burn whatever little self-esteem I still had left into a pile of ash.

I squared my shoulders as if I had to prove I was still strong while my nails dug into the palms of my hands to keep my mind off of the pain that had my chest caving in on itself.

"Please leave," I said barely above a whisper, trying my damndest to hold back the tears as I faced him.

"Jamie, please let me explain."

"I don't want to know, Liam. Please go before I call the police." I threatened, but my voice came out weak and shaky.

"You know they wouldn't come." He said, stalking towards me, making me walk back until I hit the kitchen counter. There was no way out now besides past him. "Please just listen to me." Liam stretched out his hand to touch me, immediately withdrawing as he noticed me flinch. "I'm not going to hurt you."

You already have.

The thought of his hand on my skin, of the electric current that always rushed through me under his touch, had my tears free-falling again. I'd never feel that way again. I'd never have that touch to myself.

I choked on a sob at the thought, curling into myself and sliding down the cabinets as sadness swallowed me like quicksand. My body never hit the ground, though. Before I could push him back, Liam was cradling me in his arms, rocking us back and forth while his hands smoothed out my hair. I needed it to smooth out the wrinkles in my heart.

Never again will I love this fiercely.

I was nothing but a weak girl, giving in to the only person with the ability to both break me and mend me. I wanted him. I wanted him to be mine. Only mine.

But he was taken.

"P-please. I'm begging you. I can't do this. Please leave." I sobbed uncontrollably, my whole body shaking to the rush of tears that bled straight from my heart.

He was both my drug and sobriety. The water to my desert. The oxygen to my lungs.

But I had to let him go. The longer he stayed, the harder the goodbye. I needed a clean and quick cut before I gave into temptation again.

"I hate you." I lied, but the truth cut like sharp edges, and I had already bled out.

"I know."

Liam kissed the top of my head and held me tighter against his chest. His strong grasp was all that was holding me together at this moment. It was where I belonged. Where I felt safe. But it wasn't my place to be. It belonged to another woman.

His fiancé.

I allowed myself to calm down in his arms, lying on the floor of my kitchen, trying my best to regain the ability to speak.

Time stood still as he held me, maybe taking pity on me or maybe just another harsh reminder that this was the end. My end. Who would I be after this? After him? Was there even such a thing?

I sat up straight, wiping my tears with the back of my hand before I spoke again.

"You said you didn't want to hurt me. So don't. Your touch hurts, your presence hurts, your kisses hurt, Liam." I blurted with a new flow of tears as company for my pained words. "Please leave, Liam. Please stop hurting me."

Without a word, Liam stood up and scooped me off the floor. He took me to my bedroom, and gently placed me on my bed and turned to leave, only to pause by the door. In two lunges, he was back by the bed again, his lips crushing onto mine in what felt like goodbye.

Bitter and cruel in its sweetness. Harsh but tender in its silent deliverance.

His mouth worshiped mine with a tenderness that contrasted with the urge of the tips of his fingers that bore into my skull.

"I'm sorry." He whispered against me as he pulled back, walking away and taking a piece of my soul with him.

So this is what dying inside feels like.

CHAPTER THIRTY TWO

Liam

Seeing Jamie hurt was pure agony. Seeing her hurt because of me had me tipping into a kind of madness that saw no boundaries. The Amatos could go fuck themselves. I couldn't give a shit if they came to my apartment in the silence of the night and stuck a bullet in my damn skull.

I deserved it.

For every tear she shed, for every sob that shook her. I fucking deserved it.

After leaving Jamie's apartment, I called Matt and told him exactly that. There was absolutely no way I was going through with this sham. I was all heart at the moment, clarity surely wasn't playing this hand.

So leave it to Matt to paint a fucking picture from Hell and show me exactly why I couldn't pull out. My Omertà had nothing to do with it this time. They had leverage that gripped me by the balls harder than the threat of a six-foot-three body bag with my name on it.

Jamie.

They knew about her. They knew about my obsession with this angel and that I had dragged her into this hell pit of my own making.

That fucking bartender, Jack, somehow caught wind of the predicament hovering over the Battaglia *cosca* and decided to rat us out. Apparently Jamie had made an impression on him, too, for him to be so revenge-hungry. Or, then again, maybe it was because I had his fingerprints scraped off every damn digit that dared to touch my girl. He was lucky he was wearing shoes, or that would have been twenty instead of the mere ten I had commissioned.

I'd have to revisit and square the score. Maybe make him eat those fucking fingers for pointing the Amatos her way.

I didn't mind if my life had an early expiration date on it. I just couldn't stand the idea that Jamie was in danger.

Needless to say, the Amato girl was still good to become a fucking Battaglia and snake her way into the most influential Mafiosi *famiglia* in the damn States. I could be reckless with my own safety, but I would never gamble with hers. And now that Jamie knew about the engagement, protecting her just became a whole lot more of a challenge.

I stomped into Dea Tacita, my sour mood hauling behind me and changing the normal chipper atmosphere of the pre-opening prep. Every person on the ground quieted down, their faces now matching the somberness of mine, as if I'd dragged in a cloud of toxic smoke that poisoned everything around me.

Without needing a word, Lilly poured me a double, straight up, pushing the glass forward as I walked by the central bar in the middle of the club. I grabbed it on the move, still stalking towards the stairs at the far back that led up to Matt's office. The full glass didn't even make it to the landing. In one swift move, I tipped the whole contents down my throat, needing more of that sting and double the numbness.

No! Nothing could make me forget. I could drown in booze and still feel her pain burning in my veins.

Alison stood halfway up the stairs, glaring at me with an expression I had never seen her wear. There was resentment and judgment for sure, but worst of all, there was hate there, too. Her green eyes, a matching pair of my own, should never look at me with that emotion swimming around them, but I couldn't blame her.

Again, I deserved it.

"Why haven't you explained any of this shit to Jamie?" Alison asked, her voice stern and accusatory. Any answer I could spew at her would fall on deaf ears. There was no good reason. No justification for not coming clean, even if how things had played out was very far from what I had planned.

"Not here," I warned as I walked past her and carried on climbing the stairs, my tone curt and clipped. She turned and followed me, holding her peace until we were safe in the soundproofed privacy of Matt's office.

"Why, Liam?" She pushed as soon as the door shut behind her.

Matt stood from behind his desk as we walked in, half a cigarette dangling between his fingers while the whole room smelled like a fucking ashtray. This was consuming him as much as it was me.

Matt's only addiction was nicotine, and even that was controlled. It only became evident when he was preoccupied. It was like a soothing pacifier that breathed peace into his lungs with the counter of another nail in his coffin.

"I was going to tell her everything, every fucking detail, but the Amato girl just had to fucking call the office and fuck up everyone's life, didn't she?"

I was pissed. I hadn't taken the call, so whatever she wanted to speak to me about was still unsaid. But she could have said her fucking name instead of saying she was my fiancé. Was she that eager that she was already adopting the fucking title?

"Jamie will never forgive you if you don't tell her the truth. I know it might not make much of a difference in the grand scheme of things, you're still expected to marry Francesca. But at least she'll know you didn't play her. At least you could lift that weight." She verbalized my exact thoughts.

"You should let her hate you. She'll get over you faster if she does." Matt said. He was always the most rational of the three of us.

More so in this specific case, because he wasn't in the center of the clusterfuck. Maybe his distanced perspective gave him a different understanding.

"She deserves to know!" Alison raised her voice at Matt, indignant and revolted with his opinion.

She was the only person on this Earth that could ever get away with something like that. No one else dared to raise an eyebrow, never mind their voice. His love for our little *principessa* was the lifeboat that kept her safe under any circumstance. She was simply untouchable.

"What she *deserves* is to be happy and keep her head on her shoulders. And we all know that she can't have what makes her happy right now, so let her move on. Set her free." Matt elaborated, his tone implying that what he was saying was as exact and accurate as a Math equation. He drew another sharp drag of his cigarette, the red circle glaring brighter until he stopped. "She can't do that if some part of her is still hanging on to Liam."

His words were directed at Alison, both of them discussing my life as if I wasn't even standing in the damn room. In fact, I almost wasn't. I was just an empty shell, zoning off as they debated, as if any of it was their choice.

Their voices muffled against my loud thoughts, some kind of clarity showing me the best path to take.

"Matt's right," I started out loud, cutting off their discussion with my calmness. "If she hates me, she'll be free to find happiness." Those words cut and stung like a motherfucker, leaving a bloody trail of jealousy and agony as I heard them coming out of my own mouth.

"So that's it? You just… give up?" Alison protested, her arms gesturing her ire as much as her tone was.

"I wouldn't if I knew there was any possibility of fixing this. But there simply isn't. And I can't stand seeing her hurt like this. What the fuck can I do to stop that besides this? Huh?" I angrily blurted before walking over to my sister and grabbing her shoulders. "You have to get her to go to work again. Get her back to her normal life. I'll try to stay away as much as possible, but please help me snap her out of this."

"Of course I'll help. I love her, too." Her voice was shaken, breaking with the sympathy of a true friend.

"Francesca called AD, I gather. Have you spoken to her?" Matt interrupted. Back to business, back to setting things on their right fucking track. But I wasn't having it.

"No, she did call AD, but I didn't take the call because my life went up in fucking flames. What do you think?"

"It's not her fault that this is happening. And she *will* be your wife. It's best that you start off on the right foot," Matt said, but I wasn't interested in that specific subject so I just waved him off dismissively.

"Whatever. The Amatos can wait. They'll have me for life, after all. What's another few days in the expanse of forever?"

"Don't drag it too long." He warned. There was more under those words than what meets the eye. He was referring to reassurance. Letting the Amatos know that I was on board and that they could leave Jamie out of this.

I stood there looking at the anguish in my sister's eyes and the compassion in my ruthless brother's, thinking how lucky I was to have these two to support me and help me navigate through this deep sea of shit.

Jamie didn't have such luck, she was alone. Guilt swamped my pores again for all the fucking pain I had caused her and for not being able to be there to kiss it all away.

I'd be a shadow in her darkness, night in and night out, making sure she would heal, however long that took. It was the only thing I could do, even if the idea of Jamie getting over me was revolting. The image of her slipping between my fingers sauntered through my brain, consuming my sanity like flesh-eating maggots.

I'm a selfish son of a bitch for wanting her to love me, even knowing she can never have me.

Jamie

It took five whole damn weeks for me to stop crying myself to sleep. It was a small step but a welcomed reprieve nonetheless.

That was also how long I hadn't spoken to Liam. I haven't been able to stop thinking about him, though. He was a constant thought. The last thing on my mind at night and the first name on my lips in the morning.

He had broken a lot more than just my heart. He had broken every single part of me.

My skin missed his touch, my nose his scent, my lips the delicious whisper of his name. In a short time, he had become my oxygen. The fierce force that made my heart pump blood to my veins.

He was my future. My present and the bright light that obliviated the pain from the past. Still, he had stolen my soul and sold it for less than a dime.

But I still loved him. Every fiber of my being knew I always would. I hated myself for it.

Alison had camped in my apartment every weekend since that dreadful day, keeping my mind occupied and helping me manage the crippling pain. It went without saying that any conversation related to her brother was banished from my house. I couldn't let go if I kept letting him in my life, even if it was just in tales and comments. It was bad enough that he lived rent-free in my mind.

Whatever it was, I didn't want to know.

It was an obvious lie, but still, it was the only thing I dared to make myself believe in order to survive. Because that was what life was without Liam – nothing but survival. I heard enough through office gossip already and Alison understood the unspoken rule.

Sleep, eat, work and repeat. Some days the eating portion wasn't actually necessary or even welcomed. Besides the lethargic state that came with being betrayed this way, waves of nausea were a constant. My body was reacting to losing the love of my life in ways I never thought possible.

After a couple of days, I had managed to go back to work. Back to staring at my boss's shut door. This was what Liam did now. He came in early and left late, locking himself up in his office, only showing his face in case of bare necessity.

I held my breath each time someone knocked on his door, both hoping for a glimpse of him and dreading the pounding of my heart whenever I got one.

I tried forcing myself not to feel, to turn it all off, the good together with the bad. I couldn't. His roots in me ran as deep as a bottomless ocean, and as much as I tried, I couldn't stop feeling *something* for him.

"Good morning, Miss Harden." A deep voice pulled me out of my haze. I had zoned out again, looking at my computer screen, not really seeing anything that was on it.

"Oh, huh, good morning, Mr. Dornier." That name slipped down my tongue like knives as I rushed to my feet, almost saluting the man standing tall and broody in front of me.

Instinctively, I looked past him into Liam's shut door, Mr. Dornier's eyes following mine before returning to my face again.

"I hope you're feeling better from the *indisposition* that's been plaguing you lately." His eyes were softer as he said that.

He knew! Fuck.

"Much better, thank you." I lied, forcing a small smile onto my face before swallowing hard.

"Good, good. That means that you'll be at the party this Saturday." I stared at him, trying as hard as I could to focus on his words instead of his face. He reminded me so much of Liam that my heart twisted in agony.

"Party?"

"Yes. In celebration of the Verten project. You were an essential element in closing that deal. Mr. Mercier told me how much he enjoyed your work and meeting you in LA. He specifically asked if you would be attending." My gut lurched to the sound of that. Not only would I have to face Liam for a whole damn night, now I'd have to deal with the creep, too.

"Thank you, Sir, but I'm not sure I'll be in town this weekend." It was a lie. Where else would I be? I couldn't handle a party right now, not to mention this particular one had Liam on the top of the guest list.

"Nonsense. You're my special guest, Miss Harden. No discussions. I'll send a car to pick you up at nine. See you on Saturday." With a dry smile, Mr. Dornier slammed his deciding hammer, just like my damn executioner, and walked away.

I slumped back into my chair, a new gush of anxiety spreading through my body. I picked up my phone and texted Alison, hoping she could find me a way out of this.

> Your father just cornered me into going to the party on Saturday.

> Get me out of it, please.

Welcome to my life. Adrian Dornier is a persuasive man when he wants something. But I'll be there with you.

> Please tell me your brother isn't going.

Will a lie make you feel better right now?

> No.

I'll be there. You'll focus on me and block out the rest. Okay?

She was typing another message when my eyes sensed something moving and glanced up from my phone. Liam was coming out of his office, stopping at the door as his eyes landed on mine. I swallowed dryly and averted my gaze, but it was too late. His beautiful features had burned a new hole through my chest.

He looked damn good, and somehow that hurt like a bitch.

I, on the other hand, was a horrible mess. My eyes had dark circles around them as a permanent fixture now, contrasting with my pale face and red, puffy nose. Crying every day took a massive toll on my body when all I wanted was to look as unaffected as he did.

I stared back at those three dancing dots, signaling Alison was still typing, trying my best not to break before I had the chance to hide in the bathroom.

"How are you, Miss Harden?" That voice that sounded like a damn sonnet rang in my ears, a treacherous shiver running down my spine.

Fuck I missed him.

Snap out of it, Jamie.

"I'm fine, Sir. Thank you." I coldly replied, my eyes still glued to my phone, gaining courage before I looked back up at him. It was clear there was something more he wanted to say, but instead, he pursed his lips as he took in the unshed tears brimming in my eyes. Liam inhaled deeply while his hands balled into fists, and that strong jaw pumped in pulses.

My breath was stuck in my lungs, and my eyes didn't dare to blink. I knew those tears would fall as soon as they did, so I focused on his green eyes, staring at him as if I wasn't crumbling inside.

Liam stayed silent, watching me back, thinking God knows what about my blotchy face. When I refocused on my phone as if it was more important than him, he simply walked away, crushing whatever progress I had made these last five weeks with a damn question, a tailored suit, and those green eyes filled with pity.

I hated him. I hated him so much it fucking hurt. When? When was it going to stop?

CHAPTER THIRTY THREE

Jamie

Recurrent nightmares broke me back down when I thought I was finally pulling myself out of the mud, smashing all my progress to smithereens.

I had some peaceful nights, but they were still greatly outnumbered by the devastating ones.

I would dream of him in those last ones. Liam would come to my apartment, make love to me, speak words of his undying devotion to me before we fell asleep in each other's arms.

That was the tempting dream until it was suddenly twisted into a sick nightmare. I would wake up and see him lying there naked, in my own bed, with another woman in his arms, their legs laced together. Liam stroked her hair and kissed her head, loving her as he had just done with me. I tried to pry and see her face, but I never could.

Liam treated her like a queen. Like a precious possession. Like the damn love of his life.

I love you! I heard him whisper into her ear.

Every night this dream haunted me. I'd wake up crying, suffocating on my own gasps and sobs. I'd stay awake, counting every minute and hour until the sun rose, as I tried my best to numb back the pain into some kind of submission.

If I didn't know any better, I could swear he had been in my room, his scent lingering everywhere, and instead of fading a little every night, it only got stronger. But Liam had taken my request to heart. I didn't even have to change the lock because he never came back.

As pathetic as it was, some nights I wished he would come, say he was sorry, make love to me and kiss the pain away. Those thoughts were damaging, but they were like a plague. They didn't ask for permission to exist. They simply did.

I was exhausted. Run down. A shell of the person I used to be only five weeks ago.

I could barely drag myself out of bed every morning to face the fear of seeing him and not being able to hold back the tears.

My pride hurt. My self-love was damaged. My heart was shattered into a million pieces. He'd taken the big ones, and as hard as I demanded them back, I knew they'd never be mine again.

Alison insisted on picking me up every morning. It was her way of making sure I would get out of the house and back into my life again. I had been mad at her, too. I thought she knew everything, so I blamed her for not warning me. She swore she didn't know, and I could see it on her face that she was being truthful.

It still struck me as strange how she was kept in the dark, considering the strong bond they obviously had.

She was here today, too. Giving me strength and support disguised under the pretext of us getting ready for the party together and driving there in the car her father arranged to pick me up.

"Besides, it's Saturday." She said, as if this was where she belonged on Saturdays.

If her whole wardrobe wasn't currently spread out on top of my bed, I'd be amazed. There were dresses, makeup, accessories, shoes, and everything we could possibly need scattered around the small space. She was either excited to have some fun, or she was trying extra hard to pump me up with her enthusiasm.

It wasn't working at all.

Alison practically coerced me into choosing a bright red satin gown with a plunging V cleavage that ended right between my breasts. I wasn't feeling confident enough to pull it off, but then again, I wasn't confident enough to pull off a pair of pajamas. So the statement red dress it was.

She helped me with my makeup, the dark circles all but disappearing under whatever sorcery she performed, giving me a fake glow that could fool the most attentive of crowds.

"You look so damn beautiful, J. He'll be devastated when he sees you," Alison said, her tongue slipping without dire intention.

"I'm not dressing up for him, Alison. I shouldn't even be going to this damn thing." I glared at her, the mention of Liam making me want to not leave the house.

"I know, I'm sorry. But it doesn't hurt if you see him squirm a little, either."

I didn't want reactions. Reactions meant stuff I couldn't deal with right now. I wanted to hate him with all my heart so that maybe, one day, I could free myself from him.

"Is that the reaction *you're* looking for in what's-his-name? Max, is it?" She had gone the extra mile on herself, too. The dark blue gown she had on was conservative at first glance until she bared her back, nothing but sheer lace covering her skin, ending dangerously low.

"What? Are you insane? Of course not."

"Don't lie to me, Alison Dornier. You've got a thing for him."

"That's gross, Jamie. He's like an older brother. Besides, there's nothing but mystery around him, and I don't deal well with secrets."

"I'm with you on that." It had been a secret that landed me in the land of heartbreak and misery. "Let's just go and get this over with, okay?"

"Sure." She took my hands in hers and gave them an encouraging squeeze. "I'll be there for you every step of the way."

Mr. Dornier and Matt were outside waiting for us when we arrived. Matt wasn't part of AD, but his relationship with his father was progressing to a place where he would take pride in his achievements and stand by his family to celebrate them. Family was a big deal to all of them, as Liam had once explained. They were each other's strengths and weaknesses.

Things were still a little bit weird between Matt and me, so I accepted Mr. Dornier's arm and started walking inside while Alison walked with her brother. We had only taken a couple of steps before Matt suddenly stopped.

"Wait. Liam's here." He said, Mr. Dornier pausing in his tracks.

Fuck! Do we really have to do this right here where there's no chance for escape? I have my freaking arm locked in my boss's. Please, Earth, just swallow me now!

I kept my eyes glued to the entrance straight ahead, not wanting to turn and see that devilishly handsome man my broken heart still bled for.

"Good evening," Liam said as he approached. I watched him through the corner of my eye, greeting the men with a hug first, then Alison with a kiss, finally turning to me and hesitating.

My heart pounded in my chest as if it was trying to break free. I was expecting to have had a drink or two before I had to deal with him. Maybe numbing my senses would have made it all easier.

I swallowed the lump in my throat and looked at him. He was as handsome as ever, the allure of that damn tux making my heart flutter, my eyes unable to keep from roaming over him in a feast of the senses.

Fuck, you're so pathetic, Jamie Harden.

"Good evening, Miss Harden." Liam's voice was low and gravelly, merely above a whisper, but missing the flirty tone that saying my name normally came with.

He placed a light kiss on my cheek, and my skin instantly erupted into millions of goosebumps while a heavy expression covered his face. There was regret in his eyes, maybe even pity.

Fuck that!

Revolt filled my lungs, spreading like wildfire as a reaction to that damn look on his face. I didn't need his pity. I didn't need him to feel sorry for me. I did that enough for both of us.

That was before I saw why.

I stood taller, and looking beyond the gleam of Liam's light, I saw the beautiful brunette with sun-kissed skin that stood behind him.

My breath hitched in my throat as my heart stopped beating for a whole damn minute.

The first impact was like a dark hole of nothing, sucking me into its pit as if what I had in my chest was simply gone and left a huge void that would never be filled. Jealousy hit me second, the warmth from my boiling blood contrasting with the ice that covered the place where my wounded heart once was.

This was her. His future wife. The woman I'd dreamt of being. The woman who took my life.

She was everything I feared she would be. Beautiful, elegant, and she even seemed nice. I wanted to see flaws, chips on her damn shoulders the size of a meteorite. But there were none. She wore a polite smile that contrasted with a stiffness in her body that gave away her uneasiness. I didn't think she knew who I was. Her gaze had barely glazed past me.

I sucked in a sharp breath, my arm tangling around Mr. Dornier's again as I tried my best to keep my composure.

I loved Liam, and from the bottom of my heart, I wished him happiness. I just couldn't deal with him being happier with her than he was with me.

"Let's go in before the party starts without us," Alison said, breaking the uncomfortable silence. She'd seen the panic in my eyes, and that was her saving me from breaking right here in front of an audience.

I wasn't sure what I needed right now. To scream, to cry, to disappear. Of one thing I was damn sure, I'd prefer to be standing in the middle of the fire and brimstone of Hell than to be where I was right now.

Mr. Dornier tugged on my arm, and I followed his pace, trying my best not to rush inside and hide. Thankfully he had guests to greet, leaving me free to run off to the bar and take the second-best option I had tonight – burying my feelings at the bottom of full glasses of alcohol. Alison followed my lead, rushing by my side with a heavy expression in her eyes.

"I'm so sorry, I didn't know she was coming." She apologized, her fingers lacing with mine as we made our way over to the other side of the massive hall. "Two rums, please. Top shelf, don't give me any of that weak crap I know you guys keep back there."

The waiter got busy with our order, and soon enough, I had a glass in one hand and my heart in the other. Alison looked at me worried while I held the glass against my lips without drinking. I was trying to decide what to do, and somehow, the only thing that came to mind was writing my letter of resignation on a napkin and handing it to Mr. Dornier tonight.

"Jamie, talk to me." I swerved my eyes from the counter to her, still stuck in my reverie. "Shit, why is she even here?"

"It's fine." I finally replied after gulping down the whole drink without so much as a mild flinch, slamming the glass on the counter and ordering another. "I have to get used to it anyway, right?"

I couldn't believe he would deliberately bring her here, knowing I would be here, too. But then again, he didn't owe me anything. He didn't have to rearrange his whole life to avoid hurting me. They'll be getting married soon, so I've heard. Damn office gossip. It wouldn't make sense not to bring her.

How the fuck didn't I think of that?

I had that second drink and then a third. The intention wasn't to get completely drunk. I just needed something to help me cope.

A warm hand wrapped around my arm that rested on the counter, making me startle and briskly turn around.

"It's just me," Matt said in surrender. "I just wanted to make sure you were okay. That must have been extremely hard to handle."

"I'm fine." I lied blatantly. "Nothing I wasn't expecting already!"

"Okay, so why are you trying to pass out drunk barely ten minutes after arriving?" He pried the glass from my fingers and took my hand, pulling me behind him towards the dance floor. "Come!"

"Matt, let go of me. I don't feel like dancing." I resisted, but he was too strong to even be affected.

"Jamie, come on, I'm trying to help you relax. No hidden intentions, okay?"

I tried to make myself comfortable in Matt's grasp, failing miserably to succeed. Unlike the only other time we met, Matt kept his hands in appropriate places as he held me and swayed us to the rhythm of the slow tune while his tone was nothing but brotherly.

"You're okay. You'll be okay." He whispered, feeling the tension in my shoulders. "He didn't do it on purpose, you know? The lines between business and personal aren't as clear in our lives, Jamie. They blur too easily. He wasn't trying to hurt you."

"I don't care."

"That's an obvious lie. But believe in it if it makes you stronger. Believe it until it's your unshakable truth. Be strong."

"I'm trying, Matt, but seeing him with her just breaks me all over again." I relented, unable to keep up whatever feeble façade Matt saw right through.

"I know." He held me tighter as a sob threatened to escape. "We are here for whatever you need, Jamie. Okay? Both Alison and I. If it gets too much and you want to leave, just say the word and I'll get you out of here."

I looked at him suspiciously, not entirely understanding why he was looking at me now as if I was his younger sister, protecting me as if I was family. It was strange, to say the least. Matt must have noticed the hesitance in my gaze, a comforting smile spreading across his handsome face.

"Again, no second intentions, Jamie. You are important to Alison, thus, you are important to me. We look out for our own in this family, and you're a part of it now."

I simply nodded my understanding, managing to relax slightly as we danced in silence. I closed my eyes and leaned my head on his chest, trying to calm my racing heart. How it was still beating was beyond me.

The song ended, and the crowd started clapping, acknowledging the talent of the musicians playing for us tonight, but Matt kept me in place until I was ready to pull back.

"Jamie." His father's voice sounded from behind me, forcing me to plaster a fake smile on my face, before I turned towards him and the other man I was dreading to see tonight. "You still remember Mr. Mercier, don't you?" A shiver ran down my spine as I met his piercing blue eyes, a sly and sickening smile spreading across his pale lips.

"Good evening, Miss Harden. Aren't you a sight for sore eyes?" Mr. Mercier greeted me, the kiss he placed on my knuckles making the hairs on the back of my neck stand. He looked at me from head to toe, his eyes practically undressing me on the spot.

"Good evening, Mr. Mercier." I faked my smile, trying to pull my hand from his tight grasp, my head whipping back to look at Matt. "I'm not sure you know each other. This is Matt Dornier, Mr. Dornier's older son."

"Good evening." Mr. Mercier grunted before returning his gaze to me. "Would you give me the pleasure of this dance?" The man asked, tugging on my hand that was still trapped in his clammy grip. My stomach flipped at the thought of having to be so close to him, but as Mr. Dornier studied us and gave me an encouraging nod, I didn't find much of a choice.

I looked at Matt again, my eyes glaring in a silent plea for him to save me from this torture, but he knew nothing about this man or the disgust I had for him. My salvation was not in his hands.

"Come on, Jamie. This is a party, you can have some fun." Sensing my hesitation, Mr. Dornier decided to pitch in.

"Sure, why not. *One* dance wouldn't hurt." I emphasized the word *one,* making it clear I wouldn't be enduring more than that, hoping for the song to be short.

Mr. Mercier held me tightly against him, even more than I was expecting, the repulse I felt for him making my stomach churn and my heart race.

Thankfully, not even a minute into the song, Alison came around dancing with her brother.

"Mr. Mercier, would you give me the pleasure of cutting in?" She asked without giving him time to reply, practically peeling his hand from mine.

She left Liam's arms and stepped between us, carrying Mr. Mercier far from us in a twirl. I was standing there in the middle of the dance floor, not knowing what to do, my eyes deeply buried in Liam's, before I turned my back to him and left. The night was progressively getting worse by the damn minute, my body going into overdrive from so many different emotions.

Liam reached out and grabbed my arm, pulling me back towards him. He wrapped his arm around my waist and took my hand to dance. He gently started swaying, his eyes bored into mine unrelentingly. My body betrayed me by responding to his touch with a small shiver, goosebumps radiating from every point where his skin touched mine.

Those beautiful green eyes pried into my soul, breaking to pieces any resistance I had left.

Liam felt my body reacting to his presence, those bright orbs sparkling while a small smile spread across his handsome face.

"Thank you for that," I said, trying to steer him away from thinking about how much my body still wanted this. Still wanted him.

"You're welcome. You look so beautiful, Jamie. I've missed you so much." He said with an honesty that disarmed me.

I needed to hate him. I needed to push him away, but how could I when he was saying all the things I wanted to hear? And damn the way he said it! I couldn't doubt him. I didn't want to.

But I had to. His fiancé was somewhere in this hall, maybe even watching us.

"Liam, please don't. We both know we can't do this. It's not right. You're here with your fiancé, for Christ's sake."

"I know. I'm sorry. Please just let me have you in my arms, even if it's just one dance." He pleaded, a pained look in those eyes that immediately melted whatever wall I tried to build around my heart.

I leaned my head on his chest, just as I was a moment ago with his brother, inhaling that heavenly scent of his that I missed so damn much. I felt him rest his cheek on my head, his arm pulling me closer into his hard body. I tried my best to hold back my tears, my whole body trembling and threatening to shut down under the waves of sorrow and pain that invaded my chest.

Liam held me like he never wanted to let go, and right then, I finally felt safe again. I closed my eyes, savoring the warm, tender kiss he planted on my forehead, his lips lingering on my skin.

"I love you, Jamie. I'll always love you. My heart is unquestionably yours." I looked up at him, surprised to hear those words, and without hesitation, Liam captured my lips in a soft, loving kiss. I weakly leaned into it before realizing what we were doing.

I pushed against his chest, breaking the kiss, Liam's hold tightening to prevent me from leaving.

"I'm sorry, don't go."

"I have to Liam. I can't handle this. I can't let you break whatever I've been able to rebuild these past weeks." I managed to say, stinging tears forming in my eyes.

"I guess it's my turn now." That scratchy voice came again from behind me as Mr. Mercier interrupted us, hastily pulling me to him.

I could see Liam's expression plunging into a vile darkness that reeked of danger from a distance, murder written all over his blazing features. I shook my head at him, telling him not to react to this, watching as he finally relented and walked over to where Matt, Alison, and his future wife were standing.

Liam's eyes were permanently glued to the both of us while I focused mine on him, too. But somewhere between the twists and twirls, I lost him.

"It's extremely hard to get you alone, Miss Harden." His voice had a different edge to it, something that made me even more uncomfortable lurking behind his words. "I heard you're no longer spoken for. Too bad your little boyfriend found a better-suiting tramp for him. That leaves the path wide open for me." He smiled, those yellowed teeth making me shiver in disgust while his hand roamed down my back.

"I'm sorry to disappoint you, Mr. Mercier, but I am neither available nor interested. Have a good night." I gathered all my courage to reply as I tried to leave, but he wouldn't let me, his hand squeezing mine in his painfully.

"You're only leaving when I say you can." He whispered in a low, menacing voice, spinning us around towards the back of the room. I hastily tried to break free from his grasp, my fingers being crushed by his hand in response. I groaned in pain, but he didn't seem to care.

The hand he had plastered onto the small of my back dipped into the inside pocket of his suit jacket. He pulled out a beaten red rose, crushed and flattened from being kept in there. Without a word, he placed it in my cleavage before pulling me harshly back against his body.

"AD can thank you for landing this project. I granted them this opportunity so I could see you more often, Beautiful." Shivers ran down my spine at the darkness in his tone.

His eyes were wild and scary tonight. I had tried to avoid him so much that I hadn't taken in the ruthlessness in his features. There was madness in his look, a smile that spoke of obsession and unhinged lunacy.

Fear crept up my body while I frantically turned my head in every direction, trying to find Liam or Matt. I swallowed the lump that formed in my throat, realizing I couldn't see any of them.

Mr. Mercier had successfully pushed me towards a narrow corridor and shoved me against a wall, holding both of my hands above my head in a deadly grip that made me quiver in pain. His other hand harshly roamed my skin as I twisted my body in a feeble attempt to break free.

"Please stop. Please," I begged, tears desperately running down my face now, but he either didn't hear my pleas or pretended not to.

I tried to scream, and as the first sound left my mouth, his heavy hand slapped me hard across the cheek, bursting my lip open. There was hot blood running down the corner of my mouth, already mixing with my unrelenting tears.

"Another sound and I'll be fucking you while you're out cold."

I wasn't sure that was the worst scenario.

He continued the assault on my body, spreading my legs with his knee, pushing hard so he could position himself between them. I struggled to keep them tightly closed together, but he harshly buried his fingers in my thighs, making me gasp in pain as he forced them apart.

I couldn't believe this was happening to me. He might as well just kill me now so that I didn't have to live through this, too. Every time I fought to free myself, he would tighten his grip on my wrists, making me yelp with the excruciating pain, squeezing my throat with the other.

"Look at me, Jamie." His voice was a sick sing-song, and when I didn't do as he commanded, he moved his hand to my jaw in a vice grip and banged my skull on the wall he held me up against before screaming in my face, splatters of spit landing all over my face. "I SAID LOOK AT ME."

My eyes moved up to his as the pain soared through my body. In his gaze, I saw my demise. There was no way this madman before me was letting me go.

"I like my whores to look at me while I bring them pleasure. Do you want me to pleasure you, Jamie?"

I slowly shook my head no, but he didn't care what my reply was in the least.

He grabbed my breast tightly, squeezing it in painful pulses as more tears fell from the agonizing pain and the notion of what was happening to me. He stuck his tongue out and licked the side of my face, coating me in his disgusting spit as he reached down and cupped my pussy.

"I'm gonna do you so good. I'm going to fuck you until you're raw, baby. You'll be pleading for more when I'm done with you."

"Please stop." I choked on my sobs, trying my best to twist and pull out of his grip.

"I'll stop when I'm satisfied. No one says no to me, Miss Harden. You'll be licking my cum off the floor before the end of the night, and I'm going to enjoy every fucking minute of it."

I tried to kick back and knee him in the balls, but the only thing I got was more pain, more slaps, and more bruises.

I was getting tired of fighting and it was getting me nowhere.

I tried screaming one more time before he grabbed my jaw like before and heavily banged my head against the wall again. Slowly, I felt the sweet peace of darkness sneaking in through the corners of my eyes. It came in mercy, to steal my pain away, to ease the trauma of this memory.

Suddenly I was free, my wrists falling heavily to my sides as my knees gave out from under me. I couldn't hold myself up, the pain in my skull stealing my vision and strength as I fell to the ground.

My vision was blurry, but my last memory before blacking out was an enraged Liam and his beautiful face painted in streaks of crimson.

After that?

Nothing. After that, I was finally free and plunging into darkness.

CHAPTER THIRTY FOUR

Liam

*I*t's all my fault that we're here now.

There was a weight being lifted from my shoulders each time I held Jamie in my arms.

Today was no different.

Her big brown eyes looked deep into mine, filled with sadness and torment as we danced. She looked absolutely breathtaking, but under her makeup and elegant dress, I saw her beaten features and protruding bones. Every time I saw the agony in her eyes, it killed off another piece of my soul, and I was already running low these days.

She looked at me in shock when I told her I loved her. I couldn't help but claim her as mine in one last kiss. Show her it was true, make her feel the undying love I would forever have for her.

My Jamie.

She was the one.

The *only* one.

The one who could summon my angels and ease my demons.

It's all my fault that we're here now.

Matt escorted Francesca to the hotel where she was staying while I took Jamie to the hospital. Alison came with us, in tears during the whole drive, cradling Jamie's head in her lap, trying her best to stop the bleeding on the back of her head.

The blood that painted my hands in red wasn't hers, though. And in my opinion, I had very little of it littering my clothes for comfort. I craved more. I needed a whole lot more to feel that I had even remotely avenged her.

They had to practically peel me off of that sick son of a bitch. He was barely breathing once they finally managed to. I'll need to revisit and finish the job later. Right now, I had other priorities. I had to take care of her, make sure she made it through this.

My heart was unmendably broken from what happened, from knowing what she went through. It physically hurt. The sharp pain penetrated my chest, spreading deep through my flesh, tearing me apart from the inside.

It's all my fault that we're here now.

I was sitting in the barren waiting room with Alison next to me, staring into the blue sterile floors of the hospital, not daring to blink. Time went by at an agonizingly slow pace as we both fell into despair waiting for the news. Any news.

Finally, a nurse came by saying that Jamie was taken to a room and was now resting. She led us there, her small legs taking forever to cover the length from the waiting room to the last door down the hall.

"Are you the husband?" The nurse asked before we entered her room.

"Yes, I am." I proudly replied, Alison's eyes widening at me for the shameful lie. I couldn't care less. I was hers, and she was mine, that's all that mattered at the end of the damn day. They'd never disclose any information if I said otherwise.

"The doctor will be here shortly to speak with you. We gave her a powerful sedative so she'll be able to rest right through the night. She needs all the rest she can get."

Finally, the nurse stepped out of our way, and my eyes welled up with tears as soon as they rested on Jamie.

She looked so pale in her deep slumber. So fragile. There were already bruises painting her beautiful skin in blue and black patches.

I gently caressed her hair and kissed her forehead before taking a chair and sitting by her side, holding her cold and scraped hand in mine. I couldn't imagine the terror she might have felt while that son of a bitch drove his filthy hands all over her body.

It's all my fault that we're here now.

I should have never let him take her away from me. Be relaxed while he swirled her around the fucking dance floor. I saw the way he looked at her. I knew he wanted her, craved her.

How had I not seen the sick fucker behind the corporate façade? I was too fucking slow to understand that he had disappeared with her. I lost them in the middle of the crowd.

If there was a God above, I just hoped he had gotten me there in time to prevent the worst.

It's my fucking fault we are here now!!!

The doctor finally arrived, checking her chart first before turning to us.

"Are you her husband, Mr. …?" He asked, again the same question as before, and I replied with the same confidence I did earlier as I stood up to shake his hand.

"Battaglia. Yes, I am." I purposely used that name, knowing the man would recognize it.

"Can I speak to you in private out in the hall?" His expression was somber, making me fear what was coming. My heart immediately sank from his tone alone.

I nodded and followed him outside, leaving Alison to take my spot next to Jamie, holding her hand and caressing her arm in smooth, soothing motions.

"Mr. Battaglia, we ran some tests on Mrs. Harden, and she has a mild concussion from a head injury that needed stitches. The bruising on her body is superficial and will heal over time, and there are no broken bones. That's all. There's no indication of forced intercourse." He paused, waiting for his words to sink in. I sighed in relief. That mother fucker didn't get to do what he had set out to.

"So can we take her home when she wakes up?" I wanted nothing more than to have her in a safe space where I could take care of her and make sure nothing ever happened to her again.

"Not just yet."

"But from what you just said, she has no major problem. Why keep her here?"

"Mr. Battaglia, we would like to keep her under observation. Your wife suffered a miscarriage, and we want to monitor her closely for a couple of days to watch for signs of excessive bleeding, and have her talk to a psychiatrist depending on her state when she wakes up."

A miscarriage?

I just stood there. My mouth had fallen open as I looked at the doctor in disbelief before my body collapsed onto the chairs behind me as the realization sank in, my head buried in my hands.

She was pregnant.

Jamie was pregnant with my baby.

And now… nothing.

I had never thought about becoming a father. Not that I didn't want to, but still, it was something that had never crossed my mind.

But thinking that the woman that I love was carrying *my* baby felt like the best thing in the world. And that fucker took it away from me. From us.

Did she know?

"I'm sorry, Mr. Battaglia, to break the news to you this way. She was very early on, it's possible she hadn't realized yet. It's clear that you didn't."

He mumbled a few other things I didn't quite register while I just sat there taking small, shallow breaths as grief filled me up to the brim. Grief that quickly turned into anger, closely followed by hate.

I knew exactly what I needed to do.

After dismissing the doctor, I called Mike and told him to meet me at the hospital and bring Jimmy with him. They would be guarding the door to Jamie's room until she was out of here and safely at home.

When I found the strength to get up from those chairs, I walked back into her room. Alison was still sitting beside her, whispering encouragement into her thoughts.

I took in those bruises one by one, the pain that must have come with each one, the anguish of fighting, knowing there was no possibility to win.

My grandfather always said that real men only cry when their children are born. Well I was crying because mine would never be. I'd never get to meet my child because of a sick and twisted fucker that deserved to suffer.

In two wide strides, I was kneeling beside her, pleading for forgiveness. Alison shot up as soon as she saw me enter the room, panicking when she saw my tears and dark expression.

"I'm sorry, Baby. I'm so fucking sorry." I repeated in a loop, hugging her and kissing her skin, desperately hoping my love could heal her.

"Liam, what happened? What did the doctor say?" I couldn't answer. The truth was stuck in my throat and wouldn't budge. "Liam, please. Don't tell me that son of a bitch raped her."

"He didn't," I replied, and even though it was a relief that he didn't get to do it, my heart was still twisted in agony.

I kissed her again and caressed her hair, pulling it away from her face, the cold silence growing the panic in Alison's eyes.

"She had a miscarriage." I finally managed to say, the words cutting my tongue like sharp knives while new tears stained my cheeks. Alison's eyes grew wide in shock as she gasped loudly in disbelief.

I closed my eyes tightly, resting my head in the crook of Jamie's neck, inhaling her scent and filling my lungs with power and drive. She was all the reason I needed. The strength under my wings and the madness in my veins.

"I'll take care of it, Baby. I promise." I whispered into her hair.

Mike and Jimmy arrived, and I barked out my orders, making it clear that not a soul was allowed in her fucking room.

"Where are you going?" Alison shouted as I marched out of the hospital, heading towards my fate, driven by all the darkness within my soul.

I got to my car, sped out of the parking lot way above the speed limit, and headed straight to Dea Tacita.

I had to make this right. I had to fucking solve this.

I burst into Matt's office with my gun in my hand, popping a bullet inside the chamber. My boiling blood ran through my veins, pumping my heart with an enraged heat that burned any ounce of self-preservation to ash.

I pointed the gun at Matt, angrily puffing through my clenched teeth. I was driven by rage and insanity. By regret and guilt. But most of all, I was driven by love.

"Liam, what do you think you're doing?" Matt asked, his calm voice grating harder on my nerves.

I harshly grabbed his hand and placed the gun in it, placing the end of the barrel against my head. I forced his hand tightly around it with my own, holding my thumb over the trigger, pushing the steel further against my forehead, feeling the cold metal bury into my skin.

"Shoot me, Matt. Fucking shoot me right now. I am as good as dead. I am not fucking marrying the Amato girl!"

CHAPTER THIRTY FIVE

Liam

"Calm down," Matt said, his voice low and steady, trying to diffuse the tension, pausing between words. "I know what happened."

"What? How?" I asked, confused but still driven by anger, my finger remaining firmly pressed on the trigger.

"Alison called in a panic when you left the hospital. That fucker is going to pay for what he did, Liam, and I'm here to help you make that happen. Just put down the gun. We're on the same side here."

Slowly, Matt managed to take my hands off his. He cleared the chamber and took out the magazine before setting the half-dismantled gun safely on his desk. The outcome wouldn't have been so amicable if it were someone else. My brother had a reputation to uphold, and having a gun shoved in his face, for whatever reason, never ended well for the person threatening him.

Dea Tacita had been repainted many times to cover up some artistic blood Pollocks he'd left drying on the walls to remind the whole *cosca* of what happened to people who crossed the line.

I was privileged, but having him back down wasn't my end goal when I marched into his office and made him hold me at gunpoint.

I didn't fucking care if he showed restraint or not. I wanted a solution. If there was none, he could go ahead and pull the fucking trigger for all I cared. At least that would keep it within the family because as soon as I held up my middle finger to the Amatos and their marriage proposition, either they or The Commission would sign my death warrant.

I frantically paced around the room, all the fucked up things that happened in the last few hours wreaking havoc in my mind.

They were all my fault.

If I had taken proper care of Jamie, maybe my son or daughter would still be growing inside her. Maybe she wouldn't have gone through the terror of almost being raped. Maybe she wouldn't be lying in a fucking hospital bed right now, tainted with blotches of black and blue bruises as a reminder of what that fucker did to her.

"She was pregnant, Matt. She was fucking pregnant!" I shouted, my hands pulling on my hair while anger burned a path from my heart right through to my soul. I saw his eyes burning brighter with the same thirst for revenge I had, a reaction to the despair in my voice. "I'm not leaving her, Matt. I don't care what The Commission has decided. I'd rather fucking die than see pain in her eyes again."

"I know. We'll make it right."

"This is a warning. I'm going to the Amatos tonight."

Matt's cold and calm demeanor remained unaffected as he slowly sauntered towards the chair behind his desk, sat down, and lit a cigarette.

"You're doing no such thing." He said after releasing a cloud of smoke from that first deep drag.

"I wasn't asking for permission, Matt." My reply was clipped and cold.

"I've already asked Grandpa to summon The Commission. The meeting is set for two weeks from Friday."

"I don't think you're listening. I don't give a fuck about The Commission. There's nothing they can say that will make me change my mind. I'm done." I spat, my rage blinding me from any consequences.

"It's damage control, Liam. Word is already on the street that Liam Battaglia left his fiancé alone to accompany another woman." Despite his words, Matt's tone wasn't accusatory, it was calm and neutral, which only grated on my nerves further.

"I don't think you heard me correctly. I. Don't. Give. A FUCK." They could think, say, and do whatever they wanted, I was done with living my life by other people's rules.

The Amatos were preying on what happened to Amelia, pinning it on me to achieve their goal. I wasn't going to pay for something that I didn't do. My life was not theirs to control.

"Listen, Liam." Matt stood from his chair, gripping my shoulders and steadying me from my stressed march around the room, giving me a shake as if he was making space for his words to fit into my head. "I'm trying to help you here. We're on the same side."

"Really? And exactly what the fuck are *you* able to do to change The Commission's mind?" I was hurting and aiming to hurt just as much. Matt knew exactly what I meant as I emphasized the fact that he was nobody. He wasn't Grandpa. He wasn't even a Don yet. I stared at him defiantly, waiting for his answer.

Matt released my shoulders and calmly paraded around the room, arrogantly puffing on his fucking cigarette. His calmness and eerie serenity were exasperating, contrasting greatly with my building anxiety.

"I'll make them a deal they can't refuse." He spun on his heels, his arms stretched, and his chest puffed like a fucking peacock, topping it off with a grin that would make the fucking Cheshire cat blush. "ME!"

"What?" I was sure I didn't hear him correctly.

"You heard me. I'll take your place and marry Francesca Amato, and you'll be free to be with Jamie. I'm the future Don of the Battaglia *cosca*, they won't refuse."

"And why would you do that?" I asked, dangling between hope and remorse.

Matt had never taken a real interest in any woman he'd dated, so listening to him speak about marriage came as a shock.

"It's one of Grandpa's conditions to step down and let me take over. The Commission will also accept me better if I am a family man. I'll have to comply someday. Francesca is an intriguing woman, beautiful as fuck, too. Might as well kill two birds with one stone. And you, my little brother," he walked back towards me, his hands on my shoulders again, "You'll be free."

To say I was stunned was an understatement. I could have never imagined Matt doing something like this for me. Sure, he had other motivations as well, but still. He could have chosen anyone else, and he would still get what he wanted in the end.

My older brother was a handsome fucker, filthy rich, too. The line of contenders would have been long and diverse.

Either he grew a fucking conscience, which I found unlikely, or there was something else about Francesca that he wasn't telling me.

"Did something happen between you two when you took her to her hotel?"

"No." He let go of me, taking another exaggerated puff out of his cigarette.

"You like her." It was an affirmation, I could see it in his little tell, dragging harder on the damn thing.

"No, I don't. I find her intriguing, there's a difference."

"Right."

I smiled for the first time after the clusterfuck of the last couple of hours, my breath finally slowing down to a regular pace.

"Marrying her will get me what I want. That damn seat in The Commission should be mine already."

"And that's all? Convenience and nothing else?"

"They're doing it to us, so might as well pay them back in the same fucking currency." There was more to it than what he let on. I knew my brother too well, but right now, I'd take what he was selling.

There was light at the end of this tunnel, and I wasn't feeling the slightest bit of guilt for using my brother to save me from a fate that didn't belong to me.

The question that remained was, would Jamie still take me back?

"Don't mention any of this before it's settled. Not that I'm foreseeing any resistance, but it's best to be safe. For now, you should keep the surveillance on Jamie and lay low as well. The Amatos know what you did today, and I'm sure they're not pleased."

"Sure thing, Boss." I teased with a smile before hugging my brother and finally feeling hopeful again.

Jamie

I woke up feeling drowsy, struggling just to open my eyes. My head hurt, a dull and constant pain pulsing on the crown of my skull, while my limbs felt heavy, each muscle sore from the struggle.

There was a bright light above my head, shining intensely, making it hard to see anything past it. Slowly, I turned my head to the left, my eyes settling on Liam. He sat in a chair next to my bed, his head resting on the mattress. With one hand, he held mine, while his other one rested flat on top of my stomach, the warmth from his skin radiating straight to my core.

He's here.

I took in the bare walls, painted in a faint blue, the machines that beeped in a steady rhythm, the smell of disinfectant and broken hope.

I was in the hospital.

My eyes closed again as my memory was swamped with the blurry images of the previous night. Tears formed under my eyelids, falling down my face without permission or mercy.

Did he rape me? Did he manage to finish what he wanted?

The uncertainty was killing me.

I tried to swallow the sorrow, but every time I tried, it balled back up, my throat stinging each time I insisted.

The vision of that repulsive hand squeezing the life out of me returned as if it was happening right now. I let out a muffled cry, covering my mouth with my free hand as vivid flashbacks haunted me on repeat.

Everything that happened suddenly came back. His dirty hands touching me, his fingers digging into my skin, his tongue running up my face.

Nausea hit me in heavy waves, the disgust of his touch still lingering on my dirty skin.

Liam suddenly woke up, and with a single look at me, he saw I wouldn't be able to hold it. He grabbed the trash can by the door and held it in front of me just in time for me to empty my stomach into it.

My tears were unrelenting, the pain trying to leave my body through them, but it only seemed to make it worse. I hurled again and again until there was nothing left in me.

Liam cleaned me up, a soft washcloth dampening my skin in tender swipes. I saw the fear of hurting me in his eyes, his eyebrows joined in the center with worry and caution.

He hugged me to his chest, giving me a safe and warm place to cry while he cradled my head in his arms, soothing my pain with feather-light kisses. There was something about him that, whenever he held me, all my desolation was drained and replaced with serenity.

I let myself absorb the healing magic from his touch and the peace from his kisses before breaking free and facing my demons.

"Liam, please tell me. Did he?" My voice was a broken whisper, hoarse and pained.

"No, my love. He didn't." A new flow of tears rushed from my eyes, relief filling my lungs. "But something else happened, Jamie."

I looked into his eyes, not uttering a word in expectance, waiting for him to carry on. There was this overwhelming sadness swimming around in those green pools that shattered my heart all over again. He paused, trying to control the tears from falling down his face, but ultimately losing the battle.

"You were pregnant, Jamie. You had a miscarriage. I'm sorry, Baby, I'm so fucking sorry." His voice was laced in an agony that shot straight to my chest.

I was pregnant? How?

I tried to understand as I hugged Liam back, my heart sinking deep into my chest, burning a hole right through to the other side. The devastation in his voice was soul-wrecking.

Breath was cut from my lungs once those words finally sunk into understanding.

I didn't know.

I didn't even have the chance to find out.

To feel the happiness it would have brought me, knowing that my love for this man blossomed into a perfect being growing inside me. We weren't together, and it had never crossed my mind before, but I would have happily accepted this gift and loved that baby with all my heart.

The urge to scream was crippling, a foreign pain growing wild inside me.

First I lost Liam, the love of my life, the better half of my soul. Then my dignity was wrecked at the hands of that monster, and now I've lost something I never even knew I truly wanted. Our baby.

I broke down again, holding onto Liam as he mourned with me. Time froze as we held each other, seeking solace when everything else around us only meant heartbreak and pain.

He laid on my bed, bringing me close and holding me for what seemed like eternity. I placed my head on his heart, listening to the lullaby it sang into my ears.

We didn't need words. We needed each other.

But soon I'd have to let go, stand on my own. Liam was engaged now, and his beautiful fiancé was waiting for him to get back to her.

I had to do my best to guard my heart, I couldn't let him take hold of it again. I couldn't depend on him to heal this time.

"Liam," I called, looking up at him after gathering all the courage I possibly could to push him away. That courage came with a fresh flow of tears, something else being ripped away from me. But I couldn't pretend he was mine. I couldn't expect him to be here every time I crumbled. "You should go. I can't–"

Liam cut me off, capturing my lips in his, a tender, loving kiss that set butterflies flying wild in my stomach, and I couldn't break free. This... this was my safe haven.

"I'm right here. I won't be going anywhere where you're not." He promised against my lips, sealing it with another kiss before his green eyes set on mine, prying into the depths of my soul.

"I...I don't understand."

"Let me make it clear to you then. There's only one person on this Earth I'll ever agree to marry, and that's you, Miss Harden."

CHAPTER THIRTY SIX

Jamie

They kept me under observation for three days, all of which Liam had spent beside me. I shivered each time I saw the bruises on my skin. Blue patches of shame that brought back the memories of that night.

His fingers were imprinted on my neck and wrists, his wild eyes flashing in my brain each time I closed mine.

But I was ready to move on. Liam had breathed a new reason to live into me. Even though he was adamant about not disclosing the details of what exactly had changed, I believed every word he said.

I wanted to be with him. I unquestionably knew who my heart belonged to. But there was this nagging feeling in me that wanted to know why that was now possible. I had let it go while we were in the hospital, it wasn't the time or place to press for answers. But I couldn't just sweep it under the rug and forget it ever happened.

Liam insisted on taking me back to his apartment, saying that his men were more comfortable guarding it than my place. There was also the fact that Tremont was further away from Dea Tacita. If any alarm sounded, bulky, heavily armed, angry-looking men would be at our doorstep before I could snap my fingers.

He kept checking on me. Asking if I was okay, and I knew he didn't mean physically.

The years I'd endured of verbal and psychological abuse made physical abuse much easier to overcome.

The first broke me from within. Like a small, explosive device, implanted in my brain, where every angry and harsh word shortened the fuse, making it much harder to pick up the shattered pieces once it finally went off. It killed who I was in a slow torture, taking away small portions of myself and my true essence, never to be recovered.

My bruises would heal in time. They required more patience than endurance, and from what I had gone through, I had both.

So I assured him, every single time, that with his wind under my wings, all I needed was time and his healing kisses.

As we finally arrived at Liam's apartment, I noticed most of my stuff was here. He had his men bring it over so I had everything I needed. It was a good, welcoming gift, making me feel at home in his space. I took my time breathing in the good memories I had of this place. I needed them for what I was going to push for. The truth.

I slowly took a seat on the couch, patting the place beside me and waiting for him to join me. We were finally home, and now was the time to set everything out in the open. I couldn't wait any longer for him to explain this whole mess.

"Liam, I want to know."

"Alright." He relented, taking the spot beside me and pulling my hand into his. "What do you want to know first?"

It was clear he knew my questions were coming.

"Why aren't you marrying her anymore?" I asked before thinking, but backtracking to what was plaguing me first. "No wait, first I want to know *why* you were marrying her in the first place."

My eyes detoured from his face to the couch, the feeling of betrayal creeping under my skin. I was trying as hard as I could not to feel like he had played me, desperately waiting for his answer to ease my heart.

"A few months back, I met a girl at a store, and we started talking and flirting." He had barely started and his words were already twisting my gut in jealousy. "I was distracted, I didn't realize the store was being robbed at the same time. They weren't expecting us to be there and attacked as soon as they saw us. I managed to fight three of them off, but the other two took my gun and restrained me. They were holding a gun to my head when Amelia smashed a bottle of booze on one of the guy's heads. The one holding my gun shot her with it in retribution. They ran away immediately, and I tried to stop the bleeding. I tried to save her, but it was too little too late. She was Enzo Amato's daughter, the Don of the Detroit *cosca*. We couldn't recover any of the surveillance footage because it was all staged by the owner of the store. We were the ones responsible for the protection of that damn 7-Eleven, and Amelia died on my watch with my gun, with no proof that it hadn't been me. The only way of preventing a war was with a settlement, and my sentence was set the day before we arrived from LA. I had no idea they would make me marry into their family. I feared for your safety if I refused. Because they wouldn't make it easy and just kill me, they would come after you. That's the Mafia, Jamie. Fucked up men that play with people's lives."

I sat there, listening and barely blinking, taking in all that information, a few pieces of the puzzle finally falling into place.

"Your tattoo. Forgive but never forget. It's about her, isn't it?"

"It's about all of them. Especially those fuckers who thrust me into this darkness. This happened in Tremont, close to your apartment, in fact. That's why you're never setting foot into that place again. It's too dangerous, and I won't be taking any unnecessary risks. I've learned my lesson."

"It happened in Tremont? When was this?" Liam looked at me puzzled, not understanding why it mattered.

"About a week or so before I met you."

I couldn't believe it. The coincidence was too bone-chilling to be anything but divine intervention. It was a damn shame that poor girl had to die because of it.

"That store closed down."

"Of course. I made sure of it."

"I worked there. It closed down, and I was on the street, out of a job. That's when I applied for the urgent position at AD." Shit, this was wild.

"What? You mean that I met you because of the nightmare that's been haunting my conscience ever since?"

"It seems so." I was grateful, but I couldn't help but feel guilty, too.

"Don't take this the wrong way, Baby, but when I met you, it felt like I was being punished by her ghost. There's something about you that's eerily reminiscent of her. Maybe your hair or your eyes. I don't know. But it was like I was seeing her in front of me again, only it wasn't possible because I held her in my arms as she released her last breath." I smiled weakly. I wasn't thrilled that he had thought of her when he saw me, but then again, Liam was truly scarred by the situation.

This was probably the turning point Liam had mentioned. Having an innocent girl die in his arms while he was supposed to be protecting the place. Being blamed for all of it and not having a way to prove his innocence. But why did he now feel comfortable in gambling with our safety?

"What changed? I mean, why can you decline now?"

"Matt is going to try to make a new deal with them. It's not certain yet that it will work. But he has a solid case."

"So, you might still end up having to marry her?" My eyes welled up with tears at the sound of my own words.

"Fuck no. I will protect you with all I have, Jamie. With my life, if it comes to it. You *will* be safe. But I will not agree to die a slow death by living a life away from you. I'd take a bullet to the skull any day." He replied, cupping my cheek and making me see the sincerity in his eyes.

"Why didn't you tell me? Why did you let me think that I was just another prize on your long list of hook-ups?" My breath hitched in my throat, remembering the pain I was in while thinking I was nothing to someone so important in my life.

"I tried, but at first you wouldn't listen. And then I realized that if you hated me, you would get over me sooner. Be happy. I wanted that for you, even though it gutted me to think that you could find happiness with someone else."

"I can't," I confessed. "I could never be happy without you."

"Then give Matt a chance. He'll make it right. Now let's forget about it. Come here, I've missed you." Liam leaned into me, kissing my lips, his tone playful but still guarded.

Liam was walking on eggshells around me because of what happened. He was overthinking each movement and my reaction to each one of his touches. It would take time before I healed completely, and truthfully, I didn't think some of the wounds ever would.

"So when will we know?" I asked, pulling away from his kiss but still holding on to his neck.

"Two weeks from Friday. We will know as soon as the meeting is over."

Liam

I heard her crying in the middle of the night. She did that every single night since we had come home. She somehow managed to stay strong during the day, only to crumble in the privacy that the shadows brought.

Every time I heard that sound, I wished I had killed that mother fucker.

There was no choice but to turn him in to the police since we needed the hospital to examine Jamie for forced intercourse.

I had trouble saying the fucking word. *Rape.*

We had to press charges and hand the fucker in. We had him under surveillance, knowing he would be free in less time than he deserved since he didn't get to actually go through with it. Since it was his first charge, they'd go easy on him for sure. That was the fucking justice system we had in this damn country. Rotten to its roots.

They'd set his bail, and being a fucking millionaire, he won't have any trouble accessing his funds to cover it. I was glad to at least postpone it a bit. He had been admitted to the hospital after the beating I gave him, and to me, it felt like it still wasn't enough. I wasn't about to let Jamie live in fear of what that scumbag might try to do to her.

In due time, I'd be paying that decaying fucker a nice little midnight visit.

Tonight, though? My mind had taken a small break from planning how I'd dispose of his body to make way for the anxiety that preceded The Commission's meeting. Luckily Jimmy had called asking if he could come over to talk about the mission I had assigned him. Maybe that could help me take my mind off what was happening downtown right about now.

Matt had my balls in a twist for two whole weeks, but I tried my best to be as confident as possible whenever Jamie brought up the subject.

The only way the outcome of that meeting would affect my life was whether Jamie and I could stay in New York or if we had to get the fuck out of here. I wouldn't be considering any other options. With Jamie by my side, I could be happy anywhere. Give me a cabin in the woods and the woman of my dreams, and I'd beat off any bear that tried to get to us.

I waited for Jimmy by the door, trying to hold up the calm mask I had plastered on my face for Jamie's sake.

He was the one who carried out our investigations. His exceptional skills at digging up dirt were a game-changer. He was in charge of following the leads Frank had given us after a nice hard beating. This visit meant one of two things – either he had hit a dead-end, or he found out who Jamie's father was.

I walked him straight to my home office, closing the door behind him, making sure we were far from Jamie's hearing range. I wanted to know what he had for me first before getting her hopes up.

She didn't need another fucking heartbreak right now, so I was the only one he was allowed to disclose information to. No messengers, no texts, no emails.

"Spit, Jimmy. What do you have for me?" I hastily asked as I sat down on my chair behind the desk, motioning for Jimmy to take the seat in front of me.

"Frank didn't give us much to work on besides Jamie's birth certificate. It isn't signed by him or her real father. That means he was telling us the truth about not being her father. He said a woman would send him cash every month to keep him quiet and for him to cover the baby's needs. He didn't know who sent it, but whoever it was really didn't want Jamie to be found. We checked the transfer details, and the trail leads to an offshore account. Un-fucking-traceable. We searched the house for anything that might have given us any clue. We didn't find anything conclusive." He explained.

Fuck. I couldn't believe this was it. If someone could find something, it would be Jimmy.

"But we did find this at Jamie's apartment when you sent us for her stuff." He continued, fishing in his pocket for something.

My eyes widened in shock as I saw the engraved symbol on the signet ring he handed me.

"FA. Fuck!" I grunted. "You could have started off with this. Have you told anyone? Has anyone else seen this?" I sternly asked him.

"No, Boss. You're the first." My head fell back as I let the information sink in. This couldn't be true. I'd recognize this symbol anywhere. I had seen several documents and letters with this seal on them.

Every *cosca* had one, including ours. The only difference was that ours read "FB," *Famiglia Battaglia*.

"Do you have any clue which one of them is the owner?"

Jimmy nodded his head, and as I turned the ring in my fingers, I saw why. Engraved on the inside of the ring was the inscription – *"Distintivo dell'Omerta.EEA."*

Fuck. Fuck. Fuck.

This fucking ring belonged to Enzo Emilio Amato.

CHAPTER THIRTY SEVEN

Liam

I paced around the office, Jimmy's eyes following my every step. I was trying to process the bomb I held in my hands. Literally.

"Does this mean what I think it does?" Jimmy asked.

"I think it does. It's not a fucking DNA test, but it comes pretty close."

This ring undoubtedly belonged to Enzo Amato. It was a symbol of his sworn Omertà. Even if it were made out of tin foil instead of gold, it was invaluable to its owner. It was proof of his loyalty to the Mafiosi family. A token of his respect and commitment to live by our code of honor and silence, sealed with blood, and only with blood repaired if broken.

This ring was the symbol of his ceremony. Enzo wouldn't have lost it or gifted it to someone who had no importance to him.

There was a tradition that not every *cosca* followed, where the owner of one of these would gift it to the love of his life, bonding their soul and connection through the blood spilled to receive it.

But I had to be sure this was the case before I spoke to Matt. There might not be a need for him to marry Francesca at all.

"I have to find out where Jamie got this from. We'll know then." I walked towards the office door, already rehearsing how I'd address the issue without raising any unnecessary suspicions with Jamie. "Oh, and Jimmy, I don't think I need to tell you that this remains confidential. Am I clear?"

"Crystal." I nodded and started for the door before he stopped me. "But boss? There's something else you need to know."

I was so eager to get to the bottom of this and stop my brother from sacrificing his life that I had automatically thought this was all that Jimmy had come to tell me. What more could there be?

I turned around to face him, giving him a short nod for him to carry on.

"Frank implied that Jamie's mother didn't die in childbirth as she believes. He thinks she was killed right after delivering while still in the hospital. We searched the visitor's log in their archives, and the only odd entry is of a woman called Francis Harden. Frank didn't give his name to Jamie, so Harden is her mother's maiden name. The strange thing about this is that Jamie's mother didn't have any female family members alive. No mother, no sisters, no cousins, and no aunts."

Color me fucking shocked. This whole thing was beginning to sound a lot like a commissioned murder, only confirming my suspicions that Enzo had, in fact, been involved with Jamie's mother. But who would have done it?

"See what else you can get, but be discreet about it. Report back if you find anything else. *Anything*. Thanks, Jimmy."

I led him to the door, quickly shutting it behind him.

That last piece of information was disturbing as fuck. If Frank was right and Mrs. Harden was in fact killed, it would probably be the same person who paid him to shut up and take care of Jamie.

I looked down at the ring in my hand again, inhaling deeply, and marching towards the kitchen where Jamie was busy cooking and humming to the tune of the song playing on the speaker.

"Hmmm... My God!" I inhaled her sweet scent as I hugged her from behind, my nose deeply buried in the crook of her neck. "I don't know what smells better, you or whatever it is you're making."

It was the first time Jamie was cooking here, and somehow she seemed happy. She looked better each day as her bruises faded and her skin regained its cute flush. And today of all days, when our future was depending on a bunch of old farts that took pleasure in playing God.

I, on the other hand, still had this enormous weight on my shoulders, and this meeting with Jimmy had done nothing to ease the burden.

"Why, hello there, Sir." She teased, turning her head around and placing a peck on the tip of my nose.

"Hello to you, Beautiful." I spun her around to face me, taking her lips in mine before plunging into whatever voyage this ring would take us on. "I found this ring, is it yours?" I asked, holding out the ring for her.

"Oh my God. Yes. It was my mother's." Jamie took the ring from my hand, her eyes beaming as she looked at it, not hiding the nostalgia this item brought. "It's just some cheap jewelry I guess she liked. With her and my…hum… Frank's initials. See?" She showed me the letters engraved on it, tracing them with her thumb. "FA it stands for Frank and Amanda. She must have loved it. She wore it on a necklace since it's huge. Every single photo I have of her pregnant with me, although there aren't many, she always had it around her neck." There was sadness coming afloat again, and I'd do anything to keep her in the chipper mood I had found her in just a minute ago, but I had to push.

"It's really nice. Any idea where she got it from?"

"I don't really know. Frank never talked much about her, or them for that matter. One day he just gave me a box full of her things, and this ring was inside it, together with some photos and other personal things of hers."

"It's nice that you have something of hers to remember her by." I pulled her in for another kiss as a pivot to change the subject before she asked why I was so interested in what she thought was nothing but a piece of junk jewelry. "What are you making for dinner that smells absolutely divine?"

"Lasagna," Jamie replied, wiggling her eyebrows before a bright smile illuminated her face. It was the first real and genuine smile she had flashed probably since the day we returned from LA. I fucking missed it like water in a desert.

"Oh, the cliché!" I joked, my head falling back in a theatrical exaggeration as I tried to lighten the mood and her spirits. She laughed at the gesture and I couldn't help but think that this was exactly what I wanted my life to be like. That was the sound I wanted to hear every damn day – our laughter filling the air.

We savored the perfect meal Jamie prepared for us with a lightness I couldn't remember ever experiencing that somehow managed to take my mind off the meeting that was happening as we ate. I convinced her that the dishes were my duty and sent her off to read one of those books she always kept her nose in when she wasn't working.

Halfway through cleaning, my phone flashed with the text I was anxious to receive.

> I'm downstairs. Want to talk alone or in front of Jamie?

> I'll be right down.

I never wanted to have secrets from Jamie again, but this particular issue required delicacy, and I had to speak with Matt about my discoveries before telling her everything I thought I knew.

I tiptoed out of the apartment and sprinted down the stairs. The elevator was too slow for the current of energy soaring through my body right now.

As always, Matt's demeanor gave absolutely nothing away. If he was nervous, anxious, or happy, one could never tell unless he wanted you to. To the ones who knew him better, like myself, there were small tells that could allow us to hint at what was going through that calculative mind of his.

Our fucking fate had just been written in stone, and Matt just stood there as if it was any given Monday.

"Spit it out already." I urged as soon as I reached him and no one was in hearing range.

"It's settled." He simply said, taking a drag out of a cigarette he had lit before I arrived. "I'll be marrying Francesca in two weeks, give or take. We'll stick to the schedule."

"That's it?"

"That's it. You're free, Little Brother." He smiled for the first time, pulling me in for a hug with the signature hard, manly pats on the back.

"That's fucking good to know. But we'll be changing our plans again, Big Brother."

"What do you mean?"

"This." I handed him my phone, showing him the pictures I had taken of the ring before giving it back to Jamie. "I told you about her father, right? I had Jimmy do some digging, and every fucking lead hit a wall except for this."

His mouth was wide open as he flipped back and forth through the pictures, his mind not wanting to believe what his eyes were seeing.

"That belonged to her mother."

His head whipped up like a spring, his eyes boring into mine and searching my face for any kind of uncertainty.

"That belongs to…"

"Yup," I replied before he could finish. "You don't need to marry Francesca, Matt. Jamie is an Amato, Enzo's daughter, and if I marry her, our families are tied."

Matt stood there looking at me, taking that damn thing to his mouth and inhaling until the whole cigarette was practically gone. I could see the wheels in his head turning as he thought this through, the silence between us growing in tension.

"No." He grunted, flicking the cigarette butt to the floor before stomping on it as if the damn thing was about to come alive and hunt him down. "We proceed as planned. I just need you to keep this under wraps for two weeks before you talk to Don Amato and confirm it's real. Have you told Jamie?"

"I'm sorry. Pause right there. What? You still want to marry the Amato girl?" I glared at him, watching as he scratched his perfectly trimmed beard without saying a word. "You do like her."

"I like my promised seat in The Commission if I marry her. So stop being so emotional and let's get our facts straight."

I was dumbstruck, to say the least. There was more to it than what Matt led on. His precious seat in The Commission would be just as secured by marrying Francesca or anyone else.

"What did she do to you?" I asked, intrigued, picking on him and enjoying seeing Matt getting riled up about it. He didn't want to admit it, but there was something special about her in his eyes.

"Fuck off. She can't know about what you just told me. So keep your fucking mouth shut for the next two weeks and pretend you don't know anything until after she says 'I do.'"

"Sure thing, Boss." I saluted with a grin on my face that annoyed the fuck out of my brother.

We set our facts straight and aligned our stories before I ran up the stairs with a renewed joy under my step. I couldn't get up there quick enough.

I burst into the apartment, startling Jamie, her head whipping up from the book she was eagerly devouring. She perused me intensely before placing the book down beside her and standing up in slow motion, making her way towards me.

"Really?" She asked, her face lit in a smile that came straight from her heart.

"Really," I assured, wrapping her into my embrace and kissing her as if it were the first time.

This right here was what Heaven was made of.

She pulled back from our passionate kiss, resting her forehead on mine and staring deep into my eyes, the happiness in hers making my heart swell with pride.

Jamie bit her lip and closed her eyes before inhaling deeply, "Make love to me, Liam."

CHAPTER THIRTY EIGHT

Jamie

L iam and I had both been dreading yet anticipating last night.

It wasn't just the outcome of the meeting. It was what followed, too. I wasn't sure I could allow myself to let go after what that sorry excuse of a man had done to me. I wasn't sure those images wouldn't resurface when Liam was touching me.

But thankfully, they didn't.

Liam's touch was different from all others. It was healing and not degrading, even if it was, at times, rough and demanding. I had consented to it. Craved it.

All spectrum of Liam's colors appealed to me, from the softness of his bright smiles to the ragged edges of his dark possession.

Besides, we were now free to live our lives without restrictions or imminent danger, and that was enough to loosen me up and forget the horrible past, even if just for a moment.

I gave myself to him, expecting he would take it all, but he gave as much as he received if not more.

My heart, my body, and my soul. All of it, all of me, was undoubtedly his.

When I woke up the next morning, all I felt were cold sheets beside me. Liam wasn't in bed.

I took my time enjoying the feeling of my sore muscles as I stretched out. It was the welcomed after-effect of a night well spent in Liam's arms. He had worshiped my body in every way possible, bringing me pleasure with every kiss, every touch, every flip and turn. But I couldn't help but feel that because of everything that had happened, Liam was still holding back.

I wanted to give him as much as he had given me. As much as he gave me every damn time we slept together. So as I heard the shower water running, my mind knew immediately what I wanted to do to level the field a little.

I stood by the bathroom door for a couple of minutes, admiring his glistening body as the water fell down his muscled back and splashed off every mass of perfection.

Slowly, I stepped into the shower, hugging him from behind and pressing my breasts into his back.

"Hmm." His chest rumbled content. That low, pleasure-driven groan that shot straight to my clit every damn time had my nipples hardening against his skin. "Good morning to you too, Miss Harden."

My hands traveled the length of his body, from his perfectly toned pecs and down his abs, mapping it with my fingertips, making sure to memorize every detail of this feeling.

I let my hands drop further down, tracing that sinful V of muscles that pointed straight to temptation.

His cock was starting to thicken, growing harder in my hand, rising tall just for me. Slowly, I pumped my hand up and down, leisurely teasing him until he was fully erect. Liam had both his hands on the wall in front of him, steadying himself as I worked my magic, the water working like a perfect lubricant for my paced movements.

"Wasn't last night satisfying?"

"It sure was. But with you I always want more."

Suddenly Liam turned around, his fingers lacing in my hair at the nape of my neck, pulling me closer to him, my lips only but an inch away from his.

"From me you'll get whatever you want, whenever you want." His green eyes were already clouded by lust, and his expression devious. Liam had this stern and commanding devil inside him who broke free every time he was turned on. I was always pleased to see him surface, but today I had a different thing in mind.

I took his hand away from my neck and tried to push him back against the cold tile with my hand firmly planted on his chest, my eyes never leaving his. A knowing grin spread across Liam's face before he conceded, slowly stepping back and against the wall.

There was an exhilarating feeling rushing through me, the thought of what I was about to do had my mind running wild and my pussy clenching uncontrollably.

I looked down at Liam's tall cock that was now fisted in his hand, the slow pumps making my mouth water. My tongue swiped across my lips, my need for a taste becoming clear in the hunger I was suddenly feeling.

Holding on to Liam's shoulder, I started to kneel in front of him, but with his free hand, he stopped me.

"What are you doing?"

"Kneeling to pray." I sarcastically replied with a grin on my face. "What do you think I'm doing?"

I freed myself from his grip, taking my place in front of him, his magnificent cock standing right in front of me.

"You've never done this before, Jamie. Are you sure?"

"I want to. I want to feel you against my tongue."

"Fuck, Baby." He groaned, his thumb tracing the line of my jaw before coming up to bury into my mouth and pull my bottom lip down before tilting my head up with his fingers under my chin. "Look how fucking beautiful you are, kneeling in front of me and looking at me like that."

If I hadn't ignited before, I was sure to combust now. If he enjoyed seeing me like this, imagine how he'd react when his cock was finally in my mouth.

Liam's muscles clenched at the first touch of my hand on his cock, my teasing having the exact effect I had hoped for. I stuck my tongue out, sliding it from the base to the tip, encouraged by the low groans escaping Liam's chest.

Fuck, it was doing as much for me as I assumed it was doing for him.

My heart was pumping rapidly while hot flushes traveled through my body. Finally, I wrapped my lips around his head, slowly letting him slide into my mouth.

"Jesus fuck, Jamie."

He watched me take him as far as I could go before pulling him out, only to take him in again. My eyes were glued to his, reveling in the lust that shaded his green pools.

I drove his full length as far down to the back of my mouth as possible, only stopping when I gagged. Liam's balls tensed at the feeling, and I knew the constriction of my throat was the source.

His head had fallen back in bliss, his grunts echoing against the tiles and settling straight on my clit. They had evolved from small groans into fully vocalized grunts of pleasure.

My hair was now tightly knit into his hand as Liam coached my movements, bucking his hips to meet me halfway.

My breathing was fast and getting out of control as my body responded to the sound of his satisfaction. I was aching to be filled by him, my pussy contracting, painfully empty. It seemed as though Liam could read my thoughts. Without hesitation, he pulled me up, crashing his lips onto mine in a ravenous kiss.

Before I could think, Liam spun me around and plastered my hands flat against the wall, kicking my legs apart with his foot and burying himself in me.

It was as if his cock knew the way to its favorite place, not needing to be directed before poking the entrance to where it belonged.

Inside me.

Deep inside me.

I couldn't hold the moan that escaped my mouth once I was firmly filled by him. His thickness stretching me out in a blissful sensation. Once he felt I was ready, he started pumping slowly, holding onto my hips, his fingers digging into my flesh.

Stars started rising from inside me, tingling up my neck and clouding my vision as Liam's once slow movements were now faster, harder, and deeper. I was so damn close to the edge that I would erupt any second now. Liam was there, too. His grip tightened, pulling me back into his thrusts in a rising need for release.

"Liam…" It was a plea that he perfectly understood.

"Now, Baby. Come for me."

I clenched, and he throbbed as we both rose into a bliss of epic proportions.

My God! I could never grow tired of this.

"Was it okay?" I thought he'd liked it, but I wanted to be sure he did.

"Okay? It was fucking amazing, Miss Harden."

"Good," I said with a huge smile on my face. "Cause I want to do it again. Until the end next time, okay?"

"You don't have to ask twice."

Liam kissed me with unmatched passion, my heart content and soothed, feeling like I was finally wanted and accepted for the first time in my life.

We finished our shower together, levity and familiarity warming my chilled body from within. This was the life I had always dreamed of.

"Jamie, I have to go out this afternoon. I'm going to Detroit with Matt so we can talk to the Amatos about the marriage." Liam said while we got dressed.

"What marriage? I thought it was canceled."

"It's not, actually. Matt will be marrying Francesca instead of me. That was his plan."

"Oh my God. You didn't tell me that. Why would he do that?"

"Well, for several reasons, in fact. Besides helping me dodge that bullet, I actually think he likes her. He will have to get married soon either way if he wants to completely take over my grandfather's position. It's kind of a requirement for the seat."

"And did she agree to these changes?"

"She doesn't know yet. Matt asked Don Amato if he could tell her himself and give her a proper engagement ring. I'm going for brotherly support and to back him up if shit hits the fan. Will you be fine here alone?"

"Of course. Maybe Alison can come over for some girl time." I smiled, thinking about how much I missed my best friend.

"Sounds like the perfect plan."

CHAPTER THIRTY NINE

Liam

"You nervous, Big Bro?" I teased Matt, patting him on the shoulder.

I hadn't heard a sound coming out of him since we set foot in the jet. There was nothing on his face giving away his uneasiness, no body language betraying him, but his silence spoke volumes to me.

Detroit was only a short flight away, and even though the jet was ours, Matt refrained from smoking inside. It was clear how much he needed his damn fix right now in the way his fingers wrapped and extended around the tumbler of Macallan he held in his left hand.

"No."

"Don't bullshit me, Matt. You've been quiet since we left for the strip." He could hide behind his mask of placid, unfazed serenity, but I knew him too well to be fooled. "It will be okay."

"Yeah, right." He scoffed, a huff of cynical laughter leaving his chest on an impulse, swallowed down by the shot of whiskey as a cleanser. "We're not leaving Detroit without a fight, Liam."

"A fight? What are you not telling me? Wasn't this set with The Commission?" His warning tone and serious expression had me worried now. I had come with the idea that we were welcomed.

"Yes, a fucking fight." He grunted, turning to face me for the first time. "We read this whole situation wrong, Liam. Francesca didn't want to marry into our family in the slightest. We pegged her for a status digger, but we got it wrong."

I couldn't say I knew Francesca, but from the small interaction we had before AD's party, it was clear that she wasn't there on her own free will. She liked the whole deal just as much as I did, which was the same as saying not one fucking bit.

I couldn't even begin to imagine what her reaction would be to these sudden changes. She was still unaware that her fiancé was now a four-inch-taller man with a constant broody mood and an unmatched thirst for blood and power. Francesca still thought she was marrying me.

"You're nervous your future wife will reject you?" I held back on the mockery, knowing I was treading on uncharted territory here, and I didn't want to pull a string I shouldn't.

Matt got what he wanted, come Hell or high water, and never had he worried about *how* he got it. Seeing him squirm because of a potential impending fight with Francesca was a statement itself on what ran under his curated surface.

"She's not going to reject me. She has no fucking choice but to follow through." Matt's tone was laced with tension and finality, but it was as fake as the calm façade he put on for the masses in times of war. Today, contrary to *ever,* there was a crack there, the reality under his thick skin slipping right through the crevice.

"But something tells me you don't want her to *just* follow through."

Matt had asked Don Amato to be the one to tell Francesca about the new arrangement. He had picked out an engagement ring himself, not holding back in the slightest. The fuck-knows-how-many carat ring was currently sitting in a neat box in the inside pocket of his suit jacket, probably poking into his ribs every time he moved.

"I don't know where you're trying to go with this conversation, Liam, but I don't care for it. So drop it."

"You might not want to talk about it, but I know there's something more than a sweet deal to you behind this marriage. You wouldn't have bothered to buy a damn ring and fly to Detroit to tell her yourself if you didn't care for her."

"She'll be my wife. Forever is a long time to hold a grudge. I'm just trying to shorten the sentence, nothing else."

"Prepare for landing." The pilot cued over the intercom. Matt strapped his seatbelt on, sitting straight and pretending we weren't having this conversation in the first place.

I let him be, knowing he'd be more comfortable regaining his control over his demeanor, taking this time to settle whatever demons lurked around in his mind.

By the time we were stepping out of the car in front of the Amato Manor, he was already as cool as fucking ice.

Matt had reclaimed control, burying any kind of uneasiness he had previously displayed to me in the jet. His head was held high, and his strong, dominant nature was emanating from his body in powerful waves.

Trevor and Max, my brother's shadows, stood outside while we waited for Don Amato in his study.

As I sat there, I couldn't help but think about the only thing I had bothering me – the talk I had pending with Don Amato. There was no doubt it would be a hard one.

He was still convinced that I had murdered Amelia, his only daughter. Did he know about Jamie? Did he know he had another daughter besides Amelia?

My plan was to tell him first, confirm that he didn't abandon her and her mother. Because if that were the case, this truth would be dying with me. There was absolutely no way I was going to make the mistake of making Jamie feel she was being rejected again. If her biological father was a son of a bitch, I had to protect her from him, too.

"Matt." Don Amato called from the door as he entered the room, shaking my brother's hand vigorously. "It's good to see you again. Take a seat." He motioned towards the chairs in front of his desk before hastily shaking my hand, not hiding his discomfort in his false friendliness towards me.

"It's good to see you, too, Don Amato. Thank you for having us. I'm here to speak to your niece as we agreed."

"Of course, she'll be down shortly." He said as he poured us a couple of drinks before handing them to us.

I saw the fake smile Matt directed at him as soon as he took the tumbler from Don Amato's hand. He wasn't drinking a single drop of it before Enzo did. He didn't trust him just yet.

"That one, Matt? She has a mind of her own." He continued as he took his seat, his desk posing as a barrier between us, but he made sure to keep his hands visible the whole time. "She's as precious as she is fierce. I've never seen a woman so power-hungry as her. I have three nephews, and still, given the chance, I'd choose her to take over my reign in a heartbeat." His voice was filled with pride and sincerity.

"Is that so?" Matt was intrigued. He followed the lead and took a gulp from his tumbler after watching Don Amato do the same.

"Damn right. But the Mafia is a men's only club. The misogyny runs deep. It's ingrained in its roots. Even the most capable of women would never stand the slightest chance of putting her pretty shoe in the door."

As soon as he finished his sentence, as if right on queue, the mahogany double doors to his office burst open unceremoniously. Francesca walked in, her chin held high, her shoulders squared with confidence. Both Matt and I stood, turning back to see her strutting in, the thick heels of her boots roaring with every self-assured step she took toward us.

She didn't spare us a single glance, walking straight to where Don Amato sat, placing a kiss on his forehead before acknowledging us.

"Gentlemen." Nothing above a curt nod and a dry greeting. If I didn't know any better, I'd call her a stuck-up spoiled brat, but her attitude was meant to show us we weren't welcome in her eyes. "You called me, Uncle?"

"Yes, my dear. You've met Liam and Matteo Battaglia. They came to speak with you."

Her gaze was set back on us, an annoyed eyebrow raised in protest, waiting for one of us to cut to the chase.

Matt placed his tumbler on the desk, standing to greet Francesca properly, taking her hand in his and placing a kiss on her skin.

"Miss Amato, it's a pleasure to see you again."

"Mr. Battaglia," She greeted him back, the smile on her face was put there for manners and nothing else. "To what do I owe the pleasure of your visit?"

"We came to talk to you about the upcoming wedding."

"Oh, right. That." She pulled her hand from Matt's and crossed her arms in front of her body defensively.

"Yes, *that.* The plan has suffered some adjustments. You won't be marrying Liam anymore."

"That's great news! So it's over. I'm free?" Her face had completely changed. Her eyes shone brightly with excitement, relief was clear in the honest smile that lit up her features.

"Not quite. I came here to give you this ring as a symbol of your engagement to me." Matt had pulled out the little black box, holding it out for her to take.

Francesca's face grew pale, her smile had vanished completely while her chest was caught in an inhale that didn't want to let the air back out. She was stuck looking from the box to Matt's face, frozen in her spot. Her jaw clenched tightly, and she quickly spun to meet Enzo's eyes, looking for confirmation.

"You can't be serious."

"It's true, Poppet. You'll be marrying Matt instead of Liam. At the end of the day, he's a better match for you." Don Amato's words meant to disarm, but they worked like gasoline on the already raging flames.

"You men are un-fucking-believable."

"Language, Francesca."

"No. I will not watch my language or my tone when you are tossing me around as if I'm a damn toy. I am not a *thing* you can pass around to each other as long as it suits your interests. That's bullshit."

Francesca wasn't only angry, she was hurt. She had every right to be, but it still wouldn't change a damn thing.

"And you? This is all your fault, isn't it?" She continued, jamming her finger into Matt's chest as if it were a weapon, while his only reply was a wicked grin that hid more than he was trying to let on.

"That's enough!" Don Amato roared, pushing up from his seat. "It's been decided. The Commission has agreed to this change, and the ceremony will take place as previously scheduled." He turned her to him and grabbed her shoulders firmly. "You weren't marrying for love in the first place. You weren't ever marrying for love. So what difference does it make if it's Matt instead of Liam? Don't be rude, Francesca, and just accept the gift. We don't want to insult the Battaglias."

Francesca grabbed the box from Matt's hand and stormed out of the study, my brother following hot on her trail.

I watched them disappear and couldn't help the amusement growing inside me. My big bad brother was in for the ride of his life, and somehow it seemed like he *wanted* to be in that carriage, as tempestuous as it might be.

Soon, my thoughts gave way to the feeling that I had a pair of eyes boring into my skull. I turned to see Don Amato staring at me, his eyes dead of any feeling besides disdain.

"Don Amato–" I started, hoping to finally tell him to his face what had happened that night since I had never gotten the chance.

"I know you didn't kill her." He cut me off.

"I didn't. I held her in my arms, I tried to stop the bleeding, but I didn't stand a chance. I haven't given you my condolences, and if it comes as any consolation, every single one of those bastards paid with their lives for what they did."

"I know. You got to them before I did." I looked at him puzzled. Why was he still pushing this union if he knew we had nothing to do with his daughter's unfortunate death?

"How do you know?"

"I spoke to the owner's wife. Poor woman was terrified after she saw you give her husband a shiny new Colombian necktie. Not exactly our signature, is it?"

"He got what he deserved. Might as well pin it on the Cartel." I coldly replied, remembering how none of it brought me the solace I searched for. I didn't feel guilty about the fuckers I sent six feet under. I felt guilty about the pieces of my soul that died along with them.

"Indeed. She told me about the staged robbery, but it was too late already. The issue was in the hands of The Commission by then, so now we stick to the arrangement as decreed."

Right then, Matt marched back into the office, his face covered in rage. Whatever Francesca did or said, she had managed to crawl under his skin and artfully shove him into the deep end. I had never seen my invariably controlled brother wear his emotions on his sleeve the way he was right now.

"It's set." He practically grunted, "I'll see you in New York for the wedding."

On our way out, Matt was still huffing in wrath, his jaw clenched and his muscles almost popping out of place. I had to laugh. Seeing him this worked up because of a woman was nothing short of hilarious.

Matt picked up his phone, angrily scrolling before finally choosing a number and placing it on his ear.

"Who are you calling?"

"Mom."

"Aww, running to Momma for her to kiss your booboo away? Aren't you a little too old and too criminal for that?" I teased, enjoying seeing my big bad mafia brother squirm because of a woman.

"Shut up, Asshole. I'm calling her to see how quickly she can plan a fucking wedding."

CHAPTER FORTY

Liam

Much to Francesca's dismay, my mother was an excellent party planner. She thrived under pressure and rose above expectations. No notice was too short for Teresa Battaglia to pull off the event of the damn century.

No expenses were spared, as per Matt's indication, meaning Mom had no budget to make this happen as fast as possible. Whatever Francesca said or did that day when Matt gave her the engagement ring had him obsessed about sealing the deal. Whether it was a twisted punishment or a means to ensure nothing derailed from his plan, we would never know. One thing was for sure, it was an emotional response, and that was a first coming from him.

Just a week after going to Detroit, everything was ready for my brother's big day. One week before scheduled, and having her freedom cut short was showing on Francesca's face.

It was a lot more than just a wedding for Matt. It was the first step into transforming what was once a promise of a dream into reality.

He would become the Don of the New York *cosca.*

Matteo Battaglia was a true *mafioso.* Unlike me, he had welcomed the darkness as a part of himself, wearing it like a damn badge of honor. He lived by the code, breathed power, and exuded command. This was ultimately what his marriage was about. Finally, claiming what was dangled in front of him like a carrot since he made his first kill at only twelve.

At least that was what he claimed. He could fool every single person who sat in this hall, feasting on the most expensive delicacies blood money could buy. But not me. I could see beyond the thick, fake skin he wore for deception.

Under what people saw as a ruthless smile for securing his seat in The Commission, I saw relief. He had gotten what he wanted, and it wasn't a damn seat.

It was her.

Francesca.

I couldn't blame him, though. I was obsessed with an Amato myself. Jamie sat beside me, her face shining bright with a smile I wanted to encapsulate and keep forever.

She looked absolutely stunning. My eyes stuck on her, thinking about how breathtaking she would look in a snow-white dress suited for a princess, walking down an aisle to make my dream come true.

We haven't known each other for that long, but my heart knows what it wants, and by now I had made peace with the fact that even monsters deserved to be loved.

"I'll be right back," I whispered into Jamie's ear, leaving her at our table with Alison while I sought out Don Amato for a much-needed little chat.

I had managed to snatch the ring from Jamie's stuff. It was sitting in my pocket, almost burning a hole made of anxiety.

"Don Amato, a word?" He looked at me in suspicion, reluctantly standing from his seat and following me outside to a more private spot where no one could hear our conversation.

"What's so important that you had to drag me out of my niece's wedding?" He bitterly asked. He knew the truth about Amelia, but he still nurtured an obvious grudge towards me.

I took the ring from my pocket, figuring that maybe showing him was better than trying to convince him with my words. They seemed to mean very little to him anyway.

"Is this yours?"

I handed him the ring, watching his eyes widen in shock as he took it from me. In his disturbed silence, I found my answer. It was definitely his.

"How did you get this?" Don Amato asked, his eyes in a thin line that did nothing to hide his suspiciousness.

"From the person who it now belongs to."

"Do you know Amanda? Where is she?"

Fuck, it was true. He really was Jamie's father. His face had lit up with hope, turning his normally stern expression into a much softer one. That told me that he didn't know what had happened to Amanda, meaning he most probably didn't know anything about Jamie, either.

"I'm sorry, Don Amato, Amanda passed away about 25 years ago."

I watched as disappointment and heartbreak took over his features, wiping the color from his face completely.

"How? Why?" He was lost, his visible pain unmatching the innate ruthlessness of a *mafiosi* Don.

"She allegedly died giving birth to a baby girl."

"What?" He whisper-shouted in disbelief.

"The young lady I am here with tonight, my girlfriend," I accentuated the word. "She's the owner of that ring now. The ring you once gave to her mother, Amanda Harden. Am I right?"

It was as if I had shot the man in the gut. Don Amato couldn't keep his strength, crumbling onto the chair behind him in a silent stare of shock. I gave him a moment, letting him absorb the information in silence as I took the seat beside him.

"You mean I... I have a daughter?"

His eyes welled up with tears while his trembling voice gave away the turmoil of emotion going through him. In a couple of sentences, I had taken down a criminal legend, no bullets needed.

"I think so, Don Amato. Her name is Jamie Elisabeth Harden."

I told him everything about her, especially about Frank and the money he received every month in exchange for his silence. About how badly Jamie was treated her whole life and especially about what a wonderful person she had become despite all that.

I left the most recent events with Mr. Mercier for last, emphasizing that he would soon be out of jail, hoping he'd be just as bloodthirsty as I was.

"Does she know?" His tone was soft and fatherly, concern dripping off those very few words.

"Not yet. I didn't know if it was true or what your reaction would be. I had to protect her from that before telling her. I'm sure you can understand that."

"This is… Fuck." He hissed, his hands cradling his head as he struggled to process.

"Can you tell me what happened? How come you didn't know you had another daughter?"

"Amanda was undoubtedly the love of my life, even if we were only together for a couple of weeks. After I told her what I was, she simply disappeared. There was nothing but a note saying she couldn't live with the idea of loving a criminal. I hardly knew anything about her life, I didn't even know where she was from. She was the best thing that ever happened to me. I had ended my engagement that morning to be with her. I couldn't care less about the bullet carved with my name for doing that."

This sounded so damn familiar. I could relate to his pain. I was seeing a picture of myself, had Jamie decided she couldn't love the beast in me.

"Thank you, Liam. Thank you for being there for her when I wasn't."

"I think she'd be happy to meet you one day."

"Of course. I can't make up for what I lost, but I'm here now."

"That's good to know, Don Amato. She deserves the fucking world."

We both agreed that it would be best if I told Jamie who her real father was and then set up a meeting with Don Amato when and if Jamie was ready.

I was relieved to know that he wanted to get to know her and maybe become the father she never had.

I was about to give Don Amato a moment, returning to the party and leaving him to make peace with what I had just told him, when gunshots resounded from the front of the hotel.

Instinct kicked in, making me draw my gun straight into Don Amato's face as I looked down the barrel of his gun in return.

I simply nodded, signaling that it wasn't us, and set off running towards the sound, Don Amato following hot on my trail. There was hardly enough time to fire a couple of our own rounds before the drive-by car had vanished without a trace.

Matt was on the floor, covering Francesca with his body, while I sent our men after the loaded SUV. I saw some of the Amatos joining in on the hunt before turning my attention to my brother, who was now merely a step away from Don Amato, standing taller than him in all his glorious fury.

"What the fuck is exactly right, Don Amato. First time I have you in *my* city, and this is what happens. Anything you need to tell me?" I heard him bark, not masking the animosity in his tone.

"Don't try to pin this on me. This is *your* city, as you've very well pointed out. Nothing here tells me this wasn't you." Don Amato countered.

"Accidents happen every day. Wasn't that what your nephews said?"

"They were merely comforting their sister and giving her the security she needed. You are the one with the means and opportunity here."

"It wasn't. Me." His voice dipped into a tone that exuded menace. There was a code of honor between *mafiosi* men, but that never stopped them from backstabbing a fellow Made Man. After all, above the code, we were all criminals, and deception was our second skin. "I have damage control to do and fucking assassins to catch. So if you don't mind, take your fucking progeny out of my city."

"Liam?" Jamie's voice came from behind me, and I ran to her side, guiding her back into the safety of the hotel's walls. "What happened? We heard shots."

"It's okay, Baby. Let's get you back inside. I have to get back to Matt, but we'll be done real soon, and then I'm all yours." I walked her back to the wedding hall, making sure some of our men guarded every damn entrance, not leaving without telling them to guard Jamie, Alison, and my mother with their damn lives.

It went without saying, but I'd never leave their safety to chance.

When I came back from something resembling revenge, plotting without a damn culprit, the party had died down. The air was tense, and apprehension covered the faces of every woman here while the men sported scowls of distrust.

Jamie, on the other hand, was a damn beacon of light, happily laughing and chatting with Alison. I couldn't help but fall in love with her all over again.

"Can I have the honor of this dance, Miss Harden?" I whispered into her ear from behind, reveling in the tiny goosebumps that covered her skin under my breath.

"I thought you'd never ask."

She followed me to the practically empty dance floor, not minding the dozens of eyes that settled on us.

"Is everything okay?"

"Now it is." I took her lips in mine, feeding off the delicious moan she released into my mouth. "You look ravishing, Miss Harden," I said, locking her in my arms in the middle of the dance floor, watching as a wicked little grin spread across her face. "What?"

"Do you want to know something about me you don't know already?"

I couldn't help but think that she had asked me the exact same question before. Before I could dig deeper, Jamie placed some sort of fabric in my hand, and I knew exactly where this was going.

My smile evolved into a full grin while my cock twitched in response to her teasing.

"Behave, Miss Harden, or I will have to punish you," I warned her, trying my best to dip my tone to a low, grave whisper. "I don't think you recall what happened the last time you had no underwear on in a public place."

"I don't." She feigned innocence. "My mind might need some refreshing, *Mr. Battaglia*."

That little minx. She's done it now.

Jamie

Mr. Battaglia.

Saying his name, *that* name, always granted me the undeniable pleasure of feeling the rough, possessive, and demanding hunger of a Liam he would bury under a pile of guilt.

Before I knew it, I found myself held against a wall with Liam's mouth traveling all over my neck, his hands ravenously tracing every inch of my body.

He had pushed me into an empty room, his demanding kisses and rough touch telling me I had hit that dark nerve inside him that had the devil ready to come out and play. He had practically kicked the door open and slammed me against the first wall he could find away from the prying eyes of any guest.

The pool table that sat right in the middle of the room with dangling, dim-lit lights above looked promising, especially under the blazing heat of Liam's eyes.

I did like making love to him, no doubt about that, but this raw and primal need that translated into a harsh and dominating Liam just sent electric jolts to all the right places in me.

A hot and tingling feeling rose to my core, the anticipation of how hard he'd been thrust into that pit of lust making me pool between my legs before he had even touched me.

I liked this a whole lot better.

Sex.

Hot, rough, and fucking hungry.

The possibility that someone could find us was just adding to the excitement, adrenaline pumping through my veins like rapids. I could feel my thighs dampen at each deep kiss he placed on my body while his free hand frantically roamed every piece of my skin.

"I'm going to fuck you against that pool table, Miss Harden," Liam whispered into my ear, his lips grazing my earlobe tentatively. "Is that what you wanted by teasing me like that? To get fucked at my brother's wedding?"

"Oh God." I moaned, not able to hold back on the husk of my own voice.

"What if someone comes in? What if someone sees you with that pretty mouth full of cock?"

Jesus fuck. I had no idea what had happened, but Liam was as crude as ever tonight, and I was loving every last bit of it.

My pussy clenched at the sound of that enticing possibility. I never knew I had fantasies, but that would be one of them for sure.

He slowly backed me up towards the green table, kissing me relentlessly all the way there while my hands were held behind my back in his vice-like grip.

My breathing got heavier as he devoured my lips before he spun me around, pressing his chest into my back. Liam was already as hard as a rock, showing me just how much as he rubbed his impressive erection against my ass.

"You like this, don't you, Miss Harden? The excitement of maybe getting caught? I might have to take you out more often so I can eat you in public."

I gasped as Liam kicked my legs apart and pushed my dress up my ass, exposing my naked body beneath it. My pussy clenched again from the emptiness when all it craved was just a thin layer of clothes away.

I tried bending more onto the table, searching for his body with mine, needing him to touch me where I ached for him.

"I will touch you when the right time comes and not before, do you understand me, Miss Harden?" His voice was set in a warning tone. I nodded in response. "Use your words and my name when you answer me."

"Y…yes, Mr. Battaglia," My voice trembled with lust. I was aching for him to touch me, for him to fill me, for him to fuck me just as he had promised.

At that, he fisted my hair tightly in his hand, pulling my head back towards him and whispering those words I loved so damn much.

"Good fucking Girl."

He pressed his hard cock against my pussy, a little prize for my good behavior, making me gush even further. I needed him to lose those pants. Now.

It was like he had heard my silent pleas. I hadn't noticed that he had taken his pants off before feeling the warmth of his cock pressing against my entrance. I pinned my ass out further, trying to feel more of him, but he backed out, leaving me even more desperate to have him inside me. A low, disappointed growl left my mouth at the denial of my urging need to take him in.

"Liam…" His name came out like a plea. I'd beg for it now if he wanted me to.

"Yes, Baby?" His voice hard, but oh so sexy.

"Please, I need you inside me."

"Is this what you need?" He asked, plunging a finger inside me. I gasped and swallowed hard, but still, it wasn't anywhere near enough.

"N…No. I want more. I need more." My words coming out together with my small, shallow pants.

"Then maybe this?" Another finger. "Fuck, you're soaking, baby. So fucking wet for me."

I could feel my muscles tighten around his fingers just before he pulled them out. It wasn't the perfect scenario, but I would prefer his fingers over nothing right now. I moaned as my body ached from the loss of those heavenly digits of his.

A low grunt left Liam's chest just before I finally felt him fill me up, stretching me with his girth, a feeling of satisfaction rising inside me as he slid as deep as he could go. My back arched at the intrusion, every little nerve ending lighting up like a million fucking light bulbs.

"Jesus fuck." I moaned again, desire sending shivers down my spine.

"Is this what you needed?" Liam taunted, grinding against me with his cock buried balls deep inside me. One hand on my hip, the other on my back, pinning me down onto the pool table.

He started pumping in slow, steady thrusts that pressed me into the table with every hard push as I exhaled my moans in sync with Liam's hips hitting me from behind.

I gasped in surprise when he pulled all the way out, just to have my frustration eased by the feeling of his tongue on my very needy pussy.

He plunged it inside me, then drew circles on my clit before feasting on my lips. I closed my eyes, trying to imagine the scene – Liam kneeling behind my bent body, sucking and licking my way to oblivion.

He ate me from behind without mercy until I was thrusting into his face, chasing the orgasm that grew inside my core. White, hot light filled my vision, a thousand fireflies lighting up behind my lids.

That was the first.

Before I could even come down from bliss, I felt that perfect hardness fill me again in one harsh thrust that made him reach a spot he never had until now. He spread my legs wider, repeating the deep plunge while his fingers spread my butt cheeks.

"Fuck, your pussy is still contracting." That low grunt of his settled straight onto my still-throbbing clit.

He started riding me harder, holding onto my hips tightly, his fingers sunk deep into my skin. I couldn't muffle my moans as I had been able to up until now. Neither could he. Each sound that came from his chest driving me even wilder with desire.

"I'm going to come again, Liam."

Liam stopped at the sound of that. All I could hear now was my uncontrolled breathing and my hard-pumping heart.

"You are mine, and I'm the one who decides when you come and how!" He whispered in my ear, his voice making it sound like a threat. "On your knees." He ordered, pulling me up from the table.

I did as he said, my pussy protesting at the denied orgasm that was building inside me.

"Open up, Baby."

I tasted myself on his cock as Liam filled my mouth with him. His hand was fisted in my hair, pulling and pushing until I was gagging around his cock.

"Fuck, I'm sorry."

Liam pulled back, but I wrapped my fingers around his cock and brought it to my mouth again.

"Do it again." Apparently his demanding tone was rubbing off on me. "Fuck my mouth like it deserves. Don't hold back."

I wasn't sure exactly what I was asking for, but Liam complied. He fisted my hair again as he did before, using it as reins to make me suck him as he wanted. Deep and then shallow, hard and then slow.

"That mouth. That fucking mouth will be the death of me." He said, pulling his cock out of my mouth unexpectedly, making me pout. "I can't make a mess of you, Miss Harden. Not here, not today."

Instead, Liam lifted me back onto the pool table, settling himself between my thighs, kissing me with unmatched hunger.

I grabbed a fistful of his hair, pulling him into me while he buried his cock deep inside me again. My hips met his in every thrust. Every hard pump making me moan louder as I came closer to the edge again. By then I couldn't give a fuck if someone walked in on us. They would just wish they were us.

Liam grabbed my chin between his fingers, forcing me to look into his eyes.

"Are you close, Baby?"

"Hum-um." Was all I could say.

"Open your eyes. I want you to look at me while you come. Come for me, Baby. Now."

Liam's thrusts grew wilder and harsher, pounding into me relentlessly, making me ride that wave of ecstasy along with him.

My mouth fell open as a loud moan came out straight from my core. Liam covered my mouth with his hand, trying to smooth down the sound, a devilish smile on his face, taking pleasure in knowing what he did to me. He fucked me with abandon, violently thrusting until he had emptied himself inside me.

I felt him smiling against my hair as he held me to his chest.

"What?" I pulled back, watching his face light up with amusement.

"For someone who didn't like sex that much, you've become quite a fan."

"I'm a fan of whatever it was you just did to me," I confessed between deep, ragged breaths as I tried to steady myself from the unbelievable rush of pleasure still running through my body.

"I love seeing you like this. Exposed and vulnerable, beautifully fucked, and completely mine."

"I am yours."

"And I'm yours in return. I love you, Mrs. Dornier." He said with a sneaky grin on his face before taking my lips in his in a passionate kiss.

"I like the sound of that, but not yet."

"Well, we need to change that."

His expression turned serious while his eyes glistened with a devotion that filled my heart with pride. And with his gaze buried in mine, while he was still deep inside me, he asked, and I wasn't sure I was awake in this perfect dream of us.

"Jamie Elisabeth Harden, will you give me the honor of being my wife?"

CHAPTER FORTY ONE

Jamie

A week had gone by since Matt and Francesca's wedding. More importantly, a week had gone by since I had become the future Mrs. Liam Battaglia.

I'd been on cloud nine ever since, my life finally gaining a meaning I thought it never would have.

Of course I said yes.

A million times yes.

I had no doubt in my soul that it was what I wanted. To marry for love would be a blessing. Marrying the love of my life, my soulmate, was a gift from Heaven.

As if that didn't make me the luckiest woman on Earth, Liam had found out who my real father was. Another demonstration of his love and undivided devotion to me. He had gone through all that trouble to make me happy.

Knowing he was willing to meet me was just the icing on top of the cake. I was nervous, but the simple fact that the man was interested in meeting me was already a good sign.

I had never had a real father before. Frank was… well, Frank. He put up with me for the money and the threat that came with it. There was nothing in that deal that said he had to be nice to me, never mind love me. He didn't have it in his broken heart to do so. I knew that now.

I was far from being a little girl, but a part of my heart still longed for fatherly love. For a family.

"You look amazing," Liam whispered from behind me, giving my arms a small squeeze as I reviewed my reflection once again.

I knew how superfluous wanting to look good was, but I wanted my father to like me. I wanted him to be proud to have me as his daughter, from my achievements to my personality, from my flaws to my looks. Everything.

"Are you sure you don't want me to come with you?"

"I'm sure." I smiled, trying to hide the nervous jitters that ran free in my body. "I think I need to do this myself."

It was only the hundredth time he'd asked me that. In all truthfulness, I'd be more at ease if he came, but I felt it in my bones that I needed this leap to grow. To be myself and stand on my own.

And then there was the other thing. My big bad mafia boyfriend could come on a bit strongly sometimes. It came from a place of love, but still, I didn't want my father to be intimidated into accepting me. I wanted him to do it freely. If he didn't, it just wasn't meant to be.

I shivered at that thought, Liam's hand steadying me again, rubbing my skin and pulling me back to the present.

"I'm here if you need me."

"And I love you for it."

Maybe it was Liam's unbreakable connection to his family rubbing off on me, but knowing I could have that, too, took the stakes to a place so high I got vertigo.

I could see our little family with ease, but I wanted an extended one, too, made up of the Battaglia clan and the family I was about to meet. I had all my fingers crossed and then some that it was what my father wanted, too. Whomever he might be.

There was still that part of me, that small fraction that would never completely cease to exist, telling me that there was a possibility that this man wouldn't find me worthy. And even though those thoughts of unworthiness still came to me from time to time, I could deal with them better now.

Harden was my mother's maiden name. Frank didn't bother to give me his. Ever since Liam told me he had found him, I wondered what his last name was. I'd soon get a new one. Dornier was waiting to set a date to become mine. But I was too excited about this not to wonder.

Did I have brothers and sisters? Cousins, uncles, and aunts? Did I look like my father? What did he do for a living? And then there was the ultimate question that haunted me more than all the others. Why had he never searched for me?

"Hey," Liam called out from behind me, my smile fading right before our eyes. Was it possible that my father knew about my existence and never bothered to look for me? Was I setting myself up for another disappointment?

"It will be okay. Please trust me on this." Liam saw right through me. He wouldn't send me into this meeting if I was going to come out hurt on the other side. So trusting his judgment, I straightened myself, inhaling deeply and setting my mind on the positive outcome I was wishing for.

Besides, Liam must have had Jimmy digging from here all the way to Mars to find some dirt on my father. If he was allowing me to go alone, it meant it was one hundred percent safe.

Yet somehow, there was this growing feeling in my gut, a sense of dread that amplified at every passing second.

I swallowed it down with a glass of water before grabbing my purse and kissing my soon-to-be-husband goodbye.

"Everything will be perfectly fine. I know you're nervous, but there is absolutely no reason to be. Can you trust me on that?"

I nodded, knowing he was being truthful, but I couldn't shake this bad feeling.

"Carl will leave you on 5th Avenue, and then it's up to you. I will keep my promise and let you do this alone and on your terms. The guys will step down."

"Good. I don't need the man to be scared of me before I even arrive." Liam chuckled at my remark, filling my ears and my heart with that delicious sound of happiness.

"I'm not sure that would be the case. But a deal is a deal, and I'm a Man of Honor, after all. Pun intended. Just call me when it's over, okay?"

"Yes, Boss," I teased, placing a kiss on his luscious lips and leaving for my life-changing meeting with my real father.

Soon after, Carl was dropping me off where we'd agreed, and I watched him drive off before crossing the road into Central Park. My heart was pounding erratically against my chest, the loud noises of the city muffled by the drumming of its rate in my ears.

That feeling was back. Tenfold.

A dooming sensation that something very bad was about to happen. I inhaled again, trying to shake it off, telling myself it was only my life making its way back into my brain and playing its dirty tricks on me. All those bad memories creeping back, flooding my brain and taking away all the joy of this moment.

The urge to run back home to the safety of Liam's arms was almost crippling.

Come on, you can do this. Worst-case scenario, you'll end up exactly as you are right now.

I smooth my clothes and push those thoughts aside, making a turn into the sea of green on my way to the Boathouse where the meeting was set to happen.

I wasn't ten feet into the park before the harsh clasp of a hand wrapped around my arm, pulling me back into a hard object that was now digging its way under my rib cage.

"No fuss." The man whisper-grunted into my ear, "You'll be coming with me without making a scene if you don't want this day to be your last."

His harsh, menacing words traveled down my spine together with a shiver of fear, his iron grip around my arm forcing me to walk ahead of him back towards the sidewalk. A black SUV stopped just a few feet ahead of us, and I knew that was all the time I had to get myself out of this.

Words had been lost in the midst of fear, but I had to try.

"Please, Sir. Take whatever you want. I won't even go to the police. Just please let me go." I plead, my voice coming out shaky.

The rumble of laughter that came from behind me was forged in the depths of Hell, sounding like the devil himself. Mocking and threatening at the same time.

"I'm not robbing you. I'm kidnapping you."

Tears were running down my face without me even noticing, smearing my make-up and fogging my eyes. Fear had frozen my senses, my body growing stiff, stumbling forward as the man shoved me with force.

This was it. This was the dreadful feeling I had in the pit of my stomach. My life was finally worth living, and now it would probably just… end.

I tried to override the panic that turned my breathing into a race, forcing myself to think of a way out, a way to warn Liam.

But my time was up. The distance to the car was covered, the brute behind me throwing me inside with a single shove. As soon as he was in the passenger seat, the car pulled from the curb, tires squealing from the force. My eyes were stuck on the window, trying to at least keep track of the way, yet there was a pull that made me feel observed. I feared to turn around and confirm that, indeed, I wasn't alone in this back seat.

My heart sank further into my chest, my eyes tightly shut in a failed attempt to hold back the tears streaming rapidly and freely down my cheeks.

My fate had been drawn, and luck was no longer on my side.

I didn't need to look. I knew *he* was here, and I couldn't help but shiver in both fear and disgust.

CHAPTER FORTY TWO

Liam

Mike. Are you calling to tell me the Eagle has landed?"
I joked, waiting to hear the chuckle at my stupid joke
on the other side of the line. It never came.

"They've taken her." His voice was eerily calm, caution dripping
off every word. I could hear him trying to control his ragged breaths as
he spoke.

"WHAT?" I shouted in disbelief. I stood there, frozen, the words
echoing in my mind like a relentless drumbeat.

I had sent him and Jimmy to tail her. I respected her wish to go
alone, but I cared more for her safety. The instruction was to keep a
safe distance, allow her some privacy without it turning into reckless
neglect. Bad fucking move.

"Some fucker grabbed her and shoved her into a black SUV."

Fear came first, hitting me smack center in my chest, piercing my
heart like a fucking bulls-eye. Wrath and bloodlust followed as a close
second, fighting for the front of the damn emotional race wreaking
havoc all over my body.

"Who was it? The Amatos?"

"That's where it becomes tricky. Jimmy has eyes on Don Amato
and he's still waiting at the boathouse, but the plates of the SUV are
from Michigan. Just sent you the only photo I could snatch."

Michigan, fuck! That fucking car belonged to the Amatos for sure.

"FUUUUCCCKKK!" I yelled into the speaker, shattering the half-full glass I was holding against the damn wall, crouching down, my head hanging low in defeat.

Every fiber of my being was overcome by an icy grip of fear, squeezing my heart with an intensity I had never experienced before. My breaths came in ragged gasps, and my hands clenched into fists so tight that my nails bit into my palms. The world around me blurred, and I felt like I was drowning in a sea of despair.

This can't be happening. This can't fucking be happening.

For a fleeting moment, I was paralyzed by the possibility of losing her. Images of her smile, her laughter, and the way her eyes sparkled when she looked at me flashed before me like a cruel slideshow, each frame driving a sharp knife deeper into my chest.

The thought of her in the hands of those monsters ignited a primal rage within me, but fear still clung to my heart like a persistent shadow.

But then, something snapped.

I shut my eyes as tight as they would go, forcing myself to push the fear of losing her away and focus on the rage alone. Each deep inhale fueled me with darker demons drenched in fury. I needed them all and then some.

The fear that held me captive was replaced by an overwhelming surge of determination. My mind sharpened into a laser-focused instrument of retribution. I could feel the transformation happening inside me as if the devil himself had taken residence in my soul, whispering promises of vengeance and darkness.

I pushed off the floor, composing myself as much as my heart allowed, ready to fight for the love of my life.

Striding through the dimly lit room, the floorboards creaking beneath my steps, I walked towards the other side of the office. My fingers brushed over the cold, polished wood of Matt's desk as I grabbed my Glock, a sleek and lethal extension of my will. The room seemed to darken around me, the very air growing heavy with a palpable aura of danger.

There was no room for hesitation. Every second counted.

"Get back to Dea Tacita," I barked into the phone. "Drop Jimmy off at the police station. I need to know if that fucker Mercier is out or if the Amatos have a damn death wish."

"On my way, Boss."

I killed the call with Mike and called Jimmy as I took a burner from Matt's drawer.

"Boss." He answered on the second ring.

"Do you still have Don Amato within shooting range?"

"I do. Is it time to pull the trigger?" Jimmy was always eager to get his hands dirty, but right now I needed confirmation first.

"No. Standby. I need you to flash him that little red dot when I say so. Got it?"

"Just say when."

I flicked the burner open and dialed Don Amato's number, anxiously waiting for him to pick up. I reeled it in, though. I needed a clipped tone that anxiety couldn't muster.

"Hello?"

"Don Amato, it's Liam."

"Oh. Don't tell me she got cold feet about meeting me."

"No, no. My call comes for a different reason. Look down at your chest, Don Amato. Do you see that red dot flashing right above your heart?" My voice was close to a cold taunt drenched in menace.

"What are you doing, Liam?"

"If I so much as suspect that you're lying to me, those damn swans to your left will be the last thing you see."

"What the fuck is happening?" For a man under a sniper beam, his voice was steady as fuck. The man had balls.

"Besides, picture this – Matt currently has a gun nestled between your dearest Francesca's legs. One green flag from me, and he'll shoot that cunt into the next fucking world. Am I clear?"

"Fucking crystal. Only I have no fucking clue why you're doing this."

"Because you took something that's mine. She might be your daughter, but she is my fucking fiancé. She's my whole damn world, and I will not stand by while you decide to take her from me." My tongue burned up from the acid in my words, and even though part of them were a fragile bluff, I'd personally follow through with every damn threat if needed.

"What?" Enzo's voice on the other end mirrored my rage, a low and dangerous growl. "I did not take her. Tell me what the fuck is going on right now. Who took my daughter?"

"Some fucker shoved her into a black SUV while she was on her way to meet you. The fucking car had Michigan plates. Am I supposed to believe it's a divine coincidence that a similar black SUV charged at my brother at his damn wedding? Are you still going to carry on lying to me?" I asked, signaling Jimmy on the other phone to flash the red beam again for effect.

"You can threaten me all you want, it won't make my reply any different. I didn't take her. But I sure fucking want to know who did."

He sounded as honest as a targeted man could sound, if not more. His voice didn't waiver, he didn't plead for his life, or try to bargain. Those were good signs that he wasn't lying.

"Now if you're finished threatening me, we can get down to fucking business. I want to help, where can I meet you?"

"Dea Tacita. I'll send you the location." I said deadpan, still wary if I should completely trust him. "And Don Amato? You might not have a sniper ready to take you out, but your niece is not as safe. I'd advise you not to screw me."

"Got it. She's my daughter, Liam. I want that fucker's head on a damn spike as much as you do."

"Good. Then hurry up. We don't have time to waste."

Jamie

I had no idea where we were. I wasn't familiar enough with the city to keep up with our whereabouts, so I shut my eyes tightly as I gathered the courage to turn around and confront my captor for the first time.

I focused on each inhale as I summoned the courage to face the looming nightmare. I didn't need confirmation. Deep down, I knew exactly who was behind this.

It was him – Mr. Mercier, that greasy pig.

My stomach churned at the mere thought of him sitting just inches away from me, his presence weighing over me like a sinister cloud.

I couldn't find it in me to look at him, though.

Avoiding his gaze, I kept my back turned, unable to muster the strength to meet those icy blues.

Questions clawed at my mind like ravenous beasts. Was this some sort of twisted revenge because I had refused him? Did I wound his ego so deeply that it warranted this kind of sadistic retribution?

It didn't matter, though. Understanding his motives wouldn't save me now. All I needed was to escape, to find a way out of this steel prison before the horror escalated beyond imagination, and run for help.

Desperate thoughts circled my mind like vultures. Nobody knew where I was, and it might be hours before they realized something was wrong. By then, it could be too late. The panic was rising fast and hard, threatening to overwhelm me. Shock made me stop breathing for a moment, and my vision became blurry as I was caught between disbelief and stark terror.

I couldn't control my emotions anymore. Almost without realizing, I was crying out of despair. Fear resonated with every pulse, every thought, every question, making my body shake uncontrollably.

What would he do to me? Rape me? Kill me? Both?

In this moment of terror, I realized the cruel truth – happiness was fleeting, a mirage just out of reach.

I couldn't believe that I might die before I even got to really live. Just when things were going well, something had to drag me back into darkness. My life allowed for no happiness. It was a luxury I had tasted but ultimately couldn't afford.

Every last bit of happiness had a cost, and my current predicament was the steep toll for daring to reach for something beautiful. Fate was against me, writing my story in ink, stained with pain and misery.

This was the story of my life, and I? I had no damn say in it.

Thoughts of Liam flooded my mind. His smile and roughness, the shiny glint in his eyes each time he looked at me. I thought about all the wonderful moments we shared.

If dying was the cost of those beautiful times, it would definitely be worth it. I'd rather die today than live without having ever experienced that kind of happiness.

I thought of Alison and her unwavering support, the moments of joy we had together, the undeniable sisterly bond we shared and cherished. She held a special place in my heart, and leaving her behind felt like a tragedy.

And then there was my father – the man whose identity remained a mystery. I hoped he was happy to know I existed, even though I might never meet him. I wanted to uncover the truth, to finally have the answers my heart craved for serenity.

Was this me saying my goodbyes?

"How much longer until we arrive?" The voice behind me broke my reverie, making me spin around to face the person sitting behind me. It wasn't Mercier's voice. It was a woman's. One that sliced through the air like a sharp blade. Who was she?

My eyes widened as I saw her. She was probably in her late fifties, had short, jet-black hair that matched the dark sunglasses that covered half her features. Her immaculate white suit exuded power and confidence, mirroring her unwavering gaze that was harshly set on me.

There was a familiarity about her, a feeling that I had seen this woman before.

"Just another two minutes, Ma'am," the driver replied.

Her gaze never wavered, and her lips curved into a sinister smile. With a deliberately slow motion, she removed her sunglasses, and the truth hit me like a tidal wave.

I knew who she was, but why was she here? Why would she want to kidnap me?

"Good. Is Mr. Mercier there already?"

The mention of that name had shivers running down my skin in waves of disgust. She probably knew what it did to me since her grin deepened into a malevolent expression that painted a canvas of doom. *My* doom.

"He has just arrived."

"*Perfecto*. Right. On. Schedule."

CHAPTER FORTY THREE

Liam

Enzo Amato was either being starkly honest or brutally stupid.

I watched him strut into Dea Tacita with his head held high, not so much as a slight flinch tarnishing his confidence as my men pulled a dozen guns on him. One wrong move and he'd have more holes in him than a strainer.

From the last report we had gotten only two days ago, Mercier was still waiting for his bail to be posted. We had fiddled with his files enough to have it postponed indefinitely. Some of the police officers were offered generous compensation to make sure it took as long as possible, adding an extra amount for them to tip us off if he got released.

We did the same to the media. Lining their pockets with green kept them from publishing anything even remotely related to Mercier's name. Being pals with the mayor could come back to bite us in the ass, even though I was practically sure Matt had that big fish more than hooked. Still, it was wise to avoid the news from ringing in ears that didn't suit us.

It was under control.

So shoot me for considering the backstabbing Detroit trash was behind Jamie's kidnapping.

"I have to give it to you, Don Amato. Balls of fucking steel!" I cued, walking out of the shadows towards where he stood in the middle of the huge, empty dance floor.

There were clicks of guns popping bullets into their chambers soundtracking my slow walk. That distinctive chime of metal on metal and shuffling feet would scare the best of soldiers, but not him.

Don Amato looked straight at me, holding the regal pose of someone who had nothing to lose.

"Where is she?" He demanded without a hint of fear, despite his predicament.

"I thought *you* could tell me. Is it a coincidence that the plates on the car that took her are from Michigan?" There was an accusation hidden between my words that I was sure Don Amato picked up on despite the lack of reaction.

"I don't believe in coincidences. Show me." He demanded as if his Don status couldn't fade under the threat of a foreign territory and blazing weapons eager to send him back home in a wooden box.

Pulling out my phone, I showed him the blurry picture Mike had sent me with the plate number. I watched his jaw muscles dance to the rhythm of his annoyance, yet nothing in his posture made me think he was in on it.

So I decided to make a concession.

"My guys are working on trying to trace it through the city's traffic cameras. Maybe it will take us straight to where they are holding her."

"No need." His voice was steady, unlike the muscles in his jaw that still pumped in anger.

"What do you mean?"

Had I read him wrong? Was this some sort of fucking kamikaze mission? What I wasn't expecting were the words that came out of his mouth next.

"That car is mine."

At the sound of his confession, my men started closing the circle, and before I could even think, the barrel of the Glock I held in my right hand was pushing against his forehead.

What sick game was this bastard playing?

"I'm gonna need you to start talking real fast, or I'm going to start making good on some of those promises I made to you over the phone."

My sarcasm was a reflection of a psychotic short-circuit happening somewhere in the part of my brain that controlled emotions. Or maybe it was, in fact, my emotions that had hijacked my brain because right now, I was all heart.

"I have no fucking clue what's happening, but she's my daughter. The only living memory of the love of my life. I'd never put her in any danger. Either shoot me or get that fucking thing out of my face so I can figure this out."

I paused for a second, searching his eyes for a flicker of doubt before slowly pulling back and watching his next move, still wary of the whole damn situation. Everything about Jamie's kidnapping pointed to Don Amato. Everything besides *him*.

Don Amato pulled his phone from his slacks, showing us his palms for safekeeping before angrily tapping and swiping on his screen.

"Every one of my cars has GPS tracking systems installed. I can trace that SUV." He paused for a second that took an eternity to pass. "They're not far from here." He sternly said, showing us the map on his phone indicating their location. "We should get going."

"*We* are not going anywhere until I know for sure you are not behind this. Give me some fucking answers, Amato, because from where I'm standing, bullet holes are starting to look like a good addition to that suit of yours."

Before Don Amato could say anything else, Jimmy burst into Dea Tacita, his face a blank mask that by now I knew all too well meant bad fucking news.

Jimmy stopped in his tracks, trying to read the impasse of the loaded atmosphere. I gave him a nod, eager for him to spill whatever he found out at the police station.

"Mercier was released a couple of hours ago."

My blood went cold. My heart turned to stone and stopped altogether. I'm sure I misunderstood.

"What?" I said just above an incredulous whisper, but the club had fallen into such an eerie silence that a fucking pin would sound like an atomic bomb going off.

"Someone persuaded the judge to post Mercier's bail immediately with a promise to hand in enough information to bring down two major criminal organizations within a day. One in New York and the other in Detroit."

We all stood there, unsure of what to make of this information, the scale now balancing the blame between both myself and Don Amato. Who could have done this? Who had access to such sensitive information on both sides?

"Was that bail one hundred grand?" Don Amato asked, his eyes still locked on his phone.

"How did you know?" Jimmy replied, his voice rising in disbelief.

"The money came out of my account," Enzo confessed, against better judgment. It should have been enough to have me pressing my gun back against his skull, but he wouldn't be so upfront about every detail that pointed a finger in his direction if he really was the culprit.

So I stayed still.

I was frozen for a minute, this whole puzzle making it impossible for me to understand what was happening. There were too many threads, and I had no idea which one to pull.

There was no time to waste, though. Trusting Don Amato was the only way out I could see.

"Don Amato, you're coming with me," I started, shaking my head as I came out of my silent stupor. "Everyone else, load the cars with every weapon in the armoire and follow." I picked up Don

Amato's hand and wrapped it around my loaded gun. "I trust that you are putting your daughter's safety first. Show me where she is so we can start over."

Purposely testing the outsider, I turned my back to him and walked towards Jimmy, expecting a bullet in the back at any minute. It never came.

"Are you sure about this?" Jimmy asked, concerned.

"I am. Don Amato is going to send you the location of the car that took Jamie. Go back to the station and clear her location of any patrol car. I want to be alone with that fucker. Intercept every fucking email directed to the NYPD, district attorney, or any other fucker that can bite us in the ass. Take down a fucking satellite if you have to, but no one gets any information on us or the Amatos."

"Got it, Boss."

"Let's go."

I walked out of Dea Tacita in wide strides, driven by rage and blinded by a murderous intent that propelled my every step.

I'm going to find you, Baby. Whoever took you is going to pay with their fucking lives.

All I could see was her. Nothing else in the world existed to me at this moment.

Jamie was the reason I got to smile every day. She had managed to heal the small part of my soul that I had no idea still existed. Still, she had pinned it to this Earth, preventing it from sinking further into the darkness I'd given way to.

"You told me about a woman who visited Amanda when she was in the hospital after Jamie was born. Do you know what her name was?" Enzo asked from beside me, his face contorting into disgust as if those words were sour on his tongue. I was startled by the question, not understanding why the fuck that held any importance at the moment, but I stopped and replied anyway.

"Francis Harden. Why?"

Don Amato paused for a second, his whole body going stiff, the only movement being his chest rising and falling at an increased rate.

"I know who has my car." He finally said, his hands clenching into tight fists and his nose flaring wide. "FUCK!" He shouted, kicking the gravel beneath his feet in an outburst of pure rage.

It seemed like the first genuine reaction I'd seen from this man today. Uncontrolled. Untamed. Uncut. His pure emotions flaring under his sleeve.

"Who?" I grunted, annoyed out of my fucking mind for having to ask.

"Lisa Marie Francis Amato." He slowly said before looking at me. "My fucking wife!"

Jamie

I hadn't noticed I wasn't even restrained during the whole drive. That thought only occurred to me once the tall, muscled man who had grabbed me by the park was tying my wrists so tightly together that I thought I would lose all the blood supply to my hands.

He pulled me out of the car, making me stumble onto the ground. I lost my balance from the strong, unexpected tug, falling onto the concrete floor and scraping my knees upon impact.

I looked around, trying to find something that could give me a clue about where I was. There was nothing I could see beyond old warehouses with broken windows, yellowed out by time and grease.

The air was humid, making me shiver each time a new gush swept across my skin. We were close to water, I was sure. Yet, still, I couldn't decipher exactly where this woman had taken me to.

The not-at-all-gentle giant pulled me up to my feet and shoved me forward, forcing me to follow the woman.

She walked with a calm stride as if time was in her favor. Not a damn worry in the whole world while my body ran on pure terror and anxiety. The driver walked beside her with a big gun nestled under his arm, a strap securing it to his body.

They stopped just beside a rusty door on the side of one of the warehouses, making way for myself and the huge man who had been shoving me towards my doom every step of the way.

"In you go," he said, giving me another harsh push, but this time my feet were firmly planted on the ground.

If I go in, that's the end. No one will ever find me.

I had to do something. I had to find a way to leave a trail, but how?

Craning my head, I looked everywhere for God knows what, coming to face the broken, old door and its ragged edges.

Maybe...

Looking back at the brute who captured me, I slowly shook my head, earning myself another rough shove that ended with me on my knees again. Only this time, my hands were tied, so instead of another few scrapes on my legs, my face collided with the concrete, too.

I yelped from the pain, closing my hands into tight fists and squeezing my eyes shut as tight as they could go, yet not even that held back the tears that started sprinting down my face again.

Before I could recover, he yanked me up with an iron grip on my arm, shoving me towards the open door and forcing me inside. My arm bumped harshly into the rusty threshold, the sharp edges cutting my skin deep enough to draw a decent amount of blood.

I stopped again, watching it flow down my arm, anxiously waiting for it to run enough to drip onto the ground.

"Move." The woman grunted, and as she spoke, the armed goon beside her placed the end of his weapon against the back of my skull.

Fuck.

The blood spilling from the wound wasn't going to be enough. I was hoping to at least leave behind a sign that this was where they had taken me through. Because I knew he would come. Liam would come.

Out of fear, my feet moved on their own, and before I knew it, I was standing in the middle of the warehouse.

Once I allowed myself to breathe, a distinct smell hit my senses. Nauseating. Disgusting.

Something had died inside this place and was left to rot.

Something or maybe someone.

My tears hadn't dried yet, but at that image, they gained speed. It was hard to suck in oxygen as I tried as hard as I could to control the sobs that threatened to leave my mouth. The image of my body being left in a place like this for God knows how long was more than I could take.

"Finally."

That voice. That sickening voice that lived rent-free in my nightmares broke through the space with an echo.

There he was. Mercier stood in front of a black car just a few feet away with another armed man beside him. His suit was as pristine as if he were to attend a ball. His hair slick and combed back, his attire complete with a disgusting smile plastered on his face.

That unrelenting hand was gripping my arm again, so tight I was sure it would be leaving a bruise. I looked up at the mountain of a man, pleading for mercy, but his face was nothing but a blank mask.

He was nothing but a gorilla in a suit, following orders to earn his bag of peanuts.

Pulling me all the way towards Mercier, the man didn't even spare a glance my way. To these people, I was nothing. It was like I was a bag of goods being traded off for something that benefited the lady in white.

"Oh, there she is. My little prude whore. No one will interrupt us this time, Baby." Mercier said, rubbing his thumb on my cheek, following onto my bottom lip. I tried to turn away, but his hand grasped my face and turned it towards his. "You look so pretty with blood on your face. Such a beautiful canvas to paint on. That color suits you to perfection."

"She's yours, Mr. Mercier, as promised. Now it's your turn to hold up your end of the bargain, otherwise I will have my men hunt you down and finish the job."

"Don't worry, my dear, this won't come back to bite your precious little mafia ass. I will have my fun first, and then I will dispose of the remains for good. Just as agreed."

"I sure hope so. Make my money worthwhile, Mr. Mercier."

"With pleasure," he replied, his eyes deeply buried in mine. "And you, Baby, you will cooperate, or I will make it so much worse on you. You can scream as loud as you want. In fact, please do. I like it when they scream. But today, you will give me what I want, or I will simply take it by force. It's your choice. I like it better when you squirm and kick before I can eat you up. I'll leave that for you to decide."

"Please." My voice was broken, either from the tears or the notion that my words wouldn't change anything.

Mercier leaned in and whispered in my ear, grabbing my ass so tight it hurt, "I'm going to make you lick the cum off the tip of my cock, and you are going to love every minute of it."

I'd experienced his viciousness before, and I knew I was no match for his strength. Images of that night came flashing back again, and all I could do was pray for a miracle.

"Good. I don't want to be dealing with this issue again, am I clear?" Why was this woman doing this to me?

"Crystal." Mercier's reply came with another one of those sickening grins that churned my stomach and made me gag.

I watched her turn around and start walking back out of the old warehouse, leaving me to face a certainly brutal death preceded by whatever Mercier found fit. Depraved and horrific, I'm sure.

More tears sprang down my face. There was nothing I could do to change my fate. Nothing I could do to free myself from his disgusting hold.

"Please, Mrs. Amato, don't leave me here with this rapist. Please."

"Rapist?" He grunted to my face, taking a handful of my hair and tugging harshly, angling my head so I was looking straight into those ice-blue eyes. "I bought you flowers, you ungrateful bitch. I even offered you dinner, but you were too busy getting your cunt fucked by a boy to accept."

Flowers?

The roses. They were from him. He'd been watching me all along.

Blinded by his fury, Mr. Mercier pulled harder on my hair, throwing me to the ground.

"Please help me, Mrs. Amato." I pleaded in a desperate cry, not knowing what else to do at this point. "Why are you doing this? What have I ever done to you to deserve this?"

My voice was charged with a rage I'd never heard in it before. Not even in those times I demanded to know why Frank locked me up in those tight spaces.

She stopped in her tracks as if my question had hit a sensitive nerve deep inside her. I watched her theatrically turn around and walk back towards me. Mercier stepped aside, making way for the vicious-looking woman coming towards us to say her peace.

Mrs. Amato stopped an inch away from colliding with me, crouching down as if she was about to tell me a secret, her lips curled in disgust. "You were born!"

Before I could make sense of what she was saying, Mr. Mercier yanked me back up by the back of my neck and pinned me to the side of the car.

"She's my toy now, not yours. You didn't want to stain that pretty white suit of yours, so back off and let me have her." He roared before returning those sinister eyes towards me, tracing my tears with his index. "You look so goddamn pretty when you cry."

With that, he stuck his tongue out and licked my cheek, like he'd done that night, too.

I fought the bile that rose to my throat while his hands roamed my body like a sick vice, his lips hovering over mine, too close for comfort.

Despite the weight of his body pressing mine against the car, I tried to fight him off me. I kicked and thrashed just like I had the first time, but it was too little to make him stop.

Never had I felt the urge to hurt someone as badly as I wanted to hurt him. I craved to see his lifeless body sprawled on the floor. To see his face draining of life, meaning this monster would never hurt anyone else in his pitiful life.

"That's my feisty cunt. Fight for it, Baby. You have no idea how hard my cock gets when I see you like this."

BANG!

A loud, strident sound broke his attention from me, both of us looking at the metal side door that led me into this Hell. One of Mrs. Amato's men fell to his knees before tumbling onto the ground.

Dead.

Without delay, a puddle of deep-red blood started forming around his head, making Mrs. Amato and her other goon run for cover.

BANG!

A second shot and the man who shoved me into the back of the black SUV was down, too.

I held my breath, expectant to see Liam coming through that door in all his mafia glory to save me from these shackles.

Instead, Don Amato walked through the door, darting straight towards his wife who was now standing by the wall adjacent to the entry. His gun was still tightly clenched in his hand and pointing straight at her head. Any other Monday, I'd find myself flinching, but somehow, there was relief flooding my veins.

"Explain, Lisa, or you're next. Where is Jamie?"

I was sure Don Amato hadn't come alone, and by the look on his face, Mercier knew there'd be more men coming through that door, too. He didn't wait for confirmation. Wrapping his hand around my arm, precisely on top of my fresh wound while the other covered my mouth, he pulled me along with him, away from Don Amato's sight.

I yelped in pain as Mercier stuck his fingers into my flesh and gained another harsh squeeze for it.

"Not a fucking sound, or I'll shoot you right now." He released my arm and buried his hand into his jacket, pulling out a short, black pistol.

The metal of his gun dug between my ribs, shoving me forward toward a back exit. I couldn't stop looking back, trying to see Liam walk into the warehouse, trying to look for a sign that maybe I was going to make it out of this after all.

At the sound of scraping wood, I whipped my face around to see what it was. Before I could properly register what I was looking at, everything around me suddenly disappeared.

When I woke up, I was immersed in darkness, the back of my head pounding with pain. The air was thick and humid from being breathed three times over already, but it smelled as if I was in a flower shop.

I couldn't move. I couldn't see. I couldn't hear.

Despite years of the same treatment, panic still hit me like a ton of bricks, robbing me of any rational thought that could help me.

I was trapped again, locked inside of a box.

CHAPTER FORTY FOUR

Liam

Where is she?" I urged, bursting into the building.

I was furious. The cars parked outside were in the middle of two warehouses, so we split up to cover more ground, each one of us trying our luck with a different one.

The dirty, roofless space I raided was empty. My Jamie was nowhere to be found. I didn't even need to complete the search to know she wasn't there. Those two gunshots were telling enough.

Two bodies littered the ground, bathed in their own blood, each with a hole precisely in the middle of their foreheads. It almost seemed like the man had a laser beam attached to his gun.

Clean shots with no fucking room for error. Don Amato was still at the top of his game.

The stench of death was old but clear, amplified by the humidity inside a place that had been vacant for some time now. I scanned the place with a quick glance, noticing the lines of gutters on the floor and the hooks that hung from a rail right above them.

A slaughterhouse. How fucking fitting! Somehow the weight of the air told me there were more than just pigs being killed here. These walls surely had much more macabre stories to tell.

Don Amato was holding his wife at gunpoint, yet she kept her silence, probably thinking her husband didn't have what it took to put a bullet in her brain.

But I had no such attachment, and pressing that trigger would almost feel like pleasure.

In a few wide strides, I reached them, placing my own gun against Mrs. Amato's head.

"I'm not going to ask again. Where. Is. She?"

"Right here," Mercier said, on queue with the forklift that drove into the wide space, a wooden crate precariously placed on the very tip of the metallic forks. I heard his voice but couldn't see where the fucker was. "If I drop the crate from this height, do you think she'll survive? How many splinters would pierce her body? Where will they pierce her?" The forklift stopped, and Mercier appeared from behind it. The sick grin on his face told me he wasn't playing. The fucker would actually do it. "It's a gamble, really, and I'm an all-in kinda man."

The forklift was driven by an armed man I didn't know. I dared a look over to Don Amato, and the look on his face told me he knew him. One of his, maybe? But with whom did his loyalty lie? I sure hoped it was to his Capo and not the wife.

The forks jerked, and both Don Amato and I put our hands up in surrender, Mrs. Amato taking the opportunity to run for her life.

The wife then.

"Let her go," I plead, trying with all my strength to sound submissive while my blood boiled in my veins.

Threatening my girl was like feeding lava to a volcano. Yet I had to reel in my demons and make him believe I'd behave if he put her down.

"She's innocent in all this," I spoke again, trying to lure Mercier into the open space. "Jamie has never hurt a soul in her life. Just, please, put her down, and you can have me."

"She *is* innocent. And that's exactly my favorite flavor. Don't be presumptuous. I don't want you. It's always been about her. So you gentlemen are going to watch while I place her inside my car and drive off, or she dies right here, and her spilled blood will be on you."

"You don't need to do this, Mercier." Don Amato tried.

"You're wasting precious time. That crate is lined with foil. Soon enough, your precious little girl will be out of oxygen. So please, Mr. Dornier, Mr. Amato, keep on trying to convince me not to kill her while you do it yourself."

Fuck.

There was no reasoning with a madman. So maybe controlling my own madness wasn't the right move here.

My men were standing outside waiting for a signal, after all. Mercier was outnumbered. I just had to figure out a way to keep Jamie safe while taking him out for good.

I shut my eyes, putting my hands down and cracking my neck to both sides.

Fight fire with fucking fire.

"You know what? You're on your own, Don Amato. Save your precious daughter or don't. I don't give a fuck. I have more pressing matters to attend to." It was a hard bluff, but all I could do right now was keep the straightest poker face I was capable of. I needed all my demons to step out of their shadows for this one. "Mara Mercier is waiting for me somewhere in the Verten basement, tied to a chair. How old is she, Mercier? Twenty? Twenty-one?"

He chuckled nervously, shuffling his feet while I took the opportunity to saunter closer to him like I had the upper hand here.

"I won't fall for your tricks, boy."

"Suit yourself." I shrugged while faking to look at my nails, putting on the damn performance of a lifetime. "You know fairly well *what* we are by now. No point in hiding it anymore. I'm not much into forcing myself onto women like you, but I do get a good kick from a little light torture. You know. Some wooden splinters under the nail, sanding some skin, and moisturizing with lime and salt. All green, I can assure you. We make it a point to use bamboo only. Mara will appreciate the effort."

"There's no way you could have gotten to her so quickly."

"I have my ways. But it's your gamble, really. I'm an all-in kinda guy, too. Wanna call or check?"

"Drop her!" He roared out of nowhere, the forks dropping down a whole foot before stopping.

My heart hammered like thunder inside my chest, but I kept the blank mask in place, taking a lesson out of my brother's fucking rule book.

Serenity and control.

"That was close," I teased, bringing a chuckle to my lips as if I were cheering him on, biting hard on my tongue to keep myself in check. "My turn."

With one hand stretched out towards Mercier, I fished the burner from my pocket and dialed Don Massimo on speaker before tossing the phone for Mercier to catch.

"Hello?" A thin, sweet voice called from the other side, broken and fragile with fear. They knew not to hurt her. It wasn't her fault her father was a sick motherfucker, and hurting women and children didn't sit right with me. The innocent ones, at least. But Mercier didn't know that.

"Mara!"

"Dad?" She asked again, incredulous. "What's going on? Who are these people?"

I watched his face pale further as if it didn't have the color of decaying flesh already before a rush of redness filled his cheeks.

Don Amato's eyes were fixated on the man controlling the forklift as if he were daring him to drop the crate.

The man knew that, by now, he'd fucked up enough to leave with a shiny black body bag as an accessory to his gray suit. If not today, he'd have the whole *Cosa Nostra* ready to settle the score with such a dishonorable Made Man.

By blood you enter, by fucking blood you leave.

In a fit of rage, Mercier threw the phone against the concrete floor, smashing it to pieces. He couldn't think that would fix his predicament, right?

Wrong.

"Drop her!" He roared again, and this time the machine pulled back, the forks slipping from under the crate.

My soul left my body in that instant. The motion of the crate falling cut the oxygen straight from my lungs.

No.

No!

NO! This couldn't be happening!

In less than the blink of an eye, the wooden box smashed onto the concrete, pieces flying in every direction. A twelve-foot drop was enough to destroy the fragile container and anything it held inside.

I had done this. I had driven him to drop her like she was nothing.

Both Don Amato and I ran to the pile of wood without even looking. It was an instinctual reaction. And as panic settled in our hearts and minds, Mercier ran while we faced a huge pile of broken wooden planks and nothing else.

"Fuck…" I exhaled in relief while Don Amato panted heavily beside me, his heart clearly still lodged in his throat.

"I'm gonna kill that fucker." He said, standing up and running towards his gun before taking after Mercier.

I stood with my hands still shaking. Panic, fear, rage. All of the above coursed through me like a lethal poison as self-preservation slipped through the cracks of my trembling fingers. Reaching up, I grabbed one of the metal hooks hanging from the steel rods above my head, walking calmly down the path Mercier and Don Amato had taken.

I was propelled by my fury, each step heavier on the ground as I reached that dark place not that deep inside me. Ready for the kill. Ready for the sin. Ready to be submerged deeper into my own hell. Another body to litter my conscience, but this motherfucker just had it coming.

I wasn't far behind them.

A loud shot rang through the barren space, bouncing off empty walls and rattling the windows high above. As I reached Don Amato, the guy controlling the forklift was lying at his feet, a busted kneecap bleeding profusely onto the ground.

"Where's my daughter?" His voice was a low rumble of viciousness, an eerie calm that spoke volumes of its ruthlessness.

I looked around for the scumbag that had caused all this, but he was nowhere to be found. Yet a massive truck with a metal safe on the back caught my eye. Looking back at the *idiota* on the ground, his gaze was locked on the truck, too.

I didn't need to ask again. Both the vehicle and the safe were too clean and shiny to have been sitting in this worn-out place for as long as the rusty hook in my hand had.

"She's in there." I urged, pulling Don Amato's gaze away from the man on the ground. "Can you hot wire?"

"Before you could walk." Don Amato replied, handing me his gun.

"Good. Take Jamie out of here. I'll deal with the trash." I said, pressing the toe of my shoe into his bullet wound. I had loose ends to tie, and fuck me if I was about to leave any thread dangling.

Grabbing my phone from my pocket, I called Mike.

"Boss?" He answered before it could even ring.

"Are the back doors chained as planned?"

"Yes. We have Mrs. Amato, too."

"Good. There's a truck here at the back, and I'm sure Jamie is trapped inside the safe. Don Amato is going to need help getting her out. He'll come to you through the front. Don't shoot."

As soon as I hung up, the truck roared to life, Don Amato revving the engine to get my girl to safety.

I turned back to the fucker that was now at my feet, pressing my foot harder into his knee and smiling at the strained screams he muffled into the crook of his arm. As much as I'd like to squish the blood out of him and see him pass out, I had bigger fish to hook.

"Rest in… oh wait. Fuck that. May you rot in Hell."

"Please, no…"

BANG.

He didn't get to have any last words. Worms like him didn't deserve the time of day.

I looked down the hall that led to what seemed to be a partially destroyed kitchen. There were white tiles on the walls and floor, once shiny but now covered in dirt that clung to them like grease. More of those gutters ran the length of the room, parallel to the same rods hanging overhead. This was probably the place where they gutted the pigs and left them to bleed out before moving on to the next step.

Appropriate. I thought again, looking at the hook in my hand.

Mercier had to be here somewhere. There was nowhere else to go now that the only door out was chained from the outside. Without a warning, another shot rang, and a sharp sting radiated from my leg upwards. It hurt like a motherfucker, but I was still paralyzed and sedated by the terror of almost losing Jamie when that fucking crate smashed into the ground.

"Pathetic. You can't even shoot properly to save your own life."

I'd taken note of the trajectory. He was right in front of me, behind a stainless steel counter that had definitely seen better days.

"There's only one way to eat an elephant. One shot at a time and you'll be at my feet."

I laughed. Guttural and deep, manic as if my brain was glitching.

"You're a treat, Mercier. But this is a pig slaughterhouse, so I'm thinking I'm gonna follow the house rules." The man could be a rapist, even attempt kidnapping, but he was no match for a trained enforcer. Without him noticing, I'd tip-toed over to the counter, and before he could take another breath, I dove over it, sticking the hook in his flesh and pulling him along with me.

The man shouted in pain, and fuck was it a beautiful symphony. I rolled us over and unhooked the metal from his shoulder, ready to end this nightmare once and for all.

Stephanie Amaral

"You should know by now that the house always wins. As I said, house rules, Mercier. Guts. Out."

In one swift move, I stuck the rusty hook below his stomach and forced it all the way up, tearing him in two.

CHAPTER FORTY FIVE

Jamie

For the first time, I was sure the air was going to run out. Every new breath was harder to take. It was getting hot and damp from my own breath. The scent of the roses beneath me made it all so much harder.

Each time I tried to move, a thorn pressed into my skin, making my breath quicken and waste all that much more oxygen.

Breathe in. Breathe out.

I tried coaching myself to take less oxygen each time I inhaled. My eyes were shut already, my body had stopped shaking. I was on the end of the lifeline.

Breathe in. Breathe out.

I had wished this fate before, only now I had something worth living for. Ironic, just as much as all those spoons when you need a damn knife.

Breathe in. Breathe out.

A gush of fresh air burst into my lungs just as light burned my closed lids.

"Jamie!" A voice called from above. But it wasn't him, it wasn't Liam.

The sun was blinding as I tried to peek, the humid but fresh air burning my lungs on the way in. The voice that called my name with such relief wasn't familiar, but I was free.

I was free?

Two sets of hands dove into the tight space and pulled me out, sitting me down on the rim of the metal case Mercier had locked me in. They cut the rope that was binding my hands, revealing bruised wrists. Slowly, I managed to open my eyes and see who had saved me.

Mike stood to the side, a look of concern on his face, while Don Amato was in front of me. He took my face in his hands and scanned my injuries, his brows pinching together as he turned my face around to each side.

"Fíglio di putana" Son of a bitch. His voice was deep and filled with rage.

Don Amato hugged me to his chest, cradling my head like the most precious thing on Earth. I had no reaction at first. Why was he here?

A stranger was holding me in his arms, yet somehow, I felt myself leaning into his hug. Craving the solace a tight embrace and safety could carry. Only after a couple of seconds did the panic lift, giving way to a new, fresh flow of tears, sobs, and shaking hands.

I was free!

"Jamie, are you okay?" The man I barely knew asked, pulling back again and looking right into my eyes. I nodded, no words could find their way out from my sobbing chest.

Behind him stood Mrs. Amato with a few men I'd seen at Dea Tacita. What was happening? Didn't they realize she was the one who'd brought me here?

Don Amato reached to caress my cheek. I flinched away from his touch instinctively, surely he was in on it with his wife.

"It's okay." Mike cued from beside him. "Don Amato is here to help."

"Liam?" I asked, my voice hoarse and shaky. He was the only one I trusted right now.

"I'm here, Baby." I heard the only voice that could calm my senses. I looked back towards the warehouse, watching him march out of it like a soldier returning from battle.

There was blood all over his face and hands, his shirt was more crimson than white.

"Oh my God!" I cried, not sure if he was the one it belonged to.

I wiggled off the metal box, Don Amato and Mike helping me down just as Liam got to the back of the truck. I leaped into his arms, kissing him like I had never kissed him before while crying all my panic against his lips.

"Shh, it's okay, Baby Girl. It's okay. It's all over now, you're safe."

I clung to him and didn't intend to let go, but Liam pulled me back, his hands resting on my cheeks, assessing the damage on my face and arm.

"I'm okay. Just some scratches. But you..." I trailed off, looking at his shirt.

"Not mine." I couldn't help the flinch that followed his words, even if the opposite would have been much worse. "This is me, Jamie. The real me."

Liam's face was etched with guilt, not for what he'd just done, but for how that affected me. There was fear in those pools of green.

Taking a long, deep breath, I eased my racing heart, thanking God for having someone like him in my life. Frank would never have saved me. He was the first to put me in harm's way.

"I love you. The real you. Every part of who you are." I confessed, echoing his words and kissing him again.

"You're not going to run?"

"Only if you promise to catch me."

"Explain, Lisa!" I heard Mr. Amato shout from behind me, breaking our love spell. I still couldn't understand why Mrs. Amato hated me so much to hand me over to a sick bastard like Mr. Mercier.

"You weren't supposed to find out about her!" The woman shouted. Her voice was laced with hate and pain in equal measure.

"You knew?"

"Of course I knew! I knew before she was born. I knew everything." Her face grew red, her fury driving her words through her mouth with harshness. "I overheard your conversation with Liam at the wedding. You were never supposed to know she's your daughter."

I couldn't believe my ears. Mr. Amato was my father?

"I let her live because she was a baby," she continued. "I didn't have it in me to end her life at the time. Big fucking mistake. I was pregnant with Amelia, for God's sake. But that's over, she's all grown now. And you? You were quick to replace my baby girl, weren't you?"

"Don't you dare talk about her. My Amelia was the light of my life, the best thing that ever happened to me." Mr. Amato shouted back between greeted teeth, holding Lisa's jaw in a tight grip.

"Of course. Just not from the right woman. You are replacing our daughter with a new one, just like you tried to replace me with Amanda. But you know what? It was so damn easy to drive her away from you. Even easier to kill her after she threatened to tell you about the baby." She said with a sickening grin, freeing herself from his grasp.

"WHAT?" I shouted between tears while Liam held me in place, preventing me from walking over to them. I was finally realizing what was happening and why the Amatos were here. Enzo turned to me with pity mixed with a tender look in his eyes.

"Yes, you heard me! I. Killed. Your mother!" Mrs. Amato yelled towards me. "And you? It was supposed to be you that night at the 7-Eleven. Not my baby. Not my Amelia."

"What did you just say?" Don Amato grew pale, forcing Mrs. Amato to look at him again.

Everyone stood as still as possible, hanging on every word Mrs. Amato was about to say.

"That little bitch was supposed to be working. She was the one who should have died that night. Amelia wasn't ever supposed to be there. But your fucking genes just had to make them both look the same, didn't they?"

"You killed her?" Don Amato's voice was quiet, pensive, a slow burn of hellfire, getting ready to explode. "YOU KILLED OUR DAUGHTER?"

The girl from the store. The girl they thought Liam had killed. The reason why he was supposed to marry into the Amato family.

"No! She did." Mrs. Amato insisted, motioning towards me.

"You sent those men into the store? You killed my baby girl." He was in a loop, not wanting to believe what he was hearing. Without a warning, he drew his gun from the back of his pants and placed it against her head, his hand shaking out of control.

"Tell me you didn't do it. Tell me it wasn't you."

"She was supposed to stay in Jacksonville with that sick fuck of a father. She was too close. She needed to die."

"I AM HER FATHER."

My throat was blocked with a giant lump I couldn't swallow. He was my father. I had a sister who died in my stead.

"A tooth for a fucking tooth, Lisa."

"NO!" I shouted, leaping towards them both just before Don Amato pulled the trigger. "Don't." I calmly said, even though everything inside me was shaking. "She doesn't deserve to haunt you. She deserves to live knowing that she lost everything she ever held dear."

I was staring down the barrel of Mr. Amato's gun, switching between the weapon and his tear-filled eyes.

"She killed Amelia. She killed Amanda. She almost killed you."

"Yet, here I am, because you saved me."

I motioned for Mike to take her away, drawing confidence from the smile that spread Liam's face as he looked at me. I placed my hand over the gun Don Amato held up, slowly lowering his hand. The man was a mess, all the power he exuded reduced to shambles and pain.

"You were waiting for me? You actually wanted to meet me?" I asked, making sure I wasn't in for yet another heartbreak.

"My God, yes!" He replied, finally looking me in the eye. "I'm sorry this was how you found out. But I'm your father, dear, and it would mean the world to me if you gave me the chance to get to know you."

Those words made my heart leap while goosebumps covered my skin. My real father was right in front of me, risking his life to save me, seemingly happy to see me despite everything. I closed my eyes, relishing in the touch of his hand on my cheek, thinking that now I finally had it all.

A new stream of tears sprung free, this time filled with happiness as I hugged my father tightly, feeling complete for the first time in my life.

CHAPTER FORTY SIX

Jamie

A week later

"Where are you taking me?"

Liam was being as mysterious as ever. I had asked him a thousand times before where we were going, but he didn't give in to any of my attempts.

"Be patient. You'll find out soon enough."

I sighed, sinking deeper into the lush seat of his Maybach while he drove us around town.

It wasn't exactly a smooth ride, but meeting Liam all those months ago was the best thing that happened to me.

A perfect life awaited me, and I knew that whatever came our way, I always had a hand to hold and a companion to walk alongside me.

For the first time in my life, I had a family. A father who was making a true effort to get to know me and have me in his life. Alison, my soon-to-be sister, whom I adored to the moon and back. A cousin that I was looking forward to getting to know, and a whole lot of people willing to risk their lives to save my own.

I was in a place I never thought I would ever be in. An extremely happy place. I loved these people around me, and I was loved in return.

"I need to make a quick stop. I'll be right back."

Without giving me time to speak, Liam jumped out of the car and disappeared into a coffee shop on the other side of the road. He was only in there for a minute, and before I knew it, he was opening the passenger door and offering me his hand to help me out of the car.

"If you please, Miss Amato."

I smiled at his choice of words. Pride filled my chest each time I heard it because it meant something more. I was wanted.

Taking his hand, I stepped out of the car, noticing the paper coffee cup Liam held in his other hand.

"Now can you tell me where we are going?"

"Just a few more steps and I can tell you."

I rolled my eyes at that, earning a harsh tug that had me colliding right into Liam's chest.

"Do that again and you'll be in trouble, *Smallville.*"

I frowned at the reference before it hit me.

"This place…" I said, looking around, still perfectly snug in his arms.

"And so we meet again. Care for some iced coffee on your shirt? I can help you clean it off this time."

"You brought me back to where you bumped into me."

"You bumped into *me*."

I laughed, my head falling slightly back.

"I don't think that was it. But…" Liam kneeled in front of me, opening the coffee cup and taking out a velvety black box. Inside it was the most exquisite ring I had ever seen. "I'd like to continue this argument for the rest of our lives, Miss Harden. Will you give me the honor of marrying me?"

"Yes!" I squealed, holding out my hand for him to place the ring on my finger. "I'd said yes already."

"I wanted to do this properly," Liam replied, standing to his full height and taking me into his arms again before placing his lips on mine in the most loving of kisses. "And now we can go home and address that eye roll. I told you before, brats don't do well in this part of town."

ACKNOWLEDGMENTS

This is never a one woman job, so here I am saying thank you to all the beautiful souls who helped through this book. To Michele who has edited every word, every comma, every delusion while telling me my words don't (always) suck.

To Cristina who I can always count on to slap my ass and tell me the truth, the whole truth and nothing but the truth.

To Angeliese who cheers me on and has an expert eye for catching any inconsistency left.

To my loyal GANG who's been waiting for me to get my shit together and move on with this already. You all know that this journey started from your love and support. I'd be nothing without you ladies, so a million times thank you.

A very special thank you to Xavier Guzman, who invested his time and talent into drawing the amazing image of Liam's tattoo of Dea Tacita, to make this book even more pretty. Thank you so very much for your effort and incredible talent. I love this image to bits.

ABOUT THE AUTHOR

Hi. I'm Stephanie, big dreamer and self-confessed accidental writer. This corner of the internet is where my big dreams and my "accident" meet.

Welcome!

Fall of 2020. There was nowhere to go, and little to do. I was going stir-crazy, so, I decided to use my imagination and take myself to a world where the men are confident, dangerous, powerful—and, yes, gorgeous— and the women are strong, fierce, daring, and beautiful.

What started as a way to push my boundaries and keep myself busy, turned into something I never expected when I clicked on a button with the word "publish".

Now I'm ready to start a new journey and indie publish my work. I hope my books can bring you as much joy (and angst to be honest) as they bring me.

Thank you for stopping by and joining this new dream of mine. My hope is that it will make you dream, too.

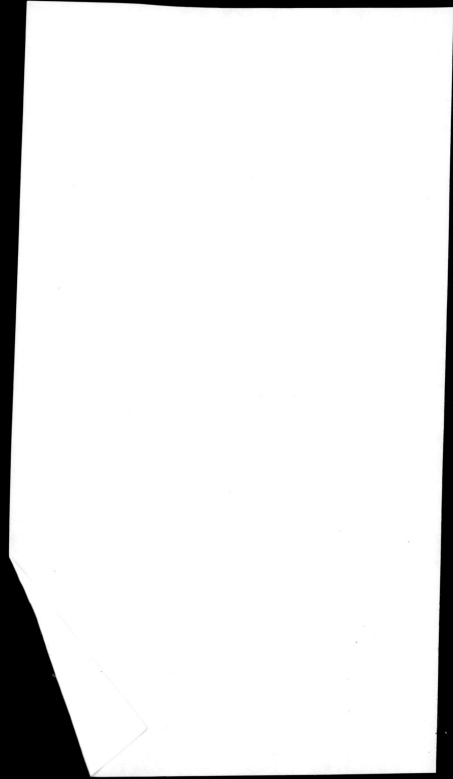

Made in the USA
Las Vegas, NV
18 November 2024

12049716R00256